Coming Around

A Second Chance Love Story

Tamala C. Jones

Line Five Publishing

COMING AROUND: A Second Chance Love Story

Updated Printing
Copyright © 2026 by Tamala C. Jones
All rights reserved.

This printing includes a newly added foreword and updated formatting. No portion of this book may be reproduced or transmitted in any form without the express written permission of the publisher or author.

Published by **Line Five Publishing**, an imprint of **Line Five LLC**

ISBN: 979-8-9985580-0-9

This is a work of fiction. Any similarities to actual persons, living or deceased, are coincidental and unintentional.

Cover image created using AI technology.

First Published: 2025
Updated Printing: 2026

Printed in the United States of America

This is a contemporary romance exploring healing, identity, and second chances in a world shaped by love, legacy, and the ties that make us whole.

Contents

FOREWORD

When I began writing *What Goes Around*, I believed I was writing a simple romance—a standalone love story about reconnection, forgiveness and choosing joy after loss. But as soon as I met the Walkers, I knew I had opened the first door to a wonderful world of Black dynamism. These people were complicated, powerful, full of secrets—I needed to know more.

So I stepped into their world shaped by inheritance, ambition, the weight of public expectation and the pain of private hurts. I found a world where love, wealth and legacy are inexorably intertwined—where each reflects burden and beauty in equal measure. I found a world where the characters are involved in the business of growing, unraveling, reckoning, rebuilding—and falling in love.

And tucked inside that world, from the very beginning, was Elizabeth Brookes.

Liz began as a side character in *What Goes Around*, her only role was to move Abe and Cassandra's love story forward. But she refused to stay in her lane. Even in her earliest scenes, there were contradictions—sharp-tongued poise wrapped in vulnerable uncertainty—she carried an emotional pull that wouldn't stay on the sidelines. She—and her mama—were the characters you all questioned, debated, judged and e-mailed me about.

You—and I—wondered: was Liz perpetrator or victim or some combination of the two? I needed to know. And she needed her story told—in all its fullness.

In *Coming Around* I was able to explore a different kind of heroine. A woman who captivated the reader, but not for the reasons expected. A woman who'd made mistakes—public, painful mistakes in front of people who were eager to define her by the worst moments of her life. A woman who wasn't universally beloved, whose protective edges were honed and sharp...whose vulnerabilities lived beneath years of survival and self-fashioning.

Liz is a Black woman written as complex, layered, flawed—and redeemed. She is allowed to love and be loved without apology. Her arc is familiar: painful, beautiful, hard won. It's about her becoming—not perfect—but whole. And that resonates deeply with me.

Then there's Warwick Walker.

Quiet. Observant. Steady and grounded. He moves through the world with strength and awareness, depth, and foundational understanding of his own value and worth. There's a generational awareness that resides in him—an intrinsic sense of where and how he fits. He's shaped by a desire to build instead of dominate; to uplift rather than overshadow. He is noble...perhaps to the point of heartbreak.

He's the perfect counterbalance to Liz's fire and the catalyst for her softening. Her sharp edges and high walls are met with gentle patience and presence—with a love that is quiet and profound. Warwick shows us that sometimes love arrives quietly, like a deep breath after years spent holding it.

Together, Liz and Warwick offered me the opportunity to explore a love story that sits differently from Abe and Cassandra's. Where *What Goes Around* is about rediscovery, ambition, and learning to claim joy, *Coming Around* is about quiet redemption. About a love that waits, a love that sees, a love that challenges us to face ourselves honestly. And then reach for what we want.

Writing this book allowed me to deepen the themes that shape the entire Walker world: Family. Legacy. Identity. The Walkers are a family who built enormous wealth, influence and reputation—but they also built walls, silences, and secrets that span generations. Their legacy is beautiful and brittle all at once. And Liz and Warwick's story embodies that tension.

Because while Abe and Cassandra's romance opened the door to the Walker legacy, Liz and Warwick's story asks the harder questions—about power, accountability and forgiveness. These questions, and the courage required to answer them, are what make *Coming Around* the emotional spine of the duet.

This expanded edition gives me the chance to situate Liz and Warwick's story exactly where it belongs: at the point where love, legacy, and truth collide. It is a celebration of everything I dreamed of writing when I was that nine-year-old girl stealing romance novels off my big sister's shelf. A world where Black love is not an exception and Black wealth is not an outlier. A world where Black families—messy, ambitious, loyal, fractured—spin narratives as sweeping and complex as any other dynasty.

I wrote this duet because I wanted to show our stories existing in every space, including the ones that once sought to exclude us. I wanted to write romances that reflect the sophistication, sensuality, vulnerability, and power of Black characters navigating extraordinary lives alongside the heartache that humanizes us all.

And I wanted to close the duet with a love story that felt like peace, like homecoming, even in the midst of the ongoing Walker saga. I hope *Coming Around* feels that way for you, as it does for me.

To every reader holding this book—whether it's your first time or your fifth—thank you. Thank you for loving this world, for loving these characters, and for allowing me to share a universe where Black love stands tall and radiant.

Thank you for walking with Elizabeth Brookes and Warwick Walker toward their second chance.

May their journey remind you that we are never too far gone to come home to ourselves.
And we are never beyond the reach of a love that was meant for us all along.

Prologue
The Gala

WARWICK

"Don't embarrass me while we're here," my mother said from the front passenger seat of the Escalade my father drove. She was turned toward the backseat, her left hand braced against Dad's headrest. It was a familiar position from which she'd been issuing warnings to me and my sister for twenty-odd years. It gave her a clear line of sight to pin Maggie and me with the stinkeye.

"Mom, we're adults–" Maggie began.

"One of us is," I muttered.

"One of us is," she immediately mimicked in a ridiculously lowered voice.

"Agreed," she said louder to our mother, and stuck her tongue out at me, "Mom, *I'm* an adult," she continued. "You don't have to warn your twenty-plus daughter about her behavior at a social function."

"Twenty plus what?" I said to Maggie, then to Mom: "I really am twenty-plus-several years and I'll keep an eye on my baby sister," a kick aimed at my shins barely missed, "so you can relax. As long as Uncle G doesn't start spouting off about how dad should've never left the family business and getting slick disrespectful."

My father chuckled as he made a slow right turn in Manhattan traffic; Mom sent him a slicing side-eye.

"If your Uncle Godrick has words to say to or about your father, your father can more than handle it." She rubbed her hand along the back of his head, smoothing his deep waves. "You two," she said, turning the full force of her maternal warning eyes on us again, "will behave."

She didn't wait for an answer, knowing that the whole conversation had been nothing more than a nod to convention. Maggie and I were both too old to start any trouble, regardless of whether there was any conversation about my father's arm of the Walker family tree deciding to branch in an unexpected direction.

That decision to branch off had been in the best interest of everyone involved; though not everyone liked to admit that fact. My father and his brother loved each other but didn't see eye to eye on several important issues that would have spelled disaster had their success depended on each other. But their differences hadn't kept me and my cousin, Godrick the third–Trey–from maintaining the brotherhood we'd begun before my father decided to move us south, to North Carolina, some twelve years ago. The move put us further from the toxicity of their sibling relationship and closer to my mom's family. Most importantly, that move had let Dad invest in the floundering hotel that laid the foundation for the hospitality business I would one day take over.

The phone in my pocket trilled. I pulled it out and tapped to answer.

"Yo, W."

"What's up, Trey?"

"Abe's flight got delayed so we're slow leaving. You'll get there before we do."

"Bet. No worries. We're pulling up in about 10. Catch you when you get here."

I cut the call and returned the phone to my jacket pocket.

"You excited to see your *boyfriend*," Maggie taunted from her side of the second-row bench seat.

"See, that's what's wrong with women these days. They say they want a man who's in touch with his sensitive side, a man who understands his emotions, but when you see two men with a healthy, supportive friendship, you trip." I shook my head in mock despair. "When will you see me for the whole person I am? When will you evolve?"

"Whatever," she sucked her teeth, then softened, "I know you're looking forward to seeing him though. It's been what? Six months?"

I thought about it, "Closer to a year. He's been running between here and Europe. And I've been focused on the southeast. So yeah, time has passed."

Mags was teasing but I truly was looking forward to seeing Trey. Seeing what kind of weight he was carrying from his father's endless expectations. The old man loved Godrick but put so much on him. It was a stark contrast to his interactions with Trey's younger brother, Abe. Uncle G seemed to almost forget Abe existed. And when he didn't, he was spewing various forms of disrespect and dismissal. I'd seen Abe's face after one of his tirades. It wasn't a good environment and it wasn't hard to understand why Abe spent little time around the family. Be he, too, loved his brother. And neither of us would miss tonight.

Trey had been featured on Forbes Magazine's Thirty Under Thirty list. It was a huge accomplishment. And as much as we didn't fuck with this side of the family, we all loved Trey. He was as opposite his father as any child could get...other than the driving need to conquer the world.

"Is he seeing anyone?" Maggie interrupted my thoughts.

"Actually, yeah. Says she's 'the one' but it's early days still."

"Well, that's exciting. You old guys need to settle down before your seed dries up."

I sputtered a laugh, "You don't need to concern yourself with my seed. And I'll settle when I'm ready."

"Mmhmm."

"Who else is going to be here, Dad?" Maggie asked.

"The usuals. You'll rekindle old acquaintances in no time."

"I don't have any old acquaintances here. I was ten when we left."

"Trey's new girl will be here," I said. "I think she's about your age. The two of you can play together."

"Again, full grown over here," she replied, skimming a hand down her front to draw attention to the fact that puberty hadn't missed her.

"Still a baby over there," I corrected, "and I'll be watching to make sure none of these soft clowns forget it."

"I promise I don't need your help, big brother."

"I promise you're going to have it regardless," I assured her. "I'll let you know if I see anyone suitable."

"Will you now?" I watched the sly light come into her eyes and wondered if I'd pushed too far. Mags was the best little sister anyone could ask for but she was sneaky and had some shit to her. If she decided she wanted to play games tonight, I could very well find myself on the losing end. I was too straightforward, too direct, to even begin to anticipate her convoluted shenanigans.

"Mags," I said in my most stern big brother voice. "Just focus on enjoying yourself."

"Nah. I think I'll focus on making sure *you* enjoy yourself." She leaned back against the soft leather seats with a self-satisfied smirk. I caught my dad's gaze in the review mirror. He just shook his head and chuckled.

The few minutes it took to reach the venue, pass the keys to the valet, and ride the elevator to the rooftop was not nearly long enough to deter Maggie from what seemed like rapidly developing matchmaking plans.

"You relax, big brother. I'll have you all set up in no time," she said as she and my mother scanned the room from the entryway. There was a sea of Black excellence in the room, one of the smaller ballrooms at the Drake Hotel. It was a historied location, well-respected, and on the list of 'places to see and be seen' for many of the elite African American crowd in Manhattan. But it was old...really old...and needed a renovation. If it were part of our portfolio, I'd do a full, but careful and respectful remodel. Then the lights wouldn't have to be kept low to disguise the slight fraying at the edges of the wealth and status it displayed.

Satisfied that the room held plenty of opportunities to get into trouble, Maggie and my mother wandered off toward one of the appetizer stations where a small group of women who looked vaguely familiar were gathered. Maggie tossed a nefarious eyebrow wiggle at me as she trailed off behind Mom.

"You set yourself up for that one, son," my dad clapped a big hand on my shoulder, as we began a slow stroll around the room, navigating the light crowd of people. I expected we'd end up at one of the nicely stocked bars I'd spotted.

"I did, didn't I?"

"She's not completely wrong you know," Dad followed up as he nodded at folks who nodded at him. "I'm not about to arrange a marriage for you like my brother is doing for Trey, but I wouldn't be mad at another daughter and some grandbabies. I wouldn't be made at all."

"Arrange?" I asked because Trey had not mentioned this.

He shrugged. "Arrange may be a strong word. But I know they've had a young lady in mind for him for several years. I understand she's who he's dating."

That was new information.

"I see you'll be following up on that," he chucked. "But back to you, don't wait so long that your mother starts taking pages from that book."

I laughed, not feeling pressured in the least. "I hear you, Dad. I'll see what I can do."

"I'm sure your mother would appreciate it. And I'll deny it til the end of my days if you tell her I said that."

"Noted. But you realize it's easier said than done."

He nodded. "Believe me. I realize. I'm not rushing you. Just providing direction," he chuckled again, clearly amused at himself.

"Well, well...Warwick Walker...my eyes must be playing tricks." The exuberant greeting had both my dad and I turning...we were both named Warwick, after all. After the requisite re-introductions and expositions about my size at the time of our last meeting, I excused myself to let my father and his acquaintance catch up.

Moving solo now, I cut a far more direct path to the closest bar. The turnout was good. I was glad to see so many folks showing up for Trey. He deserved it in every way. But it wasn't so crowded that I felt like I might crush people. I knew, objectively, that I had learned to manage my size long ago. Time spent on the basketball court and, at my mother's urging, in dance classes, had given me tight control over my body but I was still, simply put, a big man. Crowds weren't my favorite; even in light ones like this, I had to be careful not to step on some tiny person.

Like now. The woman standing in line in front of me had spun around, each hand occupied by a glass of wine, and proceeded to almost plow right into me. I easily sidestepped to avoid the collision. But she overcorrected and began to teeter on the stilettos that adorned her feet. I plucked one of the glasses from her and took her now free hand to offer stability. Which was easy because again...I'm a big man, not easily moved.

"Oh, thank you," she breathed, annoyance and relief fighting for dominance in her voice.

"Of course," I waited, holding the flute of champagne I'd taken from her, while she righted herself. She wasn't tall, but neither was she short. I was an easy six-four and I could've dropped a kiss on the top of her head without much effort. I guessed five-eight without the heels.

I watched as she moved this way and that, verifying that no stray drops of the wine had marred her dress—a long quietly golden affair that hung in a slim, body-skimming line from the thin straps that criss-crossed her bare shimmery shoulders. The gold of the dress and the sparkling brown of her skin were a stunning combination. She hadn't yet let go of my hand, and while I wasn't exactly holding it...more acting as a convenient wall while she leaned her weight on me, that weight was oddly perfect, and the place where her skin touched mine, the wiggle of her fingers resting on my hand, the absolute trust she was placing in me to hold steady while she teetered and balanced...I waited patiently for her to finish and look up...the need to know what she looked like behind the waterfall of long dark hair was growing exponentially.

Satisfied that she'd escaped unsplattered, she huffed a little breath and slid her hand from mine. My fingers clasped, reflexively, around hers at the last moment and finally, finally, her gaze collided with mine when she glanced up in surprise.

Brown. But not brown like I've ever seen it. Her eyes were a rich, bottomless brown, like molten cocoa. Dark, enigmatic, hypnotic. And, maybe, interested? *Nice. I'd like more of that, please.*

She tugged her fingers again and I released them. I watched as she wiggled them a bit. Was she trying to dispel the same tingle I'd felt as she slid her hand away?

"All good?"

"I am. Thank you again. I didn't realize you were there when I turned. I should have been paying closer attention."

"It's okay. I take up a lot of room. I should have given you more space." I let my eyes skim her face cataloguing the warm shimmer-dusted toffee brown of her skin, the pink that rode high on her cheeks, the full spread of her glossed lips. Lips that were currently turned in a rueful twist.

"Well, yes, there does seem to be a lot of you," she reached for the wine glass I still held. "I suppose you spend a lot of time apologizing for being in the way."

I laughed because clearly, she had no concerns about hurting my feelings.

"Not anymore. High school, though? That was a different story."

She grinned and my heart stuttered. Those full, glossy lips parted and the sun may as well have shone its light directly on me. I could feel my face freeze, knew I was staring stupidly but *Jesus* she was beautiful. And I knew what I'd seen when she first turned my way.

"I'm sure it was," she laughed softly and that sound matched the warm beauty of her eyes, low and melodic.

"I'd be happy to tell you about it. Regale you with tales of my trampling small children and pets," I joked, hoping to hear that velvet-wrapped chuckle again. She didn't disappoint.

"That would be quite interesting I'm sure," she said with another smile, "but I have to decline."

Fuck.

"Why?" I asked and mentally slapped a hand against my forehead.

She let one eyebrow ride up.

"Am I required to offer an explanation?"

I felt the grin spread across my face. She took no shit. "Not at all. I fully respect your decision. I'm just curious as to what they should put on my tombstone when they find me dead of a broken heart in the alley outside."

She rolled her eyes and the smile on my face spread further. *Yeah, this woman was made for me.*

"Silly."

I laid a hand on my chest, clutching my pearls. "Silly? Never that. But I am curious. You can, of course, tell me to fuck off. But what is it that's keeping us from taking the first step in the rest of our lives together?" I waggled my eyebrows at her to make that statement a little less corny.

Another eye roll. "Perhaps my boyfriend? The one I'm happily committed to and waiting for to arrive."

Fuck, again.

I'd never been one to roll up on another man's woman. That shit was low. But I know dudes who moved by the mantra 'If you leave the door open, I'll invite myself in." I wondered if her man had left his door cracked.

"Lucky man," I commented while I tried to formulate a reply that would firmly express my interest and willingness to steal her from whatever punk-ass relationship she currently thought she was in without sounding like a total asshole.

"I'm the lucky one," she said; a little smile tilted her lips. I felt an answering twist somewhere in the center of my chest. "I'm actually meeting his best friend tonight. Well, technically, his cousin."

Fuuuuuck. Please, Lord. No.

"Duece!" I heard from somewhere behind me. It was Trey. I turned to see him and Abe striding my way.

Well, shit. I turned to the woman I was trying to close to see her focused on Trey, face lit, smile bright. Whatever passing interest I may have seen flit across her face was nothing compared to this.

Trey shot me a grin, dropped a quick pound against my raised fist, and walked right past me to pull the woman into a respectful-of-her-finery hug and drop the kiss I'd been thinking about on top of her sleek head.

"You two would find each other. Liz, this is Warwick. Deuce, this is Elizabeth, my fiancee."

"Fiancee?" I felt my world tilt again, my stomach swooped before righting itself, a hard hot knot settling low in that organ.

I watched emotions play across Elizabeth's face. She was nervous, wary.

"It's an aspirational title," Trey said before coming back to me for the slap and hug of our greeting. We held the hug for a moment...it had, after all, been over a year since we'd been physically in the same room.

"It's good to see you, guy."

"You, too. You, too. We have to do better." The words were low, heartfelt.

"Agreed," I held a moment longer, another thump on the back and release. Then, to the woman who'd caused my whole future to flash before my eyes, I said, "It's good to meet you—officially– Liz."

Trey resumed his position beside her, pulling her into him. It was a position she willingly took and leaned into. I slid my hands into my pockets, contemplating. I decided to air it all out. It felt like the quickest way to dispel the faint worry that I thought I saw in Elizabeth.

Oh, you know all her moods and secret thoughts now, I guess.

I chuckled at myself before speaking again. My words were directed at Trey. My gaze was on Elizabeth. "You showed up just in time, my guy. I was just in the process of asking your girl out."

Trey laughed, unbothered. "It's your impeccable taste that has let our friendship last this long. I'd've worried about my own decision-making if you hadn't." He let his hand slide from Elizabeth's waist to take one of the glasses she still held. He sipped and took her free hand in his to hold it by his side. She leaned further into him.

"And how'd that go for you?" Abe asked, turning from the bar where he was placing his order. I signaled him to order for me, too, before responding.

"She shot me down immediately. Some shit about a wack ass boyfriend," I joked, comfortable in the knowledge that Trey knew beyond a shadow of a doubt that I would never move on his girl. Because I wouldn't. Not knowingly, at least. Lizzie–I wondered if people called her that–was now my sister for all practical purposes.

"Her taste is also impeccable." Trey quipped, his full attention on his beautiful girl.

I took a stiff swallow of the bourbon Abe passed my way. "Well, welcome to the family, Lizzie. You chose the best of us."

Moments Later

ELIZABETH

"*Welcome to the family, Lizzie. You chose the best of us.*"
I let a sigh of relief relax my shoulders and focused, not on the 'Lizzie' crooned in a baritone so deep I could barely hear it, but on the second half of the statement, *'You chose the best of us.'*

Godrick had told me about Warwick, of course. He'd painted him damn near a saint—certainly the best version of a friend a man could want. He'd been so excited for us to meet tonight. I should have known when I took in the man's sheer size that this was Warwick, best friend and cousin extraordinaire. I'd once asked Godrick whether he was closer to Warwick than to his brother, Abe. He'd looked at me in utter confusion and, now that I thought about it, had never actually answered.

"Thank you," I said to Warwick, before turning more fully to Godrick to whisper, "And I'll thank *you* to have a conversation with me before you go tossing around your 'aspirational titles'." It was a soft rebuke, jokingly made, because truthfully I would wear the title of fiancee–and wife–proudly for him. He was a wonderful man, kind and honest, thoughtful and generous with a dry sense of humor that matched mine. Plus, he could cook and didn't mind doing so.

"Oh, I have every intention of having a conversation with you. Sooner than you might think," Trey whispered in my ear.

I grinned into his brown eyes, all thoughts of the earlier interactions gone, and tightened the hold on the hand that held mine. "We've only been dating a few months. It's far too early to have 'conversations,'" I whispered back to him. "Don't tease."

"Is it?" He pondered, turning the full force of his beautiful smile on me. He was gorgeous; my heart rate ticked up. "I've been called a lot of things. Tease is rarely one of them." He considered me for a long moment before sending a look to Warwick and tugging me a few steps away.

"It has only been a few months," Trey agreed as he guided me toward a small nook that held a portrait of some pillar of New York's Black history and a small ficus. My stomach began to flutter. "And I'm not asking,"–*Okayyy*–he took the champagne from my hand and set both our glasses on the small table with the plant. "Not yet." The flutter returned. "But it's something we should talk about," he realigned our fingers, danced his along my forearms and back to clasp my hands in his much larger, much warmer ones. "It's something I would like to talk about."

I felt the color crawl up my face and tried to control the grin that took possession of my lips. "I'd like that, too."

He glanced around the room, judging the sets of watching eyes. Then he shifted slightly, blocking me from view with his wide shoulders, and dipped his head to lay a soft kiss on my lips. I eagerly accepted it, just as eagerly returned it, letting my lips cling to his and my eyes flutter closed. We both sighed into the kiss. This thing between us was easy and natural. Comfortable.

When he raised his head, his eyes were slightly darker, and, not for the first time, I wondered what it would be like to be wrapped in his arms, the recipient of all his attention. We hadn't taken that next step. I, personally, had *never* taken said step and I wondered, now that we would be having *conversations* what we would decide. The romantic in me adored the idea of waiting until marriage; the woman in me, less so.

Trey tugged my hand again, bringing me back to reality.

"Come on," he said and slipped his arm around my waist. "Let's dance. I want my arms around you and that's the only way I can make that happen in this crowd."

We spent the next ninety minutes splitting our time between the dance floor where I swayed in Trey's arms to the Motown covers being played by the band, and the table where we sat with Warwick, his sister, Maggie who was hilarious, and Trey's brother, Abe. The remaining free seats were occupied off and on by various people stopping by to congratulate Trey and catch up with Warwick who spent most of his time further down the East Coast in the Carolinas.

By the end of the night, Maggie and I had bonded over brothers (which she assured me were highly overrated) and boyfriends (for which she was currently on the prowl).

"I cannot wait to find the man that was made for me," she said to me as we shared mirror space in the bathroom.

"Do you believe that? That there's a man made just for you?"

"I do. And I'm looking for him. I want some babies and a white picket fence."

I laughed, "Babies and fences, huh? What about careers and independence?"

"Pssh," she waved that off. "I suppose I can have both, depending. But the way my man is put together, he's not going to have me out here burning the midnight oil for a paycheck. I'll be a kept woman." She leaned into the mirror to examine her lip liner.

"I wouldn't put too much stock in being kept. You have to keep yourself, because things happen. Look at Mother. When my father died, she completely spiraled. All she talks about now is remarrying well. And me? Well...," I trailed off because I was saying too much and if there was one lesson Mother had drilled into me, it was to keep family business, family business.

"Well, what?" Maggie asked predictably, pausing with the wand of her lip gloss poised for application.

I turned to her, contemplating how much more to say. She and her brother weren't part of this New York elitist crowd that measured everyone according to the price tag of clothes and cars. At least, not really. And if they were, they moved on the very edges of it all.

I sighed and said what I wanted to say. "Well. I don't know. I guess I've become a bit of an insurance policy. She's intent on my marrying well, too. Almost obsessively so."

"That's what we're supposed to do, though, right? Marry well, secure the funds, make some babies, and let the circle of life continue?"

I laughed because her summary was not at all inaccurate.

"It is, I suppose. But she's taken it to the extreme. I just thank God that Trey falls into her into her 'acceptable' category. And more, I thank God that we actually, really like each other," I blushed a little because was 'like' really the best word?

Maggie caught the color rising, "Oh you *like* each other, hmm?" She nudged my shoulder with hers and gave a little eyebrow wiggle. I shrugged and grinned and continued unnecessarily fluffing my hair.

"I can't wait to find someone I 'like'," she laughed. Then, "So what if y'all hadn't actually liked each other? Then what? Would you be forced into an arranged marriage with him?"

I shuddered, "I just thank God that we click and that he fits the bill because I honestly don't know the answer to that question."

***

"What a perfect, perfect evening," Mother gushed as we entered our home. When she was happy and excited, Mother was a sight to behold. Her brown skin glowed, her dress fit her trim fifty-plus body perfectly, her voice was melodic.

"It was very nice. I enjoyed myself," I said, peeling out of my floor-length formal coat and hanging on the coat rack before slipping onto the foyer bench to release my feet from the So Kate's I'd chosen for the evening. I massaged my grateful toes.

"I saw," she said. I caught the faintly disapproving tone in her voice and sighed. *What now?* Twenty-plus years of constant effort on my part and she was never, ever satisfied. At least that's the way it seemed since my father–stepfather–had passed away over twelve years ago.

"I saw you...kissing," she spat the word in a disgusted whisper, "at the event, like some common tramp. What were you thinking?"

I rolled my eyes. "Mother, it was Trey, obviously. And we weren't kissing. At least not really. It was one kiss. Our lips barely touched."

"Well, it was inappropriate and common," she reiterated, stalking down the hallway in her now-stockinged feet to the floor-to-ceiling wine refrigerator that snuggled into a corner of the den.

"I thought you'd be delighted. I assumed you'd use the opportunity to force your hand. Surely I've been debased and ruined by a public kiss. You can collude with Mr. Walker to force Godrick's hand into marrying me."

I was joking. Trying to show her how ridiculous she was being. But she turned to me, a speculative gleam in her eye.

"You know, you might be right," then she shook her head. "No one has morals these days. No one is concerned about a woman's honor anymore," she glanced my way as she filled a wine flute. "Least of all the woman."

Thinking to change her mood, to perhaps get us talking about a topic we would both enjoy and thus bond over, I said, "He kissed me because he'd just told me he wants to have *conversations* about getting married." I paused and let the rush of excited warmth rise again. "I told him I would very much like to have those conversations," I finished with a grin.

"Oh, that is good news," she replied, finally sounding genuinely happy. I smiled. "And it's about time. You've been dating for months. I wondered if you'd managed to drive him away."

So much for that. "Mother, we've been dating for four months. That's not very long and certainly not so long as to be disappointed by the timing of marriage talks."

"That's your problem. You always expect so little, ask for so little, are willing to accept so very little," she shook her head. "Do you have no ambition at all?"

"Mother, I'm set to marry a man who just appeared on Forbes' Thirty Under Thirty. What more could you possibly want from me?"

"I want you to want it, Elizabeth," she snapped. "I want you to understand what I've sacrificed for you and to show a little gratitude and respect."

"Okay, Mother." When she got like this, it was best to just give her space and remove myself. I knew from experience that if I stayed and tried to do anything resembling reason with her, she would escalate. I'd end up listening to her shriek at me all night about our precarious social and financial positioning. This despite her best efforts to keep Daddy's fashion house afloat (our pieces were in multiple national outlets), to keep me fed and clothed (I was more than adequately housed and nourished), and to keep the creditors away from our door (that, I had no information about). To hear her tell it, she spent her days scraping and scrounging instead of lunching and attending charity events. But whatever it was in her head, she'd pinned me as her way out. I had become, as I'd told Maggie, nothing more than an insurance policy. My value to her was directly tied to the net worth of the person I married.

I wandered off as she continued to mutter about the ungrateful daughter who was going out of her way to make her Mother's life more difficult.

I couldn't wait to marry Trey and get out of this mess. Maybe I'd call him when I got upstairs and see how he felt about getting those conversations scheduled.

Two Years Later
The Funeral

ELIZABETH

The rain was such a fucking cliche. But it matched the muddled grey swirl of despair that now resided in my brain, throughout my body. At least the fresh air waterlogged at it was, was better than the too-close cloying feel of the sanctuary. The sanctuary I'd just sat in for over an hour listening to Trey being eulogized.

The tears rose and overflowed again, streaking unchecked down my cheeks to dampen the high-necked, long-sleeved black crepe dress I wore. I was too hot, too sad, too angry, too bereft. Too everything.

I felt Mother's hand on mine. Surprised at the small comfort, I clasped it and leaned toward her.

"You're ruining your dress," she pressed a silk handkerchief into my hand. "Try to manage yourself."

I let her hand go and tried to turn my attention to the words being spoken for the interment. But my mind stuttered and rebelled, refusing to stay centered on the fact that my beloved was about to be lowered into the ground where his body would return 'to that from whence it had come. Ashes to ashes. Dust to dust.' I just couldn't. So I didn't.

I knew I would pay for it. Knew I'd hear Mother's voice incessantly about how I'd disgraced the family, shown no respect for tradition, and embarrassed her with my uncontrolled show of emotion. So be it.

I began to slip out of the row I was seated on, the row that gave me a fully unrestricted view of the obscenely ornate coffin where it sat primed for lowering. The whole show was another excessive nod to the extreme wealth Trey's family possessed. A full 50 x 50 tented structure had been erected over the grave and interment site. It was fully decorated, nearly as well-appointed as the church had been. The sides were lowered to block prying eyes but the front was open and, beyond the morbid sight in front of me, I could see out across the rest of the memorial park. Rolling green hills dotted with tiny acknowledgments of loved ones lost. I couldn't take it anymore.

I slipped past the disapproving eyes, past his parents and Abe. I could hear the chastising change in the tenor of the preacher's voice as I excused myself. But I wouldn't worry about that now. I'd add it to the bucket of things I'd concern myself with once I got this cinderblock off my chest. I pushed the heavy cotton swag of the tent aside and stepped fully into the weeping, overcast day.

I made my way toward a stone bench. It was as far as my numb legs and mind could take me. And it was far enough. I'd only needed to get out of the tent. Away from everything that was so Not Trey. I wanted to rage and scream and curse every foul spirit for the drunk driver who had slammed into Trey's car the same night he accepted the reins as CEO of HeirLoom Textiles, his family's conglomerate. It was all he'd wanted. All we'd waited for. Our lives were supposed to be beginning now. We were supposed to start planning the wedding. We were supposed to start babies. We'd picked out a condo. And now we were here. Doing *this*. I couldn't understand it.

The drone of the preacher's voice broke through. His volume had increased. I could see the tent clearly from where I was but couldn't see inside. I wondered if they'd started lowering the coffin and tears stung again. God, I needed Trey. He was—had been—my escape. We'd been that for each other, really. Pinpoints of sanity in the insanity that was our world. I could already feel myself spinning. Unsteady, ungrounded, unmoored.

"You're going to make yourself sick," the deep baritone sounded behind me. My heart thumped, startled and I turned to find that Warwick, red-eyed, and seeming a little less gargantuan than usual, had approached along the path behind me. He flipped open the umbrella he carried, took a seat on the bench beside me, and shielded me from the rain.

"The bench is wet," I said, unconcerned that he'd already sat. It had taken all my reserves to muster the energy to speak at all.

"You're still sitting on it," he observed.

I shrugged and turned back to the tent, watching as if I could see the goings on inside. I couldn't.

"Are you going back in?" He asked.

"No."

"You can't just sit here in the rain."

I turned to him, contemplated. He had kind eyes. Like Trey. Trey had the kindest, gentlest eyes. Except when we made love.

Then they were fierce and intense. "Yes. I can," I said and turned back to the tent and rolling hills. I was glad we'd decided not to wait. I was glad I had memories of being in his arms, of being that close to him. I wished I were pregnant. I was not.

"Come," he said and reached toward me, "let me take you inside the church where it's warm and dry. We can wait there until it's...over."

I shook my head, still watching the tent. I didn't want to be out there, where that still, lifeless version of Trey was. But I also didn't want to leave until it was done. Until he was resting peacefully and undisturbed.

"Then I'll wait with you," he settled more fully on the bench.

"No," I said. And that sounded harsh and hateful even to my grief-dulled ears. "I want to be alone." No, that wasn't quite right either. "I need—I need to be alone." I heard my voice crack. I was so tired of crying. So awfully tired of the hot achy eyes and stuffy nose, but mostly of the aching, gaping hole that the tears did nothing to fill. "Please leave me alone," I whispered.

Thankfully, blessedly he rose. "Okay, Lizzie." A little thump of response. A tiny, infinitesimal betrayal. Anger bloomed.

"I said, leave me alone. And don't call me Lizzie."

He obliged. But he left the umbrella.

Chapter 1

Ten Years Later

ELIZABETH

"Did you tell your brother to come here?" I whisper-hissed into the phone, even though I was the only one in the car to hear.

"What? No!" came the indignant response as I eyed the hulking pickup truck idling directly across from me in the tiny parking lot. The lot itself butted up against an exquisite brownstone with an equally exquisite Upper East Side Manhattan address out of which Allen Boone, Esquire, dispensed his legal services. This is who I was here to see.

My sleek silver Audi A5 was one of only three cars there. The parking lot was small, but the blacktop was smooth and even; the lines denoting the too-narrow parking spaces were bright white. There was no litter, no overgrowth. Unlike my nerves, everything was neat and in its place.

Except *him.* Why was he here? I scanned the lot.

The tasteful, big-bodied E-class parked closest to the entrance belonged to Boone, the attorney. The black Navigator looming over the Benz belonged to Abe and Cassandra, my sort of ex and his fiancée, who was also my maybe half-niece. This is why we were gathered here today...to evaluate the veracity of that 'maybe.'

The thought of the pending conversation made my head squeeze. On my list of top ten conversations I wanted to have in this new year of our Lord, this one was nowhere to be found.

My eyes locked on the giant king cab pickup with blacked-out windows and matted black rim. Moments ago, it rolled into the too-small lot, smoothly navigating the space, and slipped into place occupying two of the marked slots. It now rested there like some big beast caught mid-slumber...eyeing me lazily.

Why is he here? My thighs pressed together of their own accord, seeking relief from the unwelcome curl of desire that had sparked to life the moment I saw his truck.

I clutched the phone harder to quell my humming nerves and steady my shaky hands.

"Maggie?!" I hissed again. I didn't quite trust her initial reply.

At one time, when we were younger, Maggie had been a best friend, but we'd lost touch. She'd married, had a kid, divorced...done all the things I was supposed to do. Well, I wasn't supposed to do the divorce part, but certainly, the married-with-kids part. I'd been on the right track until Trey died...killed by a drunk driver on the night he'd ascended to the throne of HeirLoom Textiles as CEO. That promotion had been the nexus around which we had built our dreams; it should have signaled the beginning of our life together. Instead, it was the night that propelled me into a neverending, suffocating, overwhelming darkness that both comforted me and urged me toward an ugly surrender. I'd fought my way free, but I'd be lying if I said I didn't sometimes look back longingly at that muted, quiet place where I had been the grieving almost-fiancée. Life on the other side was markedly harder. Made more so in recent months.

Suffice it to say that my and Maggie's paths had diverged. But she'd recently returned to the area, newly divorced with her kid in tow, and we'd reconnected. It had been easy, fortuitous in a way I hadn't anticipated, and probably more than she'd banked on.

"Seriously, Liz. I didn't," Indignation rode her response.

"Maggie..." I drug it out a little bit. "You know how I feel..."

"I do. I really do. Which is why I would never send him there." She sounded sincere.

"Then why is he here?"

"I don't know," I could hear the shrug in her voice. "Maybe he's there to support Abe?"

"Abe has Cassandra to support him."

"Oh. Right." Silence. "Coincidence?"

I sat in the butter-soft, off-white leather driver's seat, gnawing gently on my carefully manicured, perfectly pointed, long-enough-to-project-a-life-of-leisure-but-not-so-long-as-to-be-gauche fingernail while I tried to make sense of his presence.

"Maybe." *Absolutely not. It's not a coincidence. You know why he's here.*

I scoffed. That's ridiculous.

No, it's not.

Yes, it is.

"Yes, what is?" Maggie asked.

"What?"

"What?"

"Maggie!"

"What?!"

"What are you talking about?"

"What are *you* talking about? You said, 'Yes, it is.' Yes, what is?"

"Nothing," I shook my head, still focused on the beast, sitting there, crouched and waiting. So out of place in the city. Nobody drove pickup trucks. Except him.

"Okay. Well. Maybe it's good that he's there. He can provide moral support."

I rolled my eyes and immediately heard Mother in my mind reminding me how terribly unladylike and uncouth eye-rolling was. *It's beneath you,* she would say.

"I don't need moral support," I said reflexively, but it was a lie. Any other ally would be welcome. I was on edge and itchy about today's meeting.

I was supposed to be okay with this situation. Adult about it, I supposed. Open to this possibility that I had a niece...who was my age, mind you...and who I knew nothing about, by a half-sister, Catherine, who I had barely known and scarcely remembered. Catherine had disappeared...gone missing...ran away...I don't know...when I was three. My parents never spoke of her; there were no pictures or celebrated special days. She had simply vanished from my experience, the fleeting memory of a child. Until this phone call asking that I provide DNA samples to verify Cassandra's identity.

"You absolutely do. And if I didn't have to convocate thirty-five hundred brand new freshmen, I'd be there with you myself, but these babies won't matriculate themselves," said Maggie, 'Dr. Walker' to the hundreds of students who would make their way through her introductory statistics classes this semester.

"Mm," I hummed, still fixated on the threat parked across from me. Still pissed at the way my pulse was racing because of it. I would just climb out of the car, ignore him, and walk confidently into the building. It wasn't rocket science. I did it every day...walking was easy. It was comfortable. It was fun.

"Liz, if he's there anyway, let him help you. I can't believe you're there by yourself anyway."

"Who else would be here?" I asked her, genuinely puzzled. I had a lot of acquaintances but very few friends. None, really. That reality had become crystal clear over the last few months when, in the midst of a breathtaking series of unfortunate events, I hadn't wanted to call a single one of the women with whom I spent countless hours, to talk. Not one. I could recite a laundry list of women to brunch with, lunch with, and shop with, but none to help carry my worries, fears, and anxieties. I wondered what it said about me that I couldn't pick up the phone to unload about anything more serious than what to include in the swag bags of whichever charity event we were coordinating. I don't know how I would have managed if it hadn't been for Maggie dropping back into my life at the perfect time. As it was, I suspected she was getting sick of me. I was getting sick of myself, so it wasn't a stretch.

She dodged the question. "Regardless. Don't be so prickly. He doesn't bite. As far as dudes go, he's a good one."

"You're biased," I said. *And I bet he does bite.* My nipples agreed.

She laughed. "I am, but I'm also right. And you know it."

I knew no such thing. All I knew was that Warwick Walker made me feel things I didn't want to feel. Big, heavy, overwhelming things that I didn't know how to manage and didn't want. And I wished he would stay away from me so I wouldn't have to figure out whether my palms were sweating as a result of the upcoming meeting or because of him. Though, I was fairly certain of the answer.

I was just beginning to see my way clear of my mother's all-encompassing, overwhelming presence, finally understanding how dependent I'd let myself become in the years since I'd lost Trey. I didn't need someone else smothering me. And that's what Warwick would do, in all his there-ness. I couldn't, and I didn't want to.

"Okay," I said, not in agreement with her suggestion but to indicate that I was ready. Ready to take the next step, literally and figuratively. "I'm going in now. I'll call you when it's done."

"Okay, babe. Call me as *soon* as you're done. I'll be out of here in a couple of hours, tops."

I tapped to disconnect the call and dropped my phone into my ridiculously tiny Anima Iris bag before I lost my nerve. I didn't check my makeup. I knew it was flawless. As was the 28-inch perfectly ombre'd sable-brown-to-honey-blonde Cambodian sew-in that tickled my lower back. I had a love-hate relationship with both the makeup and the weave...they were prison and protector.

I knew what people saw when they looked at me: an aloof, reserved, painted, and primed stereotypical representation of Black aristocracy. The right clothes, the right bag, the right shoes. Perfect hair, perfect nails, perfect makeup. Surely, I wanted for nothing. Surely, life was perfect underneath all those trappings. I'd learned, though, that there was a reason people called them 'trappings.' I felt trapped, restricted, and incorrectly defined, but I hoped today, the masquerade would help me manufacture whatever I required to get through the next hour.

Ah, it figures. In keeping with my recent luck, the moment...nay, the exact instant...I tugged the door handle to begin my trek, the door of The Behemoth—my internal name for that gaudy monstrosity he insisted on driving—swung open. And I was transfixed at the prospect of seeing the man who never failed to take my breath away, no matter how much I willed it otherwise.

I granted myself just a moment to watch, curious to see how he had adorned that big, beautiful body of his. A little shudder ran through me, my heartbeat echoing in all my hollow places, as he stepped out, slow and so damn graceful. He matched the truck: big and beautiful, immensely powerful...and merciful enough to cover it all with something shiny and easy to look at. I scanned him as he closed the door and settled a long navy coat over his shoulders. He wore a black sweater and black jeans underneath. Black boots shod the feet that were now headed my way.

God, the irony of it all. I could watch him walk toward me all day and all night but did I want him here? Nope. Not at all. Nevertheless, I was treated to the full IMAX version of his approach...close enough now to see the glint of his watch and a glimpse of the tucked gold chain he wore...close enough now to see the play of wool against denim...close enough now to see the black of his faint beard against his rich dark skin. And now close enough to enjoy a tantalizing but brief view of the bulge that lay against his thigh as he reached for the door handle and stepped back to open my door.

WARWICK

I wiped my hands on my thighs before I exited the truck. Not because I was nervous but to remind myself to keep my hands *to* myself. Elizabeth Brookes did not belong to me, no matter how much I wished it so.

So why are you here? I had no substantial answer other than I didn't want her to be alone. It had been the first thought on my mind when the sun rose and had ridden me all morning until I'd finally said *fuck it*, climbed in my truck, and made my way here. If I was also hungry to see her again, well, that was secondary and better left alone.

Decision made, I was now on-site at this meeting that could quickly turn into a clusterfuck, contemplating how to handle her sexy, prickly ass. She would *not* be happy to see me. Or at least she'd front like she wasn't. Liz Brookes and I had a complicated relationship, which is why it was equally appalling and appropriate that I was the one making sure she wasn't alone.

The last few months of her life had been the stuff of soap operas, and this was the latest episode. I'd heard from Abe, my first cousin, so I knew he and his fiancée, Cassandra, were meeting Liz today to hear the results of the DNA testing that would determine whether there was a familial relationship between Liz and Cassandra. If there were, a whole can of worms would be involved while everyone figured out exactly what it meant for Cassandra to be Harry Brookes', Liz's father's, granddaughter. It was a complicated mess, full of second marriages, step-relationships, and missing people. But regardless, if it were up to me, Liz wouldn't be managing it alone.

She *should* be leaning on her mother through it all...the two of them *should* be navigating this situation together. But her mother was a trick bitch...essentially no better than a high-dollar madam...who couldn't see the value in her own daughter beyond Liz's ability to snag a rich husband and expand the family coffers. She was the source of most of the bullshit in Liz's life...but that wasn't my place.

I'd parked my pickup directly across from Liz's little Audi coupe. I'd both driven the truck and parked it where I did to piss her off. Liz pissed was fun...and Liz pissed might feel a little less delicate in the face of what was sure to be a shitshow. So, step one of my plan was to irritate the hell out of her. It was something I excelled at.

I'd figure out step two in flight.

My boots hit the pavement, and I made my way toward her. I could make out her face but not her expression through her windshield. But I didn't have to see her expression to feel the heat being thrown my way. All fire, all the time. Every time I saw her, from the first time I'd seen her, she'd been a bundle of controlled heat and pent-up energy. I couldn't understand how people thought she was cold and aloof.

As I got closer, I saw her eyebrow rise and her lip curl. *Sexy*. Was it wrong that her scowl made all parts of me stand tall for evaluation and possible discipline?

I walked right up to her driver's side door and opened it. Then I leaned over and gave her my best shit-eating grin, perfectly curated to make her snarl at me. The thought of it landed somewhere in the vicinity of my dick.

"Not avoiding me, are you?" I asked in full asshole mode, heavy on the southern...all the better to shift her nerves directly to me and away from the bullshit I knew was swirling in her head

I watched her pupils dilate slightly before she blinked and...as I expected and hoped...snarled.

"How could I be avoiding you when I didn't even know you were here?" she declared in that snooty Upper East Side tone that made me want to haul her against me and kiss the sneer off her mouth.

"I mean, you're the one who's been sitting in her car the last ten minutes. I could only assume you were either trying to avoid me or hoping desperately that I would come escort you," I took a step back to give her room to exit the car. "So, here I am. At your service."

CHAPTER 2

ELIZABETH

"Here I am. At your service." I closed my eyes briefly. The last thing I needed was to think of Warwick at my service.

I huffed and, once again, rolled my eyes. But this time, I did it with vigor and a target.

"Go away, Warwick," I snapped, flipping the visor mirror for the lipstick check I knew I didn't need, hoping he'd heed the dismissal.

"No," he replied, low and slow, like he was dragging the words through warm molasses. "But I'll be good if you want me to."

Jesus, what was he trying to do? His voice crept under the baritones and bass of normal human communication and settled somewhere well beneath, lodged in that space between sound and vibration so that every word he spoke, I felt. Right between the thighs. Every. Single. Word.

He stepped back and held out a hand to assist me from the car, as any gentleman would.

I hesitated.

I could almost feel the dare rolling off him, so when he bent again to say gently, "Liz? It's okay. I won't bite. I promise," I was shaken—not only by the lack of snip but also by the echo of the words his sister had said earlier.

He won't bite. Humph. I still didn't believe it.

The big fingers on the big hand in front of me beckoned, and I reached out, preparing myself for the race of heat that always smoldered between us, no matter how much I, at least, ignored or denied it.

The movement from me had him wrapping my hand in his and giving me a solid, easy pull from the car. Once my feet were steady, he released my hand and touched the small of my back...setting little fires with each touch...to encourage me to take a few steps forward. Then, he reached around me to grab my bag from the car.

"You need anything else? A coat? It's cold out."

"Um. In the back," I said, trying to pretend that my entire consciousness wasn't split between my hand and my lower back, both of which were tingling following his touch. I surreptitiously made a fist and rubbed my palm, but there was nothing I could do about the hot, heavy handprint that scorched just above my bottom.

He retrieved my calf-length wool coat from the back seat and held it while I slipped in, The skirts of the rich caramel-colored fabric mingled with the wide circle skirt of my ivory wool sweater dress. I buttoned up the coat's fitted bodice and let the skirts flow together. I'd chosen the outfit carefully; I loved the strong femininity of it and needed all the Woman King vibes I could get. Warwick passed me my bag, and I slipped it over the curve of my elbow. Now, I supposed, I was expected to let him escort me inside, which would mean more touching. I sighed.

"Oh, come on. I'm not that bad, am I?" He offered his arm.

"Why are you here, Warwick?" I settled my fingers lightly on his forearm, creating barely enough contact to constitute an escort. The connection zinged through my fingertips and set off little sparkles in my veins.

"Well," he drew the word out, betraying the fact that he'd spent many years outside of New York. Warwick and Maggie had spent large chunks of their childhood down south...in one of the Carolinas. Their dad went to college and met their mom there. I knew they'd spent long summers with their mom's side every year, and Warwick had chosen to honor those roots, living much of the last ten years well below the Mason-Dixon line. I wasn't sure what had brought him back, but he'd reinvigorated the Walker hotel conglomerate breathing new life into two existing locations and renovating and launching a third within months of returning. It felt like he was making a permanent move. And that made me nervous and unsettled. Which was ridiculous because Warwick Walker's decisions had no impact on me or my life.

"Abe told me everything–" no surprise there, "–and it seems like a lot to handle alone." The timbre of his voice continued to run on the same frequency as all my ladyparts, and everything that could stand at attention did so.

"What makes you think I'm alone?" I snapped, irritated at the fact that I was even *aware* of my ladyparts as we strode the short distance across the lot and along the brief sidewalk.

He looked around us. I rolled my eyes yet again. Mother would be horrified.

"Clearly, I'm alone now, but what makes you think I'm alone-alone? I have support. I have friends." It sounded bitter and childish even to my own ears

"I'm sure you do." We climbed the short stack of five steps to reach the entrance of the brownstone before he slipped ahead and opened that door as well. "But I thought it might be nice to have someone here today. I can catch you if you faint from the news."

A tempting thought. I changed the subject.

"Don't you have work to do? Beds to make in one of your tenement homes or something?"

He chuckled. I felt the rumble of it under my skin and in my belly.

"I suppose there's always another bed to be made in one of my five-star luxury hotels," he paused for my huff, "but I do have people for that."

Before I could respond, he continued, "Well-paid people who enjoy their work and are happy to have an employer who provides good benefits and plentiful perks. But I'm happy to be here with you in your time of need."

"Did Maggie tell you to come?"

He shot me a quelling look. "No. She didn't. Which I'm sure she told you when you accused her of doing just that."

I curled my lip at him—not a lot...that would be beneath me—but just enough. I know he caught sight of it, but he chose to ignore it, which made me feel that much more childish.

"Come on. Let's get it over with."

He motioned me into the cool interior of the space, and I had to admit, I was much less nervous and upset about this meeting than I had been before. Now, I was nervous and upset about his big, warm presence heating up the left side of my body. What if it combusted? How stupid would I look with half my body aflame?

We navigated the short hallway to the meeting room at the rear of the building. Of course, Abe, Cassandra, and Allen Boone were already there. The cars in the lot hadn't lied.

I scanned their faces, noting a level of discomfort that seemed out of place even for the tenor of the conversation. I mean, I wasn't excited about plowing through this revelation, but I didn't understand why they looked so put out. Pursuing this was their idea, after all. Allen Boone's face was particularly ashen as if he'd eaten bad clam chowder.

My face must have projected my confusion because Abe began to stand, mouth opening to speak. Unfortunately, instead of his kind, soothing voice, I heard the strident sound of my mother behind me.

"Oh, you're here, finally." My esteemed mother, Juanita Brookes, entered the door Warwick and I had just walked through and brushed past us to take a seat at the opposite end of the table from the attorney, effectively signifying herself as second in command. The cloud of powdery fragrance that she doused herself in trailed behind her. It accurately represented the woman: on first impression, it was light and airy, but as time wore on, it became heavy and cloying, with faint undertones of decay.

The revulsion and hurt that had become my standard response to her merged with the prickly, sweaty tension of the day, making my armpits itch to life under the layers of wool. I'd need to shower as soon as I got home.

"Mother. Why are you here?" I asked, trying but failing to keep the impact of her presence out of my voice, pissed because I could hear the tremor. I knew it was as much from anger as anything else, but she'd use it as weakness. My body registered that Warwick had stepped closer, not by much, but I could feel his solid heat again. Normally, I would have run. Right now, his presence was the most dependable thing in reach.

She settled in her chair, straightening random items on the table in front of her...her small bag, a coaster, the glass of sparkling water that had been provided. "Well, I should think the better question is, why wouldn't I be here? Did you think I wouldn't be interested in whether or not this girl is my grandchild?"

'This girl,' also known as Cassandra, huffed and bristled. I watched Abe dance his fingers along her shoulder, offering calm.

My gaze bounced between Abe and Cassandra, "Did you invite her?"

The disgust that crawled across Abe's face matched that on Cassandra's. Clearly, they hadn't.

"Absolutely not," Cassandra spat, raising her another notch, in my opinion. Our relationship, such as it was, was polite and distant. It was not unfriendly but right on par with the relationship one would expect to exist between a man's fiancée and the woman to whom he had been previously–albeit loosely–promised. The fact that we had this other, decidedly unexpected connection kept forcing us into each other's orbit. It was uncomfortable and annoying but mostly it was just confusing.

I turned back to Mother. I hadn't called her, hadn't told her any of this on purpose. I didn't want to be around her...I couldn't figure out *how* to be around her after our last inter-actions and conversations. 'Conversations' being a euphemism for the gut-wrenching episodes where I begged, pleaded, and cried ugly, snotty tears trying to understand how she could have chosen to *physically impair* me in order to guarantee my marriage to Abe...a marriage she had wanted far more than Abe or I.

"You're being ridiculous," she'd said, "it was barely a drop. Just enough to lower your inhibitions. He got the majority."

"He got the majority?" I'd sputtered, tears streaming, refer-ring to the actual drug *she'd laced my and Abe's drinks with one night, hoping the warm fuzzies would lead to sex and matrimo-ny.*

"Yes," she'd snapped. "He got the majority. I wanted him to want you and act on it, wanted you to..." she'd waved her fingers, "I don't know...be receptive. You've become so cold since Godrick died."

She'd looked at me with such dismissive pity. "I was doing you a favor. You're letting yourself go to waste, and you need to think seriously about your future before you don't have anything worth having to offer anyone."

This, from my mother. The horror was that I might agree with her on some deeply buried level. Her methods? Absolutely, unequivocally foul and unforgivable, hence the rage making my skirts shimmer right now. The part about me being cold, reserved, and maybe wasting my life? I'd reserve judgment.

"How did you find out?" I asked calmly, taking strength from the wall of Warwick at my back.

"You honestly believe you could participate in this farce of an inquiry without my knowledge?" She scoffed and chuckled, an ugly pitying glint in her eye that belied the falsely pleasant smile she wore.

I stood there, stunned again at this woman's reach into all parts of my life. My mind swirled, trying to figure out how she could have known. She would have found out eventually, but having some control over the revelation would have been nice. The underground network of monied black gossipmongers had struck again. There was no privacy.

The attorney gave me a pitying look, which I met with what I hoped was unflinching resolve. I didn't need his pity; I needed strength. He waved a hand, encouraging us to sit.

That heavy, warm weight dropped to the curve at the small of my back again. Odd how my body could so completely hone in on Warwick's touch while my feet still worked well enough to take me toward one of the empty seats at the table.

"Let me take your coat," Warwick's warm breath whispered across my temple as he bent slightly to offer me the option. *Mint*, I registered before he spoke again. "Turn to me. Let's get you a bit more comfortable." He put slight pressure on my shoulders to spin me.

Facing him, I opened my mouth to tell him I didn't need his help, but before I could offer that setback, he caught my eyes. There was no teasing, no pity, no impatience. Just calm. Deep black pools of endless calm. He nodded at me slightly as his big fingers nimbly unfastened the buttons of my coat. The intimacy of it would have horrified me under any other circumstances. The brush of his knuckles against my chest would have sent me running...whether toward him or away from him, I couldn't say. But now, all I felt was settled under the warm weight of his hands on my shoulders, sliding along my arms as he swept the coat away. He was grounding me. By the time he turned me again, I felt a bit more in control.

Coat handled, we sat. And I listened while Attorney Allen Boone informed me that the samples we'd provided had been analyzed and evaluated and blah blah blah. I tried to concentrate—I really did—but the reality of being blindsided by Mother had left me feeling completely unmoored.

Warwick tapped a big boot against my delicate stiletto, and I tuned back in to hear the attorney say, "...based on the DNA sample results, the probability of relatedness between Elizabeth Elaine Brookes and Cassandra Williams is point one two zero eight. This means that you share twelve point eight percent of the same DNA." He laid down the paper he was reading from. "According to the accompanying interpretation specific to our inquiry, this percentage is in keeping with that seen in a relationship such as we suppose yours to be...between an aunt and niece with a half relationship between the parents as was yours, Elizabeth, with Cassandra's mother."

He paused to let that sink in. My eyes linked with Cassandra's. What did one say in such a situation? I had nothing to offer.

No one spoke. The attorney let his gaze sweep the room. I guessed he was giving someone a chance to say something. It wouldn't be me, but I wondered why Mother wasn't raising a commotion. I expected and was mentally preparing myself for the rant that should be forthcoming. I anticipated the following talking points: blaming me for the outcome of the test, blaming me for not securing Abe and thus avoiding this scenario, some highly offensive passive aggression aimed at Cassandra, ending with a completely obtuse reference to how the whole outcome would make her life more difficult.

But when I looked her way, she wasn't seething. Her still beautiful face, a warm sepia, was botoxed to within an inch of its life. Whatever she was thinking wouldn't be reflected there, but her brown eyes, so like mine, weren't angry, they were thoughtful. And that made me thoughtful. But I couldn't conceive of anything relevant that would prevent her from spewing her standard venom.

"Well, doesn't that just take the cake?" She said to no one in particular. Then, "Well. I guess we're done here? Or," and she turned a hateful, withering gaze to Cassandra—*here we go*— "do you intend to start dismantling Heritage right now?"

The test results verified what Cassandra and Abe suspected: that Cassandra was Harry Brookes's, my father's, granddaughter. As such, she would be entitled to a significant share of the quietly successful fashion house that Harry had begun with his first wife, ran as a widower for several years following her death, and continued with Mother when they married.

Sharing any modicum of anything with Cassandra would set Mother's blood to boiling. It would be the exact antithesis of every goal she's ever set for herself or me, for that matter. Her personal mission, vision, and strategic plan could be summed up in one word: *mine.*

She continued, "I really don't understand why you've opened this can of worms, dredging up memories better left buried. There's nothing for you here."

Cassandra responded by looking Mother up and down, cooly dismissing her with a raised brow and directing her full attention to the attorney. Mother huffed and seethed. I watched the color rise slightly on her brown cheeks and felt a brief smile play across my lips.

Under other circumstances, I might have enjoyed having Cassandra as a friend. I wondered what it might be like to be so bold and unfettered. To operate outside the confines of this strange life that allowed me the resources to do so many things but not the freedom to be who and how I wanted to be.

"Attorney Boone. Can you share preliminary next steps? Give us an overview, at least, of where our next conversations might lead?"

"Of course," he nodded kindly at Cassandra, then shot a resigned glance at Mother. I assumed he was buttressing himself against her next outburst. "We can take the results of this test as verification and validation of the familial relationship that exists between Elizabeth and Cassandra. As the only explanation for such a relationship is through the shared DNA passed from Harry Brookes to his daughter, Catherine, and then on to you, Cassandra," he turned his attention to me, "and Elizabeth, from Harry Brookes to you directly as your father."

He paused. Mother said nothing but I could all but hear the steam shooting from her ears. He continued. "I took the liberty of pulling documentation of Mr. Brookes's will, assuming you would want some guidance." Cassandra nodded.

"Harry did include a clause in his will," he said this slowly; the gravity of the pending revelation was apparent. Everyone's attention sharpened and centered on his next words.

"As you know, Catherine was never found," he said, referring to the horrible disappearance of Cassandra's mother. "And, I suppose a parent's love, their hope, never completely wanes," he sighed. "To that end, Harry included a clause such that, if Catherine were ever found, the distribution of assets would be amended as follows." And he proceeded to read off a redistribution of Father's material assets that, honestly left me fairly unimpacted but constituted a substantial change in Mother's portfolio. She was well cared for but some adjustments would need to be made.

"More lies. All of it," Mother spat before he could even get the words fully out of his mouth. "I've never heard of this clause."

"Mother, enough," I said, exhaustion and a faint headache rising. "If Cassandra is Catherine's daughter, then she should have her share. It's what's fair."

"What's fair is the time I spent nursing and caring for your father in his illness and old age," my eyebrow elevated. My father hadn't been particularly ill and hadn't carried himself as such. "What's fair is the blood, sweat, and tears I've poured into that business to build something for you. What sense does it make for her to waltz in here and take what's mine? What's *yours?* She'll be fine," she waved a dismissive hand in Cassandra's direction.

"She's marrying Walker money, *your* money. You should be more concerned for your future, Elizabeth."

"Should I? Or do you think I should be more concerned for yours?" I could feel ire rising and my head getting tight with the anxiety that always appeared when I engaged her. I shouldn't have said anything. We'd be that much closer to leaving if I hadn't said anything. Stupid.

"Well, that's a pipe dream, isn't it? You've always been a selfish child. Never thinking about anyone else...always only what you want."

I'd been raised in a very 'seen and not heard' household, especially after my father died. He had been a kind man, and I had very clear memories of sitting with him, reading, watching as he poured over papers at the kitchen table. Always with bins and bins of paperwork, overflowing with files and folders. He'd seemed so very busy and important. I knew he loved me. I had bright, warm memories of his love. But there had been a distant, almost absentminded quality to his love at times...a pall of sadness. As a child, I hadn't understood it, and it had made for a sometimes quiet, cloudy household.

And then he'd died not long before my ninth birthday. I learned later that it had been two strokes suffered within weeks of each other that caused his death. Without his calming buffer, the quiet cloudiness gave way to Mother's strident, demanding form of parenting. Growing up had become a job with a clear goal of marrying rich to secure the family. My assignment had been clearly communicated. But I had managed to lose my first prospect to death and the second to Cassandra. My failures had been underlined and boldfaced by Mother—her daughter's ineptitudes writ large.

"That's a bit of the pot calling the kettle black, don't you think, Juanita?" Warwick's low, slow question sounded in the room. I felt my back stiffen in preparation for the ensuing melee.

"Excuse me? I understand that you've just reinserted yourself into polite society, so I'll make some allowance for your lack of manners."

"That's not necessary," he offered in that deceptively lazy half-drawl. "My manners are fine, and I'm happy to use them in the appropriate situation. You projecting your raging self-absorption onto Liz isn't such a situation."

"Liz is my daughter, and I'll address her as I see fit. You have no business here, Warwick. I'll thank you to keep quiet."

"Keep your venom and your thanks on your side of the table, and you won't hear another word from me." Mother's mouth dropped open, then snapped shut. Before she could mount a reply, Warwick turned to Boone and said, "Continue."

Boone nodded. "Thank you. As Miss Brookes...Catherine...never, uh, returned home, we can transfer the bequeathment to Cassandra under the line of succession clause, which dictates that, as Catherine's direct descendant, Cassandra is entitled to any assets that Catherine would have inherited."

Mother's huff was just background noise.

"With your permission, Ms. Williams, I'll reach out to Mr. Brookes's estate and begin gathering relevant documents, communicating with his trust, and pursuing information regarding corporate holdings. We can reconvene in, say, two weeks to follow up." He presented it to the room as a whole.

"Be assured that I'll be contacting our family attorneys," Mother tossed out, a vague and indirect threat. She was flustered but still, not in the way I expected. Something was off; I couldn't pinpoint it though. And it could just be my own nerves causing me to see things that weren't there.

"Yes, Ms. Brookes, you should do that. There will be a number of changes that you'll want to discuss with your counsel. In fact, I'll be sure to include your counsel at our next meeting."

A beat passed, and Boone used the opportunity to wrap things up, sharing some final details and information about what to expect at our next gathering.

As we stood, chairs scraping and clothes swooshing, I did what I could to avoid Mother. Which meant actively choosing to give my attention to Warwick so she would, hopefully, take the hint and just *go.*

No such luck though. She stopped near me as she made her way toward the exit. "Elizabeth, we need to speak about this. I'll expect you for dinner this evening," she slipped her hands into the totally unnecessary gloves she wore simply because they accentuated her outfit. As she straightened them along her fingers, she let her gaze trail over me, then Warwick, then back to me.

"I won't be there," I assured her.

Her gaze turned sharp, cutting. "I assumed as much. You continue to try my patience and I see you have your little watchdog at the ready." She contemplated Warwick again before lobbing her final shot at me. "I hope this isn't where you've chosen to direct your affections, Elizabeth. If so, you're even more in need of my guidance than I'd realized." She signed, "At least I know it will be short-lived. I'm eager to see how you let this one slip between your fingers."

And with that, she stalked out.

I exhaled. I felt Warwick spin me toward him once again. This time, he used one big finger to tilt my chin up, bringing my eyes in line with his.

"You were great."

A pulse in my chest and the knot of disappointment and anxiety twisted, sending a rush of hot tears forward. I shook my head, blinking against the surge of wet heat.

His lips tightened briefly. They were full, dark, kissable.

"Let's get you out of here," he said. "Let me take you home."

Chapter 3

"*Let me take you home.*"

It was tempting. It was incredibly tempting. But no, I needed time and space to think. Warwick, wonderful though it would be to sink into the safe haven he represented, would only be a stopgap. I had to figure this out on my own. Had to learn how to withstand her under my own steam and mend the little fissures she'd wrought in my composition. Months had passed. I shouldn't still be this readily impacted; it made me angry that I was.

So, I replied, "No. I mean, yes, I need to get out of here but, no, I..." I hated sounding so ungrateful after he'd come here for no reason other than to make sure I had someone in my corner. "Thank you. I appreciate your coming. Really, I do but," I hesitated, trying to come up with words that didn't make me sound like a raging bitch, "I'll get myself home. I could use the time to regroup."

He nodded, ever the gentleman. I didn't meet his eyes because I didn't want to see or have to bear the concern—or any other emotion that might be lingering there. I turned and moved toward the door, hyper-aware of him following close behind, equally aware that I'd broken all etiquette rules by not making a proper exit. But Abe, Cassandra, and Boone were caught in quiet conversation. They'd be fine.

Outside, we quickly approached the point where our paths would diverge…I would head right to my car, and Warwick would veer left to reach The Behemoth. He paused before we parted ways, as I expected him to.

"You have a lot on your plate, Liz. I see it, and I don't want to add to it. But you need to take care of yourself, okay?" He stopped then. The silence stretched with everything he wasn't saying. When he continued, it was gently, "My offer still stands. I've heard you, and I get it. But the offer stands."

My throat caught in embarrassing fashion. The lump there was too thick to speak around; I could only send him a brief nod and a sick-feeling smile before I escaped to my car. I slid behind the wheel and cranked, forcing myself not to look up to where Warwick still stood, bulky and solid, watching me. I fiddled, checked the mirrors, set my phone in the holder, did all the things until my peripheral vision told me he'd moved on.

Sighing, I pulled out of the lot to make the hour-long drive that would take me the few miles back to the apartment I was renting in Williamsburg. I probably wasn't fit to be behind the wheel, but the vigilance needed to get out of the city, paradox-ically, allowed my brain a minute to rest. The comparative calm of the drive across the bridge and into Williamsburg, however, let other synapses start firing, and my wayward thoughts drifted to another awful instance months ago when Warwick had tried to offer solace. I'd turned him down then, too.

Rage. Hurt. Fear. Disbelief. Confusion. They all warred inside me as I paced the main floor living room of Maggie's brownstone. She stared at me...the same emotions reflected on her stunned face.

I'd just told her what I'd learned from Abe and Cassandra...that my mother had drugged Abe and myself in an effort to orchestrate a physical encounter...and, when the outcome of that effort was uncertain, she'd continued to manipulate me, feeding me something that had altered my cycle. I'd spent the last several weeks believing I was pregnant from an encounter I couldn't remember with a man I didn't love. All so she could add more zeroes to her bank account.

"Oh, God, Liz," Maggie had approached and wrapped me in her arms. I couldn't have been more grateful for her. I didn't know what I would have done or where I would have gone if she hadn't immediately said, "Come," when I'd called in tears.

"Are you sure? I mean, what the fuck?" Her questions were the same ones I'd had, but...

"Yes. They called their doctor...she was wonderful...," I finished through snotty inhalations after hiccuping the details of the multiple instant tests we'd taken. "She did a blood test right there. It was negative. They were all negative." I shredded the wad of tissues I held in my hand, trying to find a dry spot. Maggie shoved another handful at me. "She said there were ways to slow my cycle. Mother could have simply dissolved a daily birth control pill in my food. It's scary how easy it was, really." I shrugged and blew. Desperately searching for a mental foothold that would allow me to start the climb out of this initial hysteria.

"But she roofied *you? You and Abe?"*

"Something like that, I guess," I whispered, still trembling. Maggie squeezed me tight, trying to keep me from splintering into a million pieces. "It's too late to know now. But Abe said he'd gotten tested but nothing showed on his tox screen. But he'd waited nearly forty-eight hours. So, I don't know. I just don't know."

"But there has to be an explanation, right? How do they know?"

"Cassandra heard her. I called her, Maggie. I asked her."
"And?"

"She didn't deny it. She didn't say anything at all."

I'd broken down again then. Tears flowing because not only had I been tricked into believing I was pregnant, but I'd also finally accepted that fact, and now, I wasn't. Was it ridiculous to mourn a child you'd never actually been carrying? Was it ridiculous to miss that child when it had been with a man you didn't love and who didn't love you?

Not when that may have been your only chance, no.

That thought had brought heavier tears. Those hot, draining, headache-inducing tears that left you exhausted. I'd been wrung dry, nearly drifting off, when Warwick had burst into the room.

"What the fuck happened?" He'd asked. He hadn't shouted, but the question had boomed through the room, riding on that powerful baritone, squelching any sound that dared to stand in its way.

"Warwick, chill," Maggie began.

"Chill?" He'd asked darkly, his eyes sliding from Maggie to me, where I was curled on the sofa, too debilitated even to care

that he was seeing me at less than my best. "What's wrong with her? Tell me now, Maggie."

"I would tell you myself," I'd said, trying and failing to sound normal as my tear-scratched throat protested the effort. "If it were any of your business."

"You are my business," he'd responded without hesitation. My heart had leaped at the declaration before I squelched it.

"I've told you that I am not. You have no responsibility to me Warwick." I was sick of being someone to take care of, and I especially didn't want to be a to-do item on his *list.*

"I'll decide where my responsibilities lie," he'd come to kneel by me, getting far too close, seeing far too much. I closed my eyes and turned my head, effectively blocking out the sight of him but doing nothing to fortify against his clean, rich scent. I held my breath. Eventually, I felt him rise and move away.

"Maggie," he said. I peeked to see him pulling her out of the room. She glanced back at me, and I shrugged. I didn't care if she told him. He'd find out anyway if he didn't already know the meat of it. He and Abe were close. There was no reason to believe that Abe hadn't bent his ear with tales of how I'd trapped him and ruined his chances at happiness with Cassandra. What did it matter if he now learned it had all been lies built and laid by Mother?

Moments passed. If I could have drifted off, I would have. But it was no longer an option. My hand drifted to my belly, my empty womb. It had been the only potential brightness in this mess; now that was gone, too. Which meant the only thing left was the mess.

When Warrick and Maggie returned, the controlled fury rolled off him in great, slow waves; when he looked at me, all I saw was black...black eyes, black beard dusting those dark cheeks, black t-shirt and jeans, black boots...he looked like an avenging angel. If only I deserved that. But I didn't.

"Liz. Let me take you out of here so you can rest. You can't," he inhaled and let it go, "you won't... go back to Juanita's house."

He had no right to make that call. But he wasn't wrong. It was why I was here right now. When I'd left Abe's, the thought of returning home, of confronting her, had made my stomach roil.

I turned my gaze toward the ceiling.

"Again, Warwick," I repeated with as much snarl as I could muster, which wasn't much at all—in the end, I'd just sounded exhausted, "it's none of your business. I'll figure it out."

"It doesn't have to be with me," he'd tried again. "I can send you anywhere. Put you up for a while so you can go underground and think. Get some fucking space. I'll send Maggie with you." Maggie sputtered at this high-handed declaration. He tossed her a withering look.

"No," I replied.

He glared. "Liz. You're being stubborn for no reason."

"You don't get to tell me my reasons, Warwick. I said no."

He'd growled. Actually growled, before turning to Maggie, "So damn stubborn."

"Pot, kettle," she'd said. "She'll be fine. She'll stay here as long as she wants."

"You don't have the room. You have Lena."

"I know I have Lena," she'd said. I could hear the eye roll in her voice. "And I have plenty of room, as you well know."

Maggie was on the faculty at The New School, a private university in the city. She was well-known, well-paid, and able to provide very nice housing for herself and Lena. She was also the baby girl of Warwick Walker, Sr. and the mother of his only grandbaby. When she said she had space—she had space.

He'd huffed, and he'd puffed. But he'd eventually calmed down, and his energy had settled. Instead of looming over the room, prowling, ready to do battle with an enemy that wasn't there, it was now curled and coiled, watchful and protective. When he'd disappeared into the kitchen, Maggie had curled with me on the sofa, and I'd eventually drifted to sleep to the distant sounds of pots and pans clinking and clanging.

When I awoke the next morning, he was gone, but he'd left the refrigerator stocked with baked ziti and the house smelling of bacon and waffles...all comfort food of the highest order. I'd had a loosely regular breakfast with Maggie and Lena, and then the healing had begun.

I thought I'd done well, and I had. Months and months with a new therapist, one independent of Mother's recommendation, had shifted my perspective quite a bit, but it had also made it clear that I still had work to do. Of utmost importance was learning how to separate myself and my wants from hers. It was messy work because there was overlap, and I didn't want to have to create some polar opposite version of myself just to spite her. But I had to know that the things I longed for were genuine desires...not the ones that she'd taught me were appropriate. And until I was certain about that, I needed to be very careful.

My phone rang; the car display showed 'Mother' on screen. I ignored it but it rang again immediately. The Do Not Disturb feature on my phone worked flawlessly anytime I actually wanted to be disturbed, but today, when I craved the quiet Siri decided to go on strike. At the next light, I tapped and swiped to power the thing off. I'd deal with her when I got home...after a long bath and a large glass of wine.

Chapter 4

"Can you believe it?" I asked Maggie after clicking 'end' on the voicemail playback function on my phone.

"She's really a piece of work," she said, breathing heavily from our third run up the front steps of the Brooklyn Museum. Why we couldn't just sit in a coffee shop and wait while Lena's field trip took place was beyond me. But if fitness was on the menu, so be it.

"She really is. But what am I supposed to do?" I asked.

Mother had outdone herself. I had to admit I'd perhaps added fuel to her fire by not telling her about the blood test and then waiting several days before even listening to the messages she left after the meeting. When I'd finally felt ready for the foolishness and pressed play this morning, her most recent voicemail...from mere hours earlier...had played:

'Elizabeth. I understand that you are upset, but I believe I have been more than patient enough with you. I have apologized, but you continue to play the victim and push this family to the brink with your selfishness. Since you refuse to listen to reason, I am forced, as always, to do what's necessary to

preserve the sanctity of this household. I have allowed you this childish display long enough. You have ignored my repeated requests for you to return home. In light of this most recent news, it is most imperative that we present a united familial front.'

There was a pause. I let my lids slide closed in preparation, even though I knew full well what was next.

'I've suspended the monthly deposits from the trust into your account.' Another pause. I suspected she used that moment to allow herself a bit of self-congratulation. *'I'm sure you feel this is an overreaction, but I see no alternative. I'll expect you home within the week.'*

I'd be lying if I said it didn't hurt.

"Well," Maggie paused at the top of the steps, *thank God,* and we sat. She took a long drink from her water bottle before she continued. "I think first we need to determine whether it's even legal. I know it's a trust, but there are disbursement rules. If you've been allotted an allowance through your father's will and you've done nothing to violate the rules of the trust, I don't know how she could just turn it off like that."

I thought about that as I tugged my hair to tighten the ponytail I'd pulled it into. I was embarrassed for the umpteenth time that I didn't know more about the actual functioning of my adult life. I was thirty-two years old, had an MBA and I had allowed myself to be totally complacent. But shouldn't I be able to be that? Shouldn't a child be able to blindly trust their parent? Their own mother?

"You need a lawyer."

"But if I don't have any money, how can I hire legal counsel?" That seemed like an obvious concern.

"Mm. Good question. They would probably take the case based on winning it?" she shrugged, posing the statement as a question. "I don't know. But we could call Warwick; he would definitely know."

"Isn't there anyone else we could call? Don't you have an attorney?" I whined, not eager at all to pull him back into my problems or my life. It had been nearly ten days since I'd seen him at the meeting. We were set to gather again at the end of the week. I didn't know whether he thought that meant he should attend again, too.

Another shrug. "My own? No. The family attorney handles my needs. Even the divorce. Tonya manages all of it."

It would have been more surprising had that not been her answer. It was the reason I had no one to call; the only person who could answer these questions for me was Colin Lawson, our family legal counsel. Even if I called the office rather than him directly, my inquiry would get back to him and, thus, Mother.

"Have you called Lawson at all? Even if he can't change it, he should be able to give you some insight into what's going on."

"He's an ass. So, no, I haven't called him. At least not yet, but I know I need to. I'm just not sure what to ask."

"Mmm, well, Lena should be out in ten more minutes. Let's get her, and then we can go see Deuce," she said, using the pet name for Warwick that I so rarely heard. "He'll get you straight."

"Why can't we just call Tonya ourselves?" I asked. That seemed reasonable.

"We can and we will if you want," she shrugged. "But she'll definitely tell him, and then he'll call me asking about all the details and wanting to know why we didn't come to him to begin with. I'm just thinking of ways to cut through the bullshit."

She must've seen my hesitancy because she continued, "He'll behave himself. I don't know what it is between you two." I opened my mouth to say there was nothing between us, but she cut me off, "and I don't need to know. But don't cut off your nose to spite your face, Liz. He can help you, and he will. I'm sure he'll also respect whatever it is you need him to respect."

I've heard you, and I get it. That's what he'd said outside of the attorney's office a few days ago. Was that him telling me that he would do just that? Did there exist an option for Warwick and I to be just friends?

"Maybe," I said. She tossed a faintly amused look my way.

She laughed, "He will. If that's what you want." What did she mean by that? I looked her way seeking to glean her meaning from her expression, but she had already carried on, "Anyway, you can ponder it while I go grab Lena." And with that she bounced up and jogged into the building, looking for all the world like a kid herself.

If that's what you want. What did I want? While she was gone, I tied and retied my tennis, sipped from my water bottle, and began a slow march back down the steps to keep moving. It was cold out and sitting on the stone steps wasn't an enjoyable experience. I navigated the light flow of traffic while I tossed that question around. It wasn't a new question by any means, but it was one I tried to avoid when it came to Warwick.

"Are you sure this is what you want?" Warwick's voice rubbed along my senses, adding another layer to the complex web of feeling and emotion that was already wracking my body.

I nodded even though I wasn't sure. I wasn't sure about anything at all.

"You don't have to go along with it, you know. It's not the only option." He was standing too close, too warm.

"It's your choice, not hers," he said. I shook my head. Some part of me knew he was right, but it seemed so hard, so far-fetched. This would be so much easier.

"Lizzie?" that deep rumble wrapped around the nickname that, unbelievably, only he used. Just a little plea. I squeezed my eyes shut against the tumultuous rush of tears. Odd how tears originated in the chest and throat.

"Don't call me that," I said as I always did, punctuating the halfhearted order with another quick shake of my head. I couldn't think about it, couldn't even consider it because what kind of person would that make me?

Then a gentle touch along my arm...skin to skin. "Look at me, Liz."

Against my better judgment, I opened my eyes. My field of vision filled immediately with Warwick, mainly his broad chest, covered in a shirt, vest, and jacket that had been cut to his exact specifications. The exquisite fit both camouflaged and displayed his perfect body, the controlled strength, the muscles that were born of physical labor, not gym time.

"At me, Liz..."

I raised my gaze until it collided with the endless black of his. Over the years, I'd seen those eyes range from sharp, deadly obsidian honed by anger to the softest black velvet...like now...blanketing me in warm comfort I didn't deserve.

"I know we've never talked about this, about us," he paused and rolled his full dark lips in before releasing them on a sigh. He was clearly uncomfortable because this was so not the time or place. Plus, there was no 'us.' No matter how much I might want otherwise. I couldn't see my way clear to it. This was Warwick. Godrick's best friend, his closest cousin, his confidant. More of a brother than his actual brother. To even consider being with him when Godrick was lost to us, living no life at all, was the foulest betrayal I could imagine.

The fact that I wanted it desperately made it so much worse. I could never, would never, betray Godrick this way. I couldn't believe Warwick would even hint at it.

"There's no us, Warwick," I tried to laugh it off as silly and ridiculous. "What are you talking about? I need to get back." I could hear voices, Godrick's parents. Abe.

His big fingers, long with neat, short nails, traveled along my forearm, tangled with mine. "Liz, there's something here. I feel it. I've felt it for a long time."

I said nothing. He continued, "I think you feel it, too. I know you do."

I withdrew my hand, rubbed it along my thigh to silence the overstimulated nerves. It was too much. And it was wrong. "Warwick, I think you're mistaken. I value your friendship and the friend you were to Godrick..."

He interrupted almost immediately. "I loved Trey. Like I know you did. And for him, I was willing...happy, genuinely happy...to step back. And I mean that shit from the bottom of my soul. I mean," he'd given a chuckle—not bitter, but frustrated, "he saw you first, right? But he's gone," another pause, "He's been gone for a while now, and..."

"No." I stepped away. "I don't know what you're hinting at Warwick, but I'm not..."

He stepped forward then, blocking out the rest of the little vestibule we stood in so that my vision was filled with him, only him. My senses were overwhelmed with sight, sound, and scent. It was all so good, so perfectly tuned to what I wanted, what I needed. I'd thought he would kiss me. I'd wanted him to.

My mind betrayed me completely, taking me back to that moment of no return when I'd been forced to admit, to myself at least, that I wanted him. Badly. That day had occupied my dreams for too long; it still popped up from time to time when my defenses were at their lowest, obviously.

The rest of the conversation danced around the edges of my consciousness as I began the return trip up the stairs. I picked up speed. Maybe a higher heart rate would interrupt the reel playing in my head.

"I loved Trey. Like I know you did...but he's gone. He's been gone for a while now, and..."

"No." I stepped away. "I don't know what you're hinting at Warwick, but I'm not..."

"I'm not hinting, Liz. I want you. And I think—I know—you feel the same way."

He was right, then and now. There'd been this draw, this pull between us since the first time Godrick introduced us. Neither of us acknowledged it, much less acted on it because it didn't matter. I'd loved Godrick wholly and no fleeting attraction could interfere with that. Plus, we were both young and healthy, I assumed Godrick found other women attractive as well and I wasn't threatened by it. We were committed to each other; we had chosen each other, and I was happy to continue to do so.

But, Godrick had died. And, then, that weekend, Warwick had let his gaze linger, igniting feelings that I'd thought had petered into nonexistence. Feelings that still felt wrong and reeked of betrayal.

"I don't, Warwick," I had lied, "and if I did, it would be wrong—so wrong. You're his best friend, his brother."

He laughed bitterly, "And you find that worse, somehow, than being with his actual brother?" I flinched. He was right. Mother and Mr. Walker, Sr. were in there now, plotting a simple reallocation of my commitment from Godrick to his younger brother, Abe. It was a practical move that would preserve the intended merger of families and fortunes.

"It's different, Warwick, and you know it. This is just," I waved a hand, "business. It's not real. It probably won't even happen."

He looked at me like I'd grown another head. "So you're going to go along with it? Why?"

"Because it's easier! And if that's what they want, then why not?" I shrugged and rubbed my arms where the hair had been standing on end since he'd pulled me away from the group.

"Why not? Because you want me, Liz," he'd sounded so sure. He'd been right. I'd shaken my head again.

"I don't, Warwick," more lies spilling.

"So you love Abe?"

I shook my head again. At least I could be honest with this part. "No. But that's not a requirement. And love is overrated, don't you think? I loved Godrick, and look where it got me," I'd spat. "This is better. It's practical. It's smart. The family is fine with it, and so am I." And I waited, daring him to—and, terrified that he would—call my bluff.

"Liz..." He'd reached for me then, pulling me into him. My mind had resisted but my body hadn't. And when he'd caught my gaze, held it as his head lowered, I didn't move. Didn't turn my head, didn't shift away. Instead, I watched him, trying to record the moment he dipped and laid his lips over mine. But then my mind had seized at the contact from his warm, thick lips. I couldn't think, there were only swirls of color in my mind as his lips moved over mine, opening slightly, capturing my mouth in a soft kiss that immediately turned into something else when a groan escaped my lips and I pressed back against him, hungry for something I knew I couldn't have and didn't deserve. The touch of his tongue against mine sent heat racing down my spine, set off a torrent of emotion and a flood of wetness to match. I was on fire. I felt his arms tighten around me and as his head tilted to deepen the angle of this oh-so-wrong kiss, something shattered in the background. A quick curse and the sound of footsteps hauled me back to reality and I broke the contact. I didn't know whether the look of stunned shock on his face matched mine, but before he could say a word, before I could weaken and fall back into his kiss, I pushed out of his arms and returned to the sanctuary. I hadn't looked back.

I picked up the pace on the steps again, trying to outrun the heat gathering in my body...that always gathered...when that particular memory surfaced. That had been the last I'd seen of Warwick for years. Our paths had only crossed sporadically even before Godrick died, Warwick's family spending so much time in North...or was it South...Carolina. Those happenstance meetings had been even more scarce until several months ago when he'd returned to New York. Since then, functions and acquaintances had overlapped. We interacted in our stereotypically snippy fashion—mostly—when we encountered each other, but he'd made no mention of that long-ago conversation, or the kiss...not the night he'd stormed into Maggie's to find me falling apart on her sofa, and not when I'd seen him last week.

I didn't know how I felt about pressing my luck with another meeting today so when I saw Maggie exiting the building and talking animatedly with Lena about her visit, I made up my mind to take matters into my own hands. At least for the moment.

"I'll make the calls myself and see what I can find out," I told Maggie once we'd allowed Lena to take the edge off her initial excitement. "Then," I continued when she raised an eyebrow, "if I need help, I'll let you...and Warwick...know."

She raised an eyebrow, obviously ready to let me know what she thought of my plan when Lena joined the conversation.

"Uncle Warwick is a good helper, Auntie Liz." Lena offered.

"Thanks, baby girl. That's what your mom says, too."

"It's true. He helped me make my tiger layers."

I turned that over in my mind for a moment trying to decipher her meaning. In the last few months I'd become fairly proficient in Lena-speak but this one had me stumped.

"Tiger layers?" I asked.

"Yeah, I had to make a rama of tiger layers and Uncle Warwick helped. It was really good. Miss Lissa asked me to ask him if she could see his other carvings." She turned to her mom, "Did you tell Uncle Warwick that Miss Lissa wants to see his carvings, mama?"

"Oh, I told him," she answered shooting me the eye that let me know Miss Lissa was interested in far more than Warwick's carvings. But not to forget the issue at hand...

"Maggie. Tiger layers?" I whispered.

She laughed. "A diorama of a saber tooth tiger's lair," I nodded. That was an obvious one...I should have gotten it. "Warwick carved a little tiger for her to include."

"Carved?"

"Well, whittled. Warwick whittles."

"He what?"

"You know, carves things from wood with a little knife. Our gramps taught him one summer and he took to it," she shrugged. "It's a thing. He used to do it fairly often."

I was silent while I thought about that for a minute. Hazy images, reminiscent of the epic pottery scene in that one movie—of him teaching me his craft with lingering looks and touches came to mind. I blinked to clear the scene. What was wrong with me today? I definitely didn't need to put myself in Warwick's orbit again anytime soon. Getting Tonya's number and following up myself was absolutely the best approach.

"Mama, can I walk with Amanda?" Lena asked when she saw another friend and her mother headed in the same direction.

"Yes, baby, but stay where I can see you." Lena ran ahead to catch her friend and once Maggie and Amanda's mom made eye contact and waved, we continued our own conversation.

"Well, I'll send you Tonya's number and you can connect with her. Let me know if you want me around or if you need anything else. And," her voice took on a heavier quality, "you know you can stay with us, right?"

"I know. And I appreciate it. Thank you. Text me Tonya's information. I'll let you know what I find out."

And, with that, we said our goodbyes with Maggie and Lena making their way back to school and me dreading a conversation I should have had months ago.

Chapter 5

WARWICK

Desserts had just been served when Tonya Frye and I found ourselves semi-alone at the bar of Sei Less, one of Manhattan's upscale yet still accessible Asian fusion restaurants. I'd seen two actors, a senator, and a legendary rapper with his longtime girlfriend on my way to our reserved area. Since then, things had been calm.

The cocktail reception itself had been pleasant enough. The casual event was loosely arranged to celebrate the election of a long-time friend to a first district judgeship. It was a big deal. The more people who looked like us in positions of power, the better. So, I'd showed up happy to raise a glass in his honor.

Running into Tonya had been no surprise, she was a mover and shaker in her own right and I'd fully expected to see her here. For most of the evening, she'd been doing her thing, mingling and mixing while I'd been doing the same, reacquainting myself with a few faces I hadn't seen since I'd returned to the city and making promises to catch up when time permitted. For the most part, I was looking forward to the reconnections.

Once the celebration settled into little pockets of conversation, I found myself sharing a pair of barstools with a stunning trial attorney who was new to the city. We were doing the dance, feeling each other out to see how the night might end. She was my usual type: a little on the shorter side, curvy, confident, the same shade of brown as my mama, and funny. I was enjoying the conversation even if my mind flitted occasionally to a woman who was definitely *not* my usual type and had made it clear that I wasn't hers.

When I caught Tonya's eye over her shoulder, I clocked equal parts amusement and impatience. It was obvious she had something on her mind and since Tonya wasn't one to waste time...mine or hers...I concluded my business with pleasant anticipation of what could happen if our paths crossed again but no firm plans to actively make that happen.

I approached Tonya as she was slipping her phone away.

"I had an interesting phone call a few days ago," she began without preamble. She was a tall woman, beautifully imposing. Her signature afro was braided to her head today leaving long cornrows trailing down her back. Her light brown cheeks were slightly flushed and her eyes sparked under thick perfectly shaped brows.

"Did you now?" I asked, trying to read her energy. I'd known her long enough to know that the glass in her hand held some non-alcoholic concoction so whatever had her amped up wasn't chemically enhanced.

"I did. And you know I'm not one to gossip," she looked my way for confirmation, which I readily gave because she actually wasn't. At least not indiscriminately. Whatever she was about to tell me, she felt it was in everyone's best interest that I know. "But Elizabeth Brookes called me a few days ago."

My brows rose. Maggie hadn't mentioned this; we'd talked and texted multiple times over the last few days.

"Really?"

A sharp nod. "I'm walking a line here because this has nothing to do with you. But I know that family...her mother...and I know Colin Lawson, their attorney. Both are doing what they do best and Elizabeth is suffering for it."

I nodded. I wasn't surprised by her words. Or by the familiar anger that unfurled. But it wasn't my business, not unless Liz made it so, something she wasn't ready to do if her and Maggie's silence on this issue were any clue.

I sipped the old-fashioned I held. "Not my business Tonya."

"I just said that didn't I?" she retorted. She had. "But, again, I know that woman and I know Lawson. It doesn't look like Liz has her own legal advisor and she didn't retain me when we spoke. And, if what I believe to be happening is actually happening, she won't have the resources to retain anyone else."

"You can provide whatever she needs. Bill me."

She nodded. "Good enough. I'll reach out to her."

She changed the subject after that, reviewing a couple of non-critical issues we'd been discussing about Haven. I knew she wouldn't share any additional details about Liz unless I asked, and likely not even then. But I didn't want the details from her. I wanted them from Liz, if she was willing to give them to me, if she trusted me enough to share them. And so far, she hadn't.

And that was fine, I told myself. *She's just not that into you.* I chuckled, laughing at myself in spite of it all.

"Well, I'll let you get back to it," Tonya said, 'clearly your mind is elsewhere." She followed my gaze to where it appeared to be focused on Annyta. "You have a good night," she smirked and left, surely on her way home to her wife.

I didn't bother to correct her assumption–people would think what they would–but leaned in to drop a kiss on each cheek.

"Have a good night, Tonya. And thanks for letting me know about Liz. And thank you for helping her."

"Oh of course. I'd've helped her for free but I wanted to give you the chance to be a hero," she patted my chest and laughed.

"I appreciate your consideration. I'm sure my checkbook will feel more and more heroic with each invoice,"

"I'll do my best," she assured me and took her leave.

I followed soon after. My mind was focused on Liz and what she might be dealing with. I was no longer in the mood to schmooze but didn't want to head home to the empty house that waited for me.

I dropped a text to Abe and Vince to see what they were up to. I suspected Abe wouldn't be able to tear himself away from Cassandra but Vince might be free. I'd wrapped the necessary goodbyes and just stepped into the cool Manhattan air when my phone buzzed with a message letting me know that both Vince and Abe would meet me at a favorite watering hole a few blocks away. I decided to walk which meant we would like all arrive at about the same time. It was a slow stroll and it gave me time to turn some things over in my head.

Liz and I had a complicated past. Or, maybe it wasn't that complicated. I wanted her in every way imaginable. I wanted to be there for her, wanted to be the person she knew she could rely on. She thought that need was born of responsibility since she'd been Godrick's. And maybe there was a little of that there, but the core of it, the center of my need for her, had nothing to do with him; had actually lingered and eventually blossomed in spite of him. And in spite of me, too, because she was right...there was no version of life in which I would have betrayed my best friend. He was far more brother than cousin, and I had never wanted anything but joy for him. Our brotherhood was too solid for anything else.

So I'd counted it my lousy luck...and his excellent fortune...that he'd found her before I had and played my part. If I decided to pursue my graduate work down South to put a little breathing room in place, well, so be it. I'd expected them to be well and truly married by the time I finished that second degree, probably with some kids on the way, too. I had looked forward to being a godfather to those kids. But then the unthinkable happened. Trey died.

My world had crashed, leaving a gaping hole the shape and size of the brother I could no longer lean on, laugh with, argue with, or shoot the shit with. I hadn't handled it well. I'd disappeared, dropped the ball for Abe and Liz both, when I knew Trey would have expected me to do more, to do better.

Then, I'd resurfaced at a shitty time during a shitty event: a sickly entwined memorial for Godrick slash installation of Abe as the new CEO of HeirLoom. And, I'd behaved shittily while I was there, thinking I would sweep in and save the day by offering

Liz another option to the frankly disgusting plan of passing her over to Abe. She'd been right to turn me down. It had been poorly done—insensitive considering the day and presumptuous considering she'd never given any outward indication that she was interested. But I wasn't crazy. I wasn't a child, and I wasn't naive. I knew what I'd felt between us. And she'd verified it that day...even if she hadn't taken me up on the offer, she'd verified that the pull was mutual.

She'd also decided not to pursue it. The sparks were still there, still jumping like lightning between us, but I would respect her choice...there was no other option. If there were to be anything more, she'd have to come to me for it. She'd have to ask for it. And that thought shot straight to my dick because there was nothing more appealing to me or him than Liz asking for us.

And it was on that thought that I pulled open the door of Gloree and entered the low-lit speakeasy to find Abe and Vince already there, posted up in one of the comfortable seating areas. Gloree was a favorite, convenient but off the general radar it occupied the basement level of a black-owned bookstore cafe. There was a small but exquisitely curated collection of vinyl, that guaranteed that good music would flow through the speakers, tonight was no exception and the low tones of classic reggae set tonight's vibe. The intimate bar boasted an equally small and exquisite collection of liquors, for consumption inside, and cigars for consumption outside in the small heated courtyard. The faint scent of cigar smoke floated inside as patrons came and went.

We completed the requisite hand clasps and half-hugs, I put my order in with the staff person and we settled again.

"So, what's up, Wiz?" Vince started with that bullshit nickname that only he and I really understood. "Why the late-night powwow?"

"This is late-night for you? You must be getting old," I quipped, avoiding the actual question. "You could've stayed home, you know. Watched some reruns of Moesha."

"And deprive you of my riveting conversation and priceless advice. I wouldn't do that to you," Vince deadpanned.

"If you didn't have a date, just say that, man."

He chuckled, "Ninety-nine problems, and all that."

A little more back and forth before we tapped glasses and the three of us fell into standard guy conversation. We passed a comfortable hour or so debating whether the Giants would ever reach the Bowl, whether Tyson would kill Jake Paul, and how long it would take these cannabis stocks to really take off if sweeping legalization happened.

Eventually, the conversation turned to more personal topics.

"You know we're set to meet Boone again tomorrow," Abe commented.

I sipped and considered. "What time?"

"Two," he offered. "Are you coming again?"

"I don't know," I said honestly. "I don't know if I'm helping or hindering."

"I'd say helping but I'm a guy and what do I know," Abe shrugged.

"You could always ask Liz. I feel like she'd be able to tell you one way or the other," Vince offered. Always the voice of reason and practicality. But I nodded because he wasn't wrong.

"I'd say you probably need to be there because Boone has found some crazy shit. I don't know if he's shared it with Lawson yet, but he says he's going to and Lawson is supposed to be there tomorrow, too."

That piqued my interest, "What crazy shit? Is Liz about to be blindsided again?"

He didn't answer that question directly but instead said, "Brookes isn't her daddy."

I felt my head snap back. "What? What do you mean he's not her daddy?"

"Boone got access to the Heritage documents. There were some medical records in there. You know, the regular checkups verifying health and mental competency to retain the role of board chairman," he sipped, "The blood types don't work."

Vince sat forward. This was apparently new information to him as well.

"The blood types don't work?" I repeated.

He nodded. "Yeah. He probably wouldn't have noticed it if we hadn't just gotten the DNA work done. But apparently Boone was a bio major back in the day. Daddy Brookes is AB. Liz is O. He says it's impossible for an AB parent to have an O baby."

"But what about Juanita's blood type?"

"It would matter in most cases but since the old man was AB, that trumps everything. No matter what Juanita is, if daddy was AB, Liz can't be O. She could be A or B, but not O."

I sat with that for a minute. "Does Liz know?" She would be rocked when she found out.

Abe shook his head. "We just found out today."

What the actual fuck. "So Juanita, what? Just passed her off as Brookes's?"

Abe shrugged. "I guess. Liz won't be the first mama's-baby-daddy's-maybe."

Vince spoke up, "But the DNA test shows that Liz and Cassandra are related."

Abe nodded, "Correct."

A moment of contemplation, then, "The connection has to be through their fathers."

"They have to be," Abe agreed. "And we think Cassandra's father is Jacob Whyte."

Jacob Whyte was the son of Benjamin Whyte, who currently was at the helm of Whyte's, the textiles conglomerate that had been HeirLoom Textile's direct competitor since the early 1900's when great grandaddy Cyrus had sailed the ocean blue gathering material from first the Carribean, several countries in Africa including Morrocco, Algeria, and Senegal, to lay the foundation for his family's wealth. While Maggie's and my father had crafted his own path, Abe and Godrick's father had picked up the mantle and taken HeirLoom forward.

When Cassandra had first gotten her job with HeirLoom, she'd begun to receive photos of Jacob Whyte though she hadn't known who he was. Through some amateur sleuthing, with Vince's help, they'd discovered that Jacob had the same fairly rare complete heterochromia that Cassandra did. Abe's mother had pegged Cassandra as Catherine Brookes' daughter through the old school method of 'you look just like your mama'. It was also Abe's mother who had put Catherine and Jacob in similar spaces at similar times, though the reality of a relationship between a member of the Whyte family and a black woman seemed far-fetched.

The Whytes had a reputation of being less than welcoming of black business in the industry. The standard racial tension of the era had led Whyte's to try to burn HeirLoom out of the market both literally and figuratively, more than once. As time passed, the hostility and efforts at undermining were couched in legalese and constant takeover attempts.

"So if you think Jacob is Cassandra's father, then who would be Liz's father?" I asked looking between the two of them.

"No way. Not old man Whyte?" Abe just looked at me.

Vince huffed, "Well ain't that about a bitch."

I agreed with him. 'It' and Juanita were both about a bitch.

The rest of our conversation centered on how the hell Juanita could have ended up in Whyte's bed. When we finished gossiping like old women, we parted among more hand clasps and half-hugs and went our separate ways.

My phone was clasped in my hand. Should I call? Or should I mind my own business?

CHAPTER 6

ELIZABETH

The last two weeks had been an exercise in hell but I was handling it, not particularly gracefully, but I was handling it. After learning that Mother had dammed the flow of my finances, a call to Lawson, our attorney...her attorney...revealed that she was using my mental competence as the foundation for her decision. I rolled my eyes—with vigor—thinking about that conversation.

"Elizabeth, your mother has concerns about how you're managing. She's worried that your recent decisions are well out of character. You've stopped seeing your regular therapists and doctors and have cut contact with her. Unfortunately, she's determined that you may not be fully fit to manage your resources in this state. That determination is well within her rights as executor of the trust."

The obvious glee in his voice had been disgusting, as had his insinuation that he would be willing to speak with her on my behalf if I wanted to come into his office and have a 'private debrief' about my current situation. I shuddered. Lawson had been and always would be slime personified. While his light brown, angular face and well-proportioned wide features had aged well, he was easily twice my age. Even had that been my thing–which it wasn't–his approach squelched any physical appeal he may have boasted.

A less brief conversation with Tonya Frye verified that there was nothing I could do in the immediacy. I'd have to provide verification of mental competency from a doctor of Mother's choosing. This, of course, was ridiculous but I was continually learning how ridiculous Mother could be.

Even so, I could get this straightened out, hopefully, in a few weeks. The hold-up would be whether my old therapist...one who Mother had chosen for me...would be willing to honestly say that I wasn't mentally incompetent, just fed up with my mother's shit. The challenge was that she knew where her checks were coming from and it wasn't me. I couldn't be sure ethics would trump bank balances.

The more pressing concern was lodging. I was currently snuggled up with a blanket and my laptop wishing for the thousandth time that the heat did a better job of warming the condo I'd been so excited to find on short notice. After That Night, I'd moved out Mother's, stayed with Maggie for some weeks and then finally found my own place, this condo that reflected my independence–if not my style–that I had been proud to secure and pay for on my own. I scoffed, *On my own. That's a fucking joke.*

So now I was trying to work through the logistics of where I was going to go. The rent on this apartment would deplete the secondary savings I had stored. I rarely spent my whole deposit and certainly had a stash but I'd never needed to rely on it for my primary living expenses. There was no way I could live on it for more than a few weeks if I had to pay rent from it. I hadn't been irresponsible, but my real income came through the trust and investments made through the trust; I relied on that as my foundation. Why wouldn't I?

But, lesson learned. I needed to be thinking about what I was going to do for income and housing and it was stressful. Here I sat, a grown woman with no clue what to do next. Maggie had graciously offered her home as a stopgap but I'd leaned on her so hard already and honestly, it felt like a step backwards. I had recovered from Mother's horrific betrayal there and while she and Lena had been great, it reminded me of how I'd felt then...lost, undone, and alone. So, no. I didn't want to go there if I could help it, but nothing else came to mind. What the hell did people *do*?

Rather than continue to wallow, I dragged my laptop over and pulled up the work I was doing in organizing this year's Canvass fundraiser. Canvass was a nonprofit that worked to make art accessible and profitable for young people. The mission was broad but the unspoken focus was on kids from underprivileged backgrounds and households. I enjoyed the work and it took my mind off the things I should be thinking about.

The banquet was in less than a month and for the most part everything was lining up well. The music, decor, and catering were solid. The venue was, of course, in place. I'd like to have a few more options for the silent auction but we still had time. Those donations could come in until the last minute. We had previewed a few of the pieces in the invitations that had been sent weeks ago, but it was always most lucrative to present the majority of the items for bidding at the event. The people attending these things were notoriously impulsive and highly competitive especially once the drinks started to flow. I was very excited that we'd managed to secure a piece from Camille Rose, a young Black female artist new to the scene. I knew she had a few commercial endeavors but her real work, the pieces she kept for events like this, were absolutely remarkable. I expected a pretty penny to flow into Canvass' coffers because of it.

I was clicking again through my checklist when the phone rang. I'd left it on the dining table on purpose so I wouldn't spend the hour scrolling instead of thinking. But now, I'd had enough thinking and rose quickly in anticipation of a chat with Maggie. I glanced at my watch. Yep, 9:30. Lena would be in bed and Maggie would be in the mood to recap the day.

I hopped up to grab the phone, moving quickly when my barefeet encountered the cool tile that spanned the entire space. The pretty but mostly ineffectual electric fireplace and generous distribution of rugs tried to warm the place, but on cold night like this there weren't entirely successful.

Feet protected by the plush rug in the dining nook, I picked up the phone. It wasn't the goofy image of Maggie and Luna that I expected. *Cassandra W.* was written across the screen. *Huh.* What could she want? I swiped.

"Hello?"

"Um, hi. Liz? This is Cassandra." She was hesitant.

"Hi, yes, it's me. How are you?" I asked, the confusion in my voice was clear even to my own ears.

"I'm fine. I mean, yeah. I'm okay," she paused. I said nothing so she continued, "Look, there's something you need to know before we meet tomorrow. You are planning to come, right?"

I had completely forgotten that tomorrow was the next iteration of our own private Maury show. The lapse was a testament to the level of worry associated with my own problems. My presence tomorrow was perfunctory. Plus if my funds were frozen, the amount I had in those accounts was secondary. Getting access was my primary concern. I could worry about balances, later.

"Yes, I plan to be there. Two, right?" I mentally reviewed my calendar. I wasn't sure I'd actually noted the meeting, but I didn't think I'd scheduled anything else at that time. If I had, I'd need to shift it.

"Right. That's right. But, um, before you get there, there's some information you should know. I don't want you blindsided."

"Blindsided?" I repeated, taking the phone and wandering back to where I'd left the glass of prosecco I'd been sipping. I resettled myself in the corner and pulled the soft cashmere throw over my legs again.

"Yeah," she took a deep breath. I prepared myself for some more bullshit. I didn't think it would come from Abe or Cassandra. Despite the crazy circumstances, they were both good people. I hoped Abe's and my friendship could be restored and I wasn't opposed to a friendlier relationship with Cassandra. I needed all the friends I could get. These people were experiencing their own versions of the same hell and handling it with aplomb. Maybe I cold learn something.

"So you know Boone was going to pull together the paperwork to get a baseline of Heritage and start thinking about the split."

I nodded, remembered she couldn't see me, and said, "Yes..."

"Well, in the process, he came across medical records for Harry Brookes."

"Okay," I realized I wasn't being very encouraging so I added, "That seems reasonable."

"I guess. They told me that it's normal for CEOs of high-performance companies to have medical exams regularly to reassure the board of their 'vigor and competence'."

I could hear the air quotes in her voice and smiled. "I've heard the same."

"Well, blood types are in there and," she paused, then spat the rest out in a rush, "Harry was AB and you're O and they say that's just not possible."

My brain stuttered. "What do you mean, not possible?"

She sighed, "Just that. Not possible. Apparently, Boone has a background in biology and he caught it since he'd just been looking at our DNA stuff. He said he reached out to medical professionals and confirmed that an AB parent, regardless of the blood type of the other parent, cannot produce a child with blood type O. It's just not possible."

I sat. "So, you're saying..." I let it drag because I needed to hear the conclusion of this information.

"Harry Brookes couldn't have been your father."

Well doesn't that just take the cake? It was the sentence Mother had uttered when Boone read the results. She'd known. Of course, she had.

I was silent, trying to put order to my racing thoughts. And if she'd known, she couldn't have expected the DNA results to show me and Cassandra as related. That's why she'd been so smug in the beginning. She expected the results to be negative. So why weren't they?

"Liz?" Cassandra spoke my name...long moments had passed since she'd last spoken.

"But if Harry Brookes isn't my father, then how..." I asked because my mind had cramped and I couldn't understand the positive DNA test if we didn't share Harry Brookes's DNA.

An image of Harry Brookes, my father, sprang to mind. Tall and rangy, with smooth oak brown skin that defied his age. Always serious, sometimes solemn. He'd been kind and quiet and a refuge for me.

I set my wine glass down carefully. I'd forgotten it was even in my hand.

"Right. I think I'm still Catherine's daughter, though we'll have to confirm that in another fashion now. But I believe we share blood through our fathers still."

"Our fathers?" I paused, "But who's your father? Do you know?" I asked, then, "I'm sorry. I didn't mean it that way."

"It's okay, I know what you mean. And no, I didn't know until I came here. And honestly, all of this is overwhelming as fuck, excuse my French. I'd been putzing along perfectly happy as an orphan and system baby. Then I come here and have to contend with a missing mother and a father reputed to be a raging racist."

"A raging racist? Who?"

"Jacob Whyte. Benjamin Whyte's son."

That was the last name I expected to hear. I'd heard of Jacob and I knew Benjamin. Not well, but well enough to say hello and steer clear otherwise.

"Woah. How?"

"Girl, you tell me. I have no idea. But right now we're basing it on proximity and genetics. He had these weird bi-color eyes that I have and he and Catherine were here about the same time. Their circles would have loosely crossed."

"But what about me? I can't imagine Mother having an affair with a man that young. He would have been what twelve, fifteen years younger than her? And in his twenties? There's no way."

Admittedly, I hadn't known Mother then...since I hadn't been born...but given her need for propriety, I couldn't make it fit. There was absolutely no way Mother would be involved in such a relationship.

"Agreed, I guess. But what about his father?"

"*Benjamin Whyte and Mother?* That's impossible." My heart was pounding. It was impossible...wasn't it? Another mind cramp took hold, but I tossed the blanket off–it was suddenly unbearably hot–and rose to pace.

"Well. I don't know," Cassandra said with a sigh. "But I wanted you to know before you walked into the room tomorrow. Abe and I just learned today. Boone saw the discrepancy and spent a bit of time digging, checking old medical exams, and talking to folks to make sure he was right before bringing it to us. I believe him."

"That's just–," I paused. "More than I know what to do with honestly. But thank you. I appreciate your telling me before tomorrow."

I'd come to a stop in front of the sliding door leading to the balcony. The racing cars and streaking lights on the street below were the perfect complement to my jumbled thoughts.

"What do you think your mother will say when Boone shares the information? Is she coming?"

I stared blindly through the glass, focused on the darkness.

"I don't know. I don't know what she'll say and I'm not sure whether or not she's coming. I haven't talked to her since the last meeting." My head had begun to throb. I could almost feel it stretching and straining trying to figure out how to interpret and classify this new information.

"Oh. Well. Okay, then." A bit of awkward but kind silence. "I'll let you go then. Again, I'm sorry to just drop this on you but I figured you'd rather know ahead of time."

The tones of conversation wrap-up allowed my thoughts to slot into some faintly familiar pattern. I fell back on my ingrained training to politely end the call.

"I would. Thank you. I'll see you tomorrow, Cassandra."

Brief goodbyes, then I disconnected. I barely had time to let the news settle before my intercom buzzed indicating that the front door manager wanted to connect. I hadn't ordered anything recently so there shouldn't be any packages for me.

What now? I pressed the intercom button.

"Ms. Brookes, you have a visitor. Mr. Warwick Walker." Another thump of my heart. At this rate, I wouldn't make it through the night.

"Warwick? What are you doing here?" I asked.

"I came to check on you."

"Check on me? Why? I'm fine."

I heard his deep hum through the intercom. "Prove it."

I huffed. "I don't have to prove it."

"You don't. But I'll just stay here all night keeping your erstwhile doorman from other responsibilities if you don't."

I opened my mouth to send him away when he said, "I have a gift for you."

I'd like to say that that sentence didn't matter and really it didn't. Except...Warwick had a gift...for me? Curiosity crawled up my spine, wrapped and settled in my stomach. I was a sucker for gifts. And, honestly, a sucker for Warwick. Seeing him and whatever he had for me presented a far better option than spending the evening trying to unravel whatever it was that was going on with Father's bloodwork. *He's not your father.* I shook my head. I wasn't ready to consider that.

"Fine," I said, then, "Bobby, he can come up."

"Right-o, Ms. Brookes."

Moments later a knock sounded at my door.

Chapter 7

WARWICK

The doors to the fourteenth floor slid open. I took a fortifying breath before heading left to suite 1422. She hadn't asked how I knew where she lived; eventually, it would occur to her that she'd never told me. When I knocked on her door, to my surprise, it swung open readily. I'd half expected her to change her mind and leave me standing in the hallway.

Still, the giant box I held in front of me felt like a mistake. It had been impulse that made me stop, the blue and pink sign catching my attention unexpectedly. If I could disappear the box right now, I probably would. But it was too late. She'd seen it.

"Taco Bell?" She asked incredulously before I'd even stepped inside. "That's the gift?"

Shit. I stayed silent.

One perfectly arched brow climbed over lovely brown eyes. They were a true brown. Not almost black; not dark brown; not cognac or hazel. They were a true, rich, consistently brown, brown, *Like Saint's coat.* A grin spread across my face. She'd be pissed to know I was comparing her to my beloved Saint...a quarter horse of my grandfather's who I counted among my best friends. We'd grown up together during those summers in North Carolina.

"Give it to me," she grabbed for the box but I turned, blocking her.

"Let me in."

She rolled her eyes and smacked her pretty lips. "You're trying to bribe me. With *Taco Bell*. Are you serious right now?"

"You want it though, don't you?" I could barely believe it had worked. The flashing sign had triggered a long-buried memory of Trey telling me that her secret indulgence and comfort food of choice was Taco Bell and I'd swung into the lot before allowing myself to second guess the decision. The look on her face now—surprise mixed with reluctant delight—was worth the uncertainty that had hounded the drive here.

"How would you know that?"

"Trey told me."

Her eyes shot to mine, her lips quirked to the side a little before she sighed and turned, leaving the door open and offering me a view of her sweetly shaped backside, encased in a sneakily sexy one-piece sleeveless jumpsuit thing. It wasn't skintight by any means, but it seemed made for her, crafted to flow over every dip and curve. And it was pink, a pretty soft pink. Like the pink of her bottom lip. Jesus, did she have any clue how fucking edible she was?

"Come in, if you must," she said over her shoulder.

I trailed her inside and closed the door behind me. The scent of the place landed like a velvet-cloaked sledgehammer. It smelled like her. Soft and lightly floral; a hint of citrus and a touch of exotic spice riding underneath. Like a perfectly balanced French 75. The colors she'd chosen were light and soothing but not boring...a range of soft sages and muted blues accenting rich creamy fabrics. It was beautiful and feminine without being frilly and overdone. I would have expected no less.

"Well?"

"Well, what?" I asked.

"You came all this way. With Taco Bell. Why?"

She hadn't reached for the box again so I set it on the countertop and moved into her big-for-the-city kitchen area and began looking through her cabinets for dishware. She watched as I did so, arms crossed across her chest, face unreadable. Finding a platter, I set it out along with two plates and began to pull wrapped items from the box. Trey hadn't been specific. He'd only said Taco Bell. So I bought two of everything.

Before I could answer, she followed up with, "How much did you buy?"

I shrugged. "Two of everything. Four of those cinnamon twist things."

"Two. Of everything?"

I kept pulling out little wrapped packages. "And four cinnamon twists," I confirmed. "Trey wasn't very specific about your preferences."

I glanced her way, noting that underneath that sexy little one-piece, she'd lost weight. Oh, she was well on the mend from the episode all those months ago—she'd become uncomfortably slim in the weeks that had followed—now she just seemed to have dropped a pound or two. That was an easy fix.

Maybe made more so by a little thaw in the ice. "I can't believe you did this. I can't believe Trey told you."

"Trey told me all kinds of stuff about you," I teased. She obliged by shooting me a shocked and appalled look.

"Do tell." She urged as I continued to unbox the loot. Her eyes continued to track the growing pile of junk food.

"Apparently, you're funny as fuck in real life,"

"In real life?" She interrupted. "What does that mean?"

I continued, ignoring the interruption, "You can't cook for shit. You eat in the bed and leave crumbs in said bed," I caught both the open mouth and the faint blush before carrying on. "You love fresh flowers, cats and kids, some other stuff I can't tell you," I waggled my eyebrows at her. "Oh, and the pinky toe on your left foot is fucked up."

I added the last teasing bits because otherwise, it would have just been a list of all the reasons she should be with me. I'm funny, I can cook, I don't mind vacuuming the bed sheets and I also love flowers, cats, and kids. It was a match made in heaven.

She stared at me, narrow-eyed, trying to decide what to address first.

"What's wrong with my pinky toe?" She said finally, looking down and wiggling her toes, before she looked back up at me.

I lifted an eyebrow in acknowledgment of her decision not to call me on whatever else Tray may have said. "I mean, I don't know. I've never really looked at it. I'm just telling you what the streets are saying about it."

"My pinky toe is just fine, thank you very much," but she looked down again, eyebrows slightly furrowed.

"Don't worry about it. I'm sure it's okay. I mean, people live fulfilling lives every day with fucked up toes. You'll be fine."

"My toes aren't fucked up," she said knowing, surely, that she was damn near perfect.

"Let me see."

"No."

"I'll see eventually."

"No, you won't," she said and left the room. She returned in moments with pale green fuzzy slippers covering her feet. When I responded to the change with a lifted brow, she stuck her tongue out at me.

I smiled though inside I was high-fiving myself. Whatever she was dealing with, I'd brought at least a moment of levity to her evening.

"Now that we've settled that. Why are you here, Warwick?" She leaned against the entrance to the kitchen area, arms crossed in a way that highlighted her bralessness. I refocused my attention carefully on my task.

"Shall I go?" I started putting the little purple and white wrapped goodies I'd just unpacked back in the box.

"I didn't say that," she hemmed. "I'm just wondering what made you come."

"You," I answered succinctly. "I thought maybe you could use some company–someone who already knew about your pinky toe issues and was still willing to be your friend."

She glanced at me and twisted her lips. "Shut up." Then, a moment later, "You heard about my dad, I guess. Abe told you," she correctly assumed.

"He did," I didn't hesitate to admit it, there was no point in evading. But I wondered how she felt about my knowing so much of her personal business without her telling me. Maybe—if we got a little closer—I'd have to tell Abe to fall back a little bit. But at the same time, I was filling a big brother role for him; I'd need to manage both. "Are you angry?"

"That he told you? No. I should be, maybe," she shrugged, "but I'm not." She pushed away from the wall to come survey the spread of goodies. The soft scent of her shampoo cut through the greasy cheesy aromas. She settled on two cantina tacos, a beef crunchwrap and six packs of fire sauce, dropped them onto a plate, and went to sit cross-legged on the sofa.

I selected a couple of burritos and added my own plate next to hers on the low coffee table. I snagged her empty wine glass and, locating the open bottle of prosecco in the refrigerator, refilled it.

"I don't have any beer but there's bourbon in the cabinet if you want something stronger," she offered already unwrapping her selections.

"I'm fine with this." I passed her the prosecco and popped the top on the sparkling water I'd pulled from the fridge. She raised an eyebrow, watching me as she continued preparing her tacos, carefully spreading fire sauce along each one before moving along to the next.

"So, do you want to talk about it?" I asked after unwrapping the food I hadn't indulged in since high school. I wondered what revenge my body would exact once it processed what I was feeding it. Anticipating several intimate toilet sessions in my near future, I bit in, chewed, and enjoyed the moment for what it was. The shit was good, at least.

She looked at me, clearly contemplating how much to say. I couldn't blame her...it wasn't a subject easily put away once the top was popped. I waited.

Finally, she spoke. But the topic wasn't the one I'd anticipated.

"I still miss him," she said, then clarified, "Trey."

I nodded. This was, oddly enough, easier than talking about her dad. "I do, too. I don't expect it will go away." I paused, chewed. "I wouldn't really want it to, though."

She looked thoughtful but only nodded. "Me, either. It's still so hard. There are still days that I barely believe he's gone."

"Same," another few chews passed between us. The silence was a comfortable one. "Your DM took me by surprise last year," I risked mentioning the unexpected contact she'd made with me the previous year near the anniversary of Trey's death. I'd uploaded a photo of the two of us on Instagram.

The anniversary of Godrick's death had hit particularly hard last year. It had been my first year back in NY for the occasion. So I was caught up with a front-row seat to Abe's shit. Watching him turn himself inside out trying to build a dream I knew Trey didn't want for his little brother. But steering a determined Abe was like trying to redirect a freight train. That, combined with seeing Liz, watching her fight her own battles–hoping she'd decide to end this farce with Abe–well, suffice it to say I hadn't been in my best form.

The picture I'd found on my phone was of us from only a few days before Trey's death. We'd blown the day at his mom's house. Taking over her basement, watching ball, having a few beers and mostly talking about what it meant, these next steps we were both taking. It had been her idea to snap the photo. She'd sent me a digital version a couple of years after his death. The message accompanying the photo had brought me to tears. My timeline had brought the picture to the front of my camera roll and I'd posted it before I could decide against it. No caption.

I'd forgotten all about it; but then, she'd not only liked it but had also sent a direct message that read, 'It's a great picture. Thank you for loving him.'

I'd been at Haven in the middle of a conversation with Abe, had just mentioned her to him, when the message had pinged my notifications. Shocked, I had immediately walked away from that conversation to respond. But then, there wasn't much I wouldn't walk away from for her. We'd exchanged four brief messages. I'd memorized them.

<It's a great picture. Thank you for loving him.>

<Always. You good?>

<Not really.>

<Let me help you.>

Nothing more had followed. I hadn't spoken with her again until I walked into Maggie's to see her falling apart on the sofa.

"I bet. I was surprised, too. But it was a crazy time and I just needed to connect with someone who, I don't know, loved him and...didn't hate me. Things between Abe and me were so messed up at that time." A blush crept up her cheeks.

"Yeah, that's when you were playing the role of crazy, deranged arranged fiancée, if I remember correctly."

"I wasn't crazy," she chuckled and defended, "though you're right, I was definitely playing the part." She lay down the taco she'd been munching. "I can't believe how I behaved."

"Well. You were just trying to make the best of a fucked up situation." I tried to be neutral. It had been a touchy season, but yeah, she's been on one, no doubt.

"Maybe. I didn't know what else to do. Mother had made it seem that the only way out was to marry Abe. That if I didn't, I was letting her and the whole of Heritage down. I was too in my own head to see through her bullshit, although," she paused and addressed a moment I thought she'd never, ever reference in my hearing, "you tried to tell me better."

She didn't give me time to comment, but plowed right through, "She'd convinced me that Cassandra was some...I don't know...outside enemy trying to usurp what was rightfully mine. And I had to fight for what was mine." A wry chuckle slipped between her lips. "And it all started coming to a head around the anniversary of that night," she paused.

I said nothing because we hadn't talked about this. "The worst time was probably that evening Abe and I met at Haven, ugh," she took another bite, chewed, and swallowed. "I'd be traipsing all over Europe pretending I was Solange, I guess, trying to spend it away."

I chuckled. "Funny."

"And when I got back, there was Mother with her lies and Abe. Who was supposed to be my friend. I half expected when we met that day, that maybe we could talk about Trey a little. I don't know. It was a mess. I was a mess."

She continued to work her way through the taco. "But he immediately started talking about how he needed his freedom—wanted to be with Cassandra and—most importantly—was brave enough to do it. So, yeah, I behaved quite badly."

She sipped her prosecco. "I wish I could say I was totally brainwashed but I knew it was bullshit. It was just so much easier to go along with it because without Abe, without Mother's plan, what was my life going to look like?"

I nodded. "And now?"

"Now," she paused, "now, I realize that none of that was meant for me and I'm grateful to be out of it. This new situation is still crazy but at least it's teaching me to stand on my own. And that's something that's been too long in the making."

My heart thumped. I was proud of her, immensely proud. I was also glad my mouth was full because if it hadn't been, I'd have let loose with some foolishness along the lines of 'what about us', ruined the night, and earned myself and quick trip out the front door.

"My mother is insane, you know," she offered matter-of-factly. I wasn't sure how to respond because while I agreed, I knew that calling parents crazy was reserved for the children of said parents. So I just hummed. She could take it as she would.

"It's okay," she gave a little twist of her lips, "you can agree with me."

I shot her a raised eyebrow. "We'll work up to that." A little nod. Then, "I need you to know that while I might have been a bit...shortsighted about Abe and Cassandra, all the other stuff, the drugging, and the baby—or, not baby—I didn't know. I wasn't in on that."

I drew back, shocked. "Liz, I saw you that night. I know you weren't part of it."

She nodded, then, "But on to the latest news and that which brought you to my doorstep...I haven't had time to process it. Cassandra told me only moments before you showed up. So, anything I say now won't be censored."

There was a lot in that sentence. First, she didn't need to censor herself with me. I wanted raw, unfiltered, Liz. All day, every day. But, also...

"Cassandra?"

"Yes. Weird, right? I can't believe how kind she is even after I was such a bitch. I don't deserve her thoughtfulness. But she called so I wouldn't be taken by surprise tomorrow."

"Are you? Surprised?"

"Completely," she nodded vigorously, returning to pick at the crunchwrap since the tacos had been systematically demolished.

"And hurt. And angry. Not at him, but for him. I wonder if he knew."

"What about for yourself?" I asked. I couldn't imagine what she was feeling but I knew how I would feel if I learned my dad wasn't my dad. That shit would hit hard.

She opened her mouth to speak, closed it again, and pursed her lips. *Fuck*. Was she going to cry? Probably. I damn sure would.

"You wanna cry on my big strong shoulders?" I waggled my eyebrows at her and leaned back, opening my arms.

She gave me a weak, watery smile and to my immense surprise, said, "Actually, yeah, I do."

The weak smile morphed into an equally pitiful laugh at the shock that must have been written all over my face. But I rallied quickly and grabbed napkins to wipe the hot sauce and taco shrapnel off my hands. She was watching me skeptically but I took the opportunity to position my big body more deeply in the corner of her surprisingly sturdy sofa and again, held my arms out to her. I knew when to lean into my strengths as a big man; this was one of those times.

She sighed deeply, slipped in and lay her head on my shoulder. The movement obviously reminded her that she'd tied her inches up sometime that evening because her hand floated to her silk-covered head while her eyes widened at me.

"Girl, you know you're fine as fuck even with your head wrapped up so stop playing." When she huffed but settled again, I continued, "You also know you don't have to worry about being politically correct around me, right? Say what you want to say. I'm not the judgy type. Can't afford to be." There were plenty of times I'd been judged, with mistakes elevated to character flaws and opportunities for learning replaced with punishment. I wasn't trying to be the monster in anyone else's story.

"Speak your mind, Lizzie," I said. She thumped me—her standard response to the nickname I couldn't help teasing her with—and moved to get up. But I tightened my arms with a chuckle, "Relax, I'm kidding."

"I'm pissed," she said finally. She didn't cry, but I felt the anger and hurt embedded in every sibilant moment of the word.

"After everything else. After *everything* else," she stressed, "this. How could she take him from me?"

I couldn't see her face but I could feel the shudder move through her body, I could feel the weight of her settle more fully against me and I could feel the faint shimmer in her body while she tried to hold back. I rubbed her back, taking in the fine bones of her spine and shoulder blades.

"She can't take him from you. You do realize that, right? What the two of you had, it still holds." I offered the words, thinking they might bring some hint of peace if it were me in her position.

"Does it? No wonder he was so sad all the time. To think," she paused to take a small breath, "his only child disappears and now he's forced to accept this woman's outside child," she whispered. "To treat me like some sort of half-baked replacement?"

I shook my head slightly even though she couldn't see me. My heart broke for her. "Don't do that. Don't diminish that man's love for you. He wouldn't have blamed you."

She shrugged. "Maybe not. But there's no reason for him to have loved me either, is there? He was a good man. He treated me well. He didn't deserve what she did."

A few minutes passed before she spoke again. "Do you think he knew?"

It was a good question. One I'd want to know the answer to myself. "I don't know. I can't believe it would have mattered regardless. Everything I know about Harry Brookes, everything my father has ever said about him, is that he was a genuinely good and kind man. And that he lived for his daughters."

She glanced at me. "Your father said that?" She looked skeptical, "When?"

"Recently. You know this shit has hit the black gossip network like wildfire, don't you? My mother has called for 'the tea' more times than I care to admit," I told her adding verbal air quotes around my mother's requests for intel.

At that, she sat up. "What did you tell her?"

"The truth. That it's a shit show. But I can say that when we talked about Cassandra being Catherine's daughter potentially, she was happy to hear it. And they both said that you saved Harry's life. That without you, he would have just faded away. A man who doesn't love a child doesn't take that kind of strength from them, you know?"

She resettled herself at that. Her head moved under my chin in what felt like a nod. I hoped she was hearing me. I hoped she wasn't rewriting her childhood into something ugly. I told her as much.

"Don't take everything from yourself. Don't take everything from him. You each had the other to see you through your own personal challenges. You brought that man joy. You should take joy in that." I paused because she seemed to be considering my words, nodding slowly.

"Tell me about him," I urged her. "Tell me about the best times you had together."

Chapter 8

There I sat, in my own sweet nightmare, pouring out my heart and tears on Warwick's shoulder.

Warwick. Big and solid. Smelling like male heaven and setting my soul to rumbling with every word he spoke. His big hands were rubbing my back setting off little trails of fireworks amidst the comfort he offered. At five-eight, I rarely felt small and protected. Even with Godrick, I hadn't felt this sense of being encompassed. Godrick had been a bulky five-eleven, strong and masculine to be sure, but not like Warwick who was just...ginormous across the board.

And that point of comparison was enough to make me blush because if his body was this big, and his feet were that big, then...

I shifted, placing my hands on his chest to lever myself up and off because lord knows those weren't the thoughts I needed swirling in my head. The bands of his arms tightened briefly before they loosened, granting me freedom should I choose to take it. I didn't want to, but I did.

"Thank you for listening, Warwick," I said as I eased away, putting much-needed space between us. I'd spent the last who-knows-how-long curled around this man I swore I didn't want, pouring out my memories. And he'd listened with stunning attentiveness.

I watched his hands clasp, then relax. "I'm still here. Still listening, you know," he rumbled.

"I do know that. Thank you. Again. As always," I stood, my heartbeat thumping, and scrubbed the heels of my hands under my eyes, swiping away the lingering tears and giving myself a little cover. I ignored his gaze following me as I gathered my wineglass and the shrapnel from our meal to transport it all to the kitchen.

"Are you embarrassed?" He asked, cutting through my mental gymnastics with that unerring ability to see through me and equally unconcerned willingness to call me on whatever he saw.

"Embarrassed? No," I said reflexively but then paused because maybe I was. And if I were, would he take that as a cue to leave? "Well, maybe. A little. So..."

"So, what? So, you're ready for me to go now? Just use me for my body and then send me on my way, huh?" His deep chuckle skated across my senses before he went quiet.

When he spoke again, it wasn't what I expected to hear.

"Tonya Frye told me your mother cut off your funds."

Okay—I felt my head jerk slightly—that was a surprise.

"Are you angry?" He repeated his question from earlier in the evening. I hadn't been angry then because I knew how close Abe and Warwick were but I had expected some sort of confidentiality from my damned attorney. Why did everyone feel so free to discuss my affairs?

"I am," I said truthfully. "I would have expected some sort of attorney-client privilege? Why in the world would she share that with you?"

He made some sound deep in his throat and tipped his head back in agreement. But then he shrugged, " She said you hadn't retained her and she was worried about you."

"So she came to you. Why you? Why not Maggie? She's who gave me the number and I conveyed that when I spoke with her."

"Because I employ her and it's her job to keep me informed about anything that might be of interest to me."

"Anything that might be of interest to you?" My emotionally drained psyche couldn't begin to figure out how to process that.

"She's been with me for several years. She's learned about Trey," he said it matter of factly. "About people who matter to me," a brief pause before he continued. "She also knows just about everything that happens in the bougie black echelon of New York so she knows Lawson is trash. And may have similar sentiments about Juanita. But I can see how it might come off to you. She didn't mean it that way."

I nodded, processing his words, realizing that he'd just addressed every question that had fired off at his pronouncement. "I'm sure she didn't. But I still don't like it."

"Understood. It won't happen again."

I scoffed. "'I'm sure."

"Seriously. I explicitly told her to consider herself retained by you and only you. No more updates. She's your attorney now. Unless you intend to take legal action against *me*. That's different."

"I can't afford your precious attorney. As you've recently learned, I've been cut off."

"True. But she'll take you on under her standard retainer. I'll cover anything extra you may need."

"Warwick, I can't accept that."

"I'm happy to do it," he said as if the topic were closed.

"And I appreciate your happiness to do it. But I'm not interested in being beholden to someone else. I didn't retain her officially because I couldn't afford it. And I'm only interested in engaging in things I can afford myself these days. Your attorney, on your payroll, isn't what I want."

I could feel his eyes heavy on me. I took a deep breath and turned to face him. I had to learn to actually be brave and strong, not just play at it, if I were going to get my life under my control.

"I understand that. And I respect it. But don't cut off your nose to spite your face. I'm offering you help. Freely, with no strings attached." I could feel my eyebrow crawling up my forehead. He definitely saw it. Those thick sexy lips twitched in amusement. "You don't have to do it all by yourself just because you're finally realizing that you need to do it."

He made sense. It was tantamount to what Maggie had been saying for weeks. I needed to learn the difference between help and attempts to control my life. The defining line was narrow though and I couldn't think clearly. The crying jag had left my head cloudy and fuzzy. My eyes felt swollen and my skin was still hyper-sensitive from having been pressed against Warwick for those long moments.

"I'll think about it," I said. "But I need to do that alone," I sighed as my thoughts shifted to the coming day. "And I need to get it together for tomorrow."

"I'll be there." He stood, adjusted his t-shirt to fall freely across his muscled body, and began to move toward the door. A rush of disappointment-tinged relief flooded me.

"Oh, really?" I said, just to be snarky.

"Do you want me there?" he asked, then eyed the remnants of our fast food feast. There were a ridiculous amount of tacos left on the countertop. "And do you want me to take any of this with me?"

I waited a beat because *did I want him there?*

"Yes, to both," I said before I chickened out. I needed a friend and he was proving to be just that.

He gave a quick decisive nod. "I got you. Go wash your face and lay down. I'll take care of this."

I didn't go lay down, but I did slip out to lay a cool cloth over my face. The face looking back at me in the bathroom mirror was blotchy and swollen but not defeated. I dampened a clean cloth with ice-cold water and pressed it to my eyes, clearing away the tear streaks and calming the swelling.

When I returned to the living area, Warwick was gone, as were most of the tacos. He'd left two cantina wraps and one pack of cinnamon twists.

Chapter 9

Liz

"**C**an you believe she didn't show?" It was Cassandra who addressed the elephant in the room.

The fact that Juanita had chosen to go MIA for today's meeting was screwing with everyone's heads. Completely unexpected and completely out of character, her absence was a blessing and a curse. Mostly a blessing but I was pissed at the amount of time and energy I'd dedicated to preparing myself to see her.

After Warwick left last night, I'd kicked myself for sending him away. The alternative, sitting in my apartment worrying about today's encounter and trying to unravel the twisted threads of my childhood had proven terribly unsatisfying. I'd finally fallen into a fitful sleep only to wake up barely rested, bonnet lost in the covers, three hours later. After that, sleep eluded me and I'd spent the four hours between then and the start of the meeting sipping coffee, picking at a bagel, planning my outfit, and practicing scathing setdowns to use against Mother's hateful commentary.

But the session had gone quite smoothly without her there to disrupt. Much more so because Mother wasn't there. Her absence left Cassandra, Abe, Warwick, and me free to discuss the situation with Boone without her lies and constant venom contaminating the conversation. But no matter how much easier it was without her, it was there in that cool, dark office, comforting in its stereotypically lawyerly decor, that I learned there was no way Harry Brookes was my father. Boone had thoughtfully arranged for a medical professional to join us remotely. She had presented a careful, if elementary, lesson on genetics and made it clear, at least to my non-scientific mind, that genetics just didn't work that way. The man who had presented the only taste of unconditional love I could remember was not my father.

It shouldn't have mattered. Whether we shared blood or not, the feelings had been the same. The joy and quiet laughter had been genuine. The feelings of calm refuge that I couldn't put a name to back then but had sought out instinctively were real. This is what my grown thirty-something self continued to tell the child inside whose heart was breaking.

But what if those feelings weren't real? Weren't mine to claim? What if those feelings had been stolen from him, shared only because he thought I was flesh of his flesh. Would that same comfort have been so freely given had he known the lies my mother told? Had he known that I was just another of those lies? I hated the thought that he had been tricked. Duped into loving and caring for a child who wasn't his. While he should have been free to dedicate all of himself to mourning the loss of the child who was.

I couldn't stop thinking about it. Not even when Warwick laid his hand at the small of my back to usher me into Gracie's Kitchen, the restaurant where Cassandra, Abe, he, and I decided to have a late lunch and an early drink.

"I won't ask if you're okay. I can see that you're not," he grumbled into my ear sending a quick shiver across my skin. "If you want to get out of here, go somewhere private, or just be alone, you say the word. You hear?"

I nodded. It all felt faintly surreal. The kind doctor had gone on to verify what Cassandra had supposed last night. Given the DNA readings, we were absolutely related. She'd shared a few relationships that made sense given our twelve-ish percent shared DNA.

We found ourselves at a table in the back of the restaurant. I slipped into one side of the booth while Cassandra did the same opposite me. Warwick crowded his big body in next to me and across from Abe. Their opening conversation took place around me. I heard them consider drinks and appetizers, heard Warwick order a Perrier and a dirty gin martini alongside his standard Woodford Reserve. He slid them both my way when they arrived.

I hesitated, torn between the two glasses. Cassandra pushed the water my way.

"Hydrate first."

I followed her advice.

"I'm acting like my whole world just fell apart but this also means you can't prove that Catherine was your mother. I'm sorry," I said once the cool water cleared my head enough to fully consider the impact on her. She and Abe had initiated this inquiry after all. They wanted answers.

But she shrugged. "I don't know how to feel really. Part of me wishes I'd never started the process. I never thought this would happen. I'm the one who's sorry. I never meant to open this kind of a can of worms."

It was mind-blowing that she was being so kind. I didn't have enough energy to hide what I was thinking.

"How can you be so kind?" I asked, clear wonderment in my voice.

Another shrug. "Girl. You've been through hell and back. What did I really have to deal with?" she asked. "Staking claim to my man? That shit is run-of-the-mill." Was she really dismissing that whole episode as 'staking claim'? "But the shit you're dealing with? With your mother? I don't know. I tell Abe that between his father and now your mother. I know I should be all in on finding out these answers. But I'm not. I'm curious, of course, but I came to grips with not having parents a long time ago. I've had a lot of therapy over the years. Margeaux and Destiny and, now Abe, are my family. I've picked them and they've picked me.

"It must be freeing."

"Maybe. Yes, actually, it is. The circumstances of my parentage don't define me. The older I get the better I handle the days when my mind tries to convince me otherwise. But those are really few and far between now. To be honest, all this," she waved a hand, "has actually brought up more anxiety than anything else. I haven't had to think about this shit for a long time and now it's front and center again."

"So how are you managing it?"

"Honestly, I'm halfway pretending it's someone else. It's so far-fetched and far removed from anything I could have imagined. I mean, really, listen to it," she dropped into a melodramatic voice, "'A woman goes missing. Years later her daughter shows up and falls in love with her half-aunt's fiance and inherits half of a family fortune," she returned to her normal voice and shrugged, "It's all just click bait...."

I nodded and grinned, surprised I found it funny. She continued, "Now I still can't verify my identity and the only thing that's linking me to this whole crazy story is one woman's memory and another man's eyes. It's just not where I need my focus. What's far more interesting to me is that I own my own atelier and just launched a hugely successful clothing line under my own name. *That's* what I want to focus on." She took a long sip of her pink tinged drink and leaned forward, lowering her voice a little.

"But," she said, "it's different for you. This is your father, who you knew. This is all directly affecting your day to day life. And I feel horrible for dragging you into it."

"Mm," I responded. She'd said so much, dropped so many nuggets that I wasn't sure what to comment on first. The easiest was the last bit.

"First. Don't feel bad about any of this. I needed to know these things. I needed to know–need to know–who and how my Mother is. Whatever I learn about my Father, she already knows. And chose not to tell me."

"Maybe she was protecting you," Cassandra offered.

"I appreciate you saying that but I think we both know it's not the case. Nothing my Mother does is for anyone's benefit but her own. So I do want to know the answers if for no other reason than so I can prepare myself for whatever's coming next."

Cassandra nodded and leaned back so the server, who had just returned could slide several tapas onto the table.

Warwick immediately took my appetizer plate and loaded it with samples while avoiding the seafood and avocado. Yet another kindness.

"I get that," Cassandra picked our conversation up as if it hadn't paused for food distribution purposes. "But what will you do next? Have you spoken with Juanita? Does she know that you know?"

I shook my head. "No. I haven't spoken with her. I anticipated seeing her here today. The fact that I didn't makes me nervous. I don't know what it means but I'm sure she has something up her sleeve. Especially since Boone made it clear that she is aware of the findings. She must know that I've been told by now."

"She's expecting you to call her?"

"I suspect that's it exactly."

Cassandra chewed thoughtfully on her potsticker. "Will you?"

"I don't know," I traced the edge of my plate, the food on it untouched still. "I'd like to. I'd like to be able to. But I also know what I'll be walking into. I 'd prefer to delay the whole episode as long as possible. But I know that's not practical."

Warwick, seemingly engrossed in his own conversation with Abe, nudged my plate toward me, a not-so-subtle reminder to eat. When I randomly plucked something and popped it in my mouth, he turned my way, his pleasure caught in the bare softening of the gaze that snagged mine. The food suddenly tasted less like cardboard.

"I can see that. Putting it off is just as nerve-wrecking," Cassandra offered soft agreement, pulling my attention away from Warwick. But not before I saw the way his eyes dropped to my lips.

"Precisely," I responded to Cassandra. "I wish I had the distraction of work as you've mentioned. It's something I haven't figured out yet. My professional calling," I said it jokingly but it was definitely not a laughing matter. I needed to figure some things out.

She hummed thoughtfully. "How's the planning for the Canvass gala coming?"

I felt the surprise register on my face. "How did you know about that?" It came as a complete surprise that she would know of my involvement with the planning of the Canvass event.

"Abe mentioned it," she reached over to stroke his shoulder. He immediately shifted his attention to her.

"I mentioned what?" he asked, clearly unconcerned with whatever he'd mentioned, but just happy to be looking into his fiancee's beautiful face. The mix of lust and affection on his face made my heart thump. *That's not for you. Not right now.* I reminded myself. Not because of Abe—I was well past the echoes of what had never seriously been—but because I was still hungry for what the idea had represented. Security. A future I understood and could control. A family complete with a loving husband and children. But as much as it called to me, I knew

I needed to generate the first two myself. By myself and for myself. I couldn't begin to think about having someone else in my life until I–*I*–figured out said life.

"Oh yeah, Warwick told me." Abe's mention of Warwick brought my wandering mind back to the conversation at hand. What had Warwick told him?

"It was Maggie," Warwick said, recentering that devastating gaze on me.

"Maggie?"

"Who told me you were working on the Canvass project."

"Oh." That's all I said because it's all I could think of with him staring at me like that. Was it getting hot? I reached for my water but my hand moved before my eyes. Warwick reached around me to steady the glass before it could topple. The move put his upper arm in direct, if fleeting, contact with my chest. It was just enough to have me crossing my legs under the table on a back arching squirm.

"You good?" He asked, setting the glass a little further from my elbow.

I nodded, then said, "I'm good." If the words were a little breathy, I chose to blame it on the near-miss of a dousing in sparkling water. Beyond that, I could only stare into the black velvet staring back at me.

"So it's coming well then?" I turned my head slowly toward Cassandra, unable to break the eye contact with Warwick. When I finally did, it was to see blatant amusement in her bi-colored eyes. "Things are going okay?" She rephrased and gave a little nod, encouraging me to answer.

"They are," I finally responded, feeling the blush crawl up my cheeks. She'd caught me gawking. I scooted a bit to put a touch more space between myself and Warwick. It wouldn't do for Cassandra to tell Abe if she believed there was something happening. There wasn't, of course. But I wouldn't want Abe to believe I could–that I would–start a relationship with his brother's best friend.

"Maggie says it's going more than okay," Warwick chimed in. "I believe the phrase she used was 'out here taming the chaos'".

The smile that bloomed on my face was genuine. "Well, Maggie is very kind."

"Maggie is very honest," Warwick said. "I've never known her to offer empty praise."

"Me either," Abe chimed in.

"Are you planning the whole thing? I can't imagine," Cassandra gave a little shudder.

"Didn't you just plan a whole fashion show?" I asked.

"That's different and also, not really. I had a team of people...apparently like you...who took my ideas and made them reality. So maybe I visioned a show but I damn sure didn't plan one." She said it almost absentmindedly as she picked through Abe's plate and he watched her.

"Maybe. But yes, I'm responsible for all aspects of the event. Planning and design, sourcing and vendors, contracts, logistics, budgeting. I do have several very capable people working with me though. I don't want to make it seem as if I'm managing all of these tasks myself."

"But you are the project manager essentially? If it doesn't happen, it's on you, right?"

I nodded because that was certainly true. "Correct."

"How many people are you all expecting? Abe and I rsvp'd a couple of weeks ago. I'm looking forward to the silent auction. I saw Camille Rose's name on the list of contributors."

"Oh, I was so excited to get her," I said, delighted to share my girl crush with someone else. "I love everything she creates."

"Same. Even her mainstream line is head and shoulders above anything else you see out there."

"Agreed." Our side conversation meandered a bit around the world of black art before returning to her earlier question. "We're expecting around three hundred fifty guests. But melt is often as high as ten percent. So we'll see."

"You seem to really enjoy it."

"Oh, I do," I hesitated, feeling very relaxed and very much eager to continue our conversation but also at an internal cross-roads of how much to share. The rest of my response could be a polite and wholly appropriate comment. Perhaps a brief anecdote of one of the more entertaining triumphs of planning...there had been a few. Or, I could share a dream that I hadn't revealed to anyone, had barely allowed myself to ac-knowledge it in the daylight. But in the nighttime, when dreams ruled...

"I very much enjoy it. I've even thought of," another moment filled with a fortifying breath, "I've thought of starting my own business. I've planned two other events of similar size in the last two years amd countless smaller events over the years. It's always just been something to keep me busy but in light of recent events–no pun intended–it could be more. I think I have a knack for it." And I waited. Waited for her to laugh.

For Warwick to have overheard and either join her or worse, pretend he hadn't heard so he wouldn't have to respond at all.

The concept of starting my own business was both foreign and completely familiar. I'd been raised in a household supported by a self made man. Entrepreneurship should be in my veins. But when he died, my trips to the shop ended. My learning the ins and outs of the business ended. My lens was refocused to center on forming a perfect union with the perfect man. So here I sat with a whole MBA, scared shitless to do this very big thing for myself and by myself.

"Oh, that's a fabulous idea. You can plan my next show if you're available. I mean, I know I have HeirLoom's resources," she leaned into Abe, who dropped a kiss on the top of her head, "but I need to start developing my own business relationships."

"I'd love that," I answered, half-shocked, half-dismissive because she couldn't possibly be serious but at the same time, she *sounded* serious. And so immediately supportive of the idea. As if I weren't engaged in the internal struggle of a lifetime. She responded as if it were a *fait accompli* that I could and would do this.

"Have you made any moves to start yet? We can talk if you want. Oh, and with Margeaux. She's a wealth of information about starting and running a business. And she has some wild stories about being a black female business owner. There's shit you'll need to be aware of."

"I can't tell you about being a black woman in business, but whatever you need, you've got it on my end," Warwick said.

"Same," Abe chimed in. "I can't believe you haven't done this already. It makes perfect sense. You used to plan all Godrick's parties and conferences. All that shit."

I nodded because he was right. I had forgotten.

"I have an idea," Warwick said slowly. "But first, tell us more about Canvass."

Oddly excited and happy to have my mind on something positive, I told them about the project, the venue, a few stories of dealings with vendors who thought they'd take advantage of me, other stories about finding new, up-and-coming artists who I was able to give a break to. I could geek out over the whole process for hours but managed to contain myself to about fifteen minutes.

"I have a contract position for you, if you want it," Warwick said when I finished.

"What?"

"Yeah, as your first client. My events manager at Haven New York is going to be out of commission for a couple of months. I need someone to fill her shoes until she returns," he dropped that bomb then said, "Let's bless the food," before grabbing my hand under the table and launching into a quick request that God bless the four of us and the hands that had prepared the food. Then, I watched mesmerized as he cradled the huge burger he'd ordered, took a hearty bite then swiped his tongue out to capture the crumb that clung at the corner of his mouth. The man even chewed sexy. I wanted to roll my eyes at him.

"I can't work for you," I said after I'd recovered from my in-depth analysis of Warwick's eating methodology.

"Why not?" he asked, plucking a couple of fries.

"Because," I stuttered. "You don't even know if I'm any good."

"I just sat here and listened to you run down your whole process. You asked all the questions, you value relationship building, you're trying to put young black businesses on, your attention to detail is crazy, and you're smart as fuck. What else is there to know?"

"I don't even have the business set up yet."

"Well. I can hire you as a regular employee if you'd prefer but we can get your paperwork filed in a matter of hours. It'll take longer than that to process at the state but we'll rush it," he turned more fully my way. "That's if you want to. If it's what you want, I can help you make it happen."

This man. I'd never had anyone speak to me with that level of assuredness and simple focus on me. I wasn't sure what to make of it. I certainly wasn't sure how to respond to the intensity in his eyes. I knew what I wanted to do. I wanted to push the table aside and climb into his lap. I wanted to wrap myself around him and bathe in the calm that seemed to envelope him no matter what was going on around him. I wanted to go back to last night in that brief moment after the tears but before I made myself move. That moment when we just *were*.

Since I couldn't do any of that, I chose to respond to his words. "You can't possibly mean that. Surely there's a process you have to follow."

"I mean every word of it. And, you do realize that I own the place right? I make the processes."

CHAPTER 10

"I'll pick you up tomorrow. Or do you want to just meet me downtown?" Cassandra's inquiry followed the hug she gave me as we said our goodbyes in front of Attorney Boone's office. We'd spent well over three hours talking from point to point at Gracie's Kitchen and day drinking. The two-block walk back to the office had been a perfect ending. I'd taken more positivity from these three hours than any other single sitting in my life. The conversation had been easy and genuinely friendly. There were no slights, no efforts at one-upmanship. Cassandra was kind but nobody's pushover. I'd known that but we covered enough stories today that I had clear examples. I didn't take it lightly that she'd chosen to gift me her kindness. Abe had followed her lead and been equally kind and not weird at all. Warwick acted as a perfect bridge and foil. What could have been an awkward ending to an inherently stressful episode had instead created what I hoped was a new core memory grounded in genuine friendship and support.

My meetup with Cassandra tomorrow would introduce me to Margeaux so we could talk about the adventures of black female entrepreneurship in the city. I was excited about it, if a little nervous about how Margeaux would receive me. She may not share Cassandra's generosity of spirit. But I wouldn't let negativity spoil the day. Not this day.

"Whatever's easiest. Which I'm sure means me meeting you since you're far busier than I am."

"Y'all should meet at Haven." Warwick chimed in, his southern showing a little more than usual following the hyper-relaxing lunch. "That way we can get your paperwork filed and you can get a tour of the place. Since you're going to be working for me and all," he teased.

"You're awfully sure of yourself, aren't you?" I could hear the gin in my voice, making it a little brighter and more colorful than usual. Or maybe that was just happiness. I'd have to give it some thought.

"Confidence is key, Lizzie," he grumbled, letting his eyes roam me from head to toe. "Don't be scared."

I blinked. I'd almost gotten used to the teasing tone. He'd been hovering on the too-familiar all afternoon but not crossing the line enough for me to say anything. Only enough to have Abe and Cassandra tossing each other suspicious looks throughout the meal. But the flutters in my stomach had stopped going haywire each time he turned that wet velvet gaze on me and I'd even been able to uncross my legs and let my thighs breathe before the entree plates were cleared. By the time I saw the bottom of my second martini glass, I'd relaxed enough to laugh at his jokes and exchange a couple of shoulder bumps that set fireworks to sparking along my entire left side. But 'Lizzie' in that voice, with that teasing undertone? It was unfair. The regression was immediate; all my soft and wet parts were once again locked and loaded, and–fortunately or unfortunately–lubricated by two and a half martinis.

"Don't call me that," I giggled then slapped my hand over my mouth. I wasn't that much of a lightweight.

"Why not? Does it bother you? Hmmm," he replied and wiggled dark brows at me. The motion, combined with the stark seriousness on his face, sent me into peals of laughter. What was wrong with me? *Pull it together, Liz.*

"I'll meet you at Haven, Liz," Cassandra took control of the situation. "Warwick, make sure she gets home safely."

"Will do," he offered easily, shifting the toothpick he'd picked up when we left the restaurant from one side of his mouth to the other. It was crude. And sexy as hell. I rolled my eyes at him but there was no real fire behind it. I felt too good.

"I can get home safely by myself," I assured everyone, feeling good about the smile stretching my lips, even though it was met with a few raised eyebrows. "I'm not...tipsy," I pursed my lips at the doubtful expressions that stared back at me. "Okay, maybe a little, but mostly I'm just happy. This has been an unexpect-edly nice afternoon," I leaned in to give Cassandra another hug needing to do something with the energy and emotion running through me. She returned the quick embrace easily.

"Thank you, really," I told her when we stepped apart again. "I'm looking forward to tomorrow. My day is pretty open other than a few phone calls that I can easily juggle. Let me know what time works for you and Margeaux."

She said a few words in agreement and gave Warwick a quick hug before taking Abe's hand so he could lead her to their car.

"I meant what I said. I can get myself home," I began.

"I know. You're fully capable and a big girl," he stood blocking the whole damn sun so he was a giant shadow edged in light. Looking like a damn fallen avenging angel. With his big ass. He grinned as if he could hear the words running through my mind.

Then he leaned in so that his forehead was nearly touching mine. "Get in the truck, Lizzie."

I stuck my tongue out at him, but walked toward his truck as instructed. It made no sense to call a car and then sit there and wait for it to arrive when he was right here, more than willing to see me home.

I was having a good time. And that was okay. I didn't have to pull the plug on it if I didn't want to.

Luckily he was right there to steady me when my knees faltered.

***

WARWICK

Woah there, big fella. You're doing a lot right now. But she was so pretty when that little hint of red rose beneath her brown skin. And so fucking sexy when she was horny. She had no idea how clearly everything she wanted was written on her face. Not all the time, of course. But when she was relaxed, like right now? It's hard not to chase those blushes and pretty smiles.

"You good? The ground playing games with you again?" I teased her, mostly to cover the thumping of my own heart because if a little flirting had her tripping over flat ground, what would happen if I actually got my hands and mouth on her?

I fished in my pocket for a piece of gum. Elizabeth Brookes literally made my fucking mouth water. I popped the peppermint chew in my mouth just as we reached what I knew she called The Behemoth. I didn't hate it.

I reached around her to open the door then took a deep steading breath at the prospect of her climbing into my truck. Of her *being* in my truck, soaking everything with the scent of her. She paused too. Did she feel the magnitude of the moment, too?

Doubtful. It was far more likely that she was thinking about the perception of her riding with me. Probably wanted to make sure she wasn't sending the wrong signals. Maybe struggling with a little guilt, especially if she really was feeling hot and bothered around me. As much as the idea appealed to me, I didn't want to be the reason she had extra shit to deal with on her plate.

"I'm fine, thank you," she responded forcing a quick replay of the last several moments to remind myself what she was responding to.

"Clumsy and egotistical," I quipped. "The full package."

When she spun my way on an outraged gasp, I studiously ignored her glossy pink *open* mouth and instead of covering it with my own, which every nerve ending in my body demanded, I scooped her up and deposited her in the passenger seat. It was time to get this show on the road. Getting her in the truck, out of the truck, and safely in her own home was the best course of action.

I tweaked her nose, earning another gasp, grinned, and shut the door on whatever she'd been about to lash into me with. The ride to her place promised to be an entertaining one.

"I'm not egotistical," she said as soon as my butt hit leather.

"I know. If you were, you wouldn't be in my truck."

She huffed at that and I chuckled at having taken the wind out of her sails so easily. "That all you got?" I asked, settling in and checking the mirrors before pulling into traffic.

"No, but I'm not going to let you ruin my good mood."

"Good for you. You shouldn't ever let anyone fuck with your mood." I could feel her eyes on me.

"You really believe that, don't you? That you can just hold your mood regardless of how other people are behaving."

"Most of the time, yeah. Sometimes, some people make it impossible. But for those people, its usually worth it. If it's not, get them out of your life asap."

"Who are the people who are worth it?"

"The people you love. The people who love you."

"What if those aren't the same people."

"Ah, well. Then you have some decisions to make, don't you? Then you have to think about how those people are treating their hold over you. Because it is a hold, right? The ability to shift how someone is feeling is huge, impactful. It's a privilege. If people aren't treating it as such, then they don't deserve it."

"And you get rid of them," she said thoughtfully.

"Well, you don't kill them, of course," I said.

"What?" she exclaimed, "I didn't say *kill* them."

"Well, you did say 'get rid of them' in that scary quiet voice. I just wanted to be clear to the CIA who's listening that that is not what I was implying."

She rolled her eyes, "Well, CIA, that's not what I was implying either."

"But the effect should be similar. They're basically dead to you," I chuckled. "Or at least their ability to fuck with your mind is dead so, same thing."

"I wish I could do that. It'd be a handy skill to use on Mother."

"Family is the hardest. They've had the most practice and the most access."

"How's your family?" She asked. "We've spent so much time talking about the circus that is mine, I haven't asked about yours in forever."

"I'm sure Maggie keeps you up to date."

"She does, but it might be nice to hear a different perspective. So tell me, Sir Warwick Augustus, how doth your branch of the Walker clan fare?"

I laughed at her GOT impression and we spent much of the rest of the ride with me telling her about my parents' plans for their upcoming anniversary party. It was a big one for them. Logically Maggie and I should be planning their party but mom had made it clear that she had a vision and it was that vision she wanted realized. She only needed our moral support and daddy's checkbook. She and her own party planner were making it happen.

"So our only job is to show up. Dressed to the nines with something wonderful in hand for her."

She laughed, free and easy. "Well it sounds wonderful already and exactly how it should be when you're celebrating forty years of marriage. It's really a miracle, isn't it."

"Maybe. I don't know. Mom and Dad had their stuff. I know it wasn't all fun and games. I remember hearing some knock down arguments going on but even to my young ears it never really sounded scary. Just loud as hell, you know."

She nodded but I didn't think she really understood. I continued anyway.

"And the way they look at each other never changed. Even when they were clearly angry at each other, underneath it all there was something stronger than the anger. If I had to peg it now, I'd say it was respect."

"Respect. Not love?"

"Love, certainly but respect trumps love, doesn't it? People do all kinds of crazy shit to each other in the name of love. I've never heard anyone say, 'I wouldn't have cussed her ass out if I didn't respect her so much.' Nah, never heard that shit."

"You know, you're right."

"Yeah. I'd rather someone fall out of love with me than lose their respect. The first one would hurt but the second opens the door to some treacherous possibilities."

She was silent. I couldn't give her my attention to figure out why because I was slipping BigBoy into a parallel spot that was about six inches shorter than it needed to be. All I knew was that whoever was in front of and behind me better not scratch my shit.

The whole the time I was tetrising my way into the spot I could feel her gaze on me. Thoughtful and piercing.

"I'm not sure I know what that even looks like in a relationship."

"You didn't feel respected with Godrick?" I asked. Before she could answer though, I hopped out and rounded the truck to open her door. I was eager to hear her answer. Eager to keep talking to her.

"I did, definitely," she said once I'd opened her door. "But I think it was easy to feel respected at that point. We wanted the same things, had been primed for the same things. I don't know what would have happened had we not seen things so similarly."

"I'm sure you would have worked through it. Respectfully." I reached for her hand to help her down.

She smiled and slipped her hand into mine before sliding out of the truck and landing gracefully in her stilettos. How she'd been prancing around all day in them was beyond me. She and Cassandra had both strutted the two blocks to and from Gracie's like it was nothing. Women were fucking warriors.

"I'm sure we would have. But it certainly didn't hurt that we were so young. All of our growth was happening in tandem."

"Like my folks. They met when they were crazy young in college and stayed together. I asked him one time, how they'd done it. How they'd managed to stay together for so long. I must've been a junior in undergrad. I definitely remember I was pining after a girl who wasn't giving me the time of day."

"What girl could resist giving you her time, Warwick? You're a giant teddy bear."

"Teddy bear?" I growled at her low and deep. "I'm no teddy bear. A big black grizzly maybe. You disrespecting me?" I teased as she breezed past me into the warmth of her apartment building's lobby.

She giggled again, the third time today. "Never that," she waved at Bobby as we passed him. Once we entered the elevator, she said, "What did your dad say? About how they were able to stay together?"

I let my gaze drift to hers before I answered. "He said, he made sure he stayed making her climb the walls every night. He said she couldn't leave him if her legs were too weak to walk."

I watched her eyes grow round as my words sunk in. Then I watched another pretty peach blush brighten her chest and neck, turning her creamy brown skin a rich golden caramel.

"I figure that's how I'll keep my woman, too. Once I lock her down."

Then I watched her pupils dilate and her pulse quicken. I hoped it was because she was contemplating everything that might entail and how she might want to volunteer for the role. The elevator dinged open then, another heartbeat passed before she scrambled to push herself off the wall of the elevator and exit.

I followed, after giving my right leg a little shake to make room.

"I'm just going to see you in and then I'll get out of your way. Let you sleep off your drunk."

"Boy, I already told you, I'm not drunk," she said, sounding lazily unlike herself. I hoped the next words she spoke would be an invitation to hang out for a while.

"I should hope not. It's barely 4pm." The shrill commentary stopped Liz in her tracks, her back went rigid and every ounce of relaxation she'd fought and clawed for simply evaporated. Rage climbed up my spine.

I stepped in front of Liz, more than ready to slay this dragon for her. We rounded the corner of her tiny entryway to find Juanita perched at the dining table, a little laptop computer open in front of her. She was typing away, wholly unconcerned with the fact that she was an unwelcome guest in Liz's home.

"Mother," Liz said, her voice was cold and stilted, immeasurably different than it had been mere moments ago. "What are you doing here?"

"I've come to see you, obviously. Since it's become abundantly clear that you have no intentions of coming to see me."

"How did you get in? Does she have a key?" I asked directing the first question to Juanita, and the second to Liz, who shook her head.

"She does not. I'm equally curious."

"Oh so you're fine letting this man pull your chain but not the man I chose for you. I see." Juanita closed the laptop and settled her hands on top. "How I entered is none of your business, Warwick," she said my name as if she were spitting out shit. "But since you're so invested, I got in because," she paused for what I assumed was dramatic effect, "it's my building. I can get into any of the apartments. I own them after all."

"What?" Liz asked. "What do you mean, you own them? This isn't your building."

"Elizabeth, you should really make yourself more familiar with the family business. Especially now that we don't have to share it with that girl."

"What are you talking about, Mother? Proof that you were unfaithful doesn't mean Cassandra isn't his granddaughter. I assume that's where you're going with this?"

"You watch your mouth."

The old woman was quick. She got out of her chair and in Liz's face much faster than I thought she'd be able to. I stepped closer to Liz, who had drawn herself to her full height. In her sexy ass red-bottoms, she towered over Juanita by at least three inches.

"Physical intimidation, Elizabeth? That's not like you. I see you're picking up bad habits from bad company."

"Mother, you're the only bad company in my life right now. And any bad habits I have, I'm sure I've contracted them from you and you alone. I ask you again, why are you here?"

"I'm here to talk to you. Obviously, you've heard these lies about your father. I'm here to set the record straight. To let you know that they are just that. Lies. Your father is your father. He loved you."

"I believe that he loved me. My friends," she shot a quick glance my way that made my heart skip, "have given me the space to accept and believe that. But it's no thanks to you. Did he even know I wasn't his? Or did you lie to him, too?"

"Your friends," Juanita repeated on a lip-curling huff. She gave me a scathing once-over that would have felled a lesser man on the spot. *Luckily, I'm not a lesser man.* Then she turned to me. "Friend," she said, "would you excuse me and my daughter? We need to have a private conversation. One that is appropriate only for family. Not friends."

"I'll do whatever Liz wants me to do," I drawled, purposefully adding a little extra southern drag to the words. I hoped like hell that Liz would ask me to throw this woman out on her ear. Figuratively, of course, not literally. I wasn't into hurting old women.

"You'll do what I want, young man, or I'll have you removed and banned from this property. It is, after all, mine."

"Ma'am, I mean no disrespect," I offered it as I moved into the kitchen to check the fridge. I knew what was in there, nothing had changed from last night but I knew the dismissive nature of the act would drive Juanita crazy. By the smirk on her face, Liz was onto my game. "But I've said this before and while repeating myself is a particular no-no in my book, I'll do it just for you. You don't want this fight. I want it. I'm eager for it. But you? You don't want it." I pulled a beer out of the fridge. That actually hadn't been there last night. I shot a questioning glance at Liz. She shrugged and blushed again.

"I'm quite certain that was a threat," Juanita pronounced. I popped the top on the beer. It wasn't a particular favorite but it was a good brand and a solid lager. Something a beer-tender would recommend if they were asked for a recommendation. Liz had bought me beer. *You* think *Liz bought you beer.* Humph. Liz had bought me beer. I took a swig. It was nice and cold. Best beer ever.

"Regardless," Juanita's harpish voice intruded again. *Is she still here?* "I'll ask you again, politely, to excuse me and Elizabeth. I'm sure she's shared far more about our family's affairs than is appropriate. The benefit of which will be that, if you have an ounce of perception, you'll recognize that there are private matters we need to discuss. I would appeal to that ounce of perception."

Well, that was nice wasn't it? I didn't give a fuck. I took my beer and sat at the table, to the right of Juanita's laptop, and looked at Liz. I'd absolutely leave if she wanted me to. I'd absolutely stay if she wanted me to. But she was torn. And as much as I was enjoying myself, I might not be doing her any favors.

Sighing, I pushed back from the seat I had just taken and crossed to Liz. I pulled her away from her Mother, toward where I knew her bedroom was.

"Listen. I'll stay if you want me to but I think I'm in the way. Mostly in your way." I watched her trying to process, still working to switch her mindset from a lazy afternoon to this.

It made me feel good that she didn't try to hide the fact when she said, "I'm not in the right frame of mind for this right now. I don't want to do this now." She clenched and unclenched her fists. "I understand why children throw tantrums. I was having a great day and now I'm not."

"Well don't stomp too hard and hurt my favorite pinky toe. It's not her fault."

She smiled and tossed her head on an eye roll. She was angry and frustrated but so beautiful. I let my eyes roam her face for just a minute. When I returned to her brown eyes, they were soft and wary. Yeah, I was doing too much. I needed to go before I said or did something that threatened the friendship we were building. It was a friend she needed and I would be that until she was ready for...or asked for...more.

"I feel like I'm constantly thanking you," she said. Then she laid her hand on my chest gently at first. She lifted it and then placed it there again more firmly. "But thank you. You're turning out to be pretty not awful."

She was funny. "I'll take that." I studied her a minute longer. She had the faintest freckles across her cheekbones. I'd never seen them before. It was something new. I lifted a finger to touch one but she took a quick step back. She opened her mouth to say something but I spoke before she could.

"I'm going to head out. Call me. Tonight. I want to know that you're okay when she leaves."

She nodded.

"And I'll see you at Haven tomorrow."

Another nod. I sighed. Jesus she was killing me. Fighting tooth and nail for her independence and all I wanted to do was body slam any and everything standing in the way of her utter joy. Juantia Brookes included. Again, figuratively. Not literally.

She walked me to the door, where she stepped outside briefly to see me to the elevator. If we'd been on a date, it would have been the perfect setup for a goodnight kiss. As it was, I only glanced at her lips, hopefully not long enough to appear creepy, and dropped a peck on her forehead before stepping into the car. Even then I had to fight the urge to linger.

"Give her hell, Lizzie," I said as the doors slid closed.

Chapter 11

"Give her hell, Lizzie." The way his bass wrapped around the name, the sweet endearment I pretended to abhor turned into something that soaked my panties, even knowing my mother was inside waiting to rip me to shreds.

When the doors slid closed, I sighed in relief. It wasn't until that moment that I was certain I wasn't going to rip every shred of Warwick's clothes from his body and ride every part of him into oblivion. It was a shocking thought. It went against everything I'd been telling myself, every shred of decency and and every ounce of propriety but it had been on my mind all day. All night really. I told myself I hadn't slept well because I was thinking about the revelation about my parentage. But really it had been the repeated wet dreams that started with me curled in Warwick's lap crying my eyes out and ended with his head between my legs, his hips grinding between my legs, or his fingers stroking the wetness between my legs. All in the pursuit of comforting me and making me forget my troubles. Well, I had forgotten my troubles multiple times last night, all to the tune of Warwick's grumbly rumbly encouragement.

Spending all afternoon with him, watering my need with gin and vermouth hadn't been the best idea but had ultimately shaped up into a spectacular day. One that ended with me just buzzy enough to enjoy the tension of should-I-or-shouldn't-I...knowing full well that I absolutely wouldn't because I needed him as a friend much more than an ex-lover which is what he would eventually become.

But thinking about it, well, that was different. Last night proved that my subconscious didn't give a shit about decency or propriety.

I was still standing in the doorway contemplating the fantasies I might indulge in tonight when Mother burst that bubble.

"Are you going to stand there all night mooning after that boy? If I'd known you had a preference for running in the gutter, I would have looked elsewhere for your match. Perhaps I can make contact with someone from the Italian mafia if it's that ruffian sort you're attracted to."

"Mother, what are you going on about?" I asked, returning to the kitchen, every bit of the lightness and fun of the day evaporated. I felt muscles in my upper body clench and tighten as the stress that I had shaken for a few delightful hours, reemerged and settled between my shoulder blades.

"Why are you sniffing around Warwick Walker?" she asked bluntly.

"I'm not 'sniffing around him' as you so crassly put it. He's a friend. Something I have far too few of it turns out."

"A friend. Men and women are not meant to be friends, Elizabeth. You know this. If you sleep with him," she began.

"If I sleep with him, what, Mother? What? Does that make me a whore? Moreso than if I had slept with Abe who was openly pursuing another woman? If I sleep with him, what, Mother? You want me to make sure I get pregnant with his baby so I can force him into marriage and take *that* Walker fortune?"

She scoffed. "What fortune? Everyone knows Warwick, Sr. made nothing of himself. Just like his son. All flash and no substance. Mark my words, Elizabeth. He has nothing to offer you."

"Well isn't it a blessing, Mother, that I don't want anything from him? But I do want something from you." I had to get control of the conversation or the whole thing would center on me, my failures, and how the current state of the family was all my fault. "It's simple enough. The truth. Who's my father?"

To her credit, she didn't flinch when she said, "Harry Brookes is your father."

I tossed my hands up and rose from the table where I'd sat in the hopes of having a civil conversation. "So that's it? That's the party line? You have no intention of telling me?"

"I've told you all you need to know. Your father was Harry Brookes. He named you as his heir in his will."

"Is that all that matters to you? His will? I want to know whose DNA I carry. We both know that biologically I cannot be Daddy's daughter. Who was it, Mother? Whose kid did you pass off on Daddy because no part of me believes you told him the truth. You didn't did you? You let him believe I was his, didn't you?"

"Little girl, you should see yourself. All riled up in your righteous indignation. I said Harry was your father and that's all there is to it. He said he's your father as well. Are you going to go against him? Are you going to continue to go against me? I don't know what these blood tests say. As far as I'm concerned the takeaway is that there is no proof that that girl is in any way related to this family."

"How do you sleep?" I asked, honestly and incredulously. "Seriously, Mother. How do you sleep at night knowing all the lies and deceit and betrayal you've dished out. To me. To *me*, your daughter. I'm supposed to trust and rely on you above anyone else. But you're the last person can trust. The last person I can let my guard down around."

"You say that. But everything I've ever done is for us. Every decision I make is for us. For our wellbeing, to give us the lives we deserve."

"It's not us, Mother. It's 'you'. The life you deserve; your well-being. Because in what world is it in my best interest to be drugged for sex and then lied to about being pregnant."

"My God. This again. You are really quite ridiculous, aren't you? You weren't hurt. You weren't even pregnant. Nothing happened and yet you go on and on about this blip on the radar. Do you have any idea of the sacrifices I've made for you?"

"Like lying to my father about your side baby?"

I wasn't prepared for the slap. Not at all ready for the sting it left across my face. She'd never hit me and I, naively, never expected her to. My ear rang and my cheek burned with the contact.

I was stunned silent.

"I'm sorry," she said almost at once, voice trembling as she moved to the table and began to gather her things. "Clearly, this conversation has become unproductive. I'll assume from your behavior tonight that you are not coming home and thus will not be making use of the trust going forward. I am happy to allow you to stay in this building assuming all of your payments and such are up to date and remain so. If you can't manage that, you should tender your intention to vacate the premises," a brief pause before she added, "immediately."

She had slipped her laptop into her YSL tote along with her phone and proceeded to the door. There, she stopped and turned to take me in. I could only imagine how I appeared to her. My hand lay against the cheek she had slapped. I hadn't recovered enough to say anything, still processing this latest violation, sick to my stomach that she still had the power to, as Warwick put it, fuck with my day. Given everything else she'd done, why was this so hurtful? Why wasn't I raging at her? Why hadn't I, why didn't I, slap her back?

I knew tears were pooling in my eyes and I hated it. Just like I hated the hot lump that was building in my throat, forcing blood to race toward my head too quickly, so that it started pounding almost immediately.

"I really am sorry," she said and walked out.

I counted to ten. Then twenty. Then I sat back down and counted to one hundred. Then I could breathe normally again but I couldn't stop the stream of tears flowing unchecked across my cheeks. I had no mother. I truly had no mother. How did one survive like this? I lay my head on my folded arms and gave in.

***

WARWICK

Twenty minutes. Thirty. An hour. I had left Liz's apartment but not her building. I sat downstairs in the lobby chopping it up with Bobby—he was a disgruntled displaced Tampa Bay fan—while I waited for Juanita's exit. But it was coming up on an hour and a half now and she still hadn't...wait, there she was. I studied her as she crossed the lobby trying to get a read on what might have happened upstairs.

She was walking fast, head down, almost running. Was she crying? Impossible...and, alarming. Because while Liz was strong and could hold her own, she didn't have what it took to make her mother cry. She just wasn't put together that way. If Juanita was crying it was because of something else. Because of something she, Juanita herself, had done. Which meant Liz was up there alone and equally—most likely, more—upset.

"Fuck," I spat it loud enough that Juantia glanced my way. Her eyes widened slightly, then narrowed, but she didn't stop, only hurried even faster through the huge revolving glass door.

I pulled out my phone to dial Liz but paused before connecting the call. What did she need in this situation? Was it me? I didn't want to leave her and definitely didn't want her to think I'd abandoned her but I was also ready to blow some shit up and maybe that wasn't the energy she needed right now. Maybe I could be more useful elsewhere. But I wouldn't leave her alone either. I dialed Maggie's number.

CHAPTER 12

LIZ

Just like yesterday, this day was shaping up to be more than the sum of its parts. Certainly more than it had promised when I woke up, eyes swollen and face faintly marked from my Mother's hand.

I was glad that I had powered through the rocky start to the day, though. Glad that I'd taken the time to pull it together so that I matched Warwick's business casual sexy energy when we met at The Lounge at Haven. 'The Lounge' was the current, unremarkable name for the craft cocktail bar residing on the second floor of his hotel. It, along with the similarly uninspiringly named Restaurant at Haven, had been receiving rave reviews since it opened.

So far during this odd job interview, I'd seen the Restaurant on the main level–which was led by a Michelin Star chef known for creating masterpieces of classic American cuisine; the third-floor meeting spaces which were quaint in size but equipped with state of the art technology; the ballroom which occupied the entirety of the fourth floor and was a wonderfully flexible, also technologically riddled space; and, finally, the guest suites, all of which exemplified modern luxury on a scale designed to satisfy the choosiest guests.

"For all practical purposes, the only difference among the guest accommodations is size," Warwick had said when we finally entered the sprawling penthouse.

I'd found everything spectacular but Warwick had spent plenty of our time talking about his future plans which included transforming the rooftop into an oasis for guests, replete with rooftop pool and swim-up bar.

"We'll call it The Retreat once it's done but I don't expect to break ground on that project for another two years."

"And the restaurant and lounge? You mentioned earlier that you might rename them?"

"Yes," he agreed. "In keeping with the Haven theme, I plan to call the restaurant The Sanctuary and the bar, The Sanctum." He was in full business mode this morning, so instead of the broad smile that I'd been seeing more and more frequently, especially when it was just the two of us together, I only got a little twinkle in his eye when he shared his clever naming convention.

"Cute," I said in response. "The people will love it. Why didn't you name them when you first opened?"

"Good question. I wanted everything to refer back to Haven in the beginning. So folks would talk about the restaurant *at Haven*, the lounge or the bar *at Haven*. Once the name recognition is there, it'll stick. And if the names work the way I hope, they'll just reinforce the link now that Haven itself is well known across all three arms."

"So soon it'll be Haven's Sanctuary or the Retreat at Haven." It was a smart, clever approach.

"Exactly. And if it doesn't stick, no harm done at this point, but at the beginning, the branding is so important. I didn't want to water it down."

"Smart. Look at you, putting your little MBA to work."

"And look at you, about to put yours to work, too." He smoothly shifted the conversation to his hopes that I would contract with him once I'd established my business. "I hope you've liked what you've seen, that you agree we have a lot to offer each other. I have several high-profile events already ninety percent planned that you would ensure proper execution on. But there are always new opportunities that you could be fully in command of." He waited a moment before adding, "Primary among those would be the launch of the branding for the lounge and restaurant, assuming we hit it off professionally the way I expect we will."

Oh, this was new. My stomach twisted with excitement. If I decided to establish my own business—and what other choice was there—something on this scale outside of the not-for-profit arena, would be a valuable addition to my portfolio. My mind immediately started crafting possibilities. The man did not play fair.

We were strolling side by side along one of the wide hallways lined by guestrooms, engaged in a conversation that had reignited parts of my brain too long dormant.

"That seems like a lot of trust, Warwick," I said honestly. "I haven't proven myself enough for you to even mention something like that."

"Agreed. But you know me well enough to know I won't let you near it if I don't think you can handle it. And I know you well enough to know you won't accept if you don't *know* you can pull it off. So, we'll see. But first, you have to sign on for the short run." He winked then but broke character in no other way.

I smiled because his confidence in me was a thing warm and solid, blunting the sharp edges of my insecurities. He was pulling my competitive and girlie strings far too easily. "I won't hedge, Warwick. The building, the way you've renovated and appointed it, the venues you've created along with the guest amenities and rooms, it's an incredible opportunity. Creating events here would be a joy."

He let a satisfied smile tilt his lips and my breath caught ever so lightly. I allowed myself a little internal sigh and just a moment to acknowledge what I was signing up for: seeing him all day, every day and trying to resist him...all day, every day.

"Good. I'll have Marcus draw up a preliminary contract. Do you want to consider onsite lodging?"

"What?" I asked, refocusing. On-site lodging had never been discussed. "What do you mean, onsite lodging?"

"Well," he began, "for a certain level of hire, we offer relocation assistance. That can look different for different people. For some we provide a moving allowance, for others we offer a suite. For some, it's a combination. I thought I'd mention it; I heard your landlord sucks," he ended with the quip. He'd been there long enough to hear Mother's pronouncement of ownership last night.

I chuffed. "Your sources are correct. But taking a suite offline as part of a relocation package? Are you serious?"

At my dubious look, he stopped walking and offered a loose shrug. "I do what I need to do to get what I want. And I want you here. Relaxed and focused and excited about the work. Not worrying about whether your Mother is going to literally pull the rug out from under you."

"Plus, you'll be fully managing our event usage including the grounds, ballroom, conference spaces, as well as some interaction and collaboration with the lounge and restaurant. That will make you directly responsible for nearly twenty percent of the revenue we generate and connected to another thirty. It's in my best interest to have you relaxed and secure."

My eyes widened slightly at that and he peered more closely. "She's already done something, hasn't she? I knew it. All the more reason to consider the offer, Liz."

He wasn't wrong and there was no reason to pretend otherwise. I would need somewhere to stay in short order and having it already arranged would take a lot of pressure off. I could search for a more permanent option in a measure of comfort.

"I would be happy to see what the offer looks like with a suite included."

He nodded. "Good. I'll make sure it's added in the terms."

"I look forward to getting it."

By this time we'd exited the guest room wing to cross another open welcoming area full of fresh flowers and comfortable seating. On the other side of the expanse were the smokey glass doors of the lounge. Cassandra and Margeaux should be arriving soon. Maggie, too, since I'd invited her to join when she'd come to check on me last night. Which reminded me...

I didn't want to change the subject, didn't want to shift the conversation to last night's foolishness. But pretending there was no elephant in the room wouldn't keep you from getting stomped on. So I took a deep breath and plunged in.

"I appreciate what you did last night, sending Maggie. She was just what I needed. But I didn't keep her out all night," I said. "Just so we're clear."

"Noted. I heard her come in around nine. I had just put Lena down a few minutes earlier."

"You were with Lena?" I didn't know why that surprised me.

"Yeah. It was quicker that way. And since I was the one calling her for a favor, it made sense."

For some reason, the fact that he'd kept his niece so I could be comforted brought me back to the brink of tears. *What's wrong with you?*

"Well, thank you," I said feeling like I'd spent all of the last three days just thanking him for being a nice human being.

"Well, you're welcome. And if you ever do want to talk about it, you're already familiar with my ability to both listen and weather the storm of your mercurial emotions."

"Oh my mercurial emotions, huh?"

"Yeah. You're pretty high-strung."

I laughed, "Perhaps. But you're the one who keeps coming around for more."

"Guilty as charged," he agreed readily. "And until you tell me otherwise, I'll assume you like it." He said it with a slow lip lick designed to ignite lust in any human who was attracted to men.

My eyes grew wide as my panties grew wet. He gave me one hot slow blink before blinking again and returning to the wholly professional version of himself he'd been all day.

"Your girls are here," he said.

What? "What?"

"Cassandra and Maggie. And this must be Margeaux," he said as the three of them swung through the doors on a cloud of expensive fragrance and friendly chatter.

I blinked. What in the world had just happened? Had I imagined it? Was I having a fever dream?

"You're fine," he whispered. "We'll talk later. Call me."

I nodded because I was unsure what else to do.

"No, Liz. Actually *call* me." I remembered that I'd told him I would call the night before. But that was before the MMA fight.

"I will."

"I'm glad you're okay."

"Thank you, me, too."

He spent another calm moment evaluating me with those dark eyes that seemed to see too much. Then he clicked into host mode, welcoming Cassandra and Maggie and introducing himself to Margeaux whose body language showed immediate appreciation for the sexy specimen of handsome successful male in front of her.

I wasn't quite sure about the niggle of emotion that crept into my blood but I squashed it ruthlessly, chastising myself for feeling whatever feeling that had been. To make up for it, I stepped into the greetings, intent on solidifying at least one new friendship this day.

Initial introductions done, Warwick led us to a high top, then stepped away while we fell into the complementary chatter that came with a group of secure women in the beginning rounds of the friendship dance.

We distributed ourselves around the round high-top table, hanging purses and jackets on cleverly concealed nearby hooks. Warwick returned with menus, a pitcher of what looked like sangria, a large bottle of Perrier, and eight wine globes. He filled four with sparkling water, dropping a slice of lime in each. Then he filled the remaining four with the blood-red beverage and added pops of fresh fruit in those glasses as well.

"I'll have someone here in just a few minutes to take care of you all. Try not to set the place on fire with all that brainpower," he quipped before leaving us to it.

"Shall we open the games with a toast?" Margeaux asked, reaching for her glass of sangria.

It seemed as good a beginning as any.

"To Liz," she turned dark eyes on me. I felt an eyebrow creep up because was this about to be some more mess? My day had been quite nice thus far and I wasn't looking forward to it going south.

"We haven't met, but in the way of good girlfriends, Cass has informed me that you've been through some shit. Here's to shaking the shit off your Manolos and strutting into your bad bitch era." She didn't say it in the hype sista-girl tone the phrasing might suggest. Instead, she was purposeful, quiet, and intent with her words. They landed differently because of it. I was taken completely by surprise when I felt the prick of tears behind my eyes.

We raised glasses and clinked to that. While the sip was still on my lips...the beverage turned out to be sangria but with a hell of an added kick...Cassandra spoke up.

"Just to avoid any unwanted challenges as we begin this effort, Go-go you should know that Warwick and Liz are sniffing around each other."

I immediately choked on the wine and sputtered to correct her words, "No..."

"Yes," she continued. "Liz, as you've noted, has been through some shit so she's not really ready, but Warwick is doing a great impression of a patient man and giving her time."

"Oh!" Margeaux said, her full lips rounding in her dark pixie face. "Noted. Thank you for the update because, girlfriend," she leaned back and fanned herself. "I was about to put on the full-court press."

"I saw," Cassandra giggled and gave Margeaux a little high five.

"He's not," I began. "We're not...there's nothing between us," I said, lamely. "We're just friends."

"Mmm," Margeaux hummed. "I believe you. But I also believe Andi so I'll put him on my off-limits list. Until or unless you tell me otherwise–loudly and confidently. Fair?"

I started to protest again because I had no ownership over Warwick and didn't intend to make any such claim. He was a grown man, he could do whatever and whoever he wanted. I said as much.

"Even so, we're trying to build a consortium of black female power here. It wouldn't do to start off with a man in the middle. There are plenty of six-five, blick-black, thick-lipped, sexy-as-hell billionaires in New York. I'll just grab another." A sassy tilt of her head and another clink of her glass with Cassandra's put the issue to bed.

"Did you two have a good meeting? Are you going to be working with him?" Cassandra asked, making my head spin with the abrupt redirect of the conversation.

"Working with him?" Maggie chimed in. "What did I miss?"

When she showed up last night, I'd been a mess, obviously. But not nearly as much of a mess as I'd been the last time she'd had to rescue me. This time the anger took precedence much more quickly. We snapped pictures of the handprint on my face before it faded and spent some energy cursing my mother from stem to stern. Then the day caught up with me. The morning meeting, the heavy lunch combined with the heavy drinks, the heightened awareness of flirting too much with Warwick, and then the episode with Mother all combined as a weighted blanket of exhaustion. I passed out before we talked about the rest of the day. I hadn't shared anything about the meeting or lunch. I wasn't even sure when Maggie let herself out.

I'd awakened in the middle of the night cozy on my sofa. After a hot shower, I sipped a cup of warm milk and honey; it had been daddy's cure for almost everything and a comfort I needed. Then I crawled into my proper bed and slept the rest of the night. I'd awakened surprisingly refreshed and eager for the day. But, it was apparently day one of my 'bad bitch era' so perhaps that was appropriate.

I took a few minutes to bring Maggie up to speed and then caught the table up. "We had a great talk and yes, I'll definitely take the job. He's having someone named Marcus craft a contract. I'll look at it and maybe have Tonya look at it, too. I'm meeting her after our lunch to get my paperwork filed to create my LLC."

A little round of applause and 'okay, girl' brought a full grin to my face. "Yes, well," I said on a smile. "I expect it to all go smoothly. Mother said", I paused because one, I didn't want to drag the conversation down and, two, how much should I share?

"What'd that bitch say?" Cassandra asked then clapped her hand over her mouth. "Sorry, shit, Liz. What did she say?"

I nodded at Cassandra, understanding the burning need to call my Mother a bitch but acknowledging that she was still, in fact, my mother. The 'bitches' should be reserved for my use.

"Thanks. She said that since she owns the building I'm living in–" a gasp from Maggie had me turning to her to acknowledge, "I forgot to mention that part, but since she owns the building and since I'm clearly not interested in returning home or leaving off of this 'ridiculous trajectory that I'm on'...her words, not mine...that I would need to tender my intent to vacate. Unless of course, I can meet the rental payments on time. Which, I'm ashamed to say, I cannot."

"But what's changed? You've been there since you moved out."

"This new thing with Cassandra has sent her over the edge. She says I need to stand with her, show a united front. And if I can't do that, apparently, I can get out of her property."

"But don't you own it, too? Your father's will leaves you some percentage of ownership doesn't it?"

"Maybe. Probably. It's something I'l add to the list of things to talk to Tonya about."

"What will you do in the meantime? You know you can stay with me and Lena, right?"

"Who's Lena? Your girlfriend?" Margeaux asked, snared by the drama of it all.

"Nope," Maggie laughed, "my daughter. She's seven," Maggie reached for her phone to tap the screen awake displaying a closeup of Lena enraptured by something out of the frame. It was a beautiful picture capturing a rare moment of quiet.

"Oh, she's beautiful!"

"And a mess. Don't let this picture fool you," Maggie laughed. "But a mess who would love to have her Auntie Liz stay for a while."

"And I would love that, too, under other circumstances," I said with a laugh. "I need to keep moving forward and as much as I appreciate it, I stayed there after the last episode with Mother." I glanced in Cassandra's direction, "I went to Maggie's when I left your and Abe's place that night. The night Dr. Yvette came? And you were wonderful, Mags," I squeezed Maggie's hand.

"But you're not trying to come back to the recovery zone." She caught on immediately; I was grateful. "I can understand that. But what are you going to do?"

"Warwick has said that he sometimes offers relocation packages to employees and that those can include a suite of rooms for a limited amount of time."

Maggie's soft snort drew my attention. "What?" I asked.

"Nothing, I just swallowed wrong," she patted her chest. "Did he put whiskey in the sangria?"

"Maggie."

"Seriously. It went down wrong. Go on...a suite of rooms as part of a relocation package?"

I raised a brow at her and continued, "Yes. I know that I'm not actually relocating, but it's a nice option given my situation. It's convenient and helpful from both a lodging and employment standpoint. Being onsite might be quite useful in becoming familiar with the workings of Haven."

"I'm sure it will be," Cassandra added with a little twinkle in her eye.

"Mmmm," Margeaux added, "It will definitely be convenient."

I met their eyes, each pair dancing with barely suppressed laughter.

"Okay. Enough," I said, not really irritated but completely unfamiliar with being teased by women.

"We're just messing with you," Cassandra relented. "But it's clear that Warwick has a thing for you. And staying here under his nose...well, I'll just remind you that the Walker men are not to be deterred."

"We're friends," I reiterated. "You're picking up on his feelings of responsibility. He was Godrick's best friend so he feels, I don't know," I waved a hand, "honor-bound, I suppose, to look after me. I've assured him repeatedly that I do not hold him to any such commitment. There's nothing more between us."

"Godrick?" Margeaux asked. "Abe's Godrick?"

"Yea, they were actually cousins but truly best friends, brothers, all of that rolled into one. It was deep from what Abe has told me. Warwick and Godrick were the same age and had four years in the game before Abe was even born," Cassandra looked at me with understanding. I stared back.

"Well," Margeaux said, "that's a complicated situation. I can see why you're pressing pause while you figure shit out. You're going to need a clear head to handle that man."

I agreed wholeheartedly, which was why I was trying my best not to handle him at all.

"On that note, have you chosen a name for your LLC? I'm assuming Tonya is your attorney?"

I nodded at her. "She is and I haven't. I was thinking of just Liz Brookes Events."

"Mmm. Boring. And don't use your name. You don't want every move you make blatantly attached to your name. What if it flops?"

"Gogo!" Cassandra gasped.

"Well, it could," she shrugged. "My first business did. And if I'd used my name then there'd be a record of a company with my name going out of business."

"I hadn't thought about that. What was your first business?"

"Hair gel."

"Hair gel?"

"Yep. I called it 'That Sticky Icky.'"

Silence.

"Yeah. That's about how it went. But the moral of the story is that I didn't call it Margeaux Williams's Sticky Icky so no one knows that Margeaux Williams had anything to do with it."

"Williams?" I interrupted. "Are you two..." I trailed off because Cassandra's last name was also Williams.

"Yep, blood sisters," Margeaux replied and she and Cassandra both raised their right hands and pointed to matching scars on the fatty part of their palms. "We met in a group home in Maryland. I was a regular because my family couldn't get it together enough to keep me. Thandi here," she grinned at Cassandra on an inside joke, "was just a baby and needed guidance."

Cassandra rolled her eyes but the love and affection between them was obvious.

"So, I took her under my wing and the rest is history. We're blood-bonded now."

"So y'all bonded because you had the same last name, too?" Maggie asked.

"No, I didn't have a last name at all," Cassandra spoke up. "Or, rather, I was Cassandra LNU. Which stands for 'last name unknown'. Apparently, I was surrendered at a fire station somewhere in Baltimore. When I became a ward of the state, I was assigned a last name by my case worker who was not a creative sort," she shrugged. "I've learned that there are a lot of LNU's out there. When I aged out at 18, I adopted Williams since it was Margeaux's last name."

I was fascinated. "Then what happened?"

She chuckled. "Well. I went to college, met Abe senior year," she pointed at Margeaux who gave her a wink and a head tilt, "graduated college, had an amazing experience interning across Europe," she set her chin in her hand in exaggerated reminiscence, then straightened again, "plowed through some grunt work, plowed through better-paying grunt work, then landed as creative director at HeirLoom. And here I am."

I didn't know where to start. "That's impressive," I said.

"Well, there was plenty of angst, self-doubt, racism, sexism, sabotage, heartbreak," Cassandra paused briefly at Margeaux's whispered 'fucking asshole', then continued, "and debt involved. But who wants to talk about that?"

A little chorus of 'right', 'true', and 'facts' sounded.

"Wait," Maggie said. "You met Abe when you were in college?"

Margeaux's eyes lit up. "Met him, fell for him, and pined for that ni–, that *man* for damn near ten years."

"I did not *pine*!" Cassandra protested. "I moved on with my life and accomplished great things! I wasn't thinking about that man."

"Okay maybe you didn't pine, but you definitely thought about him. Luckily the fates brought you back together."

"This is a story I would love to hear in more detail," I said. "Just the part about the initial meeting though. I think I have plenty of detail about the reunion portion."

Faint surprise covered the faces of my companions. "Too soon?" I asked. Nearly two years had passed since The Embarrassement, which is how I thought about that period in my life when I was acting like a fool at my mother's behest, throwing monkey wrenches in Abe and Cassandra's love story.

Laughter erupted and I smiled. This was going to be a great lunch.

"Well, you know, what goes around..." we nodded at Margeaux's unfinished truism.

"I do believe we were fated to get back together," Cassandra said with a dreamy sigh. "But, that's a different book for a different day. This one is about you."

She clapped her hands to signal a reboot of the conversation. "Now that we know where you're going to be working, and where you're going to be living, let's wrap up the naming of your business, and then we can talk about finding out who your daddy is."

"Oh, that's on the table, too?" I asked, not sure that I was on board with pulling the topic apart here.

"Absolutely. Whoever your daddy is, that's my grandaddy, so we're going to get to the bottom of it."

"I thought you didn't really care," I reminded her.

"I don't, but you do so let's do it."

So we talked from point to point, ordered several plates to share from the restaurant kitchen, and tossed out a few company names for consideration before narrowing the choices down to 'RSVP' and 'Somebody' as in 'can't you call somebody to handle that?'.

Then, we tackled the daddy issues at the table. After the requisite utterances of disbelief and the spilling of all the tea around how this information was being revealed, we landed on the topic of how to figure out which relative Cassandra and I shared. Surely the answer would solve the mystery of both our fathers. While Cassandra and I spun elaborate plans to trick Mother into admission, Margeaux cut through all the nonsense with the sharp knife of practicality. It went something like this:

Margeaux: "So what did the online DNA service say?"

The rest of us: Blank stares.

Margeaux: "You haven't sent your spit to one of those online companies? The ones that let you build your family tree?"

Us: Head shakes and nos.

Margeaux: "Y'all are not serious. Those folks can find any-body. I guarantee if you send your sample in, you'll have hits in a week. You'll have uncle-cousin-daddy-brothers crawling out of the woodwork, I'm sure."

Us: picking up phones to search online DNA services

Once we all ordered kits, we counted that work as done. I had to admit that I was stunned by the simplicity of the plan. A straightforward DNA family tree test had never occurred to me. Could it really be that easy? I was both hopeful and fearful; the possibilities felt extreme. According to the website, results could take up to six weeks.

We spent another few moments speculating about said possibilities before the conversation turned, as it is prone to do when Black women gather, to hair.

"Margeaux, I love your hair color," I said. The short bouncy coils on her head were a blend of rich turquoise, purple, and lavender. The colors faded to skin above her ears and at her nape. It was a striking cut and an even more striking color against skin that glowed a beautiful dark umber in the low light of the lounge.

"Thanks," she said, her hand floating up to play with her curls. She pulled one and it bounced right back to her head, snuggling in with the others. "I'm surprised it's still this color. I usually change it every month or so."

"It's going on three now, isn't it?" Cassandra asked and Margeaux nodded.

"Do you do it yourself?" Maggie wondered. 'Or do you have one of your stylists do it for you?" Over the course of the conversation, we'd learned more about Margeaux's two salons and the third that was in the works.

"Oh, I do it myself. I still can't find anyone who gets it quite the way I want it. This way, if it turns out wrong, I have no one to blame but myself."

"How far out are your salons booked? I'm looking for someone new. My current stylist is also Mother's and I'm trying to cut all ties."

"They're booked out at least three months. But I'm not," she said excitedly.

"You? You still accept clients?" I asked.

"I have a few here and there," she nudged Cassandra who was clearly a loyal and permanent client. "When do you want to get it done?"

"Pretty soon," I said uncertainly. I didn't want her to go out of her way for me. "My next scheduled appointment would be in three weeks."

"Here's my number," she fiddled with her phone then laid it head to head with mine so the contact would transfer. "Let's set something up. Oh!" she said, still excited, "let's do it after hours and have a hair party!"

Maggie and Cassandra agreed and the conversation turned to planning a full-on girls' hair party complete with drinks, food and a playlist.

And, just like that, I had girlfriends.

CHAPTER 13

The hair party hadn't happened. The four of us were busy women, myself included since I'd officially started at Haven. The first date had fallen through, then the second. And now, I found myself standing outside of Margeaux's salon by myself because Sasha, the name I'd given this particular sew-in, could wait no longer.

I'd debated coming alone. My experiences with Margeaux had been pleasant enough but Cassandra had always been around as a buffer. And, truth be told, Margeaux intimidated me a little. Confident, beautiful, accomplished; I could perhaps claim one of the three for myself. Of the remaining two traits, I was consistently faking one and chasing the other. The thought of spending upwards of two hours with her had my heart beating more quickly than normal.

I could see through the huge wood-framed windows set into the red-brick front that the shop was busy. There were four spacious stations visible from the front. A technician was working at each station, but none were Margeaux. Taking a deep breath to steady myself, I tugged the heavy wooden door open and stepped inside before I lost my nerve.

Softly scented cool air greeted me along with the lovely young woman who I'd not been able to see from the front window.

"Hello," I said in response to her welcome. "I'm here to see Margeaux? I'm a touch early."

"Your name?" She asked.

"Elizabeth." I'd been preparing to give my last name when I saw Margeaux appear around a partitioning wall in the back of the salon. She saw me and waved as she made her way to me. Her heels clicked softly against the polished wood floor. Her jewelry...gold on her fingers, and at her wrists, throat, and ears...caught the bouncing light, making her look a little ethereal. A little Angela Bassett in Black Panther. She reminded me of a young version of that actress. Her cheekbones weren't as sharp...whose were?...but the beautifully defined bone structure and big expressive eyes were there. Her nose was straight and a little longer than one would expect, making her full, sharply-shaped lips look even fuller. She was stunning. She knew it, embraced it, and dressed the part.

Today, she wore barrel-cut high-waisted camo cargos that billowed around her legs and gathered at the ankle to show off impressively high strappy gold heels. She pared them with a black fitted cropped tee bearing the name and logo of the salon, *Texture*, in sparkling relief.

"Liz!" she said warmly when she reached me. "I'm so glad you found the place. Did you have any trouble?"

"None at all. Uber knew exactly where you were," we laughed and shared a quick hug and the light spattering of nerves dancing in my stomach flitted away.

"Good, good," she paused with hands on hips, scanned me up and down. "You look fantastic. Those shoes are crazy!"

I grinned and struck a little pose, foot kicked up Marilyn Monroe style. "Thank you, they look much better than they feel," I said. The funky stilettoed multi-jeweled Betsey Johnson's I'd paired with a very forties fit and flare navy dress were favorites.

"Well let's get you sitting down then. Come on, follow me."

I followed her through the salon, the cool fragranced air of the entrance gave way to a warmer space, scented with the rich herbal fragrances of the products being used. The decor combined clever lighting, chrome, and wood to excellent effect, creating a warm, bright but not shocking, relaxing space. There were all the usual accouterments, including hair dryers, steamers, and shampoo bowls and the sounds were familiar with the hum of dryers, the splash of water, and the click-clack of curling irons and fingernails. It was all held together by the quiet murmur of conversation.

When we reached the back of the salon, we made a quick right and walked into a large room fully equipped as its own mini salon... including a private sink and dryer plus some other apparatus I had never seen before. Light streamed into the room from a large wide skylight that ran from end to end along the ceiling of the room. Plants lined the walls and occupied the few places on the shelves positioned around the room that were not stuffed with books. Comfortable-looking chairs created two cozy seating areas with low tables in between. There was a hot beverage station and a wine cooler tucked in the corner. It felt a little like a library-cafe where one could get their hair done. I immediately fell in love.

"Well, I'll never look at Mother's salon the same. This is beautiful, Margeaux." I gave a slow turn, taking in the muted textured wallpaper in shades ranging from pale sage to deep browns and blues. I perused the book titles while she made fake *pshaw* noises.

"Any music or fragrance preferences?" She asked opening a long wooden box with little jars inside. "Essential oils," she said. "Lavender? Rose? Cedarwood?"

"I'm not sure. I like light scents, no musk, not too heavily floral either."

"Got it," she said and set two of the small bottles aside. "Music?"

"Surprise me." A few swipes on her phone screen and vintage Beyonce lilted through hidden speakers. It was a good, safe choice.

"Your reading tastes are pretty varied," I mentioned, seeing biographies and autobiographies for everyone from the Rockefellers to the Obamas, academic books on finance and entrepreneurship, a few self-help tomes, and fiction ranging from romance to spy novels.

"Yeah, it's my best habit," she said. "One I picked up in home. It provided the same escape for me that fashion did for Andi."

"That makes sense," I noted as I thumbed through one of the romance novels penned by an author whose name I recognized from a few best-seller lists. I hadn't read any of her work, I didn't think it would appeal to me; the few romance novels I'd read years ago had left me lukewarm on the genre. They were either weirdly date-rapey, full of silly girls and dumb jocks, or just gross. I couldn't identify with the characters and the stories made no sense to me. I slipped it back on the shelf.

"Take it with you, if you want," Margeaux said, as I continued to look at her titles.

"No, thank you. I may take you up on something else though," I said, reaching for a Martha Stewart autobiography. I'd recently watched a special about her when my streaming service had cued it up. There was a lot more to her than I realized.

"That one is good, too," she said. "Martha is a beast. I get why Snoop fucks with her."

I laughed, "Me, too. Thank you," I slipped it in my tote. "I'll be sure to return it."

"Take the first one, too," she said and I could hear the smile in her voice. "It's also really good."

"Oh, no. One is plenty," I began.

"Well if one is plenty, take that one and leave Martha here."

"Romance is not a genre I've enjoyed in the past," I said and shared my perceptions with her.

"Oh, you haven't read good Black romance until you've read this author, though. She tells our stories, and tells them with love," she walked over to pull the book and press it into my hands, "and good sex scenes," she added dropping it into my tote with the other when I continued to protest. "I promise you'll love it."

"Okay," I agreed, just to preserve the positive interaction. She wouldn't need to know I hadn't read it. "Thank you."

I set my bag on one of the chairs and peeled out of my coat and scarf to settle in her chair. The softly summery smell of the oils she'd used wafted through the air.

"So, tell me about your hair," she said, fingers kneading my scalp through my braid down.

We talked about all things hair for the next short while. The weave had been snipped out, my braids detangled and the first shampoo done before the conversation shifted, easily, to life and I learned that while Margeaux loved the written word, she'd seen the opportunity to make real money in cosmetology. She'd honed her craft and earned her certification while in college earning a degree in marketing. She said she would have studied entrepreneurship if that had been a thing back then. She'd since gathered skills as needed when her business grew.

"So how do you feel about hair though? Do you enjoy the work?"

"I do. It's another form of creative outlet, isn't it? Sometimes, especially if a client decides to give me free rein, I really love it. I like to create beautiful things," she laughs a little ruefully. "But I also need this paper. And that comes first. So being able to sort of combine the two works for me across a lot of avenues."

"And you're opening another location?"

"I'm planning to, it's not going as smoothly as I'd like. I'm trying to bring the third location further into the city but the prices are outrageous."

"Yes, they are," I agreed. "What will you do?" I was genuinely curious because she'd accomplished so much. Two profitable salons at her age was impressive in itself. To have realized such success, even on the edges of the city was almost miraculous.

Beauty and fashion ran New York; the competition was fierce and if you wanted to establish yourself as more than a hole in the wall, if you wanted to get to the exclusive clientele, you had to fight. And apparently, Margeaux had done just that.

"I'll make it work. I have the money, I just don't want to spend that much."

"How do you make it work? With so few technicians?"

"Well. One, I'm exceptional at the work," she gave a little head tilt, "two, I have six more stations upstairs. They're private, like this one. There's also a private entrance for those who want to use it. I sometimes get some pretty exclusive names, who may not want to deal with their adoring fans while getting their wigs tightened."

"That's reasonable," I chuckled at the idea.

"I've had some fuckboy use of that entrance. Bringing their girls in the back and their wives in the front," she shrugs. "Not my business as long as I get paid for both."

She paused. "I've done your mother's hair," she said. Shock stilled my breath for a moment.

"Really?"

"Yes. I don't know why I hadn't recalled before. I didn't know who she was at the time, of course. I just thought of it because she used the private entrance."

Another wave of surprise. "She did? Why?"

"Oh, I don't know. It didn't seem for any nefarious reason. Just because she wanted to."

"That sounds like her. She'd want access to whatever she deemed most exclusive." I fell silent for another moment before asking, "So she wasn't a regular client?"

"No. I only helped her the one time. I know most of the fine stylists in the area. I've made it my business to do so. They know I offer excellent service and that I don't poach. If they need to take a little load off their own books, I'll gladly help if I can without trying to steal their clients long term. I don't want or need any new long-term folks but I doubt if I'll ever completely stop hustling, given what I can make in two hours."

"It's a good model. And I know Mother's stylist well; he's an asshole."

"Well, yeah."

"They're well-matched," I say.

"Your words, not mine."

I chuckled. Then she continued, "And how is your business coming along? Is she thriving in these first few weeks?"

"She is," I said, still a little giddy at having started my own business. "I still get butterflies when I think of it." Starting the company hadn't been hard, it was a matter of filling out paperwork. But funding it? That would be more challenging. "I'm working on my business plan now so I can get some start-up funding for advertising and development. It's something I should have done years ago."

"Why didn't you? Clearly, you're talented. And you have a masters in business administration, don't you?"

I nodded while her hands worked magic in my hair. We'd moved from the shampoo bowl to one of the strange apparatus while we chatted.

"This is a steamer," she explained. It'll help the conditioner better penetrate your strands. She tucked my head under and warm steam started to billow around me. It was a facial for my hair. The machine itself was quiet and didn't interfere with our continued conversation.

"I do have an MBA, but it's a long story." Margeaux raised an eyebrow and made a show of looking at the nonexistent watch on her wrist.

"I have no real reason other than I was spiraling. Godrick died and I was so young and so miserable. I didn't know what to do. For a while, I didn't do anything. I just existed. I'd built my life around the one we'd envisioned together. And when I lost that, I had no idea how to move forward. Eventually, Mother decided it was time I 'got back out there,'" I made the air quotes with my fingers.

"She started pushing me to date and I wasn't ready. I went to school more as a distraction and an escape than anything else. She didn't like it. I think the only reason she let me go was that she assumed I'd find a husband. I didn't. And when I finished and came home, I was no closer to being ready to move on than I had been when I'd left."

Margeaux made sympathetic noises. "I can't image what you went through. To lose your fiance at that age. Early twenties?" I nodded. "Girl, I could not have." She stood from the seat she'd taken across from me while my treatment steamed. She released me and led me back to the bowl where we went through another rinse.

I shrugged. "I couldn't either. I was just going through the motions. It's how I ended up pseudo-engaged to Abe." I flashed again to that night when Warwick tried to convince me to not agree, to not even consider it. I caught Margeaux's inquisitive gaze in the mirror as she dried me.

"Mother felt it would be the easiest thing to do. And Abe's father, too. All the practical reasons were still there, the benefit to both businesses and the social implications hadn't changed. Mother was all but frothing at the mouth. I can see that now, not so much then."

"So you just...got engaged to Abe?"

"Kind of? Our parents talked about it. Thinking back and knowing what I know now, I think Abe felt obligated. And I think he was living in the same kind of dead space that I was. Neither of us particularly cared." *Warwick cared. He still does.* Does he, I wondered. He'd been wholly professional since I'd started at Haven; not even the slightest undercurrent of flirting. *But that's what you wanted, right?* And it's certainly what you need.

"Mmm," Margeaux hummed. "I guess I get that. Sometimes we find ourselves following the path of least resistance. Just letting life happen to us."

"Exactly. It was Abe finding Cassandra that woke me up. He was willing to just throw it all to the wind. Everything he thought he owed Godrick, it didn't matter anymore. Not the way it had before. It was as if he'd found himself again. I wanted that. I wanted my life back."

"So what happened with you and Abe? Why didn't you just walk away?" Margeaux worked through my now cleansed, conditioned, deep conditioned, steamed, and sealed strands, gently easing through the few tangles that dared to remain after her ministrations.

I huffed. "That's a great question." I closed my eyes while she spritzed with something that smelled delicious.

"I was scared. I knew what I should do. I knew what I wanted to do. But Mother was in my ear, telling me how I was one foot out of the grave and how Cassandra was just a fling. Cassandra and Abe themselves weren't going public, which fed into Mother's assessment. Add to it that Abe and I both had...interludes...with other people. There was no ring, no formal agreement, just a very soft understanding. It was...murky."

I sighed and then just admitted, "But mostly, I was just scared. Scared to be alone. Scared Mother was right. Scared that if it wasn't Abe, then who?"

"Warwick?" Margeaux asked sending my heart into my throat and my stomach into the ground.

I shook my head. "No. Not Warwick."

She stared at me in the mirror, the flicked the blow dryer on. A short ten minutes later and my natural hair floated around my shoulders in dark brown sheets.

"So when did you decide to let Abe go? And is that why your mom did what she did?"

I considered not answering. I didn't want to go through it all again but, there was no ugliness in her questions. And she was Cassandra's best friend, her sister. She was doing for Cassandra what I wished someone would do for me—vetting her circle, taking care, loving her. So, I answered.

"When they were in Europe, researching the launch. Some photos came out of them, walking in Paris, doing touristy things. Perfectly innocent in appearance but, I know Abe. He was in love. And she was good for him. The fact that he was out, walking the streets of Paris, doing touristy things was enough for me."

"Plus you weren't in love with him anyway," she added.

"Plus I wasn't in love with him anyway," I confirmed. "I never was, never could be. If Mother had gotten her way, if Abe and I had married, I don't know how we would have ever consummated it," I shuddered. "I was, to be honest, faintly disgusted when I thought we'd had sex."

She nodded. "Low key that was the last thing that was holding me back from welcoming you with open arms. Andi told me you were cool. A victim of circumstance, so to speak. And I get that. But I was having a hard time accepting a woman who was moving from one brother to the next. It was a lot," she said. "I'm not from this world though, and I was trying to give the benefit of the doubt. But, girl."

I laughed out loud, "I understand. Believe me. It's the strangest thing because I didn't think about it with Abe, but it's the very reason that there can be nothing between me and Warwick. He was Godrick's best friend, his first brother. I couldn't even consider it."

Margeaux had clipped my blowdried hair up and was beginning to flat iron it. We'd agreed in the early conversation that I wanted to try wearing my natural hair instead of a sew-in or wig. I was feeling adventurous, ready to throw off some of those trappings.

Now she paused with the flat iron held away from my head. "Maybe you didn't feel guilty about Abe because you didn't want Abe. Marrying him, in a sense, would have been another sacrifice made to Godrick's memory. It's different with Warwick because you actually want him. That feels different, I'm sure."

I didn't like the insight she was throwing my way. "I don't want him. Not like that. But it's true that he's completely off-limits. I couldn't even consider it."

Her incredulous eyes held mine in the mirror.

"Girl, have you lost your mind?"

I froze, "What do you mean? You just said..."

"I said, 'I had trouble with a woman moving from *brother* to *brother*.' Warwick is *not*, was not, Godrick's brother. That reasoning does not hold here, Liz."

"But,"

"But, nothing. Best friends, yes. *Like* brothers, yes. Brothers? Absolutely not. No, ma'am. Are you serious that this is the reason you're not giving that man a chance?" She resumed her curling.

I was reeling inside. I'd only had conversations about Warwick, with Warwick. And while he'd assured me that his relationship with Godrick should pose no problems well, what else would he say? *What about Maggie?* Maggie wasn't serious. And if she was, well, she was my closest friend but at the core, she was Warwick's sister. She would support whatever he wanted, let the chips fall where they may. But this woman, who I liked and respected, and as best as I could tell never hesitated to speak her mind, was telling me I was being silly.

"I mean," I hesitated, "yes. Partially. But I'm also trying to get my feet under me. I have nowhere to stay long term, no long term employment, my mother is...my mother, and I've just learned that my father is not, after all, my father. I have a lot going on. Warwick doesn't need the distractions and neither do I."

"You don't think you should let him be the judge of what he needs or doesn't need."

I rolled my eyes.

"I see how you are when he's around. You want him." She was matter-of-fact with it. "And he wants you. Seems like you're just making it difficult for the both of you."

"I'm afraid," I whispered.

She paused again, "Of what?"

"Relying on someone too much. I did that with my father and he died. I did it with Godrick and he died. I did it with Mother and well, look at how that turned out. I don't have a great track record of folks hanging around for me. Maybe that's another reason it was so easy to want to be with Abe. If he left, which he did, it wouldn't be heartbreaking."

"There's a middle ground between surrendering your independence and relying on someone. What you're describing is a surrender. You need to get your feet under you, but you don't have to do it alone. You can steer the boat but still let people help you. Let him help you."

It was the same thing Maggie had said. The same thing Warwick said.

"But if I let him help me..."

"You'll fall in love with him?" Our eyes were locked. "I wonder if it's already too late for that?"

My eyes widened.

"How do you feel when you're with him?"

"Safe," I whispered. *Was I in love with Warwick?* "Peaceful."

"Girl," she huffed. "If he's bringing you peace, why are you pushing him away?" She placed the last curl, held it a moment while it cooled, and then let it drop. "You know you had nothing to do with your father's death or Godrick's. Neither of them chose to leave you. And your mother, well, don't let her bullshit make you miss out on something good. If what you want is right in front of you, you don't have to keep punishing yourself by not accepting it."

I glanced up at her because that was profound.

She shrugged, "I saw it on Instagram."

Chapter 14

WARWICK

Not smart, Warwick. Not smart. I tried to counsel myself but my feet continued on their journey along the south wing corridor of the floor where Liz's room was located. She'd moved in weeks ago. Three, to be exact.

Since then, I'd learned that I hadn't properly accounted for how having her underfoot, in my space, in my hotel, would fuck with my head. I'd told myself it would be easy. Convinced myself that it would be actually *easier* than not seeing her. Surely, with exposure, this fascination, this thing deep in my belly that craved her, would peter out. Or at least mellow. Lessen. It had not.

The first week, I had conducted my business at Haven as usual. She'd been everywhere. In meetings, in the restaurant, in the lounge, in the hallways and meeting spaces. It was as if I had a homing mechanism set to 'Liz'. Everywhere I went, she was there. Excited, grateful, eager. Smelling like heaven. My dick had been continuously hard; the throbbing hunger a distraction that was both unwelcome and all encompassing. It was all I could do not to drag her into a broom closet and fuck her until she couldn't walk. I wanted to put my dick in every hole she had. I wanted to hear her beg for me, feel her drip for me. Make her come over and over and over again. Drink her. Maybe then she'd stop showing up every damn where I showed up.

The second week, I had limited my time at the hotel. Relying on technology and a more than competent staff to make sure business continued. I'd spent more time working from my small brownstone and showing myself at our other two locations in NY. Detoxing. From her. It hadn't worked. I'd jacked my dick raw.

The third week, I'd come in and hidden in my favorite hidey-holes like the no-pussy-whipped punk I was. I'd still conducted meetings that included her via videocall. I couldn't be held responsible for how I'd behave closed into a small space with her. But I'd needed to see her. The interactions we'd had were brief, curt, to the point. I knew I was being an ass, but I couldn't help it. I was addicted to the rise of heat, the clench in my gut, the thud in my chest...all the shit that kicked in when she was around. Even if I couldn't have her.

By the fourth week, I'd found a rhythm. I had learned to manage the constant erratic heartbeat, the semi-erection, the way my eyes always searched for her, the way the hair at my neck was an antennae for her presence. My whole body was tuned to her. And she walked around, beautiful and smart, making my staff fall in love with her. In a month she'd already moved two projects further along than we anticipated and streamlined our process for inquiries. She was fucking amazing. I'd known she would be but seeing it all in action, seeing her move my shit forward? It hinted at power couple on some 'this could be us' level shit.

Still, Heading to her room in the middle of the night was out of pocket, I told myself. *It's not the middle of the night, one. And you have reason, two.*

And so, here I was, headed to her suite at the tail end of the day to do a walk through with me with a high profile client who'd popped up unexpectedly asking to see final plans for a coming event. I'd tried to call her but she hadn't answered. Brandon, her assistant, had said she'd gone to her suite and taken the specs for the layout with her. It would be most effective and satisfying to the client if she were there, with the printed layouts. I had electronic versions but seeing the plan on screen, trying to walk the space and reference the smaller device, well, it wasn't ideal and getting the pages printed again would take too long. Plus, it would be good experience, good exposure for Liz to be part of the conversation. I'd fall back and let her manage the walkthrough. I was her only client at the moment and we both knew the position was temporary. Putting her in front of this client could help her.

I knocked.

***

LIZ

I lay on the plush sofa in the center of suite Warwick had given me as part of my employment package. It had been a godsend. Being able to walk out of my apartment without needing to beg for help from my mother had been freeing. I still acutely felt the fact that this was no permanent arrangement, but it also wasn't a handout. Margeaux had helped me acknowledge that.

My session at *Texture* earlier in the week had been therapeutic. My hair had been nourished, my soul had been nourished and now, my body was being nourished because I had just rubbed out a second orgasm thanks to this *book* Margeaux had given me. It had been a sneak attack. The romance novel had pulled me in, first intriguing with the beautiful brown characters on the cover, then holding me with wonderfully plotted, well-written, nicely developed characters so that I'd been routing for them to get together. When it looked like the story was taking them in that direction, I'd almost called Margeaux to thank her. This story of black love was food for the soul.

And then they had actually *gotten together*. Oh my god. The steam rolling off the page had melded with the fantasies I'd refused to admit I was having about Warwick. Fantasies that had noticeably increased in frequency since my visit to *Texture*. Something about Margeaux making it crystal clear that Warwick was not Godrick's brother, and that I was being ridiculous in pretending they were, had released a damn of suppressed longing. At least subconsciously. I'd woken up every night following that visit dripping wet and reaching for my side table drawer, images of Warwick, bare-chested and intense, leaning over me, leaning into me.

And now, I couldn't get enough of the book or the Warwick fantasies. I'd fucking given up. And today, when six pm rolled around, I'd eagerly taken myself to my room to pour a glass of wine, get comfortable and continue to follow the relationship unfolding on the pages, substituting myself and Warwick for the main characters. If I came to the sofa prepared, with no panties and extra clean hands, well, so be it.

I lay there replete for a moment, no longer embarrassed and no longer beating myself up for letting the images of Warwick dance behind by eyelids when my hands slipped between my thighs. He didn't have to know. I so rarely saw him these days that it was easy enough to manage. I would occasionally hear his deep voice barreling along a corridor; I secretly lived to see him, big and dark and handsome as sin, on my video screen during our virtual meetings. I could mute my camera and just watch him and ignore the fact that my nipples were hard and my panties were wet.

I hadn't decided what to do about these changes other than keep them to myself and enjoy them. It was one thing to acknowledge that perhaps I'd been purposefully denying myself something. It was quite another to say those words out loud or do anything to rectify the situation. I honestly still wasn't sure I wanted to rectify it. Margeaux had made excellent sense, but her life wasn't my life. How much stock could I really put in a conversation with a woman, wonderful though she was, who I'd only know a couple months and had one serious private conversation. It was a big ask.

But I didn't have to make a decision now. Or even think about it really. It was Tuesday. There was no reason to think I would see Warwick again until Thursday evening at the earliest.

I swung my legs to the floor and headed to the bathroom to wash my hands and clean up. In the bathroom, the shower called to me and, after wrapping my hair and making sure no moisture could get to the blowout Margeaux had blessed me with, I stepped in. I didn't even try to dissuade myself from pretending my hands were Warwick's as they glided, soapy, over my body.

When my hand slid to my neck, it was him urging me to arch. When I squeezed my breasts, teasing and pulling the nipples, one then the other, rubbing my palms across them until they stood hard and firm, it was Warwick. When I plucked and flicked them, it was his thick fingers and long tongue doing the work. My hand running across my belly and fingers slipping lower to play with my clit, to rub through the wetness that didn't come from the shower until it stood hard and hungry for my touch. All that was Warwick. And when I slid the vibrator I'd grabbed on my way through the bedroom between my thighs, cool and hard against my hot wetness, that was definitely Warwick. I sighed at the insertion, squeezed my nipples harder and harder while I pumped inside then dragged the vibrator out to hum against my clit, over and over, inside and out until maybe I screamed. *Oh, God*.

I slumped against the shower wall, and let the vibrator drop, breathing hard, ears wringing, fingers teasing myself between the thighs when it registered that someone was knocking. Not on the suite door; on the bathroom door.

***

WARWICK

"Liz!" I called out again. I was about to break the fucking door down, fuck the fact that she was in the shower.

She'd screamed. I knew I'd heard her scream.

When she didn't come the to suite door, I assumed she wasn't here. I debated but decided to open the door just to see if perhaps the plans were in plain sight. The suite was generous but it wasn't that big. I wouldn't go in her bedroom, obviously.

I'd used my master to scan into the suite. Not the best look, admittedly. But I did call out as soon as I entered. She hadn't answered but I'd both seen the plans laid on the office desk and heard the shower simultaneously. I moved to the desk to leave a note. A quick scribble, "I grabbed the layout. MH is in town and wants walkthrough tonight. Call asap. -W". Straightforward. And then I long-stepped back toward the door. She'd probably curse me out for coming in uninvited. That would be fun.

Then she'd screamed and I'd heard something clatter. I'd found myself at the bathroom door before realizing I'd moved.

"Liz!" I knocked again.

I heard the shower cut off.

"Warwick?" Her voice floated from the other side of the door.

"Are you okay? Open the door."

"I'm not opening the door! Why are you here?" Her voice was breathless, she was breathing hard.

"Liz. Are you okay? Are you having an asthma attack?"

"What? No! How did you even know I was asthmatic?"

"Godrick," we said at the same time.

"Warwick, why are you in my room?"

"I came to get the layout designs. The client is in town. He showed up unexpectedly and wants a walkthrough. I came to get you but you didn't answer."

"So you just came in."

"Yeah."

"Warwick."

"What?"

"Get out."

She was fine. I was certain of that. But now I was curious. "Why are you breathing so hard?"

"Warwick. Get out."

I leaned against the door jamb. "Are you going to come to the ballrooms when you're done? For the walkthrough?" My eyes skimmed the room absentmindedly while I waited for her answer.

"If you go away, I can finish my shower and do just that."

My eyes landed on the sofa where a blanket was strewn. She must've been taking a nap before her shower.

"What were you doing before I got here?"

"Showering, obviously," snark on level one hundred for good reason. "Are *you* okay?"

"Before that," I chuckled. I wished I could see her. She'd be all flushed and irritated, eyebrows drawn, eyes rolling.

"Reading. Will you go away so I can finish. You're keeping the client waiting."

"Oh, yeah," my eyes snagged on a book lying on the floor by the sofa, just underneath the coffee table. "What were you reading?"

The bathroom door flew open to reveal a very flushed, very bright eyed, shower-capped Liz. She was damp and soft, a cloud of clean, Liz-scented air billowed from the bathroom when she opened the door. I could literally feel the blood changing course from my brain to my dick.

"None of your business, Warwick." Her eyes darted toward the book. A slow grin spread across my face.

"What were you reading, Liz?"

"None of your business, Warwick," she repeated, enunciating each word. My eyes skimmed her beautiful face, pretty brown eyes, eyebrows drawn, faint beads of moisture still around the edges of the giant pink shower cap. I lifted a hand and slid my thumb between her eyebrows to smooth the frown.

"Your shower cap sure is big," I said adjusting my expression to show wonderment at the sheer size of the thing. "I didn't realize you were so...headstrong."

"Warwick! It is a normal sized shower cap. Get. Out."

"What were you reading, Lizzie?"

She simply glared at me, cheeks bright, eyes flashing. She looked delicious.

"Fair enough. None of my business, Liz." I paused and followed the path of a droplet of water as it emerged from behind her ear and meandered down her throat across her collarbone and the swell of her breast to finally be absorbed by the towel she'd wrapped around herself.

"But just so you know, I really was just grabbing the layout and leaving. I'd written a note," I said. "But then you screamed." Another blush raced across her shoulders and into her cheeks. "And I heard a clatter." Her eyes widened and she stepped a bit closer to me, pulled the door a little less wide blocking the direct view of the shower.

What could she possibly be blushing about? Had she fallen and was embarrassed? I looked over her head into the bathroom behind her, into the mirror that reflected the glass-encased shower. She'd definitely dropped something in the shower. It was purple. It looked like...a slow grin spread my lips and the erection that had started to subside sprang back to full life. *Dammit, Lizzy.* I wondered if she'd been thinking about me. From my thoughts to God's ears.

I looked down and her eyes were locked on me.

My teeth clenched. *Fuck.* I fisted my hands to keep from touching her because, the way she was looking at me? With those pretty brown eyes all heavy-lidded and curious, both sated and needy. Challenging me. It was about to be a situation.

"You need something, Liz?" I could hear the growl in my voice and swallowed.

She licked her lips and blinked. The deep breath she took lifted her breasts and my eyes dropped, snagged on the hard nipples pressing against the towel. I drug them back up to her face. There was hunger there. She wanted me. And unless I'd lost all understanding of social cues, she was ready to do something about it. *Almost.*

She shook her head slowly, eyes on mine. *But not quite.*

I licked my own lips. Swallowed again and nodded at her. I reached into my pocket and snagged a piece of gum. The moment it took to unwrap and pop it in my mouth was the time I needed to regain some semblance of control.

"Whenever you're ready, Lizzie," I said. She blinked.

"Warwick, I," she began.

"Whenever you're ready," I repeated and then, "I'll be in the ballroom."

***

LIZ

Jesus. That man. I glanced around the bathroom. I didn't think he had seen the vibrator, his angle wouldn't have been right for that. But he had heard me doing everything but screaming his name. *Had I screamed his name?* I had to assume not; he wouldn't have been able to resist teasing me about it.

Maybe he had though. Why else would he ask that question? *"You need something, Liz?"*

I moaned, my nipples peaked *again*, my pussy dripped *again*, and my hand crept down my body *again*. I leaned against the bathroom counter, lifted one foot onto the toilet, and slid my fingers into my wetness *again*. Slow, wide circles turned into fast, hard strokes all against the backdrop of velvety black eyes and that gravelly voice saying my name. *Whenever you're ready, Lizzie.* It had been nothing but the grace of god that had kept me from crawling up him like a tree.

Why hadn't you?

Because I needed to be sure. More sure than this at least. That I wasn't making a rash decision. Or a selfish one. I didn't want to hurt him any more than I wanted to be hurt. Sex with Warwick would be spectacular. And life-changing. But my life was already changing, and too much change might be too much change.

So, I cleaned myself up *again*, got dressed, and hurried to the ballroom to meet the man who starred in my nastiest fantasies.

CHAPTER 15

LIZ

I was, yet again, on my way to find Warwick. But it wasn't for work this time. It was personal.

I needed him. So I was going to find him. I refused to spend any more time trying to decipher the how and why of what I was feeling. At some point, I had to admit that he made me feel safe, seen, and protected. And in this moment, that's what I needed.

I tapped the elevator button impatiently and slipped through the doors while they were still opening. The gasp slipped from my lips when I caught my reflection in the mirrored panes of the elevator walls.

I couldn't believe I'd forgotten so quickly. I slipped my hand along my bare nape, touching the soft fuzz before lifting to fluff the curls that fell effortlessly in the asymmetrical bob Margeaux had blessed me with just this morning. I'd been attempting to slip into the hotel with every intention of avoiding Warwick until tonight, when he would show up on my doorstep, as he'd done every Tuesday since the night we'd dubbed The Break-In, with some tummy-tempting treat.

That same tummy flipped with the reminder of what I actually had in store for him tonight. *Me. I* was what was in store for Warwick tonight. I thought for a moment of redirecting the elevator, holding it all for tonight but no, I'd get this out of the way now, then this evening I could concentrate. On him. I licked my lips and shifted to adjust for the ever-present thread of desire that pulsed whenever he crossed my mind.

I had spent the three weeks since The Break-In torturing myself. He was everywhere, all the time it seemed. And since I'd broken the damn on masturbating to him, I couldn't stop. Every move he made, every slow deliberate step, every stroke of the beard, every lick of the lips was fodder for my memory bank. I'd turned into a pubescent boy.

It all came to a head when I visited Margeaux this morning for my now-regular shampoo and style. She had asked, as she always did, "Are you still torturing yourself?"

And the answer had been, "Yes." Yes, I was still torturing myself. Pretending that more time would somehow, what, make me want him less? Make my situation less ridiculous? Make him less imperfectly perfect?

"You know he knows all your shit and he wants you anyway. Why are you playing?" Margeaux had asked in her very direct way. I had learned over time that she had been the voice of reason for Cassandra when she and Abe had a bad patch. Because of me.

And this wasn't a bad patch, because we weren't even in a relationship but, I definitely needed to hear reason.

"Has something happened to make him not the good guy he seems to be?" Margeaux asked as she put the final touches on my blow dry.

"You know not."

"You said he's been coming by. Y'all have been talking?"

"You know we have. He's been coming to the suite every Tuesday, bringing food. We talk for hours." I shrug. "He kisses my forehead, tells me to rest well, and leaves."

"Well, I'm just asking. Trying to figure out how long you're going to leave him out there. Just because I know he's yours and am respectful enough to not push up, doesn't mean these other chicks are."

I rolled my eyes. "I don't think..." I began.

"I'm sure you don't. But that doesn't matter. Don't leave that man on ice too long. He's made himself clear, hasn't he?"

"I mean, not really."

She raised an eyebrow.

"Okay, yes. It's clear he'd be receptive. But he hasn't said anything recently."

"Are you insane? Didn't the man all but stand in your bathroom and ask if you needed some dick?" When I didn't answer immediately, she tapped my shoulder with her comb, "Well, didn't he?"

I giggled, "He did."

"Honey, you're playing with fire. You need to fuck that man and figure it out along the way."

"I don't want to hurt him. What if it doesn't work out?"

"That's a grown man, Liz. You let him make his own decisions. Tell him if you need to. Tell him you're still not sure but

that you're fiending for that dick and just can't wait any longer."
She lifted my hair and fluffed it around my shoulders before
gathering it into a knot to consider an updo. "Let him decide if
he wants to give it to you."

"Margeaux!"

"What?" She shrugged. "I'm serious. You're letting your
mother fuck with your head. She's got you out here acting like
her and you can't even see it."

I recoiled, "What?"

"I said it," she held firm. "You're taking his choices from him.
Assuming you know what's best for him. Not letting him decide.
You make your *decision and then let him make his."*

She let me sit with that for a moment before continuing,
"Plus, you're a smart woman. You know he's made his decision.
You just haven't decided whether you deserve. But you do."

"But what if he hasn't made his decision? What if I'm setting
myself up?"

"Then he'll tell you. And you get to make another decision.
That's what life is. You make a choice, see what happens, then
make another. If he turns out to be a fuck boy who's been playing
with you this whole time, then now you know and you move on.
But we know that's not the case, don't we? He wants you. He at
least wants to give it a real shot and that's all you can ask for."
She fell silent for a bit.

"Shit, right now I'd take somebody who's feeling me half as
much as he's feeling you. When we girls come into the Lounge
and he's all hovering around, mixing drinks and shit. He looks
at you the same way Abe looks at Cassandra."

I reared back in surprise. "He does not."

"Not when you're looking, he doesn't. When you're looking, he either shuts it down or gives you that 'come sit on my face' *look that gets you all giddy and flustered.*

"I do not get giddy and flustered!" I protested, horrified.

Now it was her turn to laugh. "Oh you absolutely do," she gave my head a little push with the hand that held my gathered hair.

"It's time to do something different, Liz," she said with a head tilt.

"Maybe you're right. Maybe I shouldn't be making this decision for him." I pondered it. "But can I really just proposition him? And say what? 'I don't think I can give you what you want emotionally but would you like to have sex anyway?'"

"Those might not be the words I chose but that's certainly the sentiment," she said chuckling and contemplating me in the mirror.

"I'll think about it." She grinned. I met her smile.

"Now, that that's settled, I was actually talking about doing something different with your hair."

And I'd walked out with a long asymmetrical bob cut high to reveal my nape in the back and bare my left ear and long on the right side to skim my chin, even when curly. It was sexy and fun and edgy. I loved it.

When we'd hugged at the end of the appointment, I knew Margeaux had purposefully worked her magic to free me from the weight of the fears and doubts I put on myself. I could live my life as I liked. I could make my own mistakes. I *would* make my own mistakes. I was hopeful that this decision about Warwick wouldn't be one but I had made up my mind to give myself, and him, this. I decided to talk with him tonight. Translation: I'd decided to sleep with him tonight.

I'd ask him as I always did, why he was there. And he say in the baritone that always settled between my thighs, "I just came to see if you need anything, Liz." Well tonight, I'd be needing more than the food and conversation. I just prayed he was on the same page and that I hadn't waited too long.

I'd stepped back into Haven with my mind full of thoughts of the night to come. What would I wear? I needed a wax and a mani/pedi. It had been a long time since I'd detailed in preparation for a man. My gut clenched at the thought of his appreciation for my efforts. I could already feel his beard between my thighs.

It was when I pulled my phone out to start scheduling services that I saw the notifications for the email from the online DNA company. Two emails actually. Subject lines indicating that one, my DNA had been analyzed and my profile was complete, and two, that there was a DNA match out there somewhere.

Those emails had derailed me. And rerouted me because I didn't want to open them by myself. I already knew what they held—yet more proof that the man I thought was my father, wasn't. And some familial connection to the piece of trash who might be.

Yeah. I didn't want to open them alone. I wanted Warwick there.

CHAPTER 16

I'd been in my quiet little hidey hole for nearly ninety minutes crossing tasks off my to-do list. I'd done most of what needed doing already: planned tomorrow morning's staff meeting, reviewed the guest satisfaction surveys, and reached out to a couple of the highest-dollar guests to shoot the shit for a few minutes. I'd even reviewed the inventory lists from housekeeping as tedious as that was.

The only thing left on the list was to review yesterday's financial report. I low-key loved this part–looked at it every damn day. Fully focused, fully present. I spent good money on my finance guy but I once-overed everything regularly. He got it all collected and consolidated as much as possible to make everything as straightforward as possible, highlighted trends and shit I needed to catch. But I liked to see the impact I was making. I liked to chop and screw the numbers so I could get insight to my own questions and make sure there were no surprises on the horizon.

And I needed to make sure we were on track for this second round of investment funding. Haven was doing well but I'd made bold moves in getting it off the ground. I was counting on its performance to calm the nerves of the investors who'd chosen, at almost the last minute to split their investment into two installments. The second coming available once the numbers panned out at Haven. It was stressful to say the least. They were bringing up issues we addressed repeatedly; issues they'd agreed wouldn't impact their decisions. Now here I was, feeling like I was back at the same damn drawing board I'd been at when I secured the funds to begin with. If they decided for whatever reason not to follow through, some hard decisions would have to be made. Decisions that might include a great deal of people losing their livelihoods. And I didn't want it to happen on my watch.

I sighed and checked my watch. Maybe I could get in another forty-five minutes before someone tracked me down. It was why I wasn't in my office—too high traffic—the flip side of an open-door policy that was good for morale but terrible for getting shit done. I was contemplating whether it made sense try for another round when I heard the *click click click* of stilettos across the ballroom floor.

A quick grin took over my lips. I had no doubt that it was Liz. I'd recognize that quick clip anywhere. I eagerly slid away from the six-foot folding table where I'd spread all my shit in the caterer's corner. It was a room just off the ballroom's dedicated kitchen that had no assigned purpose, but it was quiet and bright with a row of high windows that opened over the small alleyway behind the hotel. I'd discovered it in early walkthroughs of the property. I could have had it incorporated into the kitchen during renovations but something about the space spoke to me.

I knew I'd need a hidey hole at Haven and it had felt perfect. I used my office for meetings and show. I used this space to get shit done.

"Warwick?" She called my name and my eyes slid shut at the immediate throb in my groin. "Warwick, are you in there hiding?"

Another grin, broader this time, before I schooled my features into something more CEO-like. "Yes, Lizzie, I'm here. What do you need?" I heard her steps falter before regaining their regular rhythm. She appeared in the doorway a moment later, color riding high on her cheeks, a crooked smile on her face. The face that I could see in all its glory because she'd changed her hair. Drastically.

I rose and moved toward her before I realized I'd left the table. My eyes roamed her face, and back to her hair, back to her face...back to the hair. By now I stood in front of her. I stuffed my hands in my pockets to keep from touching her but at this distance, I could see the flutter of her lashes and the question in her eyes. She cared what I thought.

"Hey," she said, shifting slightly under my focused gaze.

"Can I touch it?" I asked because all I wanted to do was sink my fingers into those curls, make contact with the heat of her scalp, cup the back of her head while I dipped my tongue in her mouth and tasted her. I still hadn't kissed her. Not since that day all those years ago. Day after day of watching her, night after night of talking with her on the phone or torturing myself in her suite and I hadn't even tried. I'd done well. I'd kept my hands to myself and only engaged in the lightest of flirting.

Even though I knew she wanted me. Even though I could see her little purple vibrator laying on the floor of her shower every time I closed my eyes. Even though I could hear her scream of pleasure every time I drifted off to sleep. Even though I could scent her ever so faintly beneath the fragrance she wore and I knew she was wet for me, right now. I licked my lips and patted my pockets for a stick of gum.

I wondered what she wanted, coming in here with her sassy little haircut and her pretty smile. Soft eyes looking like she needed me. Calling my name. The spreadsheets and my to-do list were completely forgotten.

She nodded.

"Are you sure?" I asked, tilting my head, letting her see in my eyes what she was doing to me, just with her presence.

I popped the gum in my mouth and watched the pulse pick up at the base of her throat. I wondered idly, focusing on that spot, whether she was ready to stop playing yet. I'd gone into these last few weeks knowing I was risking a lot but there were signs that I liked. Not the smallest one the fact that she was clicking her mouse on a regular basis and I was cocky enough to assume I was the star of her fantasies. But I also knew fantasies weren't reality. She might be completely happy to keep me in her dreams.

I didn't think that would happen, though. I wasn't crazy. I'd been a grown-ass man for a long time; I knew when a woman wanted me. And my Lizzie wanted me. But I also needed her to trust me. And to be sure. Because when she came to me, I wouldn't be able to let her go.

Her pulse was pounding. Her pupils had dilated.

"Are you sure?" I asked again, wondering if she heard the other question—the bigger question—in my ask.

I let my gaze dip for a split second. Her nipples were pressed against the tailored longsleeved blouse she wore. This time she licked her lips.

I tilted my head. She was in a mood.

"I'm sure," she whispered. I raised my eyebrows.

"I'm sure," she repeated.

A deep breath brought another inhale of her sultry, botanical fragrance to my nose. I felt myself swell even further. If she glanced down, there'd be no question of whether I liked her new haircut.

I lifted one hand, caught one of the gold-brown-caramel streaked curls between my fingers. So soft. I tugged and released so it bounced back to dance at her chin. Her eyelids dropped slightly and the corner of her mouth tilted up.

I returned her half smile with my own lazy tilt before I slipped my hand around to her nape to touch the indent at the base of her neck. I stroked the short peach fuzz that covered that delicate skin. She shivered, goosebumps popped on her skin.

"Liz," I whispered. She nodded again and met my eyes. Hers were hot, heavy, knowledgeable. Hungry. "Yes," she said.

This time my brows dipped. I focused on her. All of her. Only her.

"I want to kiss you, too," I told her. I wanted no doubts. "Would you like me to do that?" I was looking for clear, enthusiastic consent.

She nodded once more. "Yes," she said again. I trashed the gum I'd just put in my mouth.

My other hand joined the first to plunge into her curls, reaching to her warm scalp, measuring the roundness of her skull, pulling her to me so I could cover her mouth...*finally*...with mine.

I vaguely heard the clatter of her phone when it hit the floor. I absolutely felt the heat of her body as she molded herself to me, stretched up on her tippy toes sliding her heated curves along my body, sending my dick from hard to diamond-cutter status.

I didn't want to scare her but *fuck* she tasted every bit as good as I'd imagined. Hot, liquid honey inside her mouth. I licked and sucked, trying for the life of me to capture her entire mouth, to absorb her, to take her in. She moaned, then stretched harder. I bent my knees to accommodate and she tightened her arms around my neck so that when I straightened she came with me. Feet lifting from the floor as she tried just as diligently to eat me from the inside out. I felt her tongue swipe my teeth, the roof of my mouth, before she pulled mine into her and sucked.

Her skirt was too tight to spread her legs around my hips but my hand slid to capture her ass and hold her against my erection. The movement both relieved and worsened the problem. My lips drug away from hers, slid along her jawbone to her neck. I opened my mouth on the long tendon that ran along the side of her throat. I licked then closed and sucked.

I was rewarded with her deep moan, but now she was wiggling, struggling. Some part of my mind clicked on, trying to determine whether she was trying to get away. *Idiot. She wasn't ready. You* knew *she wasn't.* I started to draw back, to release her. I was hastily trying to compose an apology...a challenging task when all the blood in my body had pooled between my legs.

Then I realized. She wasn't trying to get down. She was struggling to pull up her fucking skirt. *Goddamn.*

"Fuck, Liz. Are you sure?"

She nodded vigorously. I groaned in her ear and growled, "Hold on," before I wrapped her arms back around my neck. She squeezed, peppering my face with kisses while I shimmied her skirt up over her hips, kicked the door shut and pressed her against the flat surface. As soon as her legs were free she locked them around my hips and settled into a slow bump and grind.

Her head was thrown back, eyes closed.

"Open your eyes," I growled it. I wanted to see what happened to those pretty mocha eyes when she came. Did they go dark like cocoa or lighter like cognac?

Her eyes popped open immediately. Ah, dark, like cocoa. I propped her against the door, eased back a little so I could get to the buttons on her blouse. She met my hands with her own on my own buttons, pulling and tugging the shirt from my slacks and slipping her hands against my stomach over the black beater I wore. She groaned her frustration and I laughed.

"Oh you're all serious now, huh?"

"Why do you have two shirts on, Warwick? Take it off," she demanded.

My dick hardened painfully. *Oh shit.* I obeyed and whipped shirt and beater over my head, then returned to spread her blouse, revealing her full smooth breasts encased in pale pink silk and lace. I could see her dark nipples peeking through the lace. My mouth watered and I bent to taste her. I sucked hard because I couldn't help it. I rolled the nugget of her nipple around in my mouth, swore I could taste the sweetness of her. I shifted my attention to the other and fell into a dazed pattern moving back and forth, drugging myself with her taste, the feel of her against my tongue and teeth, and the hot thickening scent of her.

I hoisted her higher and simultaneously slid to my knees so that her legs draped across my shoulders and my face was buried between them. The tightness of her skirt kept her thighs pressed to my ears, capturing her swirling heated scent so I was lost in it.

"Warwick," she sighed as I swiped my tongue across her dripping wetness, absorbed by more pale pink lace and silk. She gasped and pressed against me, pushing herself into my mouth. "Oh my God," she hissed.

My chest swelled; making this woman feel good was my only goal. I shoved the skirt further out of the way and cranked her legs wide so I could l get to work first eating through the nothingness of her panties, then stretching them out of the way of my starving mouth. She was soon fully grinding against my face, soaking my beard, rubbing her clit across my tongue, single-minded in her pursuit of her own pleasure. I loved every minute of it. I added a thumb, sliding across her opening, teasing, massaging, circling, but not actually inserting, sucking on her nub until her thighs started to shake and her body started to go rigid. Then I did insert...and pressed...and opened my mouth over her juiciest parts so I wouldn't miss a drop as she came apart in my arms and on my tong.

I licked her through a second orgasm; it was impossible to stop when she was pouring pure honey down my throat. Arms secured underneath her thighs, my hands reaching up her back to hold her close and steady, I turned and laid her across the long table where I could spread her out, taste her thighs, kiss behind her knees, suck her ankles and the toes tipped in lavendar polish before returning to bury my tongue in the slick, sweet center of her.

My ears pounded with the force of the blood racing through my body. She drenched me again, shuddering her pleasure, sighing my name. The pounding in my ears almost made me miss her hum of contentment. I lay my head on her thigh trying to catch my breath. *Jesus*. I needed to calm the fuck down before I crawled on top of her. Give her a second to breathe. Or not, because she grabbed me by the ears and hauled me up her body, her hand sliding down as I slid up to grab me through my pants.

The table groaned, fine with her weight but not appreciating the addition of mine. A heavy stroke into her hand had the table swaying. I dropped my forehead to hers.

"The table," I groaned in her ear, trying to still my movements, "we have to get up." She massaged and licked her lips, eyes half closed.

"I don't want to," she hummed with another firm squeeze and tug. A hiss escaped my lips as I levered off her and the table.

It was for the best. I didn't have protection with me. In none of my wildest dreams...well, that was a lie...but in the realm of realistic dreams, it had never occurred to me that I'd need to be prepared to fuck Liz in my makeshift office.

She hummed again, rolled toward me and reached for my zipper. I released another hiss that matched the sound of her pulling that zipper down.

"My god, baby," I ran my fingers through the pretty curls on her head. They wrapped around my fingers the same way her taste had wrapped around my tongue. She slid from the table to one of the chairs and pulled my hips between her open legs. I gave myself a moment to enjoy the view, her wild curls all I could see as she reached into my pants, her long brown legs splayed wide, skirt hiked up so that I could see her shiny, wet pussy.

"Warwick," she breathed, clearly frustrated, working to get me out of my pants. I stilled her hands, for a few reasons. Primarily because I didn't want the first time I nutted with her to be in her mouth. And there's no way I wouldn't do that if she got those wet pink lips around my dick right now. But also, I'm a big man. Consistently. I liked to have plenty of time to make sure a woman was ready for everything I was bringing to the table. I thought she was, but I'd enjoy making sure of it when I had more time and a fucking bed that wasn't on the verge of collapse.

When I captured her hands in mine, she froze, looked up at me. I saw the immediate doubt race across her face and I knelt in front of her, "Don't fucking do that."

"Do what?"

"Whatever it is you did that put that look on your face. I'm stopping because I don't have any fucking condoms."

The doubt was immediately replaced with sunshine. "Oh, that's okay, I can..." and she went back to working on her goal. My dick jumped, urging her on. She ran her hand down the length of it, still in my compression shorts.

I stopped her again, "I don't want to come in your mouth."

I grinned at the offense she took to that and dropped a kiss on that pouting mouth. "I want inside you," I told her, the laughter fading when she saw how serious I was. And I was fucking serious. "I want to feel all that wetness drenching my dick." I slipped my fingers deep into her again, demonstrating what I wanted to do with my cock. She moaned and rotated her hips. "I want to grab that ass and suck your titties while you ride me," I removed my fingers, stood, picked her up and sat down, risking combining our weight in the chair. It was really reconnaissance for the next time she brought her pretty ass down here. I settled her on my lap, one hand riding high between her thighs. I dipped my mouth to her ear, made sure my beard did its job, lending a little scratch to her neck. "I want to fall asleep with my dick in you. We can't do that here." I eased my hand higher, slid a finger across her slick, hard nub.

"But," she began but stopped when I let my finger skate across her dripping opening, returning to circle her again. "But," she started again, "we can still do that." She spread her legs a little and I shifted a hand to her hip to hold her steady.

"How are we gonna do that here?" I asked, just to hear what she would say. I slipped my finger back down, and up again, settling into a rhythm that had her flowing again, wetting my fingers until I couldn't help but slip inside. She gasped and rocked on my lap.

"How are we gonna do that here, Lizzie? Hmm?" I asked again. "If you put my dick in your mouth," I slid my finger deeper inside, swirled. She moaned and pushed against my hand. "You think I'd be able to stop?" I asked, adding a second finger, slowly.

Her thighs fell open wider, making more room for my hand. I cupped her, held my fingers motionless inside her, the heel of my hand lay against her clit. I could feel her slow pulse and dropped my forehead to her shoulder. *Fucking Christ.* I couldn't wait to get inside her.

"Do you?" I asked again. She rocked her hips, trying to get the friction she needed. I held her still. She shook her head, I stroked her once, ground my hand against her so that she hummed low in her throat.

"Do you think I'd be able to actually take my dick out of that pretty mouth, pull it away from those pink lips?" I asked and stroked her again. And once more before stilling again.

I licked her neck, sucking the soft skin there into my mouth. I laved the warmth of her skin with my tongue. She squirmed so that her ass rubbed against my dick and her pussy dripped in my hand.

"Do you?"

"No," she whimpered and spread her legs more, rocking, grinding. She let her head drop back, exposing her long throat. I kissed it and took pity on her. I shifted her, putting her back against my chest and slipping my knees between hers so that she was spread wide.

"Oh my god," she breathed, hips thrusting upward into empty air. I lay the fingers of one hand against her apex, covering her there; then stroked two fingers into her so that both hands were full of her. Wet from her. Working together to rub and stroke until she came again on panting screams and went boneless on my lap.

I gave her a moment then rearranged her so that she was cradled. While she caught her breath, I caught mine and let myself wonder what version I would get of her when the lust haze lifted. Would she regret? That thought was enough to douse some of the remaining heat in my blood. I rubbed her thigh, a little smile danced across my lips when I noted how even her breathing had become.

Well done, my guy. I checked my watch. Three orgasms and put her ass to sleep in well under an hour. I mentally patted myself on the back. She couldn't regret that shit but so much.

I let my hand drift up her back to the nape of her neck. I really loved the cut. I couldn't wait to bury my face right there while her pretty ass bounced against my lap. I wondered if that was why she'd come to find me, to show me her new hairstyle. I grinned at that possibility. Whatever reason she'd come looking, I was grateful.

Chapter 17

Her eyes fluttered opened and immediately found mine. A little smile slid across her face and the breath I'd been holding released on a slow exhale. She was sexy as fuck, flushed, swollen, hair much bigger than when she'd walked in. Her eyes were heavy-lidded but there was no regret in them, no hint of upset, thank god.

Sadly, I'd been forced to wake her up when duty called in the form of a leaking pipe in one of the guest rooms. The guests had been relocated and maintenance was on top of the repair, but the guests were not happy about the inconvenience. And given what I knew they were paying, they shouldn't be. So I'd eased her awake.

"Hey, beautiful," I said before recognizing how corny that shit sounded. But that's what she was and it was the first thing that came to my mind.

"Hey," she whispered back and pressed against my chest to sit up. She didn't try to avoid my gaze, she met it full-on.

"Well?" She said.

I grinned. "You were right," I said. "Your pinky toe is just fine."

I laughed and leaned away from the shove she gave me.

"You make me sick," she said, her light laugh was pure heaven to my ears. She was happy. Not upset, not regretful, not angry. She shoved off my lap before I could stop her and started to shimmy her skirt back into its proper place. I stood and shifted, and following her lead, put myself back to rights, and tucked everything more comfortably in my compression shorts. I'd calmed down in the long moments she'd dozed in my arms, but by no means was I in my normal walking-around state. But that was okay. I'd happily walk with a limp all damn day. I got up to grab my shirts from the floor.

"You want this?" I asked her, holding out my undershirt, instead of following up on her statement. "There's a bathroom in the back but it's a bit of a walk."

"Oh," she looked around, "I couldn't," she hesitated. I tugged her toward me.

"You absolutely can," I said, suddenly obsessed with the idea of having her all over my t-shirt. I held her gaze while I slipped the soft fabric between her thighs, lifting her skirt one more time to reach the part of her that was still slippery, for me. I sighed and couldn't help but replace the t-shirt with two fingers. I leaned my forehead against hers and captured her soft lips once more. My tongue echoed the movements of my fingers, licking gently along the closed seam of her mouth before slipping inside to enjoy the hot, sweet depths of her. She laid a hand on my shoulder to steady herself and I pulled back to watch her eyes go dark again while I stroked her again, swirled in her wetness and then, regretfully, slid my hand away; I tightened my grip on her waist when she swayed.

"Tease," she whispered, snatching the shirt from me to clean up.

"Never," I said as I licked her honey off my fingers. I popped them from my mouth and gave a loud smack of deliciousness that made her giggle before I said, "But I do have a situation I need to handle." I wiped my hands, finished cleaning her up, then held out my hand when she looked around for something to do with her too-wet-to-wear panties. "I'll take those," I said and stuffed them, along with my t-shirt, into my laptop bag.

"Freaky ass," she muttered letting another laugh float my way. This felt too good to be true but I wasn't about to look the gift horse in the mouth. I was a grown man; I would handle the fallout when...if...it came. For now, I would enjoy the moment.

"What's the situation?"

"Why'd you come looking for me?"

We spoke at the same time but the way her face animated was enough to make me shut up and wait for her to go first. There was no way a leaky toilet could beat whatever was putting that look on her face.

"Oh! I can't believe I forgot!" I raised an eyebrow and she blushed. "Okay, I can believe it. But now that you're done mauling me," I clutched my pearls, "I came to tell you this." She retrieved her phone from where she'd dropped it, brought it to life, and tapped around a bit before handing it to me.

"These came today. I haven't read them," she said and started pulling on her blouse, buttoning away the siren who had just drenched me all over this room.

I watched until she was done, burning every frame of the process into my memory. When she'd retied the floppy bow at her throat, I turned my eyes to the phone.

"You haven't read them?" She shook her head. "Why not?"

"I'm nervous."

"So you came to me?" She nodded, an eyebrow raising in challenge. Still snarky, even with her lips red and swollen from mine.

"Good girl," I said, because I knew it would make her...yep...roll her eyes. I grinned.

"Do you want to read them now? I can go get this taken care of in say, twenty minutes." I was already thinking through the encounter with the upset guests; brainstorming how to move it along as quickly as possible.

"No, it's okay. We can talk about it tonight," she said, then stopped. "I mean, if..."

"I said stop that shit. Tonight sounds perfect. What do you want to eat?" I asked, tugging her back into my arms and filling my hands with her soft ass. I couldn't believe the turn the day had taken. I needed to touch her to verify that this was even real.

"What do you want to eat?" She asked on a sly smile that made my heart tumble.

"Bet. You make sure you keep that same energy," I grumbled and smacked her on the ass as she walked out in front of me.

***

I tapped on her suite door several hours later, dick hard, with two take-out containers from the Restaurant. The muffled sounds of her fumbling to throw the bolt on the other side had me once again gathering my willpower to bend my libido into submission. I refused to meet her at the door with a damn tent in my pants like a pubescent middle schooler. I was proud that he was only at quarter mast by the time the door swung open but *fuuuuck*.

All my efforts were for naught because my boy immediately resumed full attention when she pulled the door open wide to reveal acres and acres of pretty brown skin barely covered in a pale green...dress? Slip? Piece of tissue paper?

"Are you trying to kill me?" I asked, too stunned to move.

"Do you feel like you're dying?" She asked on a head tilt.

"Yes. And this is surely heaven," I stepped inside and kicked the door shut, momentarily at a loss because my hands were full but not with what I wanted, which was her...soft and supple in my hands. Frustration had me seconds away from dropping the damn food on the floor so I could get my hands on her, but she anticipated the foolishness and took possession of the bags turning to take them further inside to the little kitchenette area.

I trailed behind her concentrating on her barely covered ass primarily and, secondarily, keeping my literal tongue in my literal mouth. When she dropped off the bags and then turned back to me with hot eyes, I thanked the gods and moved closer in two long strides. I couldn't deny that I'd been worried in the few hours since the ballroom. I wouldn't have been surprised if she'd pulled the plug, met me at the door in a hoodie and sweats with no intention of letting me in. I didn't think things were moving too fast, but I'd been waiting for her for years. She might not see things the same way.

Our lips met hot and fast, falling into the rhythm we'd found so quickly that afternoon. I'd spent the last handful of hours licking my lips, wiping my beard, trying to catch the lingering essence of her. Sure I'd cleaned myself up...I wasn't a heathen...but her scent had lingered and her taste had teased me all day. When I rubbed my fingers together, I could have sworn her silky wetness was still caught between them.

But there was no imagination at work now, the hot sweet heat of her mouth fed mine endlessly and I scooped her up, locked her thighs around my hips. My hands gripped her ass and my fingertips brushed against her center...*fuck me*...her naked, damn near dripping center. I flexed my fingers, dipping lightly into her. She trembled and moaned into my open lips, "Warwick."

My name on her breath was the sweetest sound and I throbbed to the music of it. "Wait. We have to talk."

"Do we?" I asked, busy exploring her neck with my mouth, absorbing every part of her that I could.

"We do. I need to make sure," she paused, groaned and gyrated when my fingers danced across her exposed pussy again.

"Make sure what?"

"That you know..." she moaned.

"Know what?"

"That I want you."

The words made my dick jump, made my stomach clench.

"I can tell," I said and slipped one finger deep inside her, then immediately withdrew. I could feel her walls clench around me, trying to hold me inside.

"But," she said on a hollow breath. I hoisted her higher, captured as much of her breast in my mouth as I could and set about soaking the satin of her slip as I suckled. I made a humming noise to urge her to continue. I was trying to listen, but unless she made me put her down, I'd continue to multitask.

"But, I'm not sure I'm completely ready emotionally. I don't want to hurt you, Warwick," she whispered it and I felt her hands stroke across my back with the words.

She didn't want to hurt me? Didn't she know she was the only person walking the earth right now who could?

"I'll be fine. I'm counting it all progress."

I felt her slow exhale, "But Warwick, what if.."

I pulled back to catch her eyes, and parked her butt momentarily on the countertop. "What if what?" I asked. She blinked.

"What if I hurt you?"

"Are you planning to?"

"No, of course not but I have so much going on. My mother..."

"It sounds a lot like life to me. As long as you're not going into this intending to stomp on my little feelings, I'll continue to make my grown-man decisions."

I pushed a loose curl behind her ear. "Are you planning to stomp on my little feelings, Liz?"

She shook her head. "No, but I'm scared I might. By accident."

"The fact that you care, that you're worried about it is enough to let me know you won't. At least, not on purpose."

"You're not scared?"

"I'm not. I trust you. Apparently more than you trust your-self. You wouldn't be here, half naked and," I pulled her against me, "dripping candy on the ground, without thinking it through. If there's one thing I know about you, it's that you don't make rash decisions. I don't know what happened today to bring you to me, finally, but I'm grateful, Liz."

She laid her forehead against my chest and I waited. Kicking myself. *Grateful??* Idiot. Gratitude was not what she wanted or needed. But then I felt her head move against my chest in a nod.

"Margeaux said I should tell you where I stand and let you make your own decisions."

"Margeaux is a smart and righteous woman."

She chuffed against my chest.

"And she's right. Thank you for telling me. And I'm choosing to take the chance."

"Because you wanna fuck. But there's more to this. It could get messy, Warwick. My relationship with Godrick, *your* rela-tionship with Godrick. Maggie. Lena. We could screw things up badly."

I laughed, "I absolutely wanna fuck. All day and all night. But I'm also, as previously stated, a grown man. I know the risks. Godrick isn't here but I'd be willing to bet that after he got over his initially pissed-off-ness, he'd be on board. He loved you. And I know he loved me. He'd be okay if we," I was about to say *loved each other* but caught those words just in time, "found comfort and friendship with each other."

"And you're content with that? Comfort and friendship?"

"For as long as you are, I will be. I want you, Lizzie. All of you. For now, I'll take whatever you're willing to give. If that changes, you'll be the first to know."

Another thoughtful nod. I watched as the thoughts and worries swirled behind her eyes. I saw the moment she decided *fuck it* and exhaled.

"Are you better prepared than you were this afternoon?" She asked, tightening her arms around my neck again. I pulled her to the edge of the counter so I could press against her hot center. She rocked against me. The woman was dangerous, she had every right to wonder whether she could hurt me because she definitely could. But right now my head swam with her. My senses were full of her. I couldn't remember feeling so on the far edge of needy since those hot heady first forays into the intimacy of sex.

"Fuck, yes," I assured her and again pulled her weight into my arms.

I walked us toward her bedroom door on long strides and laid her on the bed, fished a handful of foil packets from my pocket and tossed them on the bed next to her.

"Oh, you're ambitious," she laughed breathlessly before I tugged her to the edge of the bed by her pretty ankles, spread her thighs and dropped to my knees, no prelude, no warmup. I had to have her in my mouth again. Over the course of the day I had surely exaggerated her taste; there's no way she was pouring out the luscious dreamy decadence that I remembered. I needed immediate verification.

"Nah, just realistic," I said before I dragged my tongue across her center, swirled at the top, dipped at the bottom and shoved my tongue as far into her opening as I could, dragging every drop into my thirsty mouth. I licked, sucked, swallowed everything I could reach trying to satisfy this initial drugging craving before I settled in to actually give her what she needed. "You taste...so...fucking...good. What the fuck do you eat?"

She giggled, "You should know, you're always feeding me," she ended on a gasp and a moan as I slid two long fingers inside, twisted slowly before I brought them out and licked them clean. I could spread her on my toast every morning and die a happy man. She whispered my name again.

"Yes, baby. Whatever you want."

I focused on the job in front of me and licked, stroked, and curled until this time she screamed my name while I drank what she gave me. Then I waited, painting slow, soft circles over her hot flesh until her hips started to move again, until her thighs started to tense again, until she started dripping for me, again.

Then, I slid up her body, and rested between her legs, my dick laying heavy between us, giving her something to grind against. She went to reach between us but I caught her hand and pinned it over her head. Past experience said it was better if she felt me inside her before she felt me outside her.

The positioning made it easy for me to drop my head to close my mouth over her nipple. I pulled back, teased them with the tip of my tongue, first one then the other until she was squirming beneath me, humping me from below, coating me with wetness. Finally, I slid the damn condom on and she spread her legs wide for me.

I had to pause for a minute because even with the condom I was too fucking close to embarrassing my damn self. Plus I needed to look at her, I needed to burn into my brain what she looked like, spread out beneath me, waiting for me, mouth swollen, cheeks red from my beard, titties wet from my mouth and the brown tips standing tight at attention, her stomach was rising and falling with her heavy breaths and between her thighs was heaven. Pretty, pink, open, heaven.

I propped myself over her and her eyes slid open to catch mine. She bit her lip, and pulled me toward her, "Stop teasing, Warwick." She reached down again, I pinned her hand again.

"I got you," I said and pressed against her opening, just a little, just a test. She was so deliciously wet, I trembled. And pressed again, a little more before pulling back.

She gasped and moaned against my throat where she had clamped her teeth, driving me fucking crazy. Another short stroke...just the tip...and then I heard it. The little telltale gasp that said *what the fuck is he putting in me*. I had heard it more than once. Was prepared to put more time in if she needed it. But then, she sighed and lay herself open further. I think I got harder.

"Fuck, Liz."

"Yes, Warrick," she whispered. "Please, fuck Liz."

My eyes slid closed as another full-body shudder wracked me. She was going to kill me. But I slid into her, no more pull-outs, just slow steady pressure, watching her face, until her eyes flew open to pin mine. "Warwick, Jesus."

"Too much?"

She shook her head, eyes still locked with mine. I kept going, just a little more and I'd be all the way...there. In. I stopped and held. My arms were trembling.

I could feel her fluttering around me, squeezing, relaxing, settling. Then she started to move beneath me. Tiny, slow circles, and dear god. I almost died. I let go of a long exhale and laid my forehead against the pillow under her head. I stroked, once, twice, testing her pull, testing the feel of her, then stilled again. Perfection. She was hot, wet snug perfection around my dick.

She laved my shoulders with her tongue, biting and holding as she moved beneath me, finding her rhythm, and simultaneously driving me up the wall. I held still when she hooked her arms under my shoulders and started a slow methodical grind, a dip and swirl, a lift and pivot that had my eyes rolling into the back of my head. I didn't move, was braced on my elbows, trying not to do the most while she fucked me blind from below. Dear god.

And the more she moved, the wider she spread her legs for me, the wetter she got until I couldn't *not* move. So I did, meeting her strokes with my own. Slowly at first, trying not to split her in two, trying not to slam into her like I wanted to so that my nuts clapped against her pretty ass. But then she said the magic word, "More," and since I couldn't deny her, I did as she asked, and gave her more.

"Warwick," she whispered again in my ear, her tongue skating around the outer edge before clamping on my lobe. "Fuck me. For real."

And because she was clinging to me, because she was pouring hot honey all over my dick, because she was whispering in my ear, *fuck me fuck me fuck me* on repeat, I let my hips go loose and started to swing into her, setting a deep and abiding rhythm that had us both panting, sweating, racing toward an end that seemed like it might wholly consume me.

Hot blissful moments later when her legs started to shake, and the juicy sounds of us coming together echoed off the wall, I braced myself on one hand and wrapped the other around her back to hold her to me and dug into her, trying to reach her sternum, slinging dick to the rhythm of our heaving breaths.

Then she was screaming my name, her pleasure bouncing off the walls around us while I emptied myself into her, hoping the condom held, knowing I wouldn't be horrified if it didn't.

Long pulsating moment passed. I could feel the aftershocks in her body, between her legs. Hell, I could feel my own aftershocks in the twitch of my still mostly hard erection.

I shifted to my back, pretty much smack dab in the wet spot but hell, the whole bed was a fucking swimming pool at this point. I pulled her onto me and tried to catch my breath. This was a fucking problem. This woman was a fucking problem.

"That," she eventually began and stopped.

"Yeah," I agreed and dropped a kiss on her forehead.

"How do you feel," I asked, prepared for just about anything since I'd heard just about everything in the moments after the first time with a woman.

"Well and truly fucked," she said.

I chuckled because of all the things she could have said, that worked for me.

CHAPTER 18

Well and truly fucked, I'd said. And I meant. My physical insides were delightfully stretched and exhausted, clenching around the emptiness he left when he slid out of me. And my emotional insides were all over the place, too, because I hadn't expected it to be *that* good, for him to be *that* attentive, *that* focused, and that fucking determined to turn me inside out. But he had been and I was and now what was I going to do? Because now I'd crossed every line I had said I wouldn't. I'd slept with Warwick. And even though the conversation with Margeaux had emboldened me, had made it clear that I needed to stop punishing myself by denying myself, the reality of laying here now, still catching my breath, while his big warm body cradled mine, had my head spinning.

I'd been honest with him and honest with myself. But what happens when you think you're prepared but you don't know what you don't know? I hadn't known *that*. How was I supposed to keep my wits about me knowing he was walking around with *that* between his legs.

I couldn't think. The blood that was supposed to power my brain was lodged firmly around my heart and between my thighs. Both areas were throbbing, both areas wanted more. What was I supposed to do now? Had I messed up? Did I regret it? Was I embarrassed? I couldn't process. I needed to process.

I felt his kiss on top of my head and let my eyes slide shut with a sigh. I'd deal with it later. I'd think about all of it and catalog all the ways this was a terrible choice after all, later. Five orgasms in a day were all I could handle. I felt myself start to drift when his deep voice grumbled through me.

"How about those emails?" He asked.

"Emails?"

"From the DNA people. Don't you want to find out what they say?" His long, talented fingers played in my hair, smoothing the curls, massaging my scalp.

"Oh, yeah. I guess," but I didn't move. Mainly because I couldn't fathom disengaging myself from the warmth that was Warwick to grab my phone from wherever it was. Plus, if I moved, I'd have to think and I didn't want to start thinking yet.

He chuckled. I felt it in his chest..where I was sprawled. It was a place I'd never expected to be. I decided to take advantage of the locale because I felt fairly certain I would try to talk myself out of returning to this place. I let my hands skim over him, measured the width and hills and planes of the muscles that formed the landscape of him. He was big. And hard. But not uncomfortably so. He had a faint layer of padding that kept him from looking like a freakish bodybuilder and feeling like a cement block. He also had a light dusting of soft hair across his chest that came together in an unexpectedly silky trail that led to what was already my favorite new toy. I let my fingers dance along that trail until they touched him, laying long and heavy against his thigh.

"Liz…"

"Hmmm…"

"Don't start."

"Why not?"

"You need to rest. You want a hot shower? A bath?"

I lifted my head to look at him, all thoughts of processing flitting away at the heavy-lidded look he leveled at me. *I want to sit on his face.* The thought danced through my consciousness; my insides throbbed at the thought of having his long hot tongue buried inside while I rode his beard. The unexpectedly tactile memory of said tongue moving inside me zinged through me, but it didn't shock me. Warwick had a way of pushing my limits even when he didn't know he was doing it. I twisted a little so I could prop my chin on the hands I folded on his broad pecs.

"A bath?" I repeated. "That sounds nice. Are you joining me?"

"Aren't you sore?" He asked.

I shrugged. "I guess a little." I tilted my head. "Do you think you hurt me?" He was a big boy…everywhere…and I had to admit, there'd been a moment there when things felt a little mismatched.

A black eyebrow crept up. "Not intentionally. But…maybe?" He was cute. Not that his concerns were unfounded. Had I not been so ready, were I not completely in tune with his every move, things could have easily become uncomfortable.

"Not at all. I'm good, Sir Warwick. Your mighty sword has not torn me asunder, although it is, indeed, mighty." I glanced down to where my hand trailed lightly along him and watched him start growing. I licked my lips because I intended to have him in my mouth soon and very soon.

Another chuckle, a little freer this time. "Well, I'm glad you enjoyed yourself."

"Oh, I absolutely did. Did you?"

"You have to ask?" He tilted my chin up and blessed me with a deep sex-flavored kiss.

"Not really. I was just being polite," I said when he lifted his head before he patted my ass in the universal 'let me up' signal. I rolled off and propped up to watch as he swung his legs over the bed and carried his big naked self to the bathroom. He was beautiful to watch. Long legs, thick muscles in his calves and thighs that flowed into an ass that had my mouth watering. I couldn't remember ever wanting to bite a man's butt, but here we were. The muscles in his back shifted under dark smooth skin. I knew he looked every bit as good from the front and I made sure to arrange myself so I wouldn't miss the show when he returned.

I heard him relieve himself and wash his hands before he called out to me over the sound of the running shower. "Come pee. I don't need you with a UTI on my account."

I rolled my eyes...bossy ass...but he wasn't wrong, so I forfeited my spot and padded after him to do my business and wash my own hands, all under his watchful gaze. I should have been embarrassed, every moment of my upbringing should have been screaming in horror at the casual way I was moving in front of him. But he made it all feel so easy, so sexy, so natural. When I started to slip out of the bathroom, intending to give him a bit of privacy for his shower before I had my own, he pulled me back in.

He reached behind the door to snag the same giant shower cap he'd seen me wearing that other time he found himself in my bathroom.

"Gotta take care of you," he mumbled, before hustling me into the standup shower and crowding his big self in behind me. I anticipated a hot heavy shower experience with Warwick but it wasn't what I got.

Instead, he efficiently lathered the purple shower net that hung off the shower head and set to work washing and rinsing the last hour from both of our bodies. Rather than being pressed against the shower wall and driven crazy yet again, I got instructions to turn this way or that, to raise my arms and 'give me your foot'. His hot hands, covered in the scratchy exfoliating material still set my body to humming, as did the focused spray of the handheld when he paid close attention to ensuring that no renegade soap bubbles remained where they shouldn't. But when I reached for him, intent on making the hot shower even hotter, he just winked at me, made quick work of finishing up, and then wrapped me in a fluffy towel to set me on the counter for drying and lotioning.

"Warwick?" I hummed while his hands worked Haven's rich creamy lotion into my skin. It was an interesting experience, not sexual—as I'd expected—but far more sensual. This was care being given. I liked it.

"Hmm?"

"Thank you."

His eyes popped to mine. "You're welcome, Lizzie," he dropped a kiss on my forehead. "Thank *you*," he said softly.

He finished his ministrations, which were ultimately useless because the more he patted me dry and coated me with moisturizer, the wetter I got. By the time he set me back on my feet, my body was humming again, on the edge of another orgasm.

But he pulled me out of the bathroom, sent me to find my phone while he stripped the sheets and called for room service to bring new bedding.

I wondered briefly what the staff was going to think and asked his opinion on the subject.

"My staff loves you and they're well-paid. But whatever they think, they can keep it to themselves. I don't tolerate gossip."

"I don't tolerate gossip," I mimicked his deep baritone and giggled. I was so fucking happy, too happy probably. *It won't last*...my mother's pessimistic venom snaked through the outer edges of my consciousness but I pushed that away. I'd deal with the doubt and worry later. Right now, I had big, sexy, naked Warwick Walker in my purview. He deserved all my concentration. And I deserved all his concentration.

I found my phone in the sitting area where I'd left it while I'd been nervously nibbling my acrylics, waiting for him to show up, wondering if I was doing too much with the piece of nothing I'd chosen to welcome him in. Turns out it had been just enough, I grinned to myself again and returned to the bedroom where he'd stuffed the sheeting in a pillowcase and flipped the comforter for us to lie on until housekeeping arrived.

He'd pulled on black briefs that seemed uncomfortably tight but outlined the source of my pleasure in sharp relief. Seeing him there, stretched out on the bed, taking up almost the whole damn thing, legs spread, cock forward had me stutter-stepping into the room.

"Don't get scared now," he quipped, "come on over here." He patted the bed and I climbed up and settled between his open thighs, my back to his front. It was uncomfortable in the best way.

I made a show of wiggling and settling in, "There's a pole in my back," I complained.

"Be still or there'll definitely be a pole in your something," he advised and adjusted himself. It didn't help much but I settled and pulled my phone out, angling it so we could both see.

I swiped and tapped until I got back to the emails from the online DNA company. The first email was just a notification that the analysis was complete along with a percentage breakdown of my ethnic heritage. I clicked to open the website and log into my account, then scrolled slowly to reveal 50% African ancestry...which was both expected and not. Surely if my daddy had been my daddy, that percentage would've been far closer to ninety or a hundred percent. I mean, I know most Black people have some white in them...slavery was real...but fifty percent? I kept scrolling to reveal the distribution among West, Central, and East Africa. The next swipe revealed the forty-eight percent of me that was attributed to European ancestry. I glanced up at Warwick to find his gaze locked on me.

"You okay?"

I nodded, though I wasn't really sure if I was okay or not. This was proof positive, wasn't it? Twenty-five percent British and Irish, fifteen percent Germanic European and a little bit of Scandinavian.

One more scroll revealed the source of the final two percent...of course, the Native American portion.

I pointed it out to Warwick and said, "I got Indian in my family." He chuckled, acknowledging my little effort to lighten my mood.

I closed out that message. I'd deal with it later, I guessed. I wondered what Cassandra's said. If our theory was correct, it should be nearly identical I supposed. At least on the white side.

I moved on to the next email. The subject line read, 'You have a DNA match to explore' so I'd had all day to prepare myself for something big, I just wasn't sure what. I glanced at Warwick. Yep, he was still fully plugged in, his eyes moved from the phone screen to my face. Then he squeezed my hip and snugged his bearded chin into the curve of my shoulder.

"Go ahead," he urged.

"Right," I sighed and clicked to open the email. The page loaded to show an icon of a silhouette shaded in blue to indicate the match was a male relative. I read the accompanying words out loud, "First cousin or close relative."

Then I clicked on the button to 'explore' my match. "You and Sander Scott. First cousin or other close relative. Twelve point five percent shared DNA. Eight hundred thirty cM across 14 segments."

I looked up. "What does that mean? What are cM's? And what are segments?"

"Not sure. But I think it's the twelve-point-five percent shared DNA that holds. That's the same amount you share with Cassandra, right?"

I nodded. "And she's my, what? Half niece, we think?" I tapped around again and pulled up search results for 'familial relationships that would result in 12.5% shared DNA'.

"It says here that this person and I could be a few things. Great grandparent and great-grandchild. Great aunt and great niece or nephew, or vice versa I guess. First cousins. Oh," I paused. "Half-aunt and half-nephew." I looked at him. "That would make this person Cassandra's brother, potentially."

"Have you talked to her yet? Did she get results, too?"

"I haven't. I'm going to text her now," I trailed off as my attention turned to texting Cassandra. I sent her screenshots of what I had received and waited. When she didn't immediately respond, I returned to the screens from the DNA company and started reading a little more closely while Warwick absent-mindedly stroked my thigh sending heat skittering across my still-sensitive skin. It was just enough of a distraction to make all of this palatable.

"I wish I could just go ask Mother about it all," I swiped through the ethnicity results again. "I mean, clearly there's no way my father was my father. There's no reason for her to keep lying about it. I just want to know who it is. And what white man my mama was fucking."

Warwick chuckled, "Okay with your foul mouth." He dropped a kiss on my shoulder. I snuggled deeper into his embrace, registering his rising interest but still stuck on the information in front of me.

"Ignore it," he said, realizing I had to feel him at my back.

"Ignore it?" I laughed despite myself. "Have you seen yourself? Have you *felt* yourself?"

"Yes. No? Depends on how you define 'felt'. But yeah, ignore it because I can't fucking help it. But I'm also not a cretin. This is more important," he motioned to the phone.

I cast him a dubious glance and attempted to find a more comfortable position. Truth told, what was poking me in the back seemed like a better way to spend my time than trying to decipher my mother's reasons for anything. But I kept staring at the screen because there was something I couldn't quite put my finger on. Then it clicked.

"Do you think she was," I hesitated, not wanting to voice the idea, not wanting to think about what it might mean for her...and for me. "Do you think she was raped?" I whispered it. "I mean maybe that's why she is the way she is. Maybe that's why she would want to pass me off as another man's baby? It doesn't make it right, but maybe it explains things? I can't imagine the trauma she might have experienced."

The hand stroking my thigh paused, then squeezed. "I don't know. Could be given the times but I sincerely hope not. I do know it's not going to serve you to go down that road only on supposition. Thinking the worst and building a reality around that shit is not going to help you."

He was right about that because I could already feel the anxiety creeping up my spine. I needed to think. But I also needed to *not* think.

"Hey, I have an idea," he said, voice low and comforting in my ear.

"I bet you do," I returned. I was going for humor but it fell flat under the worry that was rising too fast that I might be the product of some horrible act of violence. If the theories we were dancing around were correct, I was Mother and *Benjamin Whyte's* child. Old Man Whyte was known for a lot of things...his appreciation for Black people was not one of them.

"Seriously," he said. "You should come home with me."

Well that was not at all what I expected. "Home with you? Tonight?"

"Well, we could do that, too, though Haven is as much my home as that place I'm spending too much for. But I meant home-home, to my mama's house."

I hedged.

"I just let you in my bed and now you want me to meet your mama?"

"You already know my mama, so stop making it out to be a big thing," he started.

"It *is* a big thing," I said, squirming to turn in his arms so I could look at him. "I met your mother as Godrick's girlfriend, as your best friend's fiancee. That's how she knows me. What's she going to think if I all of a sudden show up on her doorstep. With you?"

"First of all, you're more than my best friend's fiancee. You've also been Maggie's friend forever," he said.

"But," I started to interrupt because while that was true, my and Maggie's friendship was more of a long distance relationship, forged in our late teens and early twenties. It hadn't evolved under the watchful eyes of our parents. I hadn't spent long summers in the south; I'd only encountered this set of

Walkers briefly and rarely, usually as Godrick's other half. My primary identity to them would certainly be as Godrick's almost-widow.

"She'll think it's great to see you again," he continued as if I hadn't spoken. "Second of all," he matched my raised eyebrow with one of his own, "you'd be coming for their anniversary party. So that would take the pressure off. There'll be hundreds of people there. She won't even notice you." He gave me a shit-eating grin to sell the point.

"Hundreds?"

"Easily."

"She's serious about this party."

"Very."

"What about RSVPs? I'm not interested in being a party crasher and adding stress to your mother's plate."

"I'll take care of it."

I thought about it. Maybe a little getaway would be nice. There'd be enough people there that his mother probably wouldn't be overly interested in my presence, just like he said. But what if she was? Then what?

"And what will you tell her when she's asks?"

"When who asks what?"

I rolled my eyes. Were men really that obtuse?

"When your mother asks why I'm there. With you."

"What do you want me to tell her?"

I nibbled at a nail while I thought it over. It only made sense to be there as his friend. I definitely could not attend as the women he'd been spreading like jelly all day.

I shrugged. "That we're friends. That you and Maggie felt I needed a break and so..." I waved a hand to indicate some vague, noncommittal explanation.

"If that's what you want," he said softly and ruffled my hair.

I chose to ignore the fact that that wasn't *exactly* what I wanted and focused again on the prospect of a trip south. Away from Mother and away from the uncertainty swirling around my father. A change of scenery might let my mind rest a little from the incessant worry and attempts to put a puzzle together when I already knew I didn't have all the pieces.

"When is it?"

"Next weekend."

Hmm. "I'll think about it."

"You do that. And in the meantime," he reached to gently pluck the phone out of my hands, pausing long enough that I could protest the action if I wanted to. I didn't. "You can stop ignoring us now."

"Oh, yeah? You want some attention?" I grinned at him, body already responding to the change in the timbre of his voice and the shift in his gaze. His hands sliding up my thighs felt very different than the absentminded stroking of earlier.

"Yeah. As a matter of fact, we do." And with that, he flipped me and settled his big body over mine, blocking out thoughts of anything other than his sexy, full, kissable lips as they covered mine and the stretching size of him as he worked himself steadily into me again.

Chapter 19

"**G**irl. Spill. We can see it all over your face anyway." Margeaux's urging was accompanied by nods of agreement from Cassandra and Margeaux.

I hadn't been at the table longer than five minutes before they'd hit me with varying versions of the same insistence. Apparently the smug satisfaction I'd been carrying around since I let Warwick put his hands all over me was oozing out of my pores. And my girls had picked up on it.

I glanced around the table and *fuck it*, I nodded, "Okay, yes."

And they all fell out amidst a chorus of 'I knew it', 'Mmmhmm' and 'I know that shit was good'. The last from Margeaux who popped a crab bite in her mouth before following up with, "That man looks dangerously well-proportioned."

Maggie sputtered, "Gross. That's my brother. We don't want details, only verification."

"The hell you say," she replied before turning back to me. "I want the details. So, is he?" she asked, "well-proportioned?"

"Dangerously so," I confirmed and she gave me a slow, raunchy grin.

"I knew it. Lucky bitch," she said with a congratulatory finger pointed my way.

"Again, gross," Maggie muttered.

Margeaux pffted her. "Honey, there is nothing gross about that man. I'm just happy our good sis is finally getting the regular maintenance she deserves."

The blush that had been burning my cheeks since I'd sat down intensified.

"I want the play by play," Margeaux said. "All of it."

I giggled. "I can't give you details. Maggie will have an aneurysm," I laughed at the horror that stamped her face at Margeaux's request.

"Girl, thank you," she said on a sigh of relief.

"But I will say," I continued, laughing when Maggie made a show of sticking her fingers in her ears, "everything you think you know, is true as hell. My god. That man. He's going to kill me and I'll die happy."

"We can tell," Cassandra added, hopping up to do her imitation of me walking to the table. "You walked in here like you were trying not to crease your sneakers." Her stiff-legged, careful rendition had us all dissolving into laughter.

"Forget you," I said on another laughing blush. "I won't tell you anything else!"

"Ma'am," she said, also laughing good-naturedly, "you won't have to. We can see you coming...or should I say, that you've been coming...a mile away."

"Okay, okay," Maggie interjected. "My brother is giving her the business. Can we change the subject now? I'm excited that you're coming to the party. It'll be great to have you there."

Maggie forcefully shut down the topic of Warwick's prowess and brought the conversation around to her parents' anniversary shindig.

"I'm kind of looking forward to it but I don't want to make this...thing...," I waved my hand to denote the undefined nature of whatever Warwick and I were doing, "a big deal. We talked and we're keeping it low-level. A friends with benefits kind of situation. And I don't want your parents to get the wrong idea."

They all looked at me.

"What? We're adults, scratching an itch."

More long looks.

"It's just an entanglement," I said, "because neither of us has room or time for anything more. My head is messed up, still. I need to get this thing figured out with Mother and Cassandra. Warwick is up to his eyeballs in getting Haven fully established. And," I paused because I hadn't shared this particular concern with them; I was worried how they'd react, whether their reaction would underscore my own misgivings. "And," I said again, "everyone knows me as Godrick's fiancee, and they all knew Godrick as Warwick's best friend. What will they think?"

"I mean, I'm not gonna lie," Maggie started, a rare touch of southern slipping into her speech, "the family, well, some of Mama's cousins, can be very gossipy. They'll definitely want the tea but they don't mean any harm. Plus, most of them won't remember exactly who you are unless you tell them. They'll remember Godrick for sure, he was around a lot but you only came a couple of times, right? And even if they do remember," she shrugged, "fuck them. It's none of their business. Godrick is gone and you and Warwick are grown. So, yeah," another dismissive shrug, "fuck 'em. Y'all deserve to be able to figure your shit out in peace."

I looked around to see Cassandra and Margeaux nodding their agreement. I smiled and made all the appropriate sounds but inside, I worried. I didn't want to be that woman. I knew how things could appear from the outside looking in and as much as I wished it didn't, what people thought mattered to me. I'd been raised on a steady diet of public opinion and it was hard to let that go.

"We do deserve that," I agreed, "but there are so many issues to be figured out." I could hear the note of self-pity in my near whine. "Do we really need to add another layer of a...relation-ship...on top of it all. I mean, I don't even know who I am, whose genes are flowing in my veins. And that's on top of Mother's already less-than-stable contribution. Does Warwick even need to get tangled up with me when I'm bringing that insanity plus, *Benjamin Whyte's* gene pool?"

"That part," Cassandra muttered.

I looked her way, shocked because I'd assumed she was all for this situation with Warwick.

"Oh, no," she clarified. "Not you. But yeah, I think about the same thing. I guess I've always had this guy's DNA but not knowing about it was certainly preferable. The more I hear..." she trailed off on a little shudder.

"Exactly. Is that what you want in your life, Maggie? In your family?"

"Well. One, you're not pregnant," she looked at me for con-firmation and I shook my head to confirm that no, I was not, "so we can chill with the gene pool stuff. You're not tainting the bloodlines yet. And two, you are who you've always been regardless of what you're learning now. Like Cassandra said, the blood has always been the blood. You're just now finding out about it."

"And speaking of that. What, exactly, have we found out? Cass has me up to speed on her end," Margeaux said, reclining a bit on the swanky sofa we'd sequestered in the back corner of The Lounge. We'd considered going somewhere else, the girls sensitive to the fact that this was my place of employment where I spent hours on hours each day. But when it came down to it, the food and the drinks were stellar. And since we knew the owner, it was a no-brainer. And as for me, any opportunity to see Warwick was an opportunity I didn't intend to miss.

Plus the familiarity of the place was a comfort. It felt a little like home, like we had come together in my personal lounge. I liked the soft murmur of conversations floating over the R&B that hummed in the background. I took a little solace in the easy movements of the patrons...no, the *visitors* as Warwick referred to them... as they unwound and enjoyed this space that he'd crafted just for them.

"Well," I said, reeling a little from the change of topic. Cassandra must have recognized my momentary brain stutter, because she picked up the conversation.

"We're both white. So there's that," she lifted her glass with a wry twist of her lips.

"Girl, please. Your mama's black so you're black," Margeaux announced. "You, too," she nodded at me. "But keep going."

"We both heard from the same DNA match. His name is Quinn." I shared. "I share twelve point five percent DNA with him which is the same amount I share with Cassandra."

"And she shares how much?" Maggie asked.

"Twenty-five," Cassandra and I responded at the same time. She continued, "Which likely makes he and I half-siblings and his relationship with Liz just like mine...half auntie or something like that."

"We've exchanged a couple of emails and have a video call scheduled but he seems a little hesitant. Wouldn't you say so?" I directed the question to Cassandra who nodded.

"He does. I think he's also opened a can of worms that he might not have been anticipating. We're supposed to talk in a few weeks. They're in Australia right now which has made it hell to try to connect. From what he's said so far, he doesn't have a lot of information himself. His father...we assume Jacob Whyte...refused to talk about his family, basically cut them all off, and now he...Quinn...is trying to learn more. His wife is pregnant."

"They live in Australia?"

"No, they're traveling. He said it was a last major trip before the baby comes. They live in San Diego."

"Wow."

"Yeah."

"So, we'll do a video call when they get back stateside. It's just too hard to line up the timing with them traveling."

"When do you think it'll be," Maggie wanted to know.

"A couple of weeks. Too long. Not long enough," I sipped the white wine I'd chosen when I first sat.

"Well. At least we're getting closer to answers."

"I suppose. I hope so at least. I'm ready to understand but it's so layered. And I still don't know what to feel. I keep trying to tell myself that all of this is secondary. The person I am is the person I choose to be but it's hard to focus on that when your Mother has no moral compass and your father is a racist rapist."

Shock all around. "*Rapist?* What are you talking about?" Maggie asked.

"I mean, okay, that was melodramatic but do you think Mother was willingly sleeping with him? Really?"

"Stranger things have happened," Cassandra said. "But I wonder. Abe has mentioned more than once that he's seen Juanita and old man Whyte with their heads together."

"When? Why?" I asked, surprised. I couldn't remember Mother ever mentioning the man's name.

She shrugged, "Last year sometime? He saw them talking at that wine luncheon thing where your Mom called me trash." I winced and she giggled. "And then again, not long after. He was leaving some bar and he saw them chatting it up outside of a restaurant. He didn't mention her looking particularly out of sorts."

"That's," I couldn't think of a word "odd."

"Can you ask her about it?"

I nodded. "I'm going to have to talk to her at some point. It might as well be sooner than later."

A little silence followed that pronouncement as we all sat with images of how that conversation might go.

"Anyway," Maggie brought us back to the topic, "what's the vibe going to be with this Quinn guy? How's he going to react when he sees y'all's not-white selves on the screen?"

"Does it matter, ultimately? You're just trying to find information and closure, right? It's not like you're planning to seek your status in the Whyte family tree," Margeaux said, then sat forward. "Or are you?"

I looked at Cassandra. This was something we hadn't discussed with each other.

She shrugged. "I'm not. At least not at the moment. Depends on how they act I guess."

I laughed, "What do you mean?"

"If they act like I'm not worthy, I'll see what I can do to take all their shit. I don't want it, but they better not tell me I can't have it," she laughed. "The petty runs strong in me."

"Well, I for one am tired of other people making choices for me. And I haven't decided what I want. Once I have more information, I'll talk to Tonya and see what the options are."

"I'll toast to that," Maggie lifted her glass and we all tapped and sipped.

An hour later and both Maggie and Margeaux had to take their leave. Lena and clients called for their respective attention.

"I'm about to head out as well," Cassandra mentioned. "Abe and I have tickets to a comedy show tonight and I have at least twice as much work as time left."

"I definitely understand. Work at Haven has been wonderful but it's really starting to pick up now. I'm busier than I expected to be but I love it."

"I'm glad to hear it," she offered, standing.

I walked with her toward the elevator bank. I planned to return to my office to finish reviewing the events on the calendar for the coming week. As we waited together for the doors to open, she put her hand on my forearm to halt me.

"Liz. This may be too soon and well out of my purview with you."

It was an ominous beginning and I felt my hackles begin to rise. I tried to tamp the feeling down. This woman had only been kind to me.

"It's about Warwick," she continued.

I felt an eyebrow start to crawl upwards. I liked Cassandra, and I had come to value her thoughts and opinions. I hoped she wasn't about to say something that would jeopardize our still delicate friendship.

"I think you should go for it." Okay, that's not what I expected.

"You do?"

She nodded decisively. "I do. I know you have challenges but don't all relationships? Abe and I certainly did. But I don't regret fighting for it. At all."

I didn't respond. Just waited for her to go on. "I could've easily said 'this is too much'. I actually did say that, and I did walk away and it was the worst time of my adult life. It sucked, to put it mildly. And while I don't know how all of this is playing out in your relationship, I do know that if you want him, you should fight for the opportunity to see what's up."

I sighed and let my shoulders fall a bit. "That's what I want to do but it's so hard. I feel like I don't know my own mind sometimes. Am I making decisions just to spite my mother? Am I really doing what I want? Am I flowing into open space because he makes it so easy? I don't want to use him. I don't want to hurt him. And I also don't want to hurt myself."

"I get it. But you're doing fine. And Warwick is a big boy. He knows what's up. He's choosing to put himself in the middle of it. For you. Don't take that lightly. But also don't feel beholden to it, you know?"

I nodded. "Thank you. That's not too different from Margeaux's advice. The two of you are giving me things to think about."

"Well, try to think good thoughts only," she leaned in for a hug that I readily returned. "You deserve to be happy. You don't have to punish yourself for the things that happened last year and you certainly don't have to hold yourself responsible for your mother's choices. Try to see the good things standing right in front of you, okay."

"Okay," I said on a soft whisper.

It was a long moment before I gathered myself to head downstairs and back to my work.

CHAPTER 20

WARWICK

I slid my hand between Liz's bare breasts, laid it flat on her sternum and pressed her back against me. My other hand landed near her waist, encouraging a deeper arch in her back so I could more effectively fill her up from behind. We lay on our sides, surrounded by a puddle of thick warm blankets in the master bedroom of the two bed, two bath brownstone I'd invested in when I'd found myself back in New York.

Her soft moans floated to my ears and I let my tongue roam the boundary between bare damp skin and the fine peach fuzz at the nape of her neck. Her hips stuttered and I smiled to myself. I knew we still had shit to conquer, issues to work through but one thing that was perfect as is was how our bodies worked together. I loved it.

I loved *her*.

The words pinged around in my head, not surprising, not unwanted and not new, but still...not enough. People who loved each other hurt each other all the time. We needed to figure out how to trust, how to work together, how to be there for one another and let the other in. She was hesitant, and rightfully so given all she'd recently been through; but I couldn't base my needs on her trauma. And she couldn't base hers on mine. If I wasn't what she needed, I'd have to let her go. But for now, here we were. I stroked in and out again, sucked her neck hard and felt the answering rush between her thighs.

Yep. This part, we had right.

She lifted one leg and hooked it over my hip making herself more available to my roaming fingers. I shifted one arm to provide a pillow for her head, with the added benefit that I could get my hand into the thick soft curls that capped her head. My other hand stroked her, slid through her silky wetness to swirl across her little hardness, adding another layer of sensation to the long slow strokes I was giving her. She shuddered, then pressed her hand over mine, intensifying the contact and sending us both hurtling toward completion faster than I'd intended.

I was learning the fast beautiful lesson that this woman, as reserved as she was in all other areas of her life, was not reserved in the bedroom. She chased her pleasure unapologetically, shamelessly. Sometimes she'd get shy afterward, sometimes she'd be shy on the lead up but once we got started...glorious abandon.

I felt her start to clench and flutter around me, enjoyed the sensation of her grinding her soft ass into my hips, head thrown back against my shoulder. I repositioned to cup her throat and hold her hips steady so I could find the rhythm I knew she liked. At this angle I could focus my stroke to the front and...yes...she groaned and melted around me again, drenching my efforts so that I slipped even deeper inside her. I pumped, fingers busy between her wide open thighs, mouth fastened on her throat until she went still, my name spilling from her lips, her hips pressed and shuddering around my dick and against my hand. I rocked into her once more, twice, three times and then released into her. We both stilled, sucking air. Limp and satisfied.

"How am I gonna get this sweet pussy this weekend, Liz?" I whispered in her ear, fingers still dancing, genuinely concerned that I wouldn't have access to her while she was with me at my parents'. "You gonna let me fuck you in my mama's house?" I licked the shell of her ear; she rocked against my hand and sighed.

"Absolutely," she paused and my dick jumped where it lay against her thigh, just outside of her sweet entrance, "not." She finished and I chuckled, not surprised.

"But, baby," I crooned, deepening my voice purposefully since she'd finally confessed how it affected her.

"Stop, Warwick. I am not sleeping with you in your mother's house. That's ridiculous."

"I know. I know. You weren't raised like that." I inhaled deeply, loving the smell of her. It was her natural spicy citrusy fragrance, mixed with whatever it was she wore, topped off with hot sweaty sex. My favorite.

"I wasn't either. I was just playing," I stuck my nose in that space where her neck sloped into her shoulder and nuzzled, "unless you were serious. In which case, I'd allow myself to be led by your heathenish ways." My fingers slipped into her again then eased out to coat her lips and clit with her sweet juiciness. I couldn't fucking help touching her. She arched, pressing her breasts forward, I slipped my other hand around to play with her nipples.

She sighed and rocked again, finding a slow rhythm. "You will not blame your whorish decision making on me, Warwick Walker. I'm a lady," she said before turning toward me, breaking my contact with the aforementioned sweet pussy. She snuggled more deeply into me and wrapped her fingers around my hard again, still slick from fucking her, dick. "I only do ladylike things." A long slow pulling stroke had my full attention; I watched her lick her lips as I grew even harder in her hand.

"You are very much a lady," I agreed, working to regulate my breath when she followed up with a drugging pattern of twists and pulls that had me almost ready to come again. I angled into her hand and gave zero resistance when she pressed against my chest, to push me onto my back. "Very mindful," the breath of laughter floated across my nipples; they went hard when she dragged her tongue across one, then the other. I liked it, but she didn't linger, which was fine because she was on a steady path that brought her lips closer to the fingers and the magic they were working.

"Very demure," she purred right before she wrapped those pretty lips around me and proceeded to do some very un-de-mure things.

***

An embarrassingly short time later, I followed her into my little kitchen where she plopped her fine ass on a bar stool with a cup of hot tea to watch while I pulled the necessary ingredients for breakfast from the refrigerator. Breakfast was one of the reasons we'd left Haven. I wanted the experience of seeing her, puffy-lipped, drowsy-eyed, wild-haired and smelling like me, eating the food I'd prepared especially for her. Couldn't do that at the job.

Plus we were heading to North Carolina tomorrow morning and I needed to get my fill of her before we left. I had joked around in bed, but we wouldn't have much time or opportunity to be together at home. I always stayed at my parent's house, as did Maggie and Lena. They had plenty of room, and for events like this their six-bedroom sprawling rancher would be stuffed to the gills with family and friends. There used to be kids scattered throughout from my mother's siblings and friends; Abe and Godrick had been around for more than a few visits.

The full house would make it hard to spend alone time with Liz and equally hard to find a quiet moment with my father who I needed to talk with. In person.

I cracked and whisked eggs while, despite Liz's tempting presence, my mind worried over the second round of funding for the revitalization and expansion I was leading. Normally my entire focus would be the woman at my breakfast counter, but all of a sudden shit with the Series B funding stage had started going sideways. Out of nowhere, folks were getting cold feet and it was pissing me off. I'd received communications from two primary investors talking about market volatility and over exposure in the hospitality arena. These were concerns we'd covered thoroughly, multiple times; concerns they had deemed well-addressed before we'd moved forward with the first stage. I needed to have a conversation with my pops to run it all by him. I'd wanted to keep him as far from this as possible. I was taking these steps to allow him to relax into his planned retirement and I'd encouraged him to release as much responsibility to me as possible. That meant this expansion, particularly the Haven piece, was entirely my baby. But I needed his thoughtful ear. Because it didn't make any fucking sense.

"What's got your forehead all wrinkled up like that? I thought I'd done my stress relief work fairly well," Liz's soft voice broke through my contemplations. I glanced at her over my shoulder and marveled again at how beautiful she was with her hair undone, eyes bright, face relaxed. She wore one of my shirts in the quintessentially sexy way women have worn their men's shirts since the beginning of time. It was huge on her, the open neck exposing her almost to the navel. Her smooth skin a beautiful contrast against the white of the shirt. Her hands toyed with her cup behind the thick cuffs she'd rolled into the sleeves.

"I promise that you did. But I'll never say no to a top off," I focused on the second half of what she'd said. She was so relaxed, the mood was so calm; I didn't want to bring work headaches into it. And, since I didn't really have any information to share, there was no reason to.

"Mmm. I'm sure," she sipped her tea, watching me over the rim for a long moment before she picked up the thread I'd tried to drop. "So, what's bothering you. Work? Family? Are you regretting the invitation for the weekend? Because if you are, I definitely understand and I wouldn't be hurt. At all. To just hang out here."

"Oh, so you're not trying to go see my people or something?" I asked, trying again to steer the conversation. I poured the salt and peppered eggs into a pan, followed by diced veggies, guyere cheese and a heavy shake of red pepper.

She smiled, "You know that's not it."

"So, what is it?"

"Your mother will know there's something going on between us."

I went back to the stovetop, folded the eggs over, lowered the heat.

"Probably."

"Will she ask?"

"Probably."

"And what will you tell her?"

I spoke over my shoulder as I tested the bottom of the omelet. "I'll explain that I've brought a smart, beautiful, funny woman who I care about to my home because I thought she would benefit from it. Because I thought it would do her some good. And we'll leave it at that."

I slid a plate onto the countertop and tipped the bubbling omelet onto it. She hummed under her breath, still unconvinced.

"If you say so," she offered.

"I do," I said while I made quick work of stirring up a second omelet to add to another plate.

"She will leave it at that...for the most part, at least...because while my mama is nosy as hell, she's not insensitive. And her second favorite thing to knowing everybody's business is helping anybody she can. So once she learns that I brought you for respite and restoration, she'll make it her mission for you to feel better leaving than you did when you got there."

She made a little thoughtful sound before pouring juice from the carafe on the counter and following me as I carried the two plates, now adorned with fresh fruit and toast along with the omelets, to the table.

"And who's going to make sure you're feeling better?" She asked.

"What do you mean?"

"I know I'm up to my eyeballs in my own stuff, but I see you turning something over in your head. Something's on your mind."

I opened my mouth to deny but she continued.

"And you've avoided the topic twice this morning. No need to do it again," she watched me with narrowed eyes as I chewed my food.

"Well, hell," I said chuckling after I swallowed. "You clocking me like that?"

I watched an eyebrow climb and she responded, raising her voice to that of a breathless ingenue, "Yeah, daddy, I'm clocking you like that. I just can't help it," she finished, fluttering her eyelashes wildly at me.

Laughter and orange juice erupted from my mouth. She chuckled while I set things back to right but didn't drop the subject.

"Seriously, Warwick. You can talk to me. You don't have to, of course. But you can." She said it so earnestly, brown eyes wide and intense. Something in my chest squeezed a little.

I busied myself disposing of the wad of orange-juice-soaked napkins. "It's just business," I said returning to the table.

"Well, next to me," she shot me a mischevious glance and I worried about what was going to come out of her mouth next. I set my juice down. "Business is the thing you're most obsessed with," she finished with a grin. I acknowledged the truth of that statement with a head nod.

"So, if something with the business is serious enough to have you looking like that," she waved at my face, "when you could be looking at this," she leaned back, causing the shirt to gape and my pulse to quicken, "I feel like maybe we should talk about it."

She sat forward again, eyes going softly serious. "I'd like to be there for you the way you've been there for me. Seriously."

I studied her. "It's not a contest, Liz."

"I know," she said slowly. "But reciprocity matters to me. I've just been taking and taking from you. Leaning on you. Depending on you," she said. "I feel like you're always coming to my rescue, offering your help, showing up when I don't even realize I need you." She *needed* me? They were heady, dangerous words. "Giving me a job and a place to stay," she lifted and dropped her hands. "I feel beholden to you."

That statement didn't land well with me. "You can't be serious. I didn't *give* you a job. I don't *give* people jobs. You earned it. Your work is stellar and your impact since you've been at Haven has been felt and commented upon. Shit, Amari needs to watch her damn back," I said, referring to my on-leave events curator. "And I told you, the rooms are part of the deal. As for the rest of it, I didn't do anything Maggie hasn't done. It falls under the banner of friendship, Liz."

I took another bite, chewed, before voicing the thought bouncing around in my head, "Liz. You're not here because you think you owe me something, are you? Because," something ugly and hot rose inside me at the thought that she might be doing just that.

A range of emotions crossed her face, surprise, confusion, faint insult...before she settled on self-deprecating amusement.

"No," she said slowly, thoughtfully. "I'm here because no matter what I tell myself, I can't stay away from you."

I held still through sheer dent of will and kept breathing because my body was wired to do so. But a coil of hot tension wound through me, the sound of my own heart beating filled my ears.

I heard the current of heat in my voice and tried to keep it at an audible pitch. "Is that right?"

She nodded, "I've tried. I really have. Can't do it." She licked her lips and my eyes locked on them. "I don't know what I'm thinking sometimes," her voice lowered, still thoughtful. "I know I need to focus on all these situations in my life. I know it would be much smarter to focus on therapy, getting *RSVP* off the ground, figuring out a permanent place to live. Following through on this thing with Cassandra. That's a full plate," she kind of nodded to herself. "And I'm doing all those things. But, at the same time, you're always *there*..."

"Liz." I growled it at her.

"It's true," she said, rising and coming around to my side of the table. "When Godrick died, you were there..."

I shook my head because I hadn't been. Not the way he would have wanted me to be.

"You were. I pushed you away," she said.

"I left," I corrected her.

"But you came back," she pressed. "For me." She inserted herself between me and the table, forcing me to push back to make room for her.

"When they tried to orchestrate my life, you tried to tell me better."

"I was being selfish. I wanted you for myself."

"Hmm," she murmured before she sat on my lap. "When Godrick's birthday rolled around and I finally reached out, you let me talk."

I was silent, remembering the tangle of messages that had fanned the spark in my chest.

"When I landed at Maggie's after mother drugged me, you were there."

"I overstepped."

"And you just showed up at the attorney's office. Just because you thought I might need support." She swung one leg across my hips so that she straddled me. Our noses nearly touched.

"Every time. Every single time. You're just *there*. And it irritated me...maybe. Until it didn't. I want you, Warwick. But I don't know if you should want me. I don't know if I'm good for you. Whether what I bring is worthy of what you're giving me."

"Liz," I whispered, floored by the honesty she was pouring out to me.

"I want to try, though. If you want to try."

My arms wrapped around her, tightened until her hips were pressed against my crotch the shirt gapping so that she was bared from the waist down...the single fastened button on the shirt doing nothing to preserve her modesty.

"I want nothing more," I said before I caught her mouth with mine, trying to reciprocate the words she'd given me through the kiss. My tongue devoured, filled her mouth, swept across her teeth, her tongue, and the roof of her mouth.

I felt her smile as I withdrew, and our teeth tapped. I kept my lips pressed against hers when I said. "Are you going to try with me, Liz?"

She nodded, "Yes, I am."

Chapter 21

LIZ

I had no business being up in the middle of the night creeping around Warwick's mama's house. If I got caught, I'd be mortified, despite the 'make yourself at home' that she'd offered along with a warm hug. But I couldn't sleep and even the incredibly comfortable bed in Maggie's old bedroom couldn't change that fact.

We'd arrived in North Carolina at midday yesterday. The trip had been an interesting one, made so by the cheek-numbing grin I couldn't wipe off my face after Warwick had expressed his delight with my agreement to 'try'. Thoroughly, expertly, and repeatedly. It had been a solid twenty-four hours but my thighs were still sore, my panties were perpetually wet, my clit stayed at attention, ready and eager for his tongue should he decide to bless us with it again.

It was what had awakened me tonight: this hunger for him that poured through me even, especially, in my dreams. I couldn't rest and I couldn't take care of myself in Warwick's mama's house. I knew. I'd tried. So I came down to find something to knock me out: tea, hot milk, and honey. Warwick's dick. Something. All I knew was that if I didn't get some rest, I'd be pitiful tomorrow...I glanced at the microwave clock glowing in the corner of the kitchen and winced...later today, at the anniversary party.

I made my way to the kitchen and quietly opened cabinets and drawers until I located cups and spoons. I filled the teapot that was sitting on the stove and returned it to its eye, turning the heat up to high. While the water warmed, I returned to opening cabinets, trying to find the tea. I knew it existed; Mrs. Walker didn't drink coffee, a fact that she noted at breakfast this morning. But I hadn't watched her to see where she stored her preferred hot beverage.

Ah, success! I congratulated myself when I popped open the little countertop garage to find a Teavana-worthy tea collection, complete with cinnamon, honey, and any other accouterment one might desire for their sipping.

I had just made my flavor selection...chamomile chai...when Mrs. Walker walked in. She was slipping her arms into a long robe that exactly matched the soft navy nightgown that flowed to her slipper-covered feet. She was a lovely woman of average height and weight with rich dark skin the same color as Warwick's. Her hair was covered in a bright patterned bonnet. She and her husband favored each other slightly in the way of long-married couples. Warwick and Maggie both looked exactly like whichever parent they happened to be standing next to.

"Oh, Mrs. Walker, I'm sorry. I couldn't sleep so I thought I'd make myself a cup of tea." I said, the expected embarrassment at getting caught roaming rose high.

"Psh" she waved my apology off with a dismissive tsk. "I told you to make yourself at home and so you have. I can relate to difficulties sleeping," she took her own cup from the cabinet and motioned to the kettle on the stove.

"Is there enough water for two?"

I nodded, "Yes, ma'am."

She chuckled and selected her tea with surety. She added honey and a shake or two from different bottles of spices before dropping the tea bag in the cup to wait for the water to boil.

I'd been waiting next to the stovetop for the water to boil, intent upon returning to my assigned room as quickly as possible. She settled herself at one of the hightop chairs that circled the impressive kitchen island. She sat across from where I stood, and turned her gaze upon me. The house was quiet save for the faint electrical hum of the kitchen appliances. The silence made her stare that much heavier. I tried not to squirm.

"I know why I'm awake," she said. "But what has you up and restless in the middle of the night?"

I couldn't possibly tell her I was up because I'd recently developed the need to get dicked-down by her baby boy before I could rest well. So, instead, I said, "Oh nothing in particular. It's just one of those nights," and willed the water to boil faster. I liked Warwick's mom. She was kind and thoughtful, open and funny, and successful in her own right. She was an accomplished professor of psychology at one of the UNC schools–I couldn't remember which one. She was also deeply in love with her children and granddaughter. And she was intimidating as hell. She had Warwick's direct black stare. Caught in her gaze, I felt like she was reading me from the inside out. Like she already knew all the answers to her questions and was just testing to see how I answered, how well I knew myself.

She nodded. "I understand that. When you get to my age most nights are 'those' nights," she lifted her eyebrows as proxy for the air quotes. "There's not much I wouldn't give for a full nights' sleep," she continued. "They said I'd get it back on the other side of menopause. They lied," she gave a self-deprecating laugh then fell silent for a moment.

When she spoke again, she said quietly, "I'm happy to see you again, Liz. I know we never talked much but it's good to see that you're doing well," her striking black eyes softened in concern.

"Thank you, Mrs. Walker," I said, surprised at the well of emotion that rose with her words. "I'm doing," I paused, not wanting to lie, but trying to give a fair assessment, "as well as can be expected. And better, too. Better as time passes."

She nodded. "Of course. I don't mean to bring up bad memories, but I only saw you briefly at Godrick's funeral, and not since. I wanted to let you know how sorry I am."

"Thank you," I said again, walking that strange tightrope between sorrow and exhaustion that I often felt when people offered their condolences. I didn't think my heart would ever stop responding with the heavy thump that accompanied thoughts of Godrick. But I had moved on and moved forward. Finally. The memories weren't so much painful now, as simply impactful. "It was a long time ago. And, it's taken a long time to figure life out without him but I think I'm there now."

She gave a slow nod. *Oh, God, did she think I meant that I'd figured out a life with Warwick? That I was moving on with him?* That's not what I'd meant.

"Good for you. I've done some grief counseling in my time," she said. "It's a meandering road to healing, just like any other trauma. We never really get over loss like that," she continued, "we only learn to manage," she paused. "Like Warwick has."

My ears perked and worries about her interpretation of my words faded. Warwick and I held special rank on the list of Those Who Mourned Godrick. He'd been front and center in both of our lives but we weren't immediate family, weren't quite in the inner circle of grief. I hadn't been his wife; Warwick hadn't been his brother. But almost. For both of us, almost.

"Oh?"

"Yes. It's taken him years to let go of the guilt."

"Guilt?" I asked, surprised. I had expected her to finish her sentence with the word *loss* or *sorrow*. "Why would he feel guilty?"

"Well," she said, "He had planned to leave with Godrick that night. They'd ridden together after all. But Godrick asked him not to. He asked him to stay so Abe wouldn't feel compelled to cut his evening short."

I hadn't known this. "But if Trey asked him to stay," I trailed off, falling into the familiar nickname with this woman who had been like a second mother to the man I had loved.

Mrs. Walker twisted her lips, "He feels like he should have insisted."

I scoffed lightly. "Trey would have pushed back with both hands."

"And he did. This is what Warwick has had to come to terms with. He was only doing what Godrick asked of him."

I nodded. "He beat himself up," I said to her slow nod. "I can see that; it's how Warwick is built. But there was no way he could have known Trey would encounter that drunk driver. Even if he had gone with him, he wouldn't have been able to stop it."

Mrs. Walker began to rise when the kettle whistled. I waved her back into her seat, turned off the heat and lifted the kettle to pour water into first her cup, then mine. "Precisely. But the way Warwick is—*built*, as you say—it was a hard pill to swallow."

Cup filled, I contemplated my next move. Should I stay? Should I try to politely exit? My decision was made when Mrs. Warwick shifted to settle more comfortably on her barseat and continued speaking. "It was some years before he was able to distinguish between his true grief and the feelings of betrayed loyalty," she toyed with the string of her tea bag, lifting and dunking. "I sometimes wonder if he's truly managed to release himself."

My feet were glued in place. It was the same thing I had wondered so many times. Was Warwick's interest in me genuine? Or was it the result of some misplaced loyalty? Despite myself, I set my cup on the countertop and slipped into a chair opposite hers.

"Even as a little boy, Warwick was fiercely loyal. Almost to a fault," she said. "I remember one time," she settled against the back of her bar chair, a rueful smile creeping across her lips, "Warwick must have been eleven or twelve. Yes, eleven, surely," she said thoughtfully. "It was the summer before sixth grade."

My heart thudded while she considered. Where was this conversation going? Was it simple reminiscing and sharing or her worry about Warwick because I had known and loved Trey? Or was she trying to tell me something? To warn me that maybe Warwick wasn't as ready as he thought he was. That he was still struggling with his guilt. With his loyalty. Maybe she was offering me verification that my initial concerns were not, after all, unwarranted.

I pulled my cup of steaming tea closer worried that it would no longer have the calming effect I had hoped for.

"Yes, that's it, sixth grade," she said with certainty. "There was this kid, Corey," she said, gently blowing across surface of her tea to cool it. "He was a good kid, I guess. He'd certainly visited the house a couple of times at least, spent the night, hung out playing basketball and video games and such." She blew once more, and tested the temperature with a careful sip. Deeming it satisfactory, she took a longer swallow before continuing.

"Anyway, he and his folks traveled every summer. I don't remember where," she said. "Maybe somewhere up north," she said, pondering. "No, out west. Corey's mother had a brother who lived in Oregon, near their parents. So every summer they'd spend a couple of weeks there."

I was enthralled.

"This particular summer, Corey asks Warwick if he can watch his hamster while he was gone," she chuckled and rolled her eyes. "Of course, he says 'yes', without asking me. I would have agreed, but you know, there's a process to these things," she said on a chuckle.

My faint laugh joined hers. It wasn't hard to imagine an eleven-year-old Warwick accepting the responsibility for his friend's pet.

"What happened?" I asked, finally finding my voice again.

"Oh, he brought the little thing home. Cage, food, those wood chips that go in the bottom of the cage, the little wheel. All of it," she chuckled.

"Aww," a smile crept across my lips at the thought of a mini Warwick, carefully carrying the hamster and all it's paraphernalia. Had he carried the same intense black-eyed focus then, too? "I bet he was the best pet sitter." He wouldn't know how to be anything else.

"He was. But I didn't like it."

That surprised me and I put my cup down, my attention even more riveted. "You didnt? Why not?"

"Well. Hamsters stink. And they chirp almost constantly...this weird chirp, like a crow on helium, *craa, craa...*" she chuckled. "It drove me crazy—at least at first. Warwick thought it was hilarious. And they're not really fun pets, you know. Warwick was terrified to lose it and disappoint Corey which meant he rarely took it out of its cage to play with it. He just couldn't relax," she shook her head. "I was eager for Corey to come back, so Warwick could have his summer back, you know?"

"Mm. I can see that," I said, sipping my tea. It was warm and sweet and delicious. I hoped it would have its intended effect.

"Well, Corey never did."

I sat back surprised. "Never did what? You mean, he didn't come back?"

"Exactly. The family decided to move to Oregon permanently. There was a sick parent and a fortuitous job opportunity and well," she shrugged, "they just stayed."

"They just left the kid's pet?"

She nodded. "Crazy," she said. "And that's my professional opinion."

I chuckled. "So what did Warwick do?"

"He took care of it, kept it in his room, and wouldn't hear of any other option. I offered to find it a new home, take it to the pound and have them place it. I even told him we could offer it to the school as a class pet. He wouldn't have it. He'd accepted that responsibility and he wouldn't let it go."

"Wow," I replied, not sure what else to say. There was a thin thread of uneasiness slicking it way through me. Why had she told me this story? Did she feel that Warwick was doing the same thing now...holding on to responsibility long past its expiration date?

"Mrs. Walker," I began with no clear plan for what would come next.

She lifted a finger to signal that she wasn't done. I quieted. "I watched that boy deal with that silly little hamster for three years because he'd made a promise. I was proud and irritated at the same time. Irritated that he wouldn't just let me take care of it, take the weight off his shoulders, and give him some relief. And so immensely proud because he was determined to be a man of his word. I'm still proud of him," she turned to me.

"He's still a man of his word. He's still bound by responsibility. But I think, I hope, he's learned to pick and choose how he allocates his loyalty."

I nodded, slowly.

"I asked him one time, not too long ago about that hamster and why he'd been so loyal to Corey."

"What did he say," I asked. My stomach tightened in anticipation of her response.

She smiled into her cup, "He said he wasn't being loyal to Corey."

I tilted my head in confusion waiting for her to finish.

"He said, he was being loyal to the hamster. It wasn't the hamster's fault that Corey was, as Warwick put it, 'not shit'", she huffed out a little laugh. "The hamster was just being the best hamster it knew how to be and it deserved to not lose another owner."

I smiled, "That sounds about right."

"It does. And it made me feel better."

"How so?" I asked, letting my curiosity extend the conversation.

"Well. He'd made a choice. He wasn't bound by misplaced loyalty to Corey; he understood that his responsibility to Corey had ended when Corey no longer cared himself. But the innocent hamster," she shook her head. "He made a decision to transfer that loyalty and assume that responsibility. I couldn't fault him. And it wasn't my decision to make for him."

"Huh," I said.

"It's part of who he is," she continued. "It's what makes him tick. Those of us who love him, well, it's our job to treat that part gently, acknowledge the gift that it is and make sure its not taken advantage of."

She sipped. "Anyway, that's enough chatter from an old lady. I need to get my rest so I can look my best at my party tomorrow night." She patted my hand then pushed back from the chair and got to her feet, carefully gathered her tea cup and saucer and prepared to return to wherever she'd emerged from.

"Mrs. Walker," I called as she was leaving. She paused and turned back to me. "Did Warwick ever hear from Corey again?"

She shook her head.

"What happened to the hamster."

"Well," she said slowly. "It died after a couple of years. They have pretty short life spans, after all."

I watched her. "And Warwick? How did he respond? Was he relieved?"

"Relieved? No, he was devastated. He'd fallen in love with the little furball."

CHAPTER 22

LIZ

I was crossing the central living area on my way back to my room, distractedly turning the conversation over in my head, when I staggered into the brick wall that was Warwick.

"Woah," his hands closed around my upper arms to help me maintain my balance. "Liz," he observed. "What are you doing up so late?"

"Oh," the familiar rush heated my veins, gathering and pulsing low in my belly before spreading along my skin to set it tingling. "Warwick," I breathed, a little shocked at how breathless I'd become from the mere contact.

Instead of releasing me and stepping back as I anticipated, he let his hands skate along my arms, lifting them to place my hands on his shoulders so he could gather me toward him by the hips. When we were in full contact, he caught my eyes with his.

"You okay?" He studied me, his calm black gaze watching, waiting, infinitely patient.

I nodded, off-kilter from the suddenness of his appearance—did no one in this family sleep—and the immediate intensity of my response. "I just," I paused, took a breath. It only served to pull his scent to me, heavy and male, clean with a hint of peppermint. "I couldn't sleep. I came down for tea," I lifted the half-full mug I'd almost fumbled when I'd bumped into him.

He took in the cup for a moment before returning his gaze to my flushed face.

"That's all?"

I nodded, "What else would there be?" Could he see my worry that clearly? Could he read the confusion that nagged at me after the session with his mother?

"Come on. Let's go for a walk," he said decisively, dropping a kiss on my forehead then taking my free to tug me toward the double doors that opened onto the beautiful hardscape that consumed about a third of the backyard.

It was a breathtaking but intimate area. I'd spent much of the day out here with Maggie, Lena, Mrs, Walker and a few of the female cousins. We'd sat with our feet in the pool that had been uncovered and lit for the aesthetics of the coming party. The jets were still on and the soft splash of the water broke the silence of the night. The intense quiet had been jarring when we'd arrived Friday evening; there were no sirens singing, no horns blaring, no constant underlying hum of activity like there was back home. But today, it had been a peaceful backdrop cocooning the conversations and laughter. I'd spent most of the time quiet, just absorbing the open kinship among the women who had gathered to celebrate Carol and Warwick Senior's love story. It had been an eye opening experience, hearing Mrs. Warwick speak so openly and lovingly about her husband. After all these years. Even the soft bits of vulnerable transparency she'd shared, the wry moments when she'd acknowledged that the thirty-odd years hadn't been perfect—some years, far from it—had been steeped in love. I hadn't seen this with my own parents. I had caught glimpses of what might be watching Cassandra and Abe but their relationship was still in its infancy. It had hope and a strong foundation, but it hadn't aged and matured into this rich, complex, full-bodied thing. This woman in front of me was half of a unit that had weathered time—children, loss, successes and failures, challenges and triumphs that I couldn't possibly imagine—and come out on the other side. This was what Warwick had grown up with. This is what he knew. This is what he would expect. It was beautiful but it was also intimidating. I had agreed to try, and I wanted to, but I had no example.

It took only a moment to cross the intricately paved patio and pool deck. Another several steps saw us across the lush green lawn that was currently dotted with tables and tents for tomorrow's guests. I'd learned today that the event coordinator would arrive at 7am, a mere few hours from now, to dress the tables and complete the rest of the decorations.

When we approached the edge of the lawn, the border where the grass gave way to a natural area, I balked and tugged my hand back.

"'Warwick, where are we going?" I only wore a pair of squishy rubber platform slides. They were comfortable with a treaded sole, but certainly not made for hiking.

"You'll see. It's not far. Trust me," he said, eyebrows wiggling.

I rolled my eyes—a habit I was beginning to believe Mother was right about—but relented and followed because, at the core of it, trusting him had never been the issue.

"I can carry you if you want. Piggyback style," he offered.

I seriously considered it because the thought of being wrapped around his back wasn't unpleasant but I declined out of fear that I'd just end up humping his broad back as he walked. I didn't want to sink to that level of neediness quite yet.

"I'm good," I said a little surprised at how quickly the lawn had given way to a pretty dense little natural area. But as I tipped along, I realized this area, too, had been tended to. The branches and ground cover while thick, weren't overwhelming; and there was a path hidden among the trees and fallen pine needles. Stepping stones, faintly lit by dim path lights, appeared.

"This is really nice, Warwick," I commented, enchanted by the experience. "Did your dad do it?"

His deep voice rolled on the night air, "Yeah, over time. The path itself is one we kids wore into the ground. He didn't lay the stones and open it up until we'd left for college."

"What did you do back here when you were kids?" I asked.

"Anything. Everything," he chuckled. "We would hang out back here for hours. It was like another world."

"You and Godrick?"

"Absolutely, when he was here. But also other cousins. Sometimes Maggie."

Another few steps and we made a sharp right. "Look," he said and pointed.

I followed his raised arm and saw, "Oh! A treehouse," I exclaimed, delighted. The structure was beautiful, built from what looked like the same materials used on the deck of the house, it appeared to be about a 10x10 square—much bigger than the treehouses I'd imagined based on schoolbook stories. It was held suspended among three giant trees about twenty feet above the ground.

"It's beautiful," I breathed.

He grinned down at me, "Come on."

"But how do we get up?" I asked, eyes still locked on the treehouse. My shoes had performed fine on the beaten path but climbing a tree?

"Well, you can shimmy up this rope ladder," he offered, pointing at a distressingly wobbly combination of ropes and wood planks. I looked at him skeptically. He chuckled. "Or, you can climb this set of handy dandy stairs." We walked a bit further and I saw wide sturdy planks, and a handrail, attached in a lazy spiral around the trunk of one of the broadest trees supporting the tree house.

"Your dad built this, too?" I asked as we climbed.

"Renovated," he chuckled. "We built it the summer I was fourteen, going into ninth grade."

"Who's we?"

"A bunch of us. It was a great summer. All the cousins were here at one point or another and we were so underfoot. We didn't have the pool then and as you can see, there's no one around. We'd go to our grandparents sometimes which was the best. It's a whole ass farm."

"That's where you learned to whittle?"

He turned, surprise in his eyes, "How'd you know about that?"

"Lena told me about your help with her tiger layers."

He laughed "Fair enough. And yes, that's where I learned to whittle." His excitement added a light note to his deep voice.

"But here, we'd spend the day plowing through the trees and then come back and flop around the house. Mama was sick of our funky selves."

The staircase opened onto a just-wide-enough deck that I hadn't seen from the ground. Warwick reached around me to enter a lock code and push open the door.

"Two of the older cousins—they own a construction company now—suggested we build a treehouse, so..."

My shocked gasp interrupted his flow of words. The inside was completely unexpected...maybe it shouldn't have been; after all, there was a keypad lock on the door. Inside, I was greeted by walls and floor made of knotty wood, sanded smooth and stained to let the natural tones and textures show through. Big windows and a huge skylight opened the room to the greens and blues of the trees and sky. Shelves punctuated the walls. A little kitchenette area had been carved out with a mini fridge, microwave, and a Keurig. A low-slung wide futon dominated one corner of the room. It was piled high with cushions; there was a small bookshelf next to it, loaded with paperbacks and knicknacks. The rest of the room was filled with two trim, slope-backed arm chairs with a tidy little table in-between. It looked like the house Goldilocks tried to rob.

"Wow," I had nothing else to offer.

"Yeah," he said on a long pause. "It didn't look like this when we built it."

I laughed. "I bet not."

"There's a makeshift bath now, too. The sink uses rainwater. The toilet is one of those composting things." I sent him skeptical look. "Yeah," he agreed. "There's a service."

He ushered me inside where I immediately kicked off my slides and climbed onto the futon. I still had thoughts of my conversation with his mother dancing in the background. But in the foreground, unless something went terribly wrong, I'd be laying myself open for her son on this mattress in short order.

Warwick shot an amused glance my way as I fluffed cushions and settled myself among them, expecting him to join me. He pulled one of the armchairs and sat.

I struggled into a seated position. The pillows and the blankets were heavy, they must be down-filled, I thought absently. My more salient thoughts centered on why Warwick was way over there.

"Why are you way over there?" I asked.

"Because if I come over there, I won't learn what's upset you before we screw."

"Screw?" I laughed, but at least we were aligned in purpose. "And nothing's upset me."

"Mmm. See that's what I thought you'd say. But we both know that's not the case."

I twisted my lips.

"And, you don't have to tell me. That's fair. But I do need to know if you're upset. We have to be honest with each other if this is going to work at all."

I nodded. *See? I bet that's something he learned watching the interactions in his well-adjusted two-parent household.*

"I talked to your mom," I said, dropping my eyes from his.

"Okay," he responded. When I said nothing more, he prompted, "About what?"

"You," I said, wondering immediately if he would be upset about it. I risked a glance. No upset; only curiosity. My heart thumped. "And your hamster."

"My hamster? What hamster?" His brows drew together in confusion.

"The hamster that kid Corey left you stuck with." No response. "She told me how you agreed to hamster sit then their family moved and you got stuck taking care of a hamster you didn't want. She told me how you hated it but refused to give up the responsibility because you had committed even after Corey didn't come back. Because you felt like the hamster didn't deserve to be abandoned." I took a deep breath. He still hadn't spoken. "I don't want to be another hamster, Warwick."

His face squenched in confusion for a moment before amusement took over and laughter filled the treehouse.

"It's not funny, Warwick. I know you care for me, genuinely. And independently of Godrick. But I don't want you to feel responsible for me. I don't want you to think you owe it to him to...he wouldn't want..."

"Wouldn't want what? For me to take care of you? To make sure you're safe and comfortable? To stand by you while you battle your crazy ass mother? You don't want me to owe him what? Ensuring that the brilliant, beautiful, enchanting woman he left behind knows she's all of those things? Doing what I can to remind you that you still have a whole life to live?

"I mean, no. Not if you don't really want to do it. Not if you're doing it out of some misplaced sense of loyalty," I said, heart thudding. Because what if he took the opportunity to be let off the hook? What if he finally heard what I've been trying to tell him and decided that I was right?

"First off," he leaned forward in the chair, placed his elbows on his knees, and pinned me with his start. "Loyalty to Godrick would not be misplaced. He was my best friend, my first real friend. I loved him; I still love him. And I am loyal to him. Second, and I don't want to keep addressing this—I will, because you're stubborn as fuck and you won't believe me until you decide you believe me—but this," he motioned between the two of us, "this isn't my martyring myself to uphold a promise to a friend."

"This is about me wanting you. Me wanting to be where you are, wanting to hear your voice, wanting to touch you, smell you, taste you," he licked his lips, "every time I see you. This is about me wanting to know what's worrying you and what's making you smile, what's annoying you and what's driving you, what keeps you up at night, and what makes your heart sigh. And the more I learn, the more I want to know. I want you, Liz, not because of Godrick but in spite of him."

I was mesmerized.

"So get it out of your head, Liz. Get over it," he pulled the chair closer to the edge of the futon and grabbed my ankle.

"I'm a big boy. I make my own decisions," he tugged me toward him. "I do have a very real loyalty to Godrick but it's not loyalty to Godrick that makes my dick hard every time you walk in the room. It's not loyalty to Godrick that makes my mouth water whenever I catch a whiff of whatever the fuck that fragrance is that you wear."

"It's not loyalty that makes me do whatever I can to make you roll your eyes and snarl at me. It's not loyalty that drug me out of bed tonight. It was you. Just you."

He'd pulled me to the edge of the futon, one foot propped on his knee, the other being kneaded in his big hands. "I want to touch every part of you," I raised an eyebrow and he chuckled. "Okay. I want to touch every part of you *again*. Even her," and he popped my pinky toe in his mouth, circling it with his tongue and moving on to the next until my twisting and turning giggles morphed into something warmer. He released my toes and ran the balls of his thumbs along the arch before moving on to my other foot.

"Warwick?"

"Hmm," he hummed around my freshly pedicured toes. I wasn't big on having my toes sucked but to be fair, the sloppy half efforts of past dates didn't compare to this. This was perfect suction, perfect heat, the perfect amount of his tongue dipping between my toes reminding me of what it felt like when his perfect tongue dipped elsewhere. This was an experience. An experience that had me dripping wet.

I tugged my foot, just to see what he would do. Black eyes shot to mine, he pressed the flat of my foot against his lips and bit the arch. My hips lifted and a groan escaped my lips. He soothed the bite with long swipes of his tongue before moving along to my ankles, calves, and the soft sensitive area behind my knees.

By the time he reached my core, I was weeping for him in all ways possible.

"You gonna let me fuck you in my daddy's tree house, Lizzie?" He asked, echoing the question he lobbed my way the day before.

I nodded vigorously, "Yes, please." I spread my legs to make room for his heavy hips; I started a heady grinding before he'd even settled, hungry for the pressure against my empty parts.

He pressed his bulk against me, meeting my thrusts, hard and ready, and I almost *almost* came apart right then. A shudder swept my body.

His big hand roamed down my side in a heavy, intentional caress before landing at his own hips to pull the band of his sweats down and free my favorite new toy. He ran a long, thick finger between my legs, felt the wetness collected there and swore, "Dammit, Liz. You're going to kill me."

"Fuck me before you die, please," I whispered it in his ear and was rewarded with two long fingers sinking into me. Another shudder chased the first and my legs spread wider of their own accord. My hips chased his hand, following the fingers that moved inside me, circling, pressing, building the intensity to almost unbearable levels. He withdrew. I protested. He kissed me, long and deep while he repositioned himself and settled the head of his dick against me.

"My decisions, Liz," he growled in my ear, as he began to press himself into me. My mind stuttered, as it always did, at the slow stretch to accommodate him. I felt the fullness deep in my belly. Loved it. Craved it.

"My decisions," he repeated, giving me the strokes he'd learned so quickly that I preferred. He lifted my leg, clasping me beneath the thigh...all the better to lay me open so he could get balls-deep. I swear I could feel my insides shifting to make room for each stroke.

I nodded, in encouragement and answer to his proclamation. He shifted, angling his big body so that each stroke drug his dick along that part inside me that weakened my knees and turned on my faucet. Tears of pleasure sprung to my eyes as I tilted my own hips to help.

"Fuck, Liz," he groaned, the bass in his voice vibrated along my bones. I wrapped my arms tighter around his neck and tried to absorb him. My open mouth sought his and I sucked his tongue into my mouth with the same force I was dedicating to sucking his soul from his body.

We moved at a frantic pace, he pounded into me and gladly welcomed everything that come my way. I'd be sore and slow-strolling again tomorrow. I didn't care. The sounds of our efforts bounced around the tree house, groans and sighs, soft murmurs and filthy words, the wet sounds of our kisses and him moving inside me.

I licked his neck, and clamped there, sucking, wanting to taste him while I whipped my hips on his hardness.

"Yes, Lizzie, that's it," he said low in my ear, "Come all over me, baby. Keep my dick wet with that sweet, sweet pussy."

The whimper that broke free of me was new. He heard it though, he heard every moan, every plea. He hummed at my ear,

"Good girl, you can do it." A quick lick. "Just like that. Give it all to me." I felt 'it all' begin to gather and swirl, splintering to electrify my nipples, my clit, that hot dark place deep inside that his dick kept kissing. It all coalesced into fireworks that exploded through me.

I heard my myself cry out, "Oh, God!" It was a prayer, a heartfelt thanks and definitely a little bit of blasphemy.

He captured it all, kissing me through it, trying, it felt like, to taste my pleasure, to absorb it as his own. Then he went stiff, shuddered. And I felt him empty himself in long hot spurts. I pulled him closer, lifted my hips and ground against him, riding him through his own release.

Long minutes later, I lay sprawled across the futon, Warwick's head at my breast. His tongue toyed with my nipple making me squirm. He lay a heavy hand on my hips, stopping the involuntary movement that began in response to his teasing. His fingers danced across my freshly waxed lips, a little brush to my hyper-sensitive clit.

"Girl, you're insatiable," he teased, running a finger along the wetness before turning dark, hot eyes to mine. "You have no idea how much I love playing with you," he said, then dipped a long thick finger into my pussy. He drug it out slowly then repeated the process watching me.

"You make me that way. And yes, I think I actually have a clue." I reveled in his touch.

He sighed, slow and resigned. "I'm going to have to eat you," he said on a slow head shake, resignation written all over his face.

"Are you now?" I replied. "Poor, poor baby," I comforted him as I guided him with a hand on the back of his head, to his meal.

CHAPTER 23

"**I**'m going to break into Mother's house," I announced to Warwick as we made our way through JFK. We'd landed about twenty minutes ago and had just deplaned. We were headed to meet the car that would take us back to Haven.

After the treehouse, the weekend had progressed beautifully and uneventfully. The anniversary party had been an undisputed success. Mama Walker was stunning in a gown designed by Cassandra's shop. Daddy Walker had done what men had been doing since the beginning of time...he'd shown up dressed to the nines and fawned over his beautiful woman before presenting her with an extravagant gift of flawless jewelry. He had understood the assignment perfectly and executed it exquisitely.

It had been a long and wonderful evening, made moreso for me by the memories of the time Warwick and I had spent in the trees. *My decisions*, he'd whispered again and again while his mouth left me devastated and sated. I was more than clear on the fact that he was where he wanted to be. I had accepted it. I had also come to grips with the fact that I needed to assuage the guilt that continued to lurk in the back of my consciousness. I didn't want it anymore. I wanted Warwick.

"You're going to break into your mother's house," Warwick repeated for clarification, he had slowed his long strides so I wouldn't have to trot to keep up with him.

"Yes. I'm tired of waiting for her to tell me things. It's clear that she's not going to. I'm taking matters into my own hands."

"By breaking in?"

"Well," I said, "that's an exaggeration. I have all the access codes to the house. I'm assuming she hasn't changed them. So it wouldn't be breaking in, per se."

"How would it be breaking in, exactly?"

"I plan to go while she's out of town. Which will be all week."

"Okaay," he drug the word out, clearly not on board with my idea. "And what will this accomplish?"

"I'm not sure yet," I admitted. "But I do know that if I'm going to learn anything, this is the way to do it."

He glanced my way. "So you plan to what, just randomly go through everything in the house, looking for her secret diary of dastardly deeds?"

"Not randomly. And not everything. But maybe a secret diary, yes," at his inquiring glance, I grinned. "Mother has a safe that she doesn't know I know about. At least I think she does."

He stopped walking, more interest on his face this time. "A safe?" I stepped closer to him; the crowd was flowing around him like a boulder dropped in the middle of a stream...they were less accommodating of me.

"Yes," I said, and motioned for us to continue walking. "I'd forgotten all about it actually until yesterday. Your mother mentioned needing to put her old ring in the safe since she was replacing it with that boulder your father gifted her at the party."

Warwick chuckled. "Yeah, the old man outdid himself."

"He did just fine," I chided. "It's a beautiful piece. And she deserves it."

"That she does," he held up a hand as if warding off my coming wordstorm. "You'll get no argument from me."

"Anyway, one day, not long after daddy died, I mean–," I stumbled over the word, remembering that he wasn't, after all, my daddy.

"Keep going," Warwick said. We'd reached the pick up area; he was scanning for our car. "Not long after you lost your father–," he prompted.

"I wandered into her bedroom, trying to find her for some reason or another. Probably some misguided belief that we would comfort each other," I huffed.

When our car slid smoothly to the curb in front of us, Warwick began to load our few bags into the trunk, then joined me in the back seat where I'd settled myself.

"Go on," he said, draping an arm across the back of the long seat and turning his big beautiful body toward me.

She was in the closet, didn't hear me come in even though I'd been calling for her. There was a strict rule about not playing in her room. I wasn't allowed there without her being with me. And I wasn't to enter without her knowledge. I don't know what made me wander in. Maybe when she didn't answer, I got worried. I trailed off, remembering the moment.

I stood just outside the giant bathroom with the cold floor. Mother wouldn't want me to come in without her and that was fine with me. I didn't like walking on the cold hard floor, it felt mean. I much preferred my own bathroom with the fluffy squares of rug on the floor. It had cold floor as well but I could traverse my whole bathroom without ever touching it. It was a game I liked to play.

As I stood there contemplating the broad expanse of gold hard tile, I caught movement in the mirror. It was Mother, rummaging in the closet. What was she doing? She looked almost frantic. I should go to her. Maybe I can help. *But instead of moving in her direction, I stepped back, further out of the line of sight of the mirror. I recognized the mistake the moment I made it. If she looked up now and saw me, somehow caught my reflection in the mirror as I had hers, it would be immediately obvious that I was hiding. Spying.*

But it was obvious that she wasn't paying me or anything else any attention. The clothes in the closet had been shoved aside. There was a hole. A hole in the wall? Mother was reached in again, retrieved some papers and rifled through them. Suddenly her shoulders sagged and she lifted her gaze skyward. I froze. If she turned her eyes even slightly to the right, I'd be discovered. But she didn't. She dropped her head then quickly began shoving whatever she'd retrieved back into the hole. She slammed the door shut.

A safe! I was beyond excited. We had a safe in our house! We must be spies!

There must be a special secret in there, I thought, something incredibly important.

"I remember slipping out, so excited and so convinced that we must have been a family of spies, that I used code words to write about it in my journal. And then, I don't know, I guess I just forgot about it like kids do."

"Your dad hadn't long passed away, you said," I nodded. "So it makes sense that you wouldn't remember something that happened during that time. That event was tantamount in your mind."

"That makes sense. But I also think that would be the place to look. There and maybe in Daddy's office. Oh!" I sat up, "the attic! We have an attic!"

Warwick's gaze turned amused, "I can just see your Mother scurrying about in the muck of the attic secreting away clues."

"I'm not sure if I can see it, but I definitely think it merits following up."

"Agreed. When do you want to go?"

I looked at him surprised, but not. "You'll come with me?"

"Well, you're damn sure not going alone," he said incredulously. "When do you want to go?"

I smiled and poked around inside a bit to see how I felt about his high-handedness. Yep, I was fine with it. "Whenever you can work it into your schedule. Just sometime this week. She'll be back Friday."

"And she's gone now?"

I nodded, "Yes. She's at FDNA, it's a fashion conference and runs the whole week. She goes every year and would have left yesterday if she stuck to her usual schedule."

"Well, then, there's no time like the present." He leaned forward to redirect the driver and then tugged his phone from his front pocket. "I'm going to have a friend meet us there."

***

An hour later we were standing in my mother's closet staring at the closed safe snuggled behind her clothes racks. My gate and door codes still worked. Not surprising. It spoke to how confident Mother was that I'd eventually bend to her will and return. And since she was so confident, I didn't try to hide or adjust my movements. She'd know I'd come but she wouldn't know why or what I'd done. There were no cameras inside the house.

"So now what?" Warwick asked.

I took a deep breath. I wasn't sure. I had been far more confident in the car that I might know the code to open the thing. But standing in front of it, faced with the possibility of some sort of timeout or reset function for too many incorrect attempts, I wasn't nearly as gung ho.

Warwick's phone buzzed in his pocket.

"Hey. Yeah. I'm on my way," he pocketed the phone then said, "I'm heading down to let Vince in. I'll be right back."

"Vince?" I called after him. "Abe's Vince?" Those last words were spoken mainly to myself as he'd already left the room.

I stood there nibbling a fingernail contemplating the dates that were swirling in my head. I didn't even know how many digits the code was. This had been silly.

When I heard footsteps and low male voices approach, I said as much. "Hello, Vince," I greeted. And though my confusion at his presence ran high, I instead focused on sharing my earlier concerns. "I think this may have been a mistake. I have a couple of guesses but what if there's some alarm attached to it and it alerts Mother if I get it wrong?" I worried, "I think we should just go."

"Hey, Liz, what's up?" Vince replied only to the first part of my rant. "Where's it at?" He asked. He hadn't stepped fully into the room so couldn't see into the closet.

I stepped aside and waved him in, "It's in here. But what do you know about safes, Vince? Aren't you a–" I paused because what, exactly, was Vince?

He chuckled, "A what?"

"I don't know. A majordomo, I guess."

That earned me a full laugh, "Good word, Liz." But he didn't answer the question, just leaned into the closet and studied the safe. He pulled out his phone and snapped a few pictures before wandering back into the bedroom.

"You got it?" Warwick asked him.

"Yeah, I think so. Give me a few minutes." Vince ducked his head and started feverishly working his phone.

"What's he doing? Googling 'how to open a safe'?" I asked.

Warwick chuckled, "I hope he'd doing more than that. Come on, let's give him a few minutes. You want to go look in the attic? Or your father's study?"

"We're just going to leave him? Vince isn't a safecracker. What's he going to do?"

"Vince is," Warwick paused, "a man of many talents. I don't know if he'll be able to open it. But if anyone in our circle can, it would be him."

I was skeptical. But I knew I couldn't open it. What I could do though was put the time too good use. I waved Warwick forward and we made our way to my father's study. When I pushed the door open, I was surprised that it wasn't stuffier. I'd expected dust motes and the smell of old books but it was freshly dusted and aired out.

I wandered across the floor noting the old-fashioned rug that Daddy had loved had been replaced with a broad swath of fluffy white. The office chairs had also been reupholstered. Other small changes, a new lamp, new throw pillows on the old leather loveseat, showed that Mother had been using the space. If she wasn't making it fully her own, she was certainly slowly erasing my father from the room.

I found myself at an old file cabinet that stood in the corner. I was surprised Mother had allowed it to survive. It was locked as I'd expected but if I remembered correctly—I reached around the back of the cabinet, near its base and, yes, retrieved the key. Either Mother didn't know about it, or she has ascertained that it held nothing important enough to worry about. Still, I inserted the key and unlocked the cabinet. Here was the smell of old papers I'd anticipated.

I was halfway through the second drawer, eyes blurring from random company paperwork and household documents. Nothing particularly important and nothing that shouldn't be digitally filed by now. I'd just pulled out a file labeled 'Elizabeth' from the back of the cabinet when Warwick's,

"What the fuck?" caught my attention.

I laid the file on top of the row I was thumbing through, far less excited than I had been when I'd found the first folder labeled with my name. The cabinet was organized by year and each year had subfolders related to the company, the household, myself, Mother and Daddy.

I eased over to Warwick, "What did you find?" He stood staring at a sheet of paper. "What's on it?" I peeked over his shoulder to see a list of names and phone numbers. I glanced back at Warwick trying to discern why these names were causing such a reaction in him. I could see the flex in his jaw where he was trying to hold his emotions in check.

"Who are these people, Warwick?"

"These, Liz," he said through clenched teeth, "are my investors. The ones who have been pushing back on the second round of funding, giving me excuses as to why they're getting cold feet all of a sudden."

My forehead wrinkled, "But why would Mother have them?"

"Why indeed," he asked, pulling his phone from his pocket to snap a photo.

I looked at the list again, considering.

"You think Mother is trying to tank your deal?"

"I'm not dismissing the idea," Warwick said.

"But how could she possibly influence their decisions?" Mother was a lot of things, shrewd and calculating to be sure, but she wasn't a wheeling-dealing business mogul. She had no reputation that would make any investor stop and take note of her opinion. And she had nothing with which to bargain. That I knew of, at least.

"I don't know," he said, gaze tracking to mine.

"And, why?" I asked. Even as I said the words, the realization struck that the only reason she would bother was to somehow get back at me. But she hadn't told me about it. Hadn't tried to leverage it. I shared my thoughts with him. "What good does it do her if she's not holding it over my head?"

"I don't know," he repeated, "but I'm going to figure it out. And put a stop to it." Finished with the photo, he slipped his phone back in his pocket and laid the list carefully back where he found it.

"Did you find anything?" He asked me, motioning to where I'd left the folder.

"Oh, more school files, I suspect," I said, moving back to the file cabinet and flipping open the I'd been about to review. Yep, more of the same. I put it back and moved to the next and final drawer. A quick perusal revealed nothing more interesting than the previous two drawers. Disappointed, I was about to call it a wash when Vince strode into the room.

"It's open," he said.

Chapter 24

LIZ.

We sat around the table in Mother's breakfast nook, the contents of her safe spread out on the glass-topped surface: two birth certificates, a thick stack of documents that we'd only had a chance to thumb through briefly, and, of all things, a tiny cassette recorder. The pendant was unfamiliar to me; both it and the paperwork would require some research before we knew if they held any importance to us.

The cassette recorder brought back a flood of memories of my father either speaking into his personal recorder, making business notes, or playing music. I remember teasing him about his old-fashioned tapes. He swore the music sounded better on them. I wondered if this one held his voice or his music.

Even so, it was the short stack of birth certificates that held our attention. Their importance was crystal clear.

I reached out with a shaky hand and picked up the first of the birth certificates we'd found in a file separate from the other paperwork. This file had held only the two sheets of paper. Warwick leaned near me to read again, though I suspected he, like I, had already memorized the contents. Still, I skimmed the document again. Full name of child: Nova Quinn Whyte. I traced a finger across the name.

Date of birth: March 7, 1994

Place of birth: Poughkeepsie, New York.

The line next to the mother's name read Catherine Cartwright Brookes.

"Cassandra," I whispered. "Mother knew the whole time. She knew the whole time that Catherine had a baby. Knew that Cassandra could have easily been that baby," I glanced at the paper again, "...been this Nova Quinn."

Warwick bit his lip, chewed the inside of his mouth before he spoke. His voice was even deeper than usual, gravelly. He nodded. "It seems so, yes."

"The father is listed as Jacob Quentin Whyte" I stated the obvious."The guy Cassandra and I matched with, his name is Quinn, too."

"Catherine went to Vassar. It's in Poughkeepsie," Vince noted. I nodded.

We'd have to call Cassandra the moment we finished here. We should probably call her now but first—

The other certificate was mine. But it wasn't helpful. All the information listed, including the father, was as I expected. Harry Alphonse Brooks. It was a solid man's name; a name held by a good father and a good man. I missed him so much. Still. And seeing his name there, in black and white on this official document only drove home the fact that while he *should* be my father, he wasn't.

I felt Warwick's heavy hand cup my neck; his fingers kneaded the tight muscles in my neck. "Liz," he started, but I shook my head and sighed.

I couldn't deny that I was disappointed. We'd found information that Warwick hadn't expected, but needed. And we'd essentially solved the mystery of Cassandra's parentage even if we didn't have the whole story. I was still left floundering. Knowing but not certain.

"Let's see what's on the cassette," Vince said, finally lifting his head.

"Are you good with that Liz?" Warwick asked, concern lacing his words.

"I am. Let's see what else is here," I shot him a wry expression, letting him see the swirl of emotions I was feeling. He nodded, caught the edge of my seat, and drug my chair even closer to his. His hand swept down my back, before resettling at my neck. He nodded to Vince.

Vince shifted papers to lay the cassette player in the middle of the table and pressed the 'play' button. It clicked into place and...nothing. We all exhaled, disappointment warring with relief...at least in my case. He turned the recorder over in his hands to locate the battery compartment.

"It's empty," he noted. "I might have something in my car," he said. "I'll be right back." Then he sauntered out both hurrying and not at the same time.

"He might have a battery for a thirty-year-old voice recorder in his car?'" I asked Warwick.

He shrugged. "He's a different kinda cat, for sure," the smile in his voice didn't reach his face. There was only worry there. "How are you holding up?"

"I'm okay. I really might fall apart later, but also, perhaps not. It's the thought that she knew that's killing me. How could she look Cassandra in the face in that office, knowing full well that Catherine had a child, and not even intimate that the possibility existed."

Warwick's hands caught mine and massaged, warming my cold fingers. He didn't speak.

"You're not surprised," I said. "You're not surprised that she's capable."

He finally lifted his eyes to mine. "Liz, she drugged you to make you sleep with someone you didn't want to sleep with. She tried to make you think you were pregnant. I'm not surprised by anything that she does. And I think–," he paused, searching my face, deliberating.

"You think what, Warwick?"

"I think you need to be prepared for what we might find on that cassette tape."

His words sent a chill racing down my spine. I don't know what I expected but still, even with the birth certificate in my hands showing that she knew of Cassandra's existence, my thoughts didn't automatically turn toward evil. But that's what Warwick was implying. That we'd find something horrible on that tape. Something I might not be able to manage.

CHAPTER 25

WARWICK

Vince walked back in then, carrying two small black canvas cases that he laid on the table and unzipped. Inside was some sort of electronic device. He plucked it out and connected a small flash drive to one end before plugging the device into the wall outlet. He removed the mini cassette from the recorder and slipped it into the device, tapped a couple of buttons, then finally spoke.

"It's a digital converter. It's recording the content to the flash drive."

"And you just happened to have one in your trunk?" Liz asked, incredulous.

Vince shrugged, then turned his attention back to the device to watch its progress.

Liz looked at me, I felt my lips twitch despite the gravity of the situation. "This is why we keep him around," I said, matching Vince's shrug.

Liz shook her head. "How long will it take," she asked Vince, just as the device clicked off, answering her question.

Vince returned the tape to the recorder and retrieved the second case. He set up a small sleek device, then started feeding sheets from the stack of documents into it.

"Scanner," he said.

Liz literally threw her hands up. "Unbelievable," she muttered before turning to me.

"We need to call Cassandra," Liz said. "We should do it tonight." We'd dismissed our car; Vince was taking us back to the city.

"Are you up for that?" I asked her; the fatigue was evident on her beautiful face.

"I am. It needs to happen and she deserves to know. Waiting until tomorrow won't solve anything and it's not like I'll get any sleep at all."

I nodded in agreement and put in a call to Abe. He needed to be with Cassandra when we dropped this bomb. Vince wrapped his scanned and forwarded the files. Liz and I made sure we returned everything to its original location.

When we slid to the curb in front of Haven, Cassandra and Abe were just passing their keys to the valet. Abe shared hand slaps and half hugs with Vince and me while Cassandra and Liz exchanged air kisses.

"What's going on?" I could hear Cassandra asking Liz. They stepped away whispering while Abe helped me grab bags. If he had questions about why Liz and I were arriving together with bags in tow, he didn't ask them. I assumed he was well aware of the change in status of my and Liz's relationship via Cassandra.

Once our luggage was on the curb, Vince tossed me and Liz a half wave, "Alright then...Wiz," he chuckled before thanking me for an eventful evening and pulling off. My phone pinged a moment later, and I checked it to see that he had also shared the access code to the safe and the audio file along with a text to hit him up if he could help further.

We were in for a long night and I said as much as we piled into the elevator. "My office or your suite?" I asked Liz, considering those the most readily accessible spaces with the appropriate level of privacy.

"My suite," she said, which surprised me a little but I didn't question it, just pressed the appropriate button to take us to her floor.

Once inside, we didn't waste time with preambles. Liz brought both Abe and Cassandra up to speed about our activities of the evening. While she talked, she used the glass-topped coffee table to set up her laptop. Abe and Cassandra sat on the loveseat; I sat in the accompanying armchair. Liz had pulled the angular office chair for herself. I watched her as she shared the information with icy calm. She was leaning on pedigree and professionalism to get through but her usually warm skin carried a faint pallor and her fingers weren't quite steady as she keyed her way into her laptop.

"When we opened the safe," she said, "we found a bunch of papers...which we scanned...and an ancient voice recorder...think of a Sony Walkman." As she talked, she continued to click around on her laptop, pulling up the files Vince had shared. Abe and Cassandra shifted forward, their attention on the images that appeared.

"In the documents were two birth certificates," Liz said. Confusion raced across Cassandra's face. "Birth certificates?"

Abe gave me a *what now* look before returning his attention to the tablet and the document displayed there.

"Yes. One related to me, and one with the name Nova Quinn Whyte," Liz said slowly, watching Cassandra.

"Nova Quinn Whyte?" Cassandra repeated, questioning.

"Yes," Liz answered her. "A girl. Born in 1994 in Poughkeepsie. It's where Catherine was in college."

"And you think," she trailed off, still reading the document. Liz said nothing, just gave her the opportunity to draw her own conclusions.

"You think this is me?" Cassandra finished.

"I think it's extremely likely."

"This doctor," she said, pointing to the name of the attending physician listed on the birth certificate, "do we know anything about him? Could he have more information?" She looked at Abe.

"We'll follow up on it," he said, wrapping an arm around her shoulder. "I'll get it started now." He pulled his phone out, no doubt texting Vince. I envied him the immediate opportunity to take some sort of action. I felt helpless sitting and watching this thing pour over Liz. I knew she was struggling with not having found anything solid, so far, regarding her own questions.

"The guy from the DNA match..." Cassandra said suddenly, looking up at Liz.

"Is named Quinn," Liz nodded. "It hit me almost immediately, too. And you see, Jacob Whyte's middle name is Quentin," she added carefully then trailed off, giving Abe and Cassandra time to process.

"It has to be me, right?" Cassandra asked, quietly. "It has to be. The year is right."

Abe had finished sending whatever communications he'd been working on and spoke up, "Once we find the doctor we'll know more. There'll be birth records. There'll be more information."

I shifted my attention to Liz, measuring how impacted she was so I could be better prepared to help her later.. Her focus was wholly on Cassandra; she held the other woman's hand in one of hers. I was about to go to her—I needed to touch her, feel for myself that she was holding it together and, hopefully, maybe lend some strength—when a knock sounded at the door.

"That'll be room service," I said. "I figured we'd need food and drink." I rose to take the cart and tip the attendant. I spent a few more minutes arranging things for easy access while they talked.

When I stepped back to the group, Liz had pulled up her own birth certificate on the laptop.

"But there's no useful information here. It has Daddy's name on it but we know that's not true."

"Wow," Cassandra whispered again swiping back and forth between the two documents before settling on the one recording her birth.. "I don't know what I expected to feel." She stared again, reading the information. "I'm a Pisces," she said and nodded slowly. "That feels right at least."

"Oh, when were you celebrating your birthday?" Liz asked.

"April 18," she said. "I had a counselor once tell me that birthdates in situations like mine, situations in which babies are surrendered to safe places like fire or police departments are based on the medical evaluations done on the child. Mine put me at about 10 months developmentally. But it's obviously an imprecise science," her voice trailed off again.

"Are you okay?" Liz asked. "I mean, I know you're not *okay* but are you okay? It's a lot to take in."

"It is. And I am. Or at least I will be," she said haltingly while Abe rubbed her back. "I'll keep reminding myself that I am who I am. And I'll continue to be who I've always been. I've had to shape my own existence for as long as I can remember and I'll keep doing that now. There's no reason to let this," she gestured to the screen, "make me doubt or question the person I've made myself to be."

"And the same goes for you, Liz. I know this is harder on you than it is on me. You have a family, or at least you had an understanding of who and what that family was. And it's all being shaken up and rearranged. I'm sorry for that," she said softly to Liz.

Liz smiled, "Thank you. I'm sorry for it, too," her lips twisted and my heart twisted along with them. I hated seeing her like this. I desperately wanted to hear her make some smart-ass remark, see her roll her eyes in scathing dismissal. This muted version of her was making my heart hurt.

"So what now?" Abe asked.

"Well," I said, catching Liz's eye for confirmation since this was her show, not mine. "I'm hoping Liz will call it a night and get some sleep...let me feed her first," I said gesturing to the food, "...and then tomorrow, we'll go through the rest of the documents and see what's there. Y'all are welcome to eat, too. I got plenty."

Liz didn't respond, just pulled the tablet to herself and began swiping as Cass and Abe distractedly added food to plates.

It was less than twenty minutes later when Abe's phone rang disturbing the quiet conversation we were having about what we'd already learned. It was Vince.

"I found the doctor," Vince said when Abe put him on speaker. "He's retired from private practice. And by private I mean uber-exclusive. In 1994 to see him would have meant deep pockets."

"Which Jacob would have had even if Catherine didn't back then."

"So maybe he was paying for her care," I said. "Were you able to access the records?"

"Nothing digital that I could tap into. I'm assuming they're too old, still on paper. The early 1990s would be when healthcare was just beginning to develop electronic record keeping. A private practice could go either way in terms of technological adaptation. A place like this was meant to cater to some high-dollar clientele. It looks like they leaned into paper being the safest in terms of privacy," he said. "It's not a bad choice."

He was right. Remaining analog wasn't an unreasonable decision in terms of maintaining client privacy, just highly inconvenient for our purposes. "So nothing?"

"So far. It seems they didn't go digital until the late 2000s. But I have to go that way at the end of the week. I can dig around if you want."

"Appreciate that."

Information shared, Abe switched off the speaker function and he and Vince slid into a private conversation, likely about Vince's pending visit to the doctor.

Then, "Oh, my God." It was Liz's stunned outburst. She sat ramrod straight in her chair...a far cry from the slightly dejected pose she'd assumed earlier.

"Liz? What is it?" I moved to her side, tried to read over her shoulder.

"It's DNA results," her eyes flashed to mine.

"For who?" Cassandra asked.

"Me," she said. "And Benjamin Whyte."

CHAPTER 26

LIZ

What the fuck? I didn't know how much more I could take tonight, even though two minutes ago I had been lamenting finding nothing useful regarding my own situation. I shouldn't be surprised though, this whole evening was nothing but an exercise in twists and turns. It had been a lark, deciding to go to Mother's house and open her safe. I don't think I truly believed we'd be able to do it. Oh, I knew we'd get in the house…her leaving the codes the same wasn't a surprise. It was a manipulation. But I hadn't really believed there was a safe in her closet. The memories of a child were shaky at best. I could have easily made it all up, especially given the turmoil that was my life at that age. I had actually begun to believe on the ride over that the memory was either a false narrative created by my juvenile mind, or a figment of my overactive adult imagination as it tried to identify some solution to this mess. I'd almost called it off twice and asked Warwick to send the driver directly to Haven. But it hadn't been some quirk of my mental fancy. We'd actually found the safe, right where I'd remembered it being.

And like some poorly written mystery, that safe contained all the damn answers.

I let Warwick rearrange me, pulling me onto his lap, then handing the tablet back to me.

"Well, what does it say?" Cassandra prodded.

"It's a paternity test," I repeated reading, *"DNA Test Report. Child: Elizabeth Elaine Brookes. Alleged Father: Benjamin Quentin Whyte."*

"They love that Quentin, don't they?" I quipped.

I could feel everyone's eyes on me as I scanned the page for the good part. Yep, there it was: "Probability of paternity, ninety-nine point nine percent." My eyes slid closed and I felt Warwick's arms tighten around me.

So that was it. I felt the last possibility that this could be some silly fever dream slip away. The last vestige of possibility that Harry Brookes was my father. Gone. Instead of that kind, quiet man holding the title, Benjamin Whyte, noted racist, potential rapist, held it instead. I shuddered. And my stomach heaved.

I uncurled myself hurriedly from Warwick's embrace and raced to the bathroom just in time for everything I'd just eaten to backtrack up my esophagus and into the waiting toilet bowl.

A gentle tap sounded almost immediately on the door. "Liz, can I come in?" It was Cassandra. I nodded before I remembered she couldn't see me and instead wiped my mouth with a bit of toilet tissue and clicked the lock open.

When she slipped in, I could see worry, concern and determination swirling in her mismatched eyes. The mismatched eyes that had started all this.

"I'm sorry, Liz," she said, as soon as she'd closed the door behind her. "I know this is all pulling the rug from under you. God, I wish I'd known what I was starting with all this."

She was kind. Really kind. But also had a spine of steel. I'd watched her go toe to toe with Abe's father and that was no small feat.

"It's not your fault," I told her, staring into the mirror at first my red eyes, then her wide ones. I dampened a clean cloth in cold water and pressed it against my eyes while I told her, "This is the result of a house of lies my mother has built. You just happened to pull the first card," I said, rinsing the cloth again and repeating the procedure.

"Still. I may not have pursued it had I known," she shook her head. "I should have just tossed that picture. I wish I had." She referred to the mysterious photo of a strange man that had appeared in her mailbox not long after she'd moved to the area. The photo, after much ado, had been eventually identified as Jacob Whyte; he had left the city as a young man, ostensibly to expand the footprint of the family business.

"Don't feel that way," I told her even though a significant part of me also wished she hadn't pursued it, wished she had indeed just tossed the photo. But she hadn't. And a bit of research had revealed that Jacob and Catherine disappeared at about the same time. Both were from notable families and though the Brookes' footprint was slowly growing, the Whytes' wealth far surpassed that of the Brookes', especially at that time. The children, Catherine and Jacob, would have known each other in passing, encountered each other at perhaps industry events, even attended the same schools in their younger years though they would have diverged during late middle and high school when families of this echelon farmed their children out to boarding schools during those critical years.

The connection had been formalized when Vince found old articles intimating that the younger Whyte had left the area because he'd been forced to do so by his parents' negative response to an ongoing relationship. There had been some speculation that a child was involved. This had happened the same summer Catherine Brookes disappeared from her off-campus apartment in upstate New York where she was attending college. Her disappearance with no trace and no explanation had garnered less attention than the exit of the rich playboy from the local eligible bachelor scene. But there had been no mention of a baby going missing in the few pieces of reporting on the topic. And, none of the locals they had spoken to had any knowledge of Catherine being pregnant. In fact, several people, Abe's mother included—who had initially identified Cassandra as Catherine's child through the age-old genetic testing method of 'you look just like your mama,'--had said that it was unlikely that Catherine had a child, that she was incredibly reserved and introverted.

Verification that a child had existed, would have been incredibly useful in their current efforts. Such verification may have prevented this deeper dive. If Mother had admitted the truth about Catherine, perhaps the truth about her own paternity could have remained undisturbed. So, really this was Mother's fault. Again. She couldn't even manage the proper revelation of her own lies.

"I can't help it," she replied. "I definitely feel responsible. But less about me and more about you. How can I help you?"

"I don't think you can. I think now, the only people who can help me are the people who have answers. So, that would be Mother," I met her eyes in the mirror again, "and Benjamin Whyte."

CHAPTER 27

LIZ

And so it was that I found myself standing outside the penthouse suite of the W hotel in downtown Los Angeles at damn near midnight. I had called Mother multiple times. Ironically, we had switched places in each other's lives now: I was hounding her to pick up the phone while she studiously ignored my calls.

So I tracked her down. I knew she was attending FDNA the full week. I had tried to wait until she returned but the five remaining days of the conference loomed ahead like insurmountable obstacles. I needed to talk with her, preferably face-to-face, preferably right-the-fuck-now.

I knocked. Again. And finally, the door swung open. The curse I heard spilling from my mother's lips as she opened the door was bright and colorful. When she recognized that I was the reason for the disturbance, the words died on her lips.

"Mother," I said in greeting and pushed past her to enter the room. I was furious. The six hours in the air had only served to fan my ire.

"Elizabeth," she said, gathering her robe about her. "What are you doing here?" Her surprise was obvious and expected. I could see that she was having trouble figuring out how to school her features. She wasn't in control here and wasn't certain how to process my presence.

"Are you well?" she asked, lip curling in disdain at the athleisurewear I'd thrown on once I'd made the ridiculous decision to fly cross-country to confront her.

"I'm quite well. I'm here because you haven't been answering your phone." I set my bag on the counter and immediately pulled out my laptop. "And I have questions that you need to answer. Now. Tonight."

"Elizabeth, surely whatever has you all worked up...so worked up that you've hunted me down like some sort of animal...can wait until this conference is over."

"It cannot, actually." I pulled up the paternity test and shoved the screen in her face. "What is this?" I asked.

I watched as she scanned the screen. I watched as her eyes widened. I watched the color drain from her face. I watched her struggle to come up with an explanation. Her eyes darted to mine, then back to the screen, then around the room lighting briefly on different objects. Trying to find a foothold for her thoughts, I supposed, or the foundation of another lie.

"I'll tell you what it is since the cat seems to have gotten your tongue." I zoomed in on the document, highlighting the indicated percentage probability of parenthood. "It's a DNA test that says my *father* is *Benjamin Whyte*." I nearly screamed the words, all semblance of control had flown out the window while

I watched her struggle to compose a lie that would explain what was written in clear black and white in front of us both.

"Elizabeth," she said, her usually strident voice raspy, "you don't have to yell. I'm sure there's no reason for the neighbors to be part of this conversation."

"Oh, are we going to have a conversation, Mother? At long last?" I snapped the laptop shut and sat on one of the plush chairs scattered throughout the overly luxe room. It briefly occurred to me that this room was beyond even Mother's usual performative choices. Was she staying here all week?

The thought flitted away, my thoughts couldn't remain on anything other than the issue at hand for more than a fleeting moment. "If that's the case, I'm eager to hear what you have to say. Go on." I encouraged with a sarcastic wave of my hand.

"Elizabeth, I'm not interested in your attitude. You will not just barge into my room, making ridiculous accusations," she began. And while the words were standard fare, her tone was off, I could hear the discomfiture beneath.

"They are not accusations, Mother. They are facts. But I agree that they are ridiculous. I agree that it's ridiculous that you had a baby with *Benjamine Whyte* and passed it...passed me...off to a good man as his child. Why, Mother?" I asked. "How?"

She was silent. I wanted to believe it was because she was selecting her words, trying to figure out how to share some deep painful truth with me. I wanted to believe that this–tonight–would mark the beginning of a new relationship, a new level of honesty. I wanted to believe that she was about share some long-buried revelation that would explain everything, all the choices she'd made, all the manipulations, all the damage she'd inflicted.

"Where did you get that? Where are these lies coming from, Elizabeth?" My shoulders slumped. So that was the way it was going to be.

"From you, Mother. From your safe," I said as she made her way to the seating area. Were her steps a little less steady than usual?

"What safe? What are you talking about?"

"Mother, you can stop. Just stop. I know about the safe in your closet. I've known for years, since daddy," I chuffed, but repeated the title, refusing to have that small comfort taken as well, "since daddy died. I saw you in your closet one day, not long after the funeral."

"You were spying," she said.

"I was a little girl in pain, looking for her mother," I said, the anger riding my voice. She looked faintly chastised but said nothing.

When the silence stretched, I continued. "We went there yesterday."

"We?" she said. "Who have you had in my home? I imagine that degenerate Warwick. That branch of the Walker tree was never worth their salt. I suppose he was more than willing to help you burgle my home."

"It's my home, too, Mother. As you've pointed out repeatedly in your efforts to leash me to the place. So, yes, I and Warwick went to *my* home. And this is what we found," I said, motioning to the computer. "Verification that Benjamin Whyte," I spat the name, disgusted at them both, "is my father. And," I continued, "verification that Catherine had a baby by his son." She flinched.

"What's going on, Mother? Why are we so wrapped up with that family? What do they have over you." I paused, remembering the fleeting thought I'd had when we were still speculating about my paternity.

"Mother, were you," I paused, loathe to say the word, "raped? Did Benjamin Whyte rape you?"

"No," an unmistakably male voice sounded from behind me. I spun in my seat to see Benjamin Whyte, also robed, standing in the doorway of what was obviously the bedroom. "I didn't rape her."

Chapter 28

LIZ

My brain stuttered to a stop, misfired, then came back online in such a rush that dizziness swept through me.

I watched, stunned, as he padded over to take a seat beside my mother. He was barefooted and somewhere in the back of my mind I noted how odd his pale, blue-veined feet looked next to my mother's brown pedicured ones.

"I'm not a rapist." He said, pale green eyes pinning me to the chair I'd taken when he walked in the room. "But I am your father."

My mother started and he patted her hand. My gaze strayed to where his hand covered hers. It was a familiar touch, long practiced. Whatever this was, it wasn't new. It was time-worn and comfortable.

"I don't understand," I whispered.

"What don't you understand, dear?" Mother said, far more steady in herself now that I was so very unsteady.

I looked between the two of them. "How long?"

"Over thirty years, obviously," Whyte said, turning an amused glance to my mother who...blushed and fawned over the attention.

"But why?" Thousands of questions tumbled about in my brain, I tried to snag hold of one or two good ones. "What about Daddy?"

"Harry knew," Mother said curtly. She offered nothing else.

"Mother!" I exclaimed, coming to my feet because I simply couldn't stay seated any longer. "Say something! *'Harry knew,'*" I mocked her scant words. "At what point do I get a fucking explanation? Why were you fucking this man when you were married to my daddy? Why did you pass me off as his? Why did you *lie* about it? Why are you continuing to lie?"

"Elizabeth, lower your voice and watch your mouth. Sit down."

The rage flowing in my blood was nearly overwhelming but I knew I'd get nothing if I didn't calm down. My anger was sustenance to her. Until I could manage it, she would simple feed off it and wallow in it.

"You're right, Mother, I'm overreacting to the revelation that this man," I gestured toward Whyte in disgust, "is my father." I sat. "At your leisure, I'd appreciate an explanation."

"I can hear that you're being deliberately flippant. It's your attitude, Elizabeth that continues to be your problem," she allowed.

"My problem is not my attitude, Mother. It's you. It's your constant lies, your constant manipulation. Your neverending willingness to treat me like a pawn in whatever game this is that the two of you have going on."

"There's no game, child," Whyte spoke up. "This is very much our lives. Very much your life as well."

"If that's the case, then tell me how we got here. Tell me how, why, my father knew he was raising another man's child and was okay with that."

"You forget that I raised his child with another woman as well,"

"He was a widower, Mother, hardly the same thing."

"But selfless, nonetheless, wouldn't you say?"

Whyte chuckled. "Of course, it was, my dear," he squeezed her hand. "Regardless, no one said he was okay with it, but, as the younger generation says, it was what it was. I suppose the money provided some solace."

"Money?"

Whyte looked to Mother, who shrugged. "Just tell her. It doesn't really matter anymore anyway."

"You're right, dear. It doesn't."

"There was no rape," Mother began, sharing a sickeningly soft glance with Whyte. "But there was a baby. You. But Benji was married, you see." *Benji?* My stomach rolled.

"And I was not," she continued, "Neither was a good scenario. Harry had been sniffing around me for months. As if he had anything to offer, anything that I would be interested in," she scoffed.

"The man can't be faulted for his taste," Whyte added. "He wanted a nurse and a nursemaid," he shrugged. "He got both."

I ignored him, instead directing my response to Mother. "Daddy was neither ill nor incapable. And he was successful. The business, *Heritage*, it's successful."

"What would you know about it? He died of heart problems. It was my burden to care for him through his illness. And Heritage," she piffed dismissively, "it was limping along, nearly dead when I came into his life. Any success it's seen is only because of Benji," she said.

Whyte picked up the story. "You, my dear Elizabeth, were an inconvenience we needed to manage. Harry was available." He shrugged. "I do have to say though that he wasn't as gullible as I'd anticipated. He was smart, too."

Juanita nodded. "Yes, he picked up on the same blood typing concerns your lawyer found. They do say the blood always tells."

"They do say that, don't they?" Whyte commented.

"So he did know," I said. Trying to reconcile the fact that he was aware that I wasn't his with the kindness he'd always shown me.

"He knew. And to his credit, he made noises about leaving. But you were a cute little monkey," Whyte chuckled, "It was no wonder he became attached. And it was for the best, I suppose since he really had no other choice."

"What did you do?" I asked, too overwhelmed to even address the monkey comment.

"I funded his floundering business in exchange for his giving you and Juanita here his name. *Heritage* wouldn't exist without me. But I couldn't have Juanita living as a single mother. The disgrace would have destroyed her."

Mother lay her head on Whyte's shoulder. My eyes bled.

"So you paid my father to care for me and marry Mother."

"Stay married," he corrected. "Your mother did a fine enough job of getting married by herself. And who wouldn't want to be with her? Look at her."

Mother blushed again. What the actual fuck was happening right now?

"You," I said. "You didn't want to be with her."

Mother pished, "Oh Elizabeth. That would have been impossible and I understood that. I still do. Benji has a reputation to uphold, a business empire to manage. Divorce wouldn't do. Nor would an acknowledged mistress."

"And you're okay with that? To be his hidden what? Side piece?"

"You don't understand. We wouldn't expect you to but I do expect you to be respectful to your mother," Whyte spoke.

I reared back. "Are you trying to...*parent* me?" I asked incredulously. I rolled my eyes in dismissal and turned my attention back to Mother.

"So let me understand. You were, what? Having an affair with a married man," I paused. "How did you even meet?"

"My Mary hired her," Mother glanced at him and smiled sweetly. "Brought this angel into our home as a house manager. I was immediately smitten." Mother's lashes fluttered furiously.

"Okay," I said before my eyes rolled out of my head. "So you fell for the *maid*," I stressed the word toward Mother, "and you two began an affair and produced me. Rather than own up to it, you seduced and married my father and tried to pass me off as his. When he discovered the deceit, you blackmailed him with funding for his dreams to keep me."

"I was not a maid," Mother clarified. "I was a home professional. A role I continued for some years, you know. And, there was no blackmail. We agreed to terms. He agreed to terms."

"Continued? You mean you were still going into that house, continuing the affair, while Daddy was alive?"

"Of course, dear. Benji and I are fated," Mother said. I thought I was going to be sick to my stomach.

"And when he died? Why wouldn't you tell me? And what's the point of the secret now?" I turned to Whyte, "Your wife is dead, too. Why the secrecy?"

"I would never sully Mary's name by implying that I had extramarital relationships. Certainly not one that produced offspring such as yourself." *What the hell did that mean?* "Nor am I interested in dragging your Mother through the scrutiny such a revelation would cause."

He squeezed her hand. Nausea continued to bubble in my stomach.

"And we certainly don't want Harry's legacy tinged with such talk. Do we? As far as the world knows, *Heritage* was built by the blood, sweat and tears of his hard work and perseverance. It's a regular rags-to-riches success story. Think of the impact on the Black community if it were revealed that my white money made it all possible." Whyte chuckled again.

I was stunned. There was no other word for it. They were insane, their minds functioning on some plane just adjacent to the actual reality everyone else experienced.

"And what now?" I asked. "Because now I do know. And I have this document so I could blow your little secret to kingdom come."

"To what end, Elizabeth?" Mother asked.

She was right. To what end? I'd have to think about it. And think about it putting myself first. Did it really matter who my father was? Did it matter whether the world knew what they had done? What did I want and need?

"What about the rest of it Mother? The drugging? The pushing me at Abe? What was the point of all that? What was the point of you constantly pushing me to marry well? To line the coffers? If you had *Benji's* money to fall back on, why?"

"Oh, that," she pish-poshed. "Benji here wants *HeirLoom*. He always has," she patted his hand this time. "If you married Abe, then it would be all but his, wouldn't it? Perhaps then, we would have told you who your real father was. Can you imagine?" She looked up at Whyte with glowing eyes. "Can't you just see the look on old Godrick's face?" She giggled...actually *giggled*. "He'd be positively apoplectic."

Whyte smiled at her indulgently.

"But you've blown that, haven't you?" Whyte picked up the thread. "Not to worry, though. I want *HeirLoom*, it's true. Now, I'll just have to get to it through the other brother. I have to say you've added a layer of complication I hadn't anticipated. But it's good for the old noggin. I'll get it unraveled and in the end, I'll have a little hospitality venture in addition."

What we he blathering on about? Then it struck me, it wasn't Mother behind the challenges to Warwick's second round of funding. It was Whytye.

"You think pulling the rug from under Warwick will somehow lead you to *HeirLoom*?"

He'd laid his hand along the settee behind Mother and one hand toyed with the shoulder of her robe. "Brotherly commitment and all that. If the one fails, the other will leap to his rescue thereby putting his own company at risk." He shrugged. "Or not. Either way, it'll be endlessly entertaining."

He was banking on Godrick, Sr., Abe's father and founder of *HeirLoom*, bailing out Warwick's father if the second round of funding fell through.

I just nodded. There were words vying for position in my brain, trying to arrange themselves into some reasonable order, an order that would allow me to ask the perfect question to make logical sense out of all this. But no such question was forthcoming.

"It could have been avoided, you know. Had Godrick simply not died," Mother shuddered….

"Messy business," Whyte muttered.

"Had Godrick not died?" I repeated. "Are you insane?"

Mother's lip twisted. "Language, Elizabeth. I simply mean to say it would have been so much easier had you followed through with marrying him. It was all in place but then the accident happened and you went through your little depression."

"My little depression? You mean the period of time when I thought I would die because I'd lost the love of my life?"

She carried on as if I'd said nothing. "And just as we got back on track, that girl comes along. And you *helped* her." Mother pouted at me. "I just can't understand how you let that gutter trash usurp your position.

"She's not gutter trash. She's smart and accomplished and most importantly, the woman Abe loves, Mother. And she's your granddaughter."

Mother scoffed. "I share no blood with that girl."

I looked at Whyte. "Yours, too." There was no surprise on his face. He knew. *Good grief. What else were they hiding?*

"How long have you known?" I asked them both.

"Oh, I knew as soon as I saw her at that damned winery event. The eyes, you know. And that face. She really is a beautiful girl, as was her mother."

He patted Mother's shoulder when she turned up her nose in disagreement.

"Did you send the picture that started this whole thing?" I asked him.

"Picture? No, I've sent nothing to anyone. Why would I want to stir that hornet's nest. Best to let sleeping dogs and lost children lay."

"But you knew Catherine had a child. Knew that child was alive."

"We knew of the child," Mother answered. "But it, like Catherine, disappeared. We don't know what happened to them but good riddance."

"Good riddance?"

"She was a layer between you and what was rightfully yours. After me, you're the sole beneficiary for Harry. Or at least you were."

I needed to get out of there before I became physically ill.

"I see," I said as I stood and slid my laptop into my bag, hands shaking with the effort of controlling my bile.

Mother stood as well; she was much more confident and sure of herself now than she had been when she'd opened the door to my insistent knocking. As always, the more off-kilter she left me, the more grounded she was.

I moved toward the door and she trailed behind. I could feel her smug righteousness at my back. One hand on the doorknob, I paused to study her. It might very well be the last time I shared space with her purposefully. She looked soft, easy. There was an ugly relief in her eyes. She was glad that I knew; equally unconcerned with and fascinated by the hurt she'd caused. But there was nothing more. I saw no hopefulness that we could build a relationship now that the truth was out; no remorse for having held such secrets for so long; no shame at having railroaded my daddy into caring for me.

"One more question," I said.

"Of course," she replied easily.

"What's on the tape?"

"Tape?" Her head tilted.

"The one in the safe. We copied the recording but the data was corrupted. We haven't been able to listen to it." That had been a disappointment.

Her face blanched. "Oh, that's nothing that would interest you," she said.

I sighed and rolled my eyes. Nothing was easy with this woman. "What's on it, Mother?"

She threw a glance over her shoulder to where Whyte still sat on the settee.

"It's just an old recording of your father's. Of Harry's," she clarified, laying a hand on my forearm.

I looked down at the spot where she touched me and back to her face. She'd drawn her features into some semblance of what I supposed was meant to be sorrow.

"I did care for him you know, though I'd never tell Benji, of course. He was kind. He used to make tapes for us, don't you remember? I kept this one because it was the last one he made for me. It was special, but you're right, it doesn't play anymore. I think the ribbon was somehow damaged."

"Why would he be so kind knowing what you'd done?"

"Because," she said, "as I said, he was a kind man."

I didn't believe her. I didn't trust a word out of her mouth. We needed to play the tape. It was that thought that hounded me as I rode the elevator down to where Warwick waited.

Chapter 29

For better or worse, the next several days were over-whelmed with work. Despite my personal issues, Haven continued to thrive. It called for Warwick's attention and mine. I'd hoped to go back to Mother's and take the tape and recorder from the safe. Now that she was aware of my access to the safe, there was no reason to play coy. But the return flight, the jet lag, the sheer emotional exhaustion and work conspired to absorb three days before I could make my way to Mother's house again.

"And when I got there, it was gone."

"What do you mean, gone?"

"Just that. Gone. Not there. Removed. Disappeared."

"But she's still in LA?"

"She was at the time. I don't know if she's back now or not."

"And Whyte was still there, too?"

I shrugged. "I don't know."

It was midday on a Sunday. Cassandra, Margeaux, and I were at Cassandra and Abe's house. Maggie and Lena had both been felled by whatever bug was making its way through Lena's school. The weather had just begun to warm slightly even though spring had officially begun a little over a month ago. As usual, the change in seasons brought a bunch of sniffling and sneezing with it. Haven, whose processes were already exceptional, had added an additional daily disinfecting of all the common spaces in the establishment. I had to admit, I'd never been in such a public space on such a regular basis before. I had already fended off one cold. I wasn't eager to deal with another on top of everything else.

Warwick was out of town for the week. He'd left this morning after giving me three delicious orgasms designed to hold me for the duration of his absence. They absolutely would not, but I had memories and my purple friend from the bedside drawer to take the edge off.

He was visiting his investors, 'getting in their faces' as he called it. When I'd told him that Whyte, in addition to Mother, was behind the trouble he was having, he'd been furious. I'd told him then that I'd understand if he wanted to put some distance between the two of us, that such a decision might take some of the heat off of him. He'd replied by telling me I sounded ridiculous, tossing me on the bed and proceeding to eat me out like he was searching for the secret of life.

I'd been quite reassured.

But, aside from a quick video chat, I hadn't had the opportunity to debrief with the girls. And today we were on schedule to have the first video chat with Quinn, the man who was Jacob Whyte's son.

"So now what?" Margeaux asked.

"Well, Vince is working on it," I shrugged.

"That could mean anything," Cassandra commented.

"So I'm learning," I replied. "But otherwise, I don't know what to do. Criminal investigation is not my forte."

We had decided to set up in the sun room where we could enjoy the clear blue skies and light breezes that were flowing through the three screened-in walls. Cassandra moved to the fourth wall where a stunning glass fireplace stretched from one end to the other. The glass surround allowed us to see into one of the casual living areas of the house on the other side. She pressed a button and blue flames leapt to life to combat the slight chill that the New York spring air still carried.

Margeaux and I set out a couple of brunch trays I'd picked up along with a bottle of prosecco. We settled, poured drinks, and piled plates with mini chicken and waffle skewers, scrambled eggs, and fresh fruit. Cassandra grabbed a remote and started up the big-screen television that hung over the fireplace.

"I cannot believe they've been having an affair. All this time," Cassandra said while she navigated through the TV's smart settings. We would conduct the video call on the larger screen rather than huddling together in front of a laptop.

I nodded. "Imagine my horror when he walked out of the bedroom." I shuddered. "Sick."

"And no remorse?" Margeaux asked.

"None. Zero. They were smug and self-righteous and just, all the things I've come to expect from her. I don't think I can be surprised anymore."

"Well. I'm very curious about what we'll learn today," Cassandra said. "It feels like we're almost at the end of it, doesn't it?"

"It really does."

"What else do we need to figure out?" Margeaux asked. "Let's make a list so we know you've covered it all." She dashed back inside to dig through the oversized bag she was rarely without. She returned with a digital notepad, keyed it to life.

"Okay, we now know with certainty who Liz's daddy is. And we know with certainty who Cassandra's daddy is."

"Well," Cassandra interrupted. "We know with certainty that Nova Quinn's daddy is Jacob Whyte. We are still assuming that I'm Nova, since it's the only way Liz and I could be related and likely the only way this Quinn and I could be related. I'd still like to pin that part down. I want to know for sure whether I'm Nova Quinn."

Margeaux's head tilted. "I suppose that's true. Men can make many babies at once. I suppose it's possible that old Jacob seeded more than one field in the same span of time."

"So, to clarify, we know Liz's daddy and Nova's daddy. We also know the how and why behind Liz's situation. We know that you and Liz are related. We need to verify that you're Nova," she pointed at Cassandra. "We also need to figure out what happened to Catherine."

"And who sent me that fucking photo that started all this mess."

Margeaux scribbled 'source of photo' on her list. "Is that it?"

"I think so. I think that would tie it all up: who's your mother and who sent the photo, right?" I summarized.

"How will we ever verify my connection to Catherine though? She's gone and Harry's gone. Are there any other relatives I could test my DNA against?"

I thought about that for a moment. "You know what? Yes. I don't know why I didn't think of it before."

"Probably because you were discovering that your daddy isn't your daddy and that you mother was sleeping with the ghost of Christmas past."

I laughed. "Probably. But your grandmother," I pointed to Cassandra, "Daddy's first wife, her name was Harriett, definitely has or, at least, had a sister."

"Wait just a minute," Margeaux interrupted. "Wasn't your dad's name Harry?"

I nodded.

"And he married a woman named Harriett?"

I nodded again.

"Okay," she said. "Carry on."

I grinned at her but carried on. "And I know she had children. I remember her visiting Daddy when I was young. She sometimes brought her children and I wanted to play with them so badly."

"You didn't?" Margeaux asked.

"Mother hated it when she visited. I don't know if it was because she reminded Daddy of his first wife or what it was. But she always made sure I had something else planned. Some lesson or class that was far too important to cancel just to 'run around with hooligans.'"

"Do you remember her name?"

"Gwendolyn," I said without hesitation. "I always thought it was the most beautiful name, like something a fairy would have, and she was so regal looking to me. She was long and slim like Daddy. The name fit," I shared the information between sips from my glass of bubbles. "She lived in Philadelphia. I remember because Daddy would always tease that she hadn't brought him a cheesesteak. And," I said triumphantly, "she was still a Brookes at the time, too. It was one of the things Mother talked about...her having two children but not being married. It was the worst of sins in her eyes, obviously."

"When was this?" Cassandra asked.

I gave Cassandra the relevant years. "She didn't visit after Daddy passed that I can remember."

"Younger or older than your dad?"

I thought about that. "I'd say much younger looking back on it. It seemed like her children were close in age to me. I feel like she was at least ten years younger but that's just my impression from all those years ago. She seemed older than Mother, though."

Cassandra pulled her phone and started typing. A moment later my phone pinged. It was an alert for the group chat we'd created. We called it the Maury Chat. Cassandra had shared the information we'd just discussed.

"Maybe Vince can find out where she is."

We passed just under an hour continuing to work through details and turn over what we already knew. Plenty of that time was pure gossip as we speculated about my mother's state of mind all those years ago and what thirty years of an affair with a man who refused to acknowledge you must do to your psyche. I wondered how much of her crazy was a result of her situation and how much was innate. I also wondered how much of it was hereditary.

When Cassandra's phone pinged with an email from Quinn saying he was ready to join the video call, we all sobered up. Literally and figuratively, though we'd shown restraint in preparation for this important conversation.

My nerves were raw as we waited for the call to connect and Quinn's face to appear on the screen in front of us.

When the screen came to life, we found two people staring back at us. Margeaux leapt up to fiddle with the angle of the camera we were using, making sure that Cassandra and I were centered, sharp, and looking our best in the afternoon sunlight. Margeaux wasn't officially joining the call. She was there for moral support and bottle service.

"Hi," the man, who I assumed was Quinn said. I looked to Cassandra because it was obvious that they were related. More than the eyes, the shape of the face was the same, the winged eyebrows were the same. "I'm Quinn."

"Hi," Cassandra replied. "I'm Cassandra. This is my aunt...our aunt, I guess...Elizabeth Brookes."

"Well, I guess the first question is answered," the man quipped. His voice was strong and pleasant. Comforting. It was a little odd, seeing Cassandra's familiar features on this man whose pale skin and blond hair showed no other potential connection.

"Oh?"

"It seems obvious that we're related. The eyes, of course, but there's something else there, too, I think."

"The face and the eyebrows certainly," the woman who shared the screen with Quinn spoke up. "But the other features, you look just like her."

"Her?" Cassandra sat up straighter. "Who is 'her'?" She directed the question at the woman. She was older than Quinn clearly and, if the obvious were to be believed they, too, were related. They shared the same streaked blond hair and at least one of Quinn's eyes matched her soft brown ones. Faint lines showed around her eyes and the corners of her mouth. She had a friendly, if reserved, look about her.

"I'm sorry," Quinn said. "This is my mother, Natalie."

"Hello," Natalie said, her voice soft but clear. "I'm sorry to horn in your meeting but when Quinn told me, I just had to. You see, I think I have information that you may need. If you're looking for answers, that is."

"We are," I said. "We definitely are."

"Let me first say, I think I've done you a disservice, Cassandra. Actually, seeing you now, I know I have. But, you see, I was trying to protect Jacob. To make sure he wasn't opening himself up to something ugly."

Quinn turned to her. "It's okay, mom. You didn't know."

"What happened?" Cassandra asked, leaning forward.

The woman nodded and tucked long strands of softly waving hair behind her ears. "It's a bit of a story. But here goes," she said.

She went on to tell us how she'd met Jacob years ago when he first moved to the West Coast. He'd been lost, angry, hurt, and blazing a self-destructive path through the city. She'd recognized his pain because it had mirrored her own and for a while, they'd both been drugged out, seeking relief from pain and nothing more. Eventually, they'd gotten pregnant, gotten clean, gotten married, in that order. But the demons chasing

Jacob had never fully relented. His heartbreak had never fully healed.

"Because, you see, he thought himself responsible. Thought he was responsible for the death of the woman...and child...he'd loved beyond all else."

We sat riveted, while the breeze and warmth of the fire, brought her words to life. Some part of my brain registered that this woman was an excellent storyteller.

"He carried that for the duration of his life. I hope he is at peace now. I hope he is reunited with her." We watched as Quinn patted her hand, offering comfort. They sat on a nubby grey sofa in front of a wall covered in simple, elegantly patterned gray and white wallpaper. We could see little else beyond the edges of a table in front of them and a collection of generic photo prints on the wall behind. They were both nicely if not expensively dressed. Natalie wore a simple navy dress with a pale blue cardigan. Quinn displayed a similar style with a green and navy striped polo and khakis.

"Why did he think that?"

"Because he loved her. And he knew his parents didn't approve of that. He never really told me all of it, not all at once, at least. It came out in spurts and fits. Some of it he shared during those first months we were together and I admit I may have forgotten parts because I was out of it for so long." She looked at Quinn.

"But you got clean. Both of you and you were both great parents, Mom."

She smiled at him before turning back to the camera.

"And after that time, well it was so painful for him. I thought it best to leave it alone, try to let time work its magic. But it never did. He never did get past it. Not really. He loved me, you see, but he was in love with your mother, Cassandra." She shared this with no bitterness; it was simply fact.

"How do you know the woman he loved was my mother?"

"Did you send the picture," she asked Quinn.

"Not yet. I wanted you to meet first. I'm sending it now," he directed the last to the screen.

Cassandra's and my phones pinged and we hurried to swipe open. There were two photos there. One of a young couple, a black woman and a white man, they had to be in their very early twenties, if that. They were both beautiful and both clearly in love. The photo was taken outside where they lounged on a blanket spread in what seemed to be an open field. There were no buildings in sight, no signs of other life. They'd obviously been enjoying a picnic and each other. The young man was propped on one elbow, the young woman seated in front of him with her legs curled under her; his free arm circled her hips and she leaned back into his chest, clearly easy with his touch. Their shoes were cast aside and she wore a bright yellow sundress; one strap fell from her shoulder. They were grinning into the camera. I wondered who had captured the moment.

The second picture was taken in what looked like a medical facility. Not so stuffy as a hospital, the room looked much more homey and comfortable. The same woman was in the photo but she was wearing a printed hospital gown, sitting in a recliner holding a tiny bundle of baby. She held the baby in the crook of one arm. With the other hand, she held the blanket that wrapped the baby away from the child's face so it was fully revealed in the photo. She was looking into the camera, exhaustion and delight on her face; love emanated from her eyes. I supposed it was Jacob behind the camera this time.

They were old photos. Worn with time and handling.

"These are printed photos. You can't see the back of the images but they're both dated. Those dates line up with the information you shared online and with Quinn. The baby's name is Nova. Nova Quinn. It's why we named Quinn, Quinn. To honor her."

"And you believe that's me? That I'm Quinn."

"There's no other explanation. If you share 25% DNA with my Quinn here, you have to Nova. But I will do what I can to help you verify that. I, of course, have old things of your father's...of Jacob's. I'm sure there's something there we can use for a paternity test. But, I know he wasn't seeing anyone else. He loved her. It took two years for us to," she trailed off, blushing. "And even then, he felt guilty. I think it was Quinn's birth that healed him somewhat." She laid a hand over Quinn's.

"Cass, look at her. Look at the pictures," Margeaux urged.

"I am. I see," she said, quietly, studying her phone. The resemblance was uncanny. Particularly since the woman in the photo, Catherine, wore her hair just as Cassandra tended to wear hers. The same way she had it now. Full and bushy, wild curls all over the place. The faces under those curls were remarkably similar though the woman in the photo was a darker version of Cassandra. The similarities I'd seen between her and Quinn faded into nothingness in light of the nose, cheekbones, and eye shape that she shared with this woman.

"Also," Natalie continued. "He believed you were her, too."

Cassandra's eyes sprang to the screen. "What? What do you mean?"

"Well. There are a few things you should know first. First, Jacob suffered from early-onset dementia. I think it was a combination of his early drug use and a broken heart...I don't know... but it started when he was around forty and progressed quickly. Second, he and his parents were estranged. When he showed up here, he rarely spoke of them except to rail against how they'd treated his relationship with Catherine. He refused to contact them. Even after Quinn was born, he refused to let me reach out to them so Quinn could build a relationship. He said Quinn was better off without them. 'Away from their evil' were the words he used to use."

"So when he came to me, weeks before he died, telling me he had found you, had found Nova, well, I thought it was a by-product of the dementia. It had gotten bad by then, he had only a few lucid episodes a week by that point. He wasn't mean, like some of the stories you hear, he was sad, nostalgic. He spent a lot of time with you, with Catherine, in his head. So when he started saying he'd found you, I thought..." she trailed off.

"It's okay, Mom," Quinn said again. I'd only met these people moments ago and already I envied the relationship between them. What must it be like to have a supportive loving mother? To feel free to give that same love and support back?

"He'd put together a mailer and addressed it to you, Cassandra, there in New York. I found it because I always went through the mail, especially as he got sicker," she explained. "People are mean, you see. They try to take advantage and you have to keep a lookout for scams and such. Anyway, I came across it in the outgoing stack and opened it. The address was unfamiliar and it wouldn't have been the first time Jacob responded to something he'd seen on TV or online during his illness."

"Nevertheless, I opened it," she shrugged. "What I found inside seemed to be the collection of a tangled mind. At least that's what it looked like. There was a headshot from his younger days. He'd done some modeling, during that time that we can barely remember, when we both did whatever for a while. He was blindingly handsome, you know." A sweet smile shaped her lips before she continued. "And at that time, no one cared about the mental and physical wellbeing of their models. His drug use added to the appeal...that cocaine glam," her lips twisted at the memory.

"Anyway, there was this headshot and a letter. A rambling, confused mess."

"Wait," Cassandra interrupted. "I received the headshot. But there was no letter inside. It was just the photo."

Natalie nodded. "Hence the disservice I mentioned earlier. I tried to stop the mailing from going out. I was looking at it all, reading the letter when Jacob found me going through his mail. He was furious. It was the first time I'd seen him like that. He took it all, packed it back up, and mailed it before I could stop him. But he was still confused. He didn't realize, or it didn't occur to him, that I still had the letter. That's why all you received was the picture. I'm sorry. But, honestly, I don't think you would have been able to make heads or tales of it."

"Do you still have it?" Cassandra asked.

"I do. I don't know why, but I do. I'll mail it to you today."

"Thank you," she whispered.

"I am sorry, dear. I just, I was just trying to protect him, his dignity, his final days. It was...a lot."

"I understand," Cassandra told her. "You've helped a great deal by just telling me. And you did keep the letter. I'm happy I'll get to read it."

"I am as well. I'll send you these photos, too," Natalie said referencing the pictures of Jacob, Catherine, and Nova. "And we'll figure out how to get your paternity tested but I really don't think we need to. Seeing you now, it's obvious. And, he knew...I should have trusted that."

"Thank you," Cassandra said again. She was quiet after that. We both were...just processing.

Margeaux, a little out of camera shot, motioned to get our attention. She held up the list she'd made earlier. It had a giant check mark beside 'Is Cassandra Nova?'...she had circled in red 'What happened to Catherine?' and was pointing at it, reminding us that this was the last piece of the puzzle.

"Natalie," I said, "did Jacob know what happened to Catherine and Nova? Did he tell you anything?"

She shook her head. "He said they were gone. I believe he believed his parents did something. I think he hoped she was paid off but suspected far worse. The most I was able to put together was that he showed up at her apartment one day as planned and she was just...gone. Everything. All signs of her and the baby. He never told me anything more. It was the not knowing I think that was his undoing. Sometimes I wish he'd just confronted them. As it was, as much as he wanted to distance himself, they were always there, bottled up with his pain."

It was a painfully emotional afternoon. There were tears and regrets. There was a little bit of laughter. The conversation ended with the lot of us agreeing to connect soon and making loose plans for an in-person meeting. I wondered about these people, wondered if they would make better family than the one I had.

Chapter 30

WARWICK

I tossed my truck keys to the valet at Haven, something I never did, but I wasn't interested the additional delay of parking myself. A week had passed, seven days too long, since I'd seen Liz. We'd talked, of course. Texted. FaceTimed. Enjoyed wild video phone sex that had done nothing more than whet my appetite for her.

But now, even though I desperately wanted to get my hands on her, I mostly wanted to *see* her. To *experience* her in living color. I wanted to see the nuances in her eyes that the camera blurred. I wanted to smell the airy spice of her when her skin heated. I wanted to watch her fight to keep her brow smooth when she really wanted to scowl at me. I wanted to see that flutter in her pulse when I stood too close; that blush that climbed her cheeks when she watched me but thought I didn't know. I wanted all that shit and I wanted it now, dammit.

I also need to lay my damn eyes on her after the week she'd had. Her recap of the conversation with Quinn and Natalie had been something off Baller Alert. She'd sounded steady, looked steady on screen. But again, I needed to see her live and in color to set my mind at ease.

The flight had taken too long, delays on the tarmac added two hours to my arrival time. Then the fucking drive had taken too long with traffic snarling and snagging with the singular purpose of slowing me down. I'd intended to be back late afternoon, it was now well into the sunset hours. So, yeah, I tossed the keys, instructed the valet to have my things put in my office—another first-time request—and strode through the front doors of Haven on a mission.

Through the lobby, around to the back where the offices were tucked away from client eyes. I peeked into her office; she wasn't there. I took the back elevator to the floor her room was on, fingers thrumming against my thigh, impatient even at the twenty seconds it took the elevator doors to slide open. I tapped on her door; no answer. With a little burst of memory at the last time I'd done so, I keyed in and called out her name. Still no answer and, unfortunately, no running shower.

I closed the door and pulled my phone from my pocket to call her again. I'd tried twice since landing. Still no answer. Frustration crawled along my spine and I felt the growl rising in my throat. I was not one for tracking down my employees or my love interests, so I chose not to examine my actions too closely when I dialed my operations manager.

"Yes, Mr. Walker," the voice on the other end answered briskly. "I hope your travel was uneventful."

"It was, thank you." I replied, trying to remain civil, knowing that my voice often sounded more curt than I felt. This particular manager had been with Haven since its remodel and while

I was onsite every day, as I always was with a new launch, when we moved on to the next location, it would be she who I elevated to general manager at this location. She knew me well, but I still attempted to temper my tone. "Have you seen Ms. Brookes?"

"Not in the last hour or so but Mark Hoyt's event has begun. I suspect she's in the ballrooms or the fourth-level terraces."

"Ah, I'd forgotten." I thanked her, ended the call and re-traced my steps to the elevators. It spoke directly to the way Liz was consuming all my thoughts that I'd forgotten about the event; we'd just talked about it last night. It was set to be a four-day mashup of ridiculous, revenue-generating, excess in celebration of Mark's daughter's nuptials. It was this event that had taken me to Liz's room the night of The Scream. She'd eventually admitted what had caused said scream, and I'd eventually admitted that I'd known, having seen her purple vibrator on the floor of the shower. I'd since met and employed that tool with her to both of our immense enjoyment. I was eager for a repeat performance. Tonight. Now.

When the elevator doors swung open again, I was dumped into a noisy melee of richly attired folks, enjoying music and drinks, as they moved between the lavishly decorated ballroom and the less ornately adorned but equally elegant outdoor ter-races. It was an overdone display of gratuitous extravagance but hey, I couldn't say I wouldn't do the same for my only daughter. If I had one. Especially if that daughter had the same soft brown eyes as her mother.

And that thought brought me to a full stop. I tilted my head as I considered the heavy sense of rightness that settled on my shoulders when I gave the notion my full attention. It had been a long time since I'd thought about kids in any context other than how to avoid creating them. But I wasn't averse, not with the right woman. Apparently, my subconscious had identified that right woman as Liz.

I wasn't mad at it. And I wasn't mad at the idea of Liz being swole up and snarky carrying my babies. And I definitely wasn't mad *at all* at the prospect of putting them in her.

I scanned the room for the woman I was looking for, not a challenging task among the less-melanated gathering in the room. She was not here. But Mark was. And the moment that man saw me, he made immediate haste in my direction.

I applauded myself for not immediately hitting an about-face and I hoped my face wasn't as unwelcoming as my spirit at the moment. He was not the person I wanted to be engaged in conversation with but he was my highest paying client of the quarter so when his nasally, "Walker! It's good to see you!" rang out, I replied with, "Mark, you, too." And proceeded to lose another fifteen minutes of my life.

Finally free, I returned to the task of tracking my woman. It was back to the elevator bank for the second time. As I debated whether to head up, to check her room again, or down, to the main levels, the elevator doors slid open and there she stood.

Draped in bright green that left her shoulders and arms bare, she was stunning. And what I saw in her eyes when they collided with mine caused my heart to tumble then soar: surprise, delight, relief, desire, and...something softer, warmer, grounded, steady. Something that made me want to pull her close in the night and rest my chin in the curve of her shoulder while we slept. I wanted that look in her eyes, directed at me, forever.

"Warwick," she exclaimed on a breath.

"Lizzie," I pitched my voice to a higher octave to match hers and stepped into the empty elevator with her. The doors slid closed. I pressed the button for her floor and turned, reaching for her.

"Wait," she said. She pulled the tiny earbud I knew she sometimes used to stay in contact with her events team from her ear and dropped it in her also tiny purse. No wonder she hadn't answered my calls.

"Okay. Now," she said.

Then, she was stepping into my arms, holding nothing back when our lips met. I turned, took a wide stance against the wall and pulled her into me, one hand at the back of her head to hold her mouth steady while I reacquainted myself and the other full of her soft bottom encased in silky green fabric. Her arms wound around my neck and she pressed against me, raised herself another half inch over her already impossibly high heels.

I groaned at the contact and swept my tongue further into her mouth, living for the slick sweetness inside. She matched me stroke for stroke until we heard the soft ding in advance of the doors opening again.

"I missed you," she finally said, as we parted, a small smile playing around her now smudged lips. She knew what the admission would do to me. The last week, while hard as hell, had perhaps been good for us. We had talked on the phone far too late in the night, every night. We had, of course, pulled apart the happenings with Juanita and Whyte and Cassandra and Quinn. We'd brainstormed, plotted and debriefed the meetings I'd had with the investors this week. But we'd also talked about us, about those years when we hadn't been in communication.

In a quiet voice she shared how hard it had been to break free of the depression that had followed Godrick's accident, about how hopeless and lost she'd felt, barely able to get out of the bed for long stretches of time. I'd been surprised at her honesty. She'd given herself to me physically and I was honored, grateful. But she'd whispered about the deep ache that threatened to consume her, about the thoughts she'd had and shared only with her therapist. I was humbled.

We talked about the self-destructive path I'd taken after the same loss: the aimlessness and wastefulness, the crazy 'adventures' I used to fill the gap before my father had made it clear that I was worrying my mother and better get my shit together before he got it together for me. I would *not* put another gray hair on his wife's head.

That's when I'd started seriously working the business, starting in the housekeeping department at one of my father's hotels. I'd worked through all the departments in one capacity or another and when I'd emerged, I was hooked. The combination of service and savvy that it took to be successful appealed to me. That experience had been the catalyst for the first stages of rebranding and reintroducing Walker Hospitality to the world.

The week had been torture, not having her in my bed after finally getting her there, but we'd laid ourselves bare in a way that was far more impactful than the physical intimacy we'd already shared. And I knew more than ever that this was the woman I wanted and needed.

"I missed you, too," I admitted readily. My eyes roamed her face.

"You look good," she said and my lips quirked up. I'd never tire of hearing Liz Brookes tell me she liked how I looked.

I let my eyes dip from her pretty face to trail down her body. From the gold choker at her throat that secured the lush green fabric, I noted where the gown revealed strips of flesh along her sides, and gathered between her legs thanks to the long slits in either side of the dress. I caught glimpses of her green-tipped toes before I started the return journey.

"You do, too," I replied. "I really like your dress."

"Thanks," she said. "Cassandra."

I nodded. When the doors started to slide shut again, I took her hand, led her out and in the direction of her room.

"How much time do you have?" I asked, knowing she was on her way down to the event to work the room and ensure everyone was having a good time.

"Plenty. I've done the rounds. Mark is in hog heaven," she said, faintly breathless. I smiled to know I'd put that breathlessness in her voice.

I nodded again, "He looked well taken care of."

"You saw him?"

"Yes. When I was looking for you," I said with a slightly chastising note.

"You were looking for me?"

"Who else would I be looking for?"

"Why?" she asked as we walked down the hall. She turned to walk backward toward her suite, hips swaying, eyes dancing and daring me. She was feeling herself and I loved every minute of it.

"So, we could talk." I said, happy to indulge, struggling to contain the limp she was causing me.

"You want to talk?" She asked with a seductive tilt of her head.

"It's a euphemism," I growled, lengthening my stride to reach her and scoop her up just as we reached her door.

I swiped us in.

***

"I love the idea," Liz was saying. I heard her words but my attention was focused on her mouth, soft and sweet as it was.

"When do you want to do it," she asked against my lips, her body stretched across mine so that her breasts pressed into my chest. The first ten minutes of our reunion had been spent with her pinned against the front door, legs wrapped around my waist while I did my best to climb inside her dick first. Now we were wrapped in that still horny, lazy period between rounds.

"Soon. Labor Day Weekend," I said referring to the investors' weekend we'd decided to host after my hopscotch tour across the country. My voice was lazy, slow, maybe a little more country than usual but I was so damn good right now that it was all I could manage. My hands slid down her back to cup her butt and squeeze. She gave a little squirm and moan. I did it again.

"Interesting choice," she said, pressing away a bit to catch my eyes. The movement caused her bare breasts to shift against my chest. *Soft*, I registered. "Busy weekend."

My visits had been partially successful. I hadn't moved the needle as far as I would have liked with all six, but had secured commitments to visit Haven in advance of the scheduled annual investment meeting, which was a much drier, business-oriented affair. I wanted them to see their money at work in person, enjoy the amenities as patrons.

"But it would be an excellent opportunity to show them how Haven operates at full capacity. How well the machine runs. Plus we have three events that weekend to show off." She levered herself higher and watched me as I watched her.

I nodded. I knew she'd get it. If we could make it work, they'd be sold.

Liz's revelation that it was really Benjamin Whyte behind the trouble I was having was eye-opening but also clarifying. It made no sense that Juanita Brookes could influence the people I was working with. Whyte on the other hand was far more powerful, far more well-connected. He would be real trouble, as I was finding out. But I knew that there was no way they could see what I was doing here on site and walk away thinking it was bad for their money.

The real challenge though would be whether they loved it enough to go against Whyte.

"Yep," I agreed and ran my tongue across my bottom lip. She'd repositioned herself so that she straddled my waist, thighs against my ribs. The green dress had been discarded; an easy task since it had been held together only at the neck and waist. She'd been naked underneath.

Now, as she found her seat on my torso, I watched her titties sway for me. Her nipples, just a shade darker than the smooth tawny brown of her body were already hard. I licked my thumbs then cupped them, and laid my wet thumbs against her nipples. Her hips bucked then settled into slow circles. *Beautiful.* I shifted beneath her so that her thighs spread wider and she pressed more fully against me and I could better feel the heat of her.

"We'll have a formal event. People love to dress up," she whispered, voice breaking only a little.

"Good idea," I offered, rewetting my thumbs and carefully returning to my task of pulling, tweaking, teasing her until pebbles pressed against the pads of my thumbs.

She arched into my hands and I covered her breasts fully, stroking and squeezing, loving the play of my skin...dark and damn near light absorbing...against hers, lighter brown and warmer now because of the blood riding so near her skin's surface.

"Invite them to spend Memorial Day. We have events planned at Haven," she said on a long slow roll that had my dick reaching for her again, "it could be fun."

"Could be," I put my hands on her waist and pressed her hot wetness against my bare stomach, stamping myself with her, before I pulled her up and toward me so I could suck her breast into my mouth. She groaned and rocked back, trying to connect her wetness with the tip of my dick that was straining toward her, equally eager to make contact.

"Brunch and a tour," she breathed. "On Saturday."

"Of course," I said, but held her away from her goal. Instead, I switched to her other breast, paid it the same attention until it was wet and straining in my mouth. Back to the first and a thumb on this one.

"Warwick," she breathed and that shit sounded like the angels singing.

I let her nipple slip free, wet and shiny, from my mouth, and drug her upward. Only letting go of that sweetness because I needed to taste the rest of her, all of her, immediately.

"Warwick," she said again and braced her hands against my chest.

"What?" I asked, pausing, catching her eyes to make sure her body and mind were in agreement.

"What are you..." she breathed, staring down at me, pussy damn near dripping on my chest.

I grinned against her leg, laid an open-mouth kiss on the skin I could reach. "Now, Lizzie, I think we both know what I'm doing," I said, bringing her just close enough to kiss the top of her opening. I inhaled deeply, absorbed the rich scent of her, and kissed her again, adding a little swipe of my tongue for encouragement.

It worked. She stretched forward and settled herself, thighs by my ears, pussy hovering over my mouth. I grinned, "Keep talking, baby," I said before I covered her, tongue sweeping, lips working to get at all the goodness inside her.

"I'm listening," I hummed against her.

"Oh, my God," I heard her whisper, music to my ears, inspiration to my mouth. I licked her, as deeply as I could, alternating pressure but always aiming high for that sweet spot inside her, swallowing and returning and making sure she could feel every inch of my tongue over every inch of her.

When I felt her knees quiver, I retreated and slid my tongue and lips over her clit, sucked, swirled, dipped again, repeated the process, sinking into the rhythm of it all until I felt that sweet release slide down my throat. I pulled her into me, buried my nose, my beard, my everything and just existed while she flew.

And then she was kissing me, lips and tongue hungry on my mouth while she essentially ate herself. I felt her hand close around my dick, firm and sure, before she sank onto it, easing inch by torturous inch until she was seated so fully that it took my breath away. I could feel the cool wet slickness of her against my groin. My brain was melting but I pried my eyes open to watch her, to watch when she pushed back and rode me, rocking and undulating her hips, chasing what she wanted. Stretches of her skin filled my vision, a warm bronze glow shone beneath the light brown and I lay one hand against her collarbone to feel the warmth of her. The other hand landed at the soft curve of her hip. She arched and my hands roamed again, returning to her breasts, to pull and tease her nipples, timing my work to the sway of her movements.

And she flowered open and sank another quarter inch.

Jesus. I repositioned my mouth under hers and let one hand slide to her thigh. My thumb drifted down to gather wetness and then circle her slick peak. I pulled away to lick the the fingers of my other hand before slipping it around her hips to dip the middle finger between her cheeks, to give a slow massage to her other opening. She whimpered and bit the side of my neck; I felt her tongue sweep across the bite before she returned her lips to mine. I played with her there until her hips whipped into a frenzy and she pulled my tongue into her mouth matching the rhythm of her sucking to the stroke of my hands.

She came apart. I matched her.

Every fucking time. I thought, then slept.

Chapter 31

I was in love. There was no denying it and no doubt in my mind. I'd been in love before so the feeling, the draw, the foundational desire to be near was not new. What was new was the depth to which the feeling had seeped into my bones. What was new was the level of exposure I felt. There was a lot more to me than there had been when Godrick and I were together. I'd loved him wholly and completely. With the totality of my twenty-ish years. I wasn't discounting that love; it was core to who I was.

But this? This *thing* with Warwick? It felt so true, so complete. Like he'd seen my soul, like I'd willingly revealed it, he'd held it, turned it this way and that and then returned it to me tranquil and soothed.

I felt the smile dance around my lips as I pulled my little Audi in beside The Behemoth behind Warwick's brownstone. I hopped out and all but danced up the stairs. The back door swung open as I walked climbed the steps. I felt my smile grow wider when Warwick's big frame blocked most of the light pouring out of the kitchen. I wasn't able to and didn't even try to keep the delight off my face. This thing we'd agreed to try, to feed and water, had grown. It was thriving and I'd finally begun to trust that it was good. And good for us...for both of us.

And it seemed that nothing could impact the joy I was feeling. Planning this investor event on a shoestring timeline, continuing to unravel the mess that was my life? It was all just a beautiful backdrop to the happiness that I was finally allowing myself to experience. Good things were happening in the midst of all the turmoil. Tonya had worked miracles with my trust—I couldn't wait to sit with her in hopes of getting a blow by blow accounting of that process—and I could expect my funds to start flowing again within a couple of weeks. Including retroactive payments. I'd have a nice nest egg on autopilot because I would never ever again be solely dependent on those funds. I'd begun to look at apartments; modest places that I could afford on my own. It felt good.

And, Cassandra had been in touch with Quinn and Natalie again. They'd rushed the DNA comparison using hair samples from some of Jacob's things. The results had been conclusive. Jacob was definitely her father. She been on a bit of a roller-coaster learning of him, learning that he had loved her and her mother deeply; knowing that he'd only died recently, within the year. She could have met him had Natalie not interfered but that wasn't the way Cassandra's spirit worked. She didn't seem to be holding a grudge but I did know she was working through some things. I was glad she had Abe.

But I was also making it my business to be there for her, which was making the balance a little hard to maintain. What was making it easier though was this place and coming here, every night, since Warwick had returned.

When I reached the top step, he slid his arm around my waist and laid those full soft lips against mine. When he pressed for me to open my mouth, I did it readily, welcoming his tongue inside me. I couldn't imagine not doing so, not anymore. When he finished his exploration with a last lick across my teeth, he stepped back and ushered me into his kitchen where I was hit with the rich tangy smell of what I thought must be spaghetti sauce. He was going to double the size of my ass if I let him.

I jumped when his hand landed gently but with a little pop on the underside of said ass.

"Welcome home," he said and dropped another quick kiss on my lips.

"Thank you," I replied, feeling the heat in my cheeks that always rose when he tossed endearments in his intoxicatingly rich baritone. I completed the ritual I'd developed over the last two weeks, taking my shoes off, storing my work items, stopping in the bathroom, then the bedroom, shedding the day as I went. When I rejoined him, I wore short shorts and a tank in acknowledgment of the rising temperatures.

I climbed onto a bar stool to watch him work his magic and update him on the happenings at Haven and progress in planning the investors' event.

"I'll be relocating my items to 607 tomorrow so the suite can be prepared for Friday arrivals, and that," I said on a flourish, "pretty much wraps it up."

"And you're feeling okay about relocating to 607?"

"Well, yeah, but I plan to move back once they're gone assuming that's still okay?"

"It's not actually. I've been thinking."

"Oh?" I said, taken aback but not surprised. The room hadn't had pent-up demand but I also knew I couldn't just stay there forever, though he had made it seem as though I could. My moving this time was just because we had so many on the investment team. Six in total. We always held our most luxurious rooms in reserve for VIP guests who had unpredictable schedules and extravagant tastes. But the Presidential tier would be perfect for rolling out the red carpet for them. So, I'd planned to move out with intention of moving back afterward.

"Well, I've been on the lookout for a place," I said, "as you know. I know the areas I'm interested in. I'll move along at a faster clip next week, once we're on the other side of this weekend."

"I don't think you need to do that. You can move out of the Presidential. Move that shit here," he said, not breaking the rhythm of his stirring. As if he hadn't just asked me...what, *exactly*, had he just asked me.

"Here?"

"Yeah, here. Move your shit out of the Presidential. Here," he looked over his shoulder and used the pasta stirring spoon he held in one hand to emphasize the location.

"But," I started, then stopped. "But moving it all here, and then back to the hotel. That seems like a lot, and I don't know how long it'll take to get an apartment. They go so quickly."

"Liz. I don't care. And I don't want you to move back to Haven and you don't need to go to some other apartment. Unless that's what you prefer. And then I'll help you find something. Close by. Next door."

He'd rounded the countertop when he started speaking and now stood before me, big and hulking, nearly looming, almost intimidating but for the hint of vulnerability that danced in his eyes.

There'd been a time when I would have never considered it, never even let him get the words out. But now, I heard myself say, "Okay."

His eyes grew, his beard split in a grin and his arms, big and strong came around me. "Okay?"

"Okay," I verified with a nod and a grin. I tilted my head to meet his kiss and everything in my world slipped and slotted into place. Finally.

The sound of the oven timer followed closely by Warwick's phone buzzing broke the moment.

But we'd parted with goofy grins on both our faces; I was still wearing mine. A little niggle of doubt crept at the edges...it had barely been a month since we'd decided to try. And now I was agreeing to move in, even if it was potentially temporary.

"Stop worrying, Lizzie," Warwick said as he pulled his phone out and swiped. "We'll do a trial run."

I laughed. He knew me so well. "How long is the trial?" I asked.

He just winked at me and spoke into the phone, "Vince. What's up?"

He listened for a moment and said, "Yeah, she's here. Putting you on speaker now."

"Hey, Liz."

"Hi, Vince. How are you?"

"No complaints, no complaints," he said with his patented calm. "Listen, a couple of things. I already spoke with Abe and Cassandra. I found Gwendolyn."

I gasped, "Really? How is she?"

"She's well. Feisty as hell. I showed her Cassandra's picture and she said, and I quote, 'I knew in my soul that baby wasn't dead.' She and Cassandra are going to make contact."

"Oh, that's wonderful. I hope to see her again, too."

"She asked about you, too. She wanted to know if—again, her words, not mine—'that woman had managed to ruin that sweet baby'. She said to give you her number if I thought you'd be interested. It sounds like you are so I'll text it over."

I felt tears sting my eyes. "Thank you, Vince." Warwick pulled me into his arms where he leaned against the counter. The phone lay beside us.

"The other thing," he started, "is that I got the recording to play. Sent it to a friend who was able to save most of the file. There are still some pieces with no sound but you can listen to it now when you're ready. I'm sending it over."

"Have you listened? What's on it?"

"From what I heard, it's music. But I didn't listen from end to end, just enough to verify that I worked. I didn't want to come up on some personal shit that wasn't for my ears."

I felt Warwick's deep chuckle under my ear. "I hear you. We'll give it a listen and see what's there."

"Music? Maybe Mother wasn't lying after all. Just this once."

I felt Warwick's skeptical gaze and couldn't blame him. I irritated myself with my continued need to give her additional chances, even when I didn't mean or want to.

"You want to listen to it?"

"Sure," I shrugged. "Daddy did like to listen to music and I don't really have anything of his. If it's really a tape he made, I'd like to hear it."

"Good enough," he said and clicked around on his phone to download the file and then connect to the Bluetooth speakers in the kitchen.

Music, a little staticky, filled the space. It was an old Earth Wind and Fire song, We grinned at each other and leaned into the chorus when it came up. The song flowed from one oldie to the next, providing the background music as we ate dinner, and flirted through the topic of how my lacy panties would look next to his boxers.

We'd finished the food, rinsed the dishes, loaded the dishwasher and relocated to the sprawling sectional in front of the TV Warwick had installed before he'd even purchased the sofa, according to his sister. I'd begun to doze off, tummy full and body warm where it was snuggled against him, when voices filled the house. We both started, alarmed until we realized they were coming from the speaker. The music had ended some time ago without our realizing it and now we heard...voices.

"What did you do?" A strong, familiar voice said. It was Benjamin Whyte.

"What else could I do, Benji?" Verification, noted. *Benji?* It was a woman's voice, but it was muffled, not clear and strident as was Whyte's.

"It was a disgrace," she said. *"An abomination."*

"But Jacob..." Whyte began.

"Will get over it," the woman's voice said, sharp and clipped.

"Tell me," Whyte said, the weight in his voice telling. *"Tell me everything so I can fix it."*

And we listened as a horror story unfolded.

CHAPTER 32

My nerves were on edge and no matter what I did, I couldn't get them to settle. I stood in front of the mirror in the master bathroom at Warwick's...and my, according to him, brownstone. He'd had all my belongings moved in, unpacked and placed the day after I'd agreed to move in. That had been three days ago.

Two days ago, we had sat with Abe and Cassandra and played the end of the digital recording of the tape from Mother's safe. She and I had held each other. The men had held us.

Yesterday, we'd pulled ourselves together and we'd come up with a plan. We'd also welcomed the six donors Whyte and my Mother had been attempting to sway against Warwick. Day One of Project Wine and Dine the Donors had been flawlessly executed. They'd loved their accommodations, the dinner The Restaurant had specially curated and the live jazz after-dinner cocktail hour Warwick had arranged.

This morning, Warwick had golfed, taking the four men and two women to the club Abe most often frequented when he did that kind of thing. I'd spent the morning directing tagalong spouses and bored children to the gardens and pool, downtown for shopping and to nearby parks so little legs could better stretch themselves.

The afternoon tour of the facility had been the perfect segue into free time before tonight's banquet and presentations. And before the execution of The Plan. It was risky and perhaps poorly and too hastily conceived. It wasn't too late to pull the plug though...wouldn't be too late until the last possible moment.

"Are you worried?" Warwick's big body appeared behind mine in the mirror. I reached up to unwind the curling rods Margeaux had taught me to use on my natural hair. The molded curls sprang free and bounced around my chin.

"Worried? No. Cautious? Yes. Mother is unpredictable at best and we really have no bead on Whyte at all. We don't know what he'll do."

"But we do know what he's done."

I nodded. This was true. And what he'd done needed revelation. But to what end.

He laid a kiss on my bare shoulder and met my eyes in the mirror. "If you don't want to..."

"I think it's more Cassandra's choice. It's her mother, after all."

When his arms slid under mine to meet around my waist, I leaned back into him. His scent enveloped me...both the cologne that never failed to make me go wet and the underlying maleness of him. The strength of him. I wasn't worried about the fallout of this thing because I knew, knew in my heart, that he would be here, rock steady, waiting for me. And I would be that for him. Whenever and however he needed me to be.

"I'm ready," I said. I fluffed out my curls and surveyed my face in the mirror.

I'd gone light on the makeup. It was a warm evening and the excitement of the Plan had my body temperature running high. A lighter hand with the face made sense. But more than that, I felt no need for the mask, for the layers between me and wherever I might have to face tonight. That strength would come from the man standing at my back and from my own damn grit.

My heels clicked along behind him as we crossed his hardwood floors and exited to climb into The Behemouth. When Warwick handed me up into the high cab, he let his hand linger along my hip, along the curve of my thigh when I settled into the seat.

He tapped a finger on my nose before dropping a light kiss there. I wrinkled and swiped the tip, tickled and completely unprepared for the words that accompanied his second kiss.

"I love you, Lizzie Brookes," he said before he captured my lips, soft against his, slightly parted in surprise at his words. It was just like him to say them, then kiss me, to both scramble my brain and give me time to process.

But I didn't need time, not *this* time. I knew what I felt for this man who had been both infinitely patient and relentlessly demanding. I wanted him. I needed him. I deserved him.

He drew away slowly, kissing me softly, sweetly again, and again, and once more before he leaned away far enough to let me see the soft black velvet of his eyes. I lay my hand along the softness of his beard and made sure he was watching me, seeing me see him, when I replied.

"I love you, too, Warwick Walker." The softness in his eyes sharpened, fine-tuned to midnight crystal. If I'd thought I'd seen possessive heat in his eyes before, I was wrong. This, this was something that would scald my soul in the most wonderful way. And I wanted it. So I repeated myself.

"I love you, Warwick Walker," I said it fiercely and kissed him this time, just as fiercely until his tongue was dancing with mine, pulling me into him. I wanted to wrap myself around him. To seal this new level with my body clinging to his while we climbed together.

When we broke apart it was with unspoken hot promises to seal this deal later. He shut my door, rounded the truck and climbed in behind the wheel. He navigated onto the road and headed us toward Haven.

Several minutes passed before I asked him, "Why would you tell me that when you know we have somewhere to be?" I could hear the frustration in my own voice.

"Fuck if I know," he growled. "Just piss poor planning on my part."

"Agreed," I grumbled, shifting in my seat and turning my attention to watch the street lights and people whip by.

***

Abe and Cassandra met us at the door. She was stunning as usual, the tension in her face only mildly obvious. Abe on the other hand was prowling like a caged tiger. He and Warwick both. They were ready but they were wary as well.

We entered the Terrace Room where the evening banquet was being hosted. My nerves retreated as the event planner in me rose to the forefront. My eyes scanned the room, first taking in the soft golden light that bathed the room, twinkling from the warm chandeliers that hung from the ceiling and the candles scattered across the cocktail tables. Strategically placed greenery and wide-flung patio doors brought the outside in. I exhaled when I saw the room was nearly full. We'd worried, the invitations had gone out so late and it was a holiday weekend after all. We'd hoped, because many of the same people had rsvp'd to the next day's Memorial Day day party, that they'd also be available this evening before.

We split, Cassandra and I drifting one way, Abe and Warwick the other.

"So, you and Warwick," Cassandra looped her arm through mine as we nodded and smiled at guests we both knew. "It looks like a done deal. You keep arriving places together."

I smiled. "We do, don't we. I suppose it makes sense," I hedged with a secret smile, "since we're living in the same house."

A gasp followed by a face-splitting grin spread across her face. Before she could comment, we found ourselves stopped for a few moments by one of the investors, a short, kind woman who had seemed on board with the whole affair from the beginning. She'd made little secret of the fact that she was here for the vacation. The woman took the moment to share her delight with everything from the weather to our dresses, patting both our hands and raving over the food once more before releasing us to continue our slow lap around the room.

"When did this happen?"

"Two days ago," I told her. "This event was the catalyst. We needed to free up my suite. I was going to just move into another room but he said he wanted me with him," I said, feeling the color warm my cheeks.

"And you said?"

"I said, yes."

"But?"

"But nothing. I still worry whether my feet are really under me but that's just my life. I'm learning is never going to be perfect. I can't keep running away from the best parts of it."

"Oh, listen to you," she said on a laugh. "That sounds like a Margeaux-ism."

"It is. Believe me. She's better than any therapist I've ever had."

"And Warwick is the best part, huh?"

"Definitely top two," I quipped.

I saw Warwick and Abe engaged in deep conversation on the other side of the room. I drew Cassandra's attention to them. "What do you suppose they're talking about?"

"You," she said without hesitation.

I looked at the scene again. My eyebrows drew together. "Me? Why?"

"I think Abe is checking Warwick's intentions toward you."

My eyebrows shot up. *His* intentions toward *me*? "What does he think his intentions are?"

"I don't know. He sees how quickly things are moving. He doesn't even know about your living together. And he knows you're dealing with a lot." She shrugged. "He cares about you.

He always has. That's what made all that other stuff," she waved a hand, "so hard for him."

I nodded. "But Warwick has only ever taken care of me," I said. I felt her look at me.

"Did your and Warwick's relationship start before now?" She asked, a teasing look in her eye. "How long has it been going on?"

"No, it...I...not really. I mean, there was one time. No. No!" I stuttered through an answer to the tune of Cassandra's delighted laughter.

"Well. It looks like it's all working out in the wash," Abe and Warwick were doing that slap-handshake-hug thing that guys do. The hug part lasted long enough to make me smile. Godrick would be happy to see it.

Over the next thirty minutes the waitstaff steered the guests seamlessly through hors douevres on the terrace and back into the main room for dinner preparation, during which Warwick would guide guests through a interactive presentation about Haven, where it had come from and where it was going.

We'd then retire, depending on how completely the evening blew up, to the terrace.

But none of it would matter unless, ah there. Mother walked in on the arm of Lawson, the family attorney. I had been unsure whether she would join. Benjamin was already here. I'd avoided him and his gaze, though Warwick had met him and exchanged handshakes. I wasn't sure how he'd managed not to puke on the other man's shoes. I'd watched Whyte though. Seen how he'd been careful to avoid initiating any contact with the investors.

Waiting until he was introduced and then in most cases feigning no or only passing familiarity. He was full of shit, I thought.

Mother glanced my way, hesitated, clearly uncertain as to her reception. Equally uncertain as to why she was here but the curiosity—scratch that, flat out nosiness—wouldn't let her miss it. I wondered whether she was more eager to see Whyte or to see what Haven was up to.

I walked to her, slipping through the guests who were moving to take seats for dinner...and the show. When I reached her side, she slid her arm from Lawson's to step toward me, shielding her words from his ears.

"I'm glad you've convinced that girl to let these things rest. Lawson says he's not heard anything else from their attorney."

Already, Mother? The moment we're within earshot? "I don't know anything about that, Mother. I assure you I have no influence over Cassandra's legal decisions."

"Well, you should," she fell silent for a moment, scanning the room taking in the guest list. I watched her preen. Never once questioning the fact that she didn't actually belong in this room, with these people who made deals that changed the course of the economy on a daily basis.

"Well, Mother. We've invited the investors in Haven to have a weekend. As you know, Warwick's had a little pushback.This is the closing event, if you will. We thought to keep it small, fairly intimate. Keep the guest list to the quietly influential. Like yourself." She searched my eyes. I struggled to keep the sarcasm in them at bay.

"Well. Where have you seated me?" She tilted her chin a little higher.

"Over here, Mother," I took her to the table where we'd seated Whyte, in the forward middle of the room, and left her there to greet the table. It was unforgivably rude but I didn't care. I wouldn't waste my breath on either of them. He was only there because, given the guest list, to not invite him would have been noted. And Mother was, well, my Mother. She made it her business to be anywhere the money resided. To not invite her would have stirred even more conversation and we wanted all attention on Warwick's presentation. The fact that their presences played into our goals was perfect.

The expectation was that the word would spread and even if the investors he'd been working with pulled out, others would step in and take their places. I had no doubt it would happen that way. Particularly once the presentation ended.

The guests finally settled, the first course on the table. Warwick leaned in from where he was seated next to me and kissed me. "Here goes nothing," he said and rose to move to the mic that had been set up in the corner of the room. A screen slowly descended in the front of the room.

He walked through his interactive presentation, the guest laughing at the right times, oohing and ahhing when the dishes set before them coincided with the locations Warwick planned for expansion. When he finished to thunderous applause my heart swelled for him. This would work.

He had stepped from behind the podium, was shaking hands of the folks who were approaching him asking the questions we'd all hoped would be asked...how can they be part of the expansion...when the familiar scratching, then a strident voice again broke through.

"What did you do?"

My eyes shot to the table where Whyte and Mother sat. Her back went rigid, the response immediate. She knew. Whyte's posture didn't change. He hadn't realized yet.

"What else could I do, Benji?"

Now he sat up straight. The hum of excitement shifted to confusion. The lights in the room fell and the screen glowed under a directed spotlight. The screen that displayed the written captions, making sure that everyone in the room clearly understood each and every word spoken.

"It was a disgrace. An abomination," the woman said, her voice ugly and spiteful.

"But Jacob," Whyte began.

"Will get over it," she spat.

Silence. Then, Whyte: *"Tell me. Tell me everything so I can fix it."*

"I don't know the details," the woman said. *"I sent Matthew to handle it."*

"The baby?"

"Especially the baby," she screamed at him. The murmurs in the room intensified as people began to recognize the speaker.

"Mary," the gasps sounding throughout the room made it clear that Whyte's recently late wife was well as known among the patrons in the room as he. *"What exactly, were your instructions to Matthew."*

Movement stilled and voices silence as the attendees were captured by the drama, eager to hear what she'd told Matthew.

"I told him to kill them. Both of them," her words were clear and hateful. *"And to get rid of it all. Make it like it had never happened."*

"Do you blame me, Benji?" she asked, voice taunting and ugly. *"Do you? Did you want him saddled with* her *with* them *the rest of his life?"*

"Of course not," he snapped and the room recoiled. Whyte looked around, finally responding to the palpable shift in the air.

"Is that what you wanted for the Whyte name? To have some half-breed trash sitting in your seat?"

"I said 'no', Mary, but you have to be smart. This. This wasn't smart, Mary. This could come back on us."

"Then you make sure it doesn't. You hear me? And you make sure that Jacob never knows."

The recording scratched and skipped but you could hear continued background sounds, voices and then doors slamming.

The recording clicked off and the screen went blank.

The room burst into chaos.

Epilogue

18 Months Later

Liz

I swung my brand-new midnight black Audi Q5 into the neat little parking lot beside The Behemoth. I'd only had the SUV a couple of weeks; already though, the extra room was making all the difference. It was so much more comfortable. Plus, Warwick hadn't liked me riding around in that 'little ass tin can'. These days, he didn't want me driving at all, he'd prefer to chauffeur me around—but we'd had to meet today rather than travel together since we were coming from opposite sides of the city.

Warwick left the brownstone this morning to walk the new location he'd recently identified for Haven 2, several blocks from the first location. With plenty of backing, he was able to move quickly and decisively. The seller was responding by accepting an offer well below the asking price, a move that placed Warwick well on-track to dominating the rising hospitality industry in the city. Watching his ambition translate to action and outcome was sexy as hell.

I smiled when I saw his truck door swing open. His big boots hit the ground and I was treated to the sight of long muscled legs shod in his preferred black denim as he came around to open my car door.

I took the hand he offered and slid out. "Hey, baby," I purred and leaned into the sweet kiss he laid on my lips, hummed when he slipped me just enough tongue to make me sway.

"Hey, yourself. You ready for this?"

"I am. But I can't believe it's happening." Today was the final technicality in the process of splitting Heritage between Cassandra and me; and Whyte's among Quinn, Cassandra, and, again, me.

"I can believe it. When a CEO gets arrested, charged, and convicted of failure to report a crime, obstruction of justice, accessory after the fact, evidence tampering, and misprision of felony, I mean," Warwick shrugged, "that's what happens. They lose all their shit."

I twisted my lips in agreement. The judge had not been lenient and had enacted the strictest sentences on Whyte. And stacked them. Even though Whyte himself hadn't planned Catherine's murder or Cassandra's attempted murder, he would spend the next twenty plus years in prison. His board had quickly voted to remove him from all positions and revoke his holdings.

Warren Sloane hadn't fared any better, only avoiding a life sentence because he'd been able to show an airtight alibi for the period surrounding Catherine's murder. There was no doubt he'd orchestrated it all. But the hired help who'd done the deed was long gone. Why that person hadn't finished the job on Cassandra, we'd never know. But thank God he hadn't.

"Fair enough. Plus there's all the other stuff," I shuddered. The court proceedings had revealed a far more extensive list of Whyte's dirty deeds than we'd anticipated.

Warwick pulled my coat from the back of my baby SUV and twirled his finger to indicate that I should spin for him. I did and he held the coat so I could slip my arms in. When I turned back, he fitted my collar and buttons. "There. All bundled up. Let's go get this money of yours."

I grinned, "Let's." And followed him inside where Abe and Cassandra were waiting. Quinn was there as well via video chat with Natalie and their attorney.

"Welcome, Ms. Brookes. Mr. Walker. It's good to see you both looking well."

"Thank you, Boone," we both said before exchanging hugs and cheerful greetings with Cassandra and Abe. The energy was wildly different than the last time we were here. I took a seat and laced my fingers with Warwick's as Boone read through the particulars.

Later, paperwork signed and holdings transferred, we walked back out into the cool air.

"I'll see you this weekend?" Cassandra asked, taking Abe's hand as they prepared to walk to their car.

"You will. Margeaux said she's making ox tails."

"She is," Cassandra laughed. "You'd better get there early, though. Maggie ate more than her fair share last time."

I'd missed the last girls' night. Warwick had made me lose all track of time and once I realized how late I was, well, I decided 'in for a penny, in for a pound.' I'd been read the riot act by the girls the next day. If Cassandra could walk away from a hot and horny Abe, she informed me, I could damn well do the same with Warwick. I'd agreed. Girls' night was sacred and I would do a better job of managing my time. Warwick would have to start earlier.

"We'll probably just get a car together."

"Bring clothes. We can make it an overnight," she offered.

Warwick cleared his throat and she laughed, "Okay, okay. Maybe not. We'll play it by ear."

Once they took their leave, I climbed into Warwick's truck with him, loathe to separate again because I knew it would be a late night for both of us. I was meeting a new client for RSVP and he had a dinner meeting.

"You gonna miss me, Lizzie?" he asked, sweet, teasing affection lacing his baritone.

"Are you going somewhere?" I teased back, leaning in to lay my lips against the soft cushion of his.

"Never that. Not unless you're trying to get rid of me," he nibbled my lips, making me shiver.

"Never that," I answered back.

The little makeout session we settled into was interrupted by the samba-flavored ringtone of my cell.

We groaned, both aware that we were in the middle of the workday. And since we both worked for ourselves, we were always on the clock. When the upbeat tune repeated itself,

Warwick, dropped kisses along my neck and growled, "Answer it."

The commanding tone and the kisses had me ready to do whatever he suggested, so I dug around in my Telfar bag...they really needed to put compartments in these...and found my phone. I glanced at the screen and froze.

Warwick, always attuned, pulled back to look at the screen.

"Woah. That's unexpected,"

"It is."

"It's been over a year," he said.

"Yes. It has." I slid fully back into the passenger seat and slid my thumb along the screen to connect the call.

"Elizabeth?" Mother's voice in my ear was quiet, hesitant.

Curiosity bloomed. But that was all. No upset, no sense of being unmoored or derailed. I'd settled my feet so firmly beneath myself and learned so much about my capabilities over the last two years that I felt invincible. Unshakeable. But I was certainly curious. A full year had passed since Mother and I last interacted face-to-face outside of the investor's gala when she'd made it clear that she never wanted anything else to do with me. I'd reminded her that she'd not been identified on the recording, was in no way implicated in that moment, but that Whyte needed to be held accountable. I'd assured her that her punishment would not be severe. This was something that Warwick and I had consulted extensively with Tonya Frye about. I didn't want my mother rotting in prison, I just wanted her to get some help. Because for all of her mistakes, I recognized that as long as she lived, there existed some chance to salvage our relationship. Watching Cassandra mourn parents who had loved her but whom she'd never met threw a lot of things into interesting perspective.

I—rather, Tonya—had been right. Mother had fared much better than Whyte and his attorney. In exchange for having the charges dropped, she confessed that she had worked in the Whyte household for years, even after the affair began. She made it a habit to record conversations as an insurance of sorts. *You never knew what you might discover*, she'd told the courts. When she realized what she had on this one, she knew she had hit paydirt. But she hadn't disposed of the others; hadn't disposed of any of them. It turned out that mother had some twenty mini cassettes of random taped conversations from the Whytes. She'd given them all to the authorities. They'd found evidence of insurance fraud, tax fraud, assault and battery, and possibly two additional murders.

When it was all said and done, no matter what she'd sacrificed for Whyte, no matter the strange relationship they shared, she hadn't trusted him and felt no qualms about giving him up to protect herself. Her offering had yielded her five years probation, mandatory psychiatric intervention, and fees exorbitant enough that she'd needed to humble herself enough to ask for my help. The alternative was five to seven years of jail time. She'd chosen Door Number One. But liquidating her assets to address the fees had left her destitute; she didn't have the resources to maintain her own housing. Though we didn't interact, Warwick and I agreed that we would put her up in a small two-bedroom apartment in Lower Manhattan. It was, admittedly, ironic.

"Elizabeth," she repeated. "Are you there?"

"Yes," I said slowly, already exasperated with the anticipated interaction. "I'm here, Mother."

I heard her inhale. Then, "Elizabeth," she began but stopped almost immediately. "Elizabeth," she started again, "I'd hoped we could talk, but...," she paused and then started again. "There are some things I need to say to you." Another pause.

This was...weird. Her words were familiar, but her tone was odd. Resolve mixed with uncertainty.

"I mean, there are some things I hope you'll be willing to hear." Mother's wry chuckle filled the car. "This is harder than I anticipated," she said quietly—almost to herself—before the determination returned. "Dr. Armstrong says I've made a breakthrough."

The thread of curiosity grew into a vine.

"A breakthrough?" My heart thumped and I raised my eyes to Warwick's before flipping the call to speaker. Whatever she said, I didn't want to keep it from him. He'd be helping me unpack it all later anyway. He raised his eyebrows and slid one big hand over to lay on my thigh. From pinky to thumb his hand spanned my leg from knee almost to groin. I nearly lost focus.

"Yes," she said, sounding faintly relieved that I'd spoken again. "I've hurt you," she said.

I widened my eyes at Warwick, who shrugged in confused amazement.

"The doctor says I should start there. With acknowledgment." Her voice was still hesitant, introspective. Calm. My heart ballooned. "And that's not a surprise to me. I knew you were hurting, but," she paused a moment, then continued, "but I do understand now that...well...I understand that the ends don't justify the means." Another soft chuckle. "And apparently, we don't even have to agree on the ends." She sounded almost mystified at that concept. "I won't pretend to fully understand all of your sensitivities, but I do know that we engage with life differently and that my attempts to manage things have been...misplaced."

"Mother, I," I stopped because I didn't have anything to say. I could barely process the words I heard. "I didn't mean to interrupt. Go ahead, Mother."

"Yes, well, okay," she said in the vocal equivalent of brushing her skirts. "If you're willing, Dr. Armstrong says you can attend one of my sessions. Or maybe more than one...if it seems pro-ductive."

"What is happening?" I mouthed to Warwick.

He shook his head and squeezed my thigh.

"Well," she said, relief at having made it through evident in her voice. "I guess that's all I have. Um, you can call Dr. Armstrong's office if you'd like to join. I, um, I hope you have a nice day and–hello, Warwick." And she hung up.

If that wasn't the most surreal, discomfiting experience.

"What the hell was that?" Warwick asked as soon as the call disconnected.

"I don't know. I truly don't know. Do you think it was real?"

"Does it matter?" He asked, rubbing my thigh, making it hard to think. "You'll never be able to predict whether she's sincere."

"And I have to decide independently of her actions what I want, what I'm willing to risk."

He nodded. "That's my girl."

"What do you think I should do?" I asked, already knowing his answer and already knowing what I was going to do. I was going to a therapy session with my mother. I would be careful, but it wasn't an opportunity I could pass on. Especially not now.

He smiled at me knowing, too, that I'd already made a decision. "I think you should do whatever your soft, sweet, heart tells you to do."

"And if it turns out to be a mistake?"

"You learn. You grow. And I'll be right here, learning and growing with you," he rubbed a thumb along my jawline, tilted my chin to better position my lips for his quick kiss.

I smiled against his mouth, overwhelmed again by the twists and turns of fate that had blessed me with him. I cupped his face and let my lips move over his slowly, softly, with gently lingering kisses that sought to convey how very much I loved him...independent of the raging lust he consistently fired in my belly. I needed this man to know how much I felt about him. How much I wanted him and how much I needed him in my life. I wanted there to be no questions.

He growled low. "Lizzie..."

I sat back before he could pull me into his lap. "Wait," I said and his hands on my arms stilled.

He laced his fingers with mine, still sending soft shockwaves dancing along my skin. "What's on your mind, Lizzie?"

"You. Always, you," I said with a soft smile. "But I do have something I need to tell you."

Instant concern covered his face. "What is it? Is everything okay?"

"Yes," I said, smiling and cupping his face again. "I'm okay. We're okay."

"Good." He smiled back and rubbed his thumb along the back of my hand, patiently waiting to hear what I would offer next.

"You know, I've changed a lot...grown a lot...these last couple of years. I'm not the same woman I was when you showed up then. A lot of that has to do with you." He began to shake his head, but I continued. "Most of it has to do with me, but a lot has to do with you. You saw strength and ability and good in me when I wasn't sure those things existed in me," I said. "You've taught me patience and kindness, what it means to love but not smother, what it means to support without shackling. I've wasted a lot of time—or, maybe not wasted, but I look back and certainly wish I'd moved things along a little sooner, a little faster."

"Lizzie," he said. "No regrets. Ever. Past Liz was taking care of Present Liz. She was doing her job."

I nodded. "She was. But now Present Liz wants to take care of Future Liz and that means making sure Future Liz and Future Warwick are..." I trailed off.

He dipped his head, chucked my chin, "Are what?"

"Together. Us."

"We will be, as long as you want us to be."

"Mmm," I hummed. "I hear you. But that's a little uncertain for me so," I paused, pulled my Telfar tote closer, and again dug in the bottom...they really, *really*, needed compartments...until I felt it. I tugged the box out and turned more fully toward Warwick.

"Warwick Walker," I said as his eyes grew. "I know you've been waiting for me. Waiting for me to be whole and be ready. You haven't rushed me, even when I probably needed rushing," I said, struck by how true that statement was. He always knew what I needed before even I did. I felt heat gather behind my eyes as I thought about how infinitely patient he'd been. Simply loving me...and showing me how much I deserve to be loved. "I'd intended to hold this until tonight. Or tomorrow night. Or whenever my nerves let me get it out. I know you've been waiting," I said again. "Waiting for me to be sure." I held his gaze so he could see the truth in my eyes before I continued. "You probably have a whole proposal event arranged, just waiting for your word."

His eyes flickered and I laughed at the truth revealed there.

"Well, you can tell them to cue it up because I am sure, Warwick. Every part of me is certain. I want to wake up every morning fighting with you for the covers and I want to go to sleep every night with my butt snuggled into your lap. So," I drew a deep breath, watched the slow grin spread across his face, "Warwick, my love, will you marry me?"

He reached across the console to draw me carefully, gently, to him, lifting me across the gear shift so it didn't dig into my tummy. His lips came down on mine, firm and possessive, hot and insistent. His tongue swept into my mouth, stroking and laving until I got dizzy. Finally, finally, he set me back in the passenger seat and wrenched the ring box from my stunned, frozen fingers. *Holy fuck.*

He slid the ring onto his left ring finger and grinned. "Yes, Lizzie Brookes, I'll marry you." He smooshed another kiss onto my lips and then just sat looking at his ring finger and grinning like a loon.

"You like it?" I asked, needlessly; but my grin matched his while I watched him admire his new jewelry. Warwick wasn't a flashy sort but something in me had wanted to stake my claim. Margeaux's words from so long ago had resonated. She might respect my relationship but these other chicks...they may need more incentive to stay in their lane. So the ring that wrapped around his finger was a wide platinum band encrusted with tiny pave diamonds. It was, essentially, a disco ball with a hole drilled for his finger...with a masculine edge. It was highly effective at announcing his status as taken.

"I love it. For so many reasons. But mainly because you gave it to me. You have no idea how fucking patient I've had to be."

"Oh, I know," I assured him. "And I'm very, very grateful."

Warwick's eyes turned dark and intense. "Are you now?"

I nodded.

He cranked the car, "Fasten your seat belt."

I laughed because he and I both knew I couldn't go wherever he wanted to take me. I had prior plans. "Where are we going?"

"Home."

I pulled him to me and tried to match the heat of the kiss he'd laid on me earlier. "You know I can't."

He growled his frustration at me.

"Why?" He asked as he snuggled his nose into my neck, inhaling and causing the need to erupt along my skin.

"Client meeting. Big client," I said, then repeated, "Big, big client," to remind myself of this meeting's importance because

Warwick's long suck at the junction of my neck and shoulder had me questioning all my entrepreneurial pursuits.

"Why would you ask me to marry you when you know I don't have time to properly accept?" The question was vaguely reminiscent of the one I'd asked him the night he told me he loved me—in his truck before we had a major event to attend.

I gave him the same answer he'd give me then, "Poor planning on my part, I guess."

"Tonight, then," he promised.

"I should hope so," I returned.

***

Tonight came more quickly than I'd imagined. The client meeting had gone swimmingly well. We'd met in my new small but beautiful showroom. I'd balked at opening a physical location but the girls had convinced me that some physical setups along with large mounted graphics of past events would be helpful for clients to imagine the possibilities. They hadn't been wrong. I still did most of my business online, but when people saw the showroom?---they always became clients.

Regardless of how successful the day had been though, I was exhausted and ready to be home. With Warwick, The door to the brownstone swung open before my foot hit the bottom step as it often did when Warwick beat me here. I loved that he watched for my arrival.

He met me at the door with a sweet kiss and arms ready to take the weight of my laptop bag and purse. "We're going to have to figure something else out, baby. This bag is heavy as shit. You need to stop carrying it." He gathered all my items and carried them inside.

"It's a Macbook," I teased him, following him through the mudroom and into the kitchen. "I can't get any lighter than that and still do the work," I said. Happy to receive both the kiss and the lightened load, I slipped my hand around to my back to ease the ache that was beginning there. Warwick noticed.

"Go get comfortable. Dinner's up whenever you're ready."

"You had time to cook?"

"No, but I ordered in from Sei Less. Kung pao chicken and szechuan beef. I have it in the warmer."

"Oh," I groaned in pleasure. "Perfect. I'll be back in two seconds." I turned to head to the bedroom where I'd peel out of the slightly too snug bodycon sweater dress I'd pulled on that morning. It had been easy and comfortable when the day started but now, I felt constricted.

Warwick snagged my hand before I'd taken the first step to pull me back into his arms. "You think you're just going to prance in here and ignore the fact that I'm your official fiance? No kiss? No pat on the ass or anything?"

I giggled and snuggled into his embrace. I lifted my lips to kiss him thoroughly, "There's your kiss." I let my hands roam around to his perfect, firm, butt and gave it a grasp and squeeze, though there was no give there. I wrapped it up with a firm smack. "And there's your pat on the ass. Better?"

He growled in my ear and bent to scoop me up. "Warwick!" I shrieked. "Put me down. We're too heavy."

He tossed me a skeptical look as he carried me to the bedroom and deposited me carefully in the center of the bed.

"You'd need to be carrying quadruplets before you get too heavy for me to carry, Lizzie. And even then, I'd get my weight up."

"Would you?" I purred when he knelt at the end of the bed and began to unbuckle the ankle straps of the stilettos I needed to stop wearing. Once the shoes were off, his big hands began to massage my slightly swollen feet.

"If my feet keep swelling at this pace, I'll be a giant roly-poly by the time the baby comes," I didn't really care, but I thought the fact was worth mentioning.

"And you'll be the most beautiful roly-poly to ever rolly pole." Warwick kissed my puffy ankles before pulling me toward the edge of the bed, my thighs opening around his firm–still flat–waist.

"Lizzie, you have no idea how happy I am, do you?" He sprinkled kisses on my swollen belly to punctuate his words. I was well aware how happy he was because my own happiness was a joyful reflection of his. But I wasn't above hearing it again.

So, I said, "Hmmm," and tilted my head, thinking. "I don't." I draped my arms over his shoulders. "You should tell me about it."

He nodded. "I think I should. I think I will." His hands slipped underneath my dress to tug my panties down over my hips and off. Another soft stroke of his big hands across my tummy, then he put a hand in the center of my chest and gently pressed me back onto the bed. He lifted my feet to put my heels on the edge of the bed, pushing my dress to my hips in the process.

"This is how you tell me how happy you are?" I asked.

"Are you complaining?"

"Not at all."

"Your mother is a complainer," he said to my stomach.

"I am not!"

"She's not," he corrected and kissed my belly softly again before trailing those kisses further down toward my open thighs. A broad swipe of his tongue along my inner thighs had me angling them open further, feeling myself begin to weep in anticipation of his contact.

"You taste so good," he groaned after the first long swipe of his tongue. "How can you possibly keep getting sweeter?"

I gasped out a laugh. He'd been saying this since we found out about our baby four months ago. According to him, he'd known something was up because my body had changed, the taste of me had changed. I hadn't doubted him but Dr. Yvette–who had been delighted to share that I was truly pregnant this time–had confirmed that the pregnancy would indeed change my body chemistry which could translate into a different flavor profile.

"I think you're biased."

"Maybe. But I'm also right," he mumbled and settled into his work. Lips, tongue, and fingers combined to bring me to a quick orgasm that left my legs shaking and the stress of the day nonexistent. Warwick got to his feet, repositioned me on the bed, then sat beside me, one arm across my body so that my vision was filled with him and the heat of him rolled over me.

I reached up because I couldn't help but touch his handsome face. His eyes were soft black velvet again. Warm, encompassing.

"I love you, Lizzie."

"I love you, too."

He nodded. "I love our baby."

I grinned, "Same."

"You should wear this," he said, producing a small black box from...somewhere. Granted, my senses were overwhelmed, and my powers of perception were less than sharp.

I propped up on an elbow. "I should wear what?" I asked, teasing and eager, because I wanted his ring on my finger *so badly*. Especially now that he was wearing mine.

He popped open the box to reveal a giant sparkling cushion cut diamond, set incredibly low in a platinum band that let the shine of the diamond blend with the lustre of the metal. No side stones, no distractions. Stunning in its simplicity, breathtaking in its presence.

"Oh, Warwick," I breathed. "It's beautiful."

"No more so that you, Lizzie. No more so than you."

He pulled the ring from the box and slid it onto my finger. "I would say that I can't wait to start this life with you but we've already started, haven't we?" His hand cupped my growing belly. "You are my life, Liz. You have been since long before you even knew it. When I met you, I knew you were mine. I didn't know how—and I never could have predicted this—but here we are. And I am *happy*."

I slipped my arms around his neck and kissed him, tasting myself and his love on his lips. "I love you, Warwick. We, too," I patted his hand on my stomach, "are insanely, immeasurably, uncontrollably happy." My stomach growled. "And hungry. Feed us, please."

More kisses. One on my lips, one on my sparkling ring finger, one on my belly. Then he tugged me up. "Come on. Let's get y'all fed."

A Note from Tamala

Thank you for stepping into Liz and Warwick's world.

Coming Around was a deeply emotional book to write—unexpectedly so. Liz's journey was uniquely her: a complicated, heartrending exploration of self and commitment to self. She has carried the weight of legacy, loyalty, expectation, and heartbreak for most of her life, and yet, she still chose to fight for her own voice. Her own desires. Her own joy. She's so special to me.

Warwick surprised me, too. Beneath all that Southern sensibility and sexy swagger is a man shaped by loyalty, loss, and a quiet hunger. He, too, is searching—his need to care, to provide, to shelter wants a home...needs a home. His patient intentionality provides the type of safety and security Liz needs to bloom. Warwick, more than most, is someone who has learned that love doesn't always show up at the right time, but when it does, it asks for truth, vulnerability, and courage.

If you met Liz in *What Goes Around*, I'm sure you had questions. You may have judged her, may have wondered how her story could possibly unfold with style and grace. I wondered, too. But that's the magic of second chances—sometimes they belong to the people who need them most. This book is a story about rewriting the scripts we inherit and reclaiming narratives we didn't choose. It's about finding love in the unexpected space between who we are and who we dare to become.

Thank you for taking this journey with Liz and Warwick—for sitting with the ache, the heat, the hope, and the healing. Thank you for letting these characters matter to you.

With gratitude and love,
Tamala

About the Author

Tamala C. Jones is a Southern girl through and through—born, raised, and educated in North Carolina by a high school English teacher and a U.S. Army Master Sergeant who jumped out of planes with the 82nd Airborne.

She started her first romance novel at twelve, already hooked on Harlequin paperbacks and sweeping historical love stories. Even then, she wanted to see herself reflected in the pages she devoured. She paused the dream long enough to earn a doctorate and build a career in academia—but she never stopped craving stories where smart, complex Black women took center stage.

Now, she writes contemporary romance for grown folks: stories full of heat, heart, emotional tension, and characters navigating real-life stakes. Her books are intentionally crafted—rich in story, sharp in dialogue, and unapologetically sexy. Because Black women deserve love stories that make you think, make you feel, and occasionally make you need a cold shower.

These days, Tamala lives her own love story with the man who swept her off her feet over Colt 45 and homemade spaghetti. Together, they're raising three beautiful kids, two cats, and a dog. When she's not writing love stories, she's reading them—or doing the work that (for now) still pays the bills.

ALSO BY:

WHAT GOES AROUND: A Love, Legacy & Second Chances
Novel
(Contemporary Romance)

THE BILLIONAIRE'S ACCIDENTAL HEIR
(A Sexy, Fast-Paced Standalone Romance)

THE LOVE, LEGACY & SECOND CHANCES DUET
What Goes Around
Coming Around

www.ingramcontent.com/pod-product-compliance
Lightning Source LLC
Chambersburg PA
CBHW060818120726
47909CB00006B/1973